○ ○ ○

THE WHOLE CREATION

○ ○ ○

○ ○ ○

Also by Theodore Morrison

THE DEVIOUS WAY
THE DREAM OF ALCESTIS
THE STONES OF THE HOUSE
TO MAKE A WORLD

*Translated and Edited
by Theodore Morrison*

THE PORTABLE CHAUCER

○ ○ ○

The Whole Creation

by

THEODORE MORRISON

New York · 1962

THE VIKING PRESS

To my brother

HOWARD A. MORRISON

in memory

Contents

○ ○ ○

PART ONE

∘ ∘

A Mixture of Elements

o o / o o

Fortunately the rain had cleared after three days of downpour, and the wind had turned west. If it had not, a sudden column of smoke that rose from the industrial outskirts of Fullington, swelling out like a balloon inflated in mid-air, would have enveloped the whole city in an acrid cloud. The cloud would have smarted in the eyes and nostrils of doctors and patients in the Stoughton Hospital, just across the river from the manufacturing district. It would have spread west and north over the business section, over storefronts, offices, churches, tenements, movie theaters, over the fifteen-story insurance building and the twelve-story commercial hotel, crowded on irregular spokes of streets about the hub of a small municipal park graced by brownstone statuary. Pushing still farther, it would have seeped into the classrooms and lecture halls, libraries and museums, of Rowley University. It might even have reached the residential area that climbed the knolls and disused quarries above the traffic artery that bounded the northern edge of the Rowley campus. As it was, the October wind, bright as water running over clean sand, carried the baggy balloon away, bent it in a long greasy horn eastward over the truck gardens and stretches of scrub wood that led from city to country.

Fullington was about to think of winding up its working day and going home. The world was beginning to sigh, stretch, yawn, and divert its anxieties or its libido toward whatever the evening might offer. But the smoke produced among several thousand people, willing and unwilling, a turbulence, a whirl of contrary motions like its own. Halfway up the river drive a

3

fire-chief's car, its lacquer immaculately scarlet, emerged from its cell even before the roll-up door had clicked to rest on its carriage. Hard behind the chief's car a rescue truck roared out on the cement apron in front of the firehouse and made a breakneck turn into the drive. Tons of equipment formed in procession and rocketed southward, the brass fittings on the trucks glittering in the sunlight, the drivers accelerating with military single-mindedness: attack the enemy before he can develop his strength. Last in line came the enormously long extension ladder. When the river drive cramped at the foot of town into a narrow street lined with drugstores and food-shops, the driver catapulted through as if recognizing no difference, catapulted on around the sharp left turn past the hospital and up the steep bridge across the river. The tons of centrifugal force behind him must surely jackknife and plow into the bridge abutment; no, the auxiliary helmsman at the rear, sitting straight-backed at his big horizontal wheel, applied the needed counteraction, and the ladder went bee-line up and over the bridge. Police cars, ambulances, reporters, and a photographer from the city newspaper joined the attacking brigade.

All these forces of organization did not go unopposed. Anticipating their attack, intermingling with it, heedless of disrupting it, streamed the forces of disorganization. In cars till cars could no longer move, on bicycles, on foot, young and old, spry and halt, with faces of indefinable craving, they choked streets, poured from alleys, sprang by spontaneous generation from the ground. Fire. Where? Is it a factory? Have they got everyone out? Look at that smoke, all greenish and terrible! You can see flames in it now. That's a big one, a big blaze. If the wind changed, it would burn up half the town. What does the man say? Just a lot of empty buildings? A shade of disappointment at this anticlimactic news; yet if only empty buildings were going up, you could just relax and enjoy the havoc to the utmost. A good conflagration satisfies needs older than history. The terror and the triumph, the destruction and purgation, are as worship.

In the plant of the Fullington Chemical and Pharmaceutical Corporation, along the industrial flats by the railroad and not

4

far east of the river bridge, the afternoon had begun without any disturbance of routine. In the company's research labs molecules were at work combining in patterns that might turn out to have remedial or at least marketable properties. Their reactions were watched by young graduates of the best technical schools, who would report their findings to management and to advertising, where grave heads would consider them in terms of cost and profit. Here was a process that would ensure the uniformity of an ingredient in a popular drug, but it would increase costs. Could the public be induced to pay more for a better product, or would sales be lost to competition? What advertising slogan, what new gimmick in TV presentation, would persuade the buyer to accept a higher price? Here was a way of producing a skin lotion more cheaply. Should the economy be silently accepted, or could sales and profits be increased by slightly reducing the price? In production buildings workmen watched dials controlling flow and pressure and viscosity. In packing rooms women supplied automatic machines with tubes to be filled with unguents or bottles to receive tablets. In the business offices paychecks issued from IBM machines, to be verified and stacked by girls who possessed, whatever their human cravings, a sort of cool, prophylactic union of mental and digital accuracy. In his third-floor room in the dingy old brick shell that still served as headquarters for management, Kent Warner, Executive Engineer, sat looking at the plans for the new office building he had designed as a replacement, a structure that would be in keeping with the growth of the company into a multimillion-dollar enterprise.

For some reason a lurking dissatisfaction was making it hard for Kent to concentrate. He tried to focus on the plans beneath his eye. After all, the boss had not only approved of the new office building, he had been positively genial about it. The boss, in fact, was so genial at lunch that by the time he ordered a third round of martinis, just as the waiter was heaving into view with the oysters, the executives hunched about the table with him in a private dining room of the City Club uptown had progressed from calling him Mr. Stockwell to calling him Herman and finally Stocky. The stories and the kidding, the jibes

5

and the wheezes, went thick and fast around the table. Kent supplied his own share, mostly hunting and fishing yarns from the days when his old man had taught him to use rods and guns in the country around Amity, back in the days when he was growing up. Old Stocky fell for that sort of stuff, even though the only time someone had pursuaded him he ought to go to New Brunswick and get his deer in the fall, his guide had refused to take him out after the first day for fear of being shot. Finally the table got down to business, and Stocky said that while the Directors were enthusiastic about Kent's design, they had to think about costs. They had to prove to the stockholders that they kept a vigilant eye on economy, so Kent would have to knock a couple of hundred thousand off his estimates, chiefly in office space and conveniences for executives.

Cheeseparing, Kent's judgment told him; fool's economy. More noise, harder working conditions, less efficiency; and by the time the construction job was finished, the cut in preliminary estimates would have vanished anyway in actual costs. You could do your best to keep contractors honest, but they always cheated on specifications unless you watched them twenty-four hours a day, and then they claimed their costs had gone up despite the corners they cut. Costs always exceeded estimates. For that matter the contractor often had his case. Like Fullchem itself, he had to contend with feather-bedding, wildcat strikes, grievance committees that ate up hours of time in a world where time was a race against inflation. Higher wages, cost-of-living increases, more holidays with pay; security, pensions, living on the government; rugged individualism was a phrase you couldn't pronounce any more in decent society.

Well, you could still see some of it in Old Stocky. Kent had been told to cut down on the comforts of lesser executives, but the allotment for the President's office and the adjoining Directors' Room in his new building, so far from being lopped, had been steeply increased. Fifty thousand dollars for imported British oak paneling! He could see Abby's face when she heard about that. She would say things about crudeness and materialism and what could you expect from a man of Stocky's education?

Kent wished the word education hadn't come into his mind. It touched too closely on the nagging discontent that was keeping him from getting ahead with his work. He pictured Old Stocky as he would sit at the Directors' table in the new oak-paneled room, bending forward with his burly shoulders and short arms, with his heavy head, broad at the top but narrowing down to an underlip like a dyspeptic trout. Old Stocky, President of a corporation doing an annual gross of sixty million, and how had he started? Quit high school after two years and clawed his way up the ladder with his bare hands. Old Stocky couldn't design a henhouse for himself, but he knew how to hire an expensively trained engineer who could. Kent thought of the money his patient father had borrowed to put him through the best technical school in the country. Where had education got him? He was doing well enough by some standards, of course. His salary probably amounted to twice or three times as much as the pay his brother-in-law got as a top professor at Rowley. He was allotted a tolerably good cut in profit-sharing, and he'd built up more seniority than he cared to think about in retirement benefits. To a hod-carrier on a weekly paycheck his position might look like the pot at the end of the rainbow. But lay it up against the hundred and fifty thousand a year that Old Stocky took out of the company in salary alone! As a matter of fact, Stocky was probably among the last of a vanishing breed. Nowadays a kid had to sport an A. B. to get a job sweeping floors, and young Ph. D.s could start at salaries that would have enabled a man to retire at fifty in days not long past. The more everyone had to be educated, the less distinction education conferred. Kent felt uneasily that his father's sacrifices had been cheapened.

Money wasn't everything, Abby told him; the world couldn't get along on nothing but material values. He agreed, within limits. He didn't think Stocky was happier or more successful in his family life for the money he had that he didn't need. There was a lot to be said for simplicity, for old-fashioned Yankee thrift, in the way kids were brought up. At the same time, if a man went into American industry as a career, if he believed in the country and the free-enterprise system, he played for the stakes in the game he had chosen. Reward ought to be commensurate with work and ability, and in business the reward was money. The trouble was that the big rewards went to management, and management dealt not in technical but in profit-making decisions. You could be the best plant engineer on the market, you could have judgment and business sense besides, and still be frozen out of top management. Or take one of the higher-degree geniuses in the research lab: if he found out how to extract a new hormone from mouse glands or a wonder drug from old potato skins, he'd still be nothing but a hireling. Sales and profits counted. Look at the salary of the advertising director, the budget he had to spend on TV sponsorship. Some guy like Stocky, who didn't know the difference between tension and compression, made the big decisions and got the credit.

Kent's eye came back to the plans on his desk. Abby was always trying to reassure him that his job was constructive. Sometimes he had his doubts. He lost the sense of what was constructive about manufacturing thousands of gross of tablets for dyspeptics or millions of bottles of tranquilizing pills. But to solve a tricky production process or design a building that would meet complex needs was a different matter. Here was the work he liked to do. The word constructive applied, or a man could feel that it did. Kent was just beginning to see how the heating pipes in his new office structure could be rerouted when he heard the siren of the chief's car as it swung over the bridge by the hospital.

Kent thought briefly of the latest inspection reports on Fullchem's alarm and sprinkler systems. One of the points on which he could pride himself as engineer in charge of plant was the steady reduction of industrial accidents. He didn't think any division of Fullchem was bringing the chief's car wailing over the bridge, but a fire of serious proportions in the manufacturing district wouldn't be something to overlook. He got up from his desk and went to the window.

The room faced roughly north, looking down on a wire fence, bedraggled with sooty woodbine, along the marshaling yards of the railroad. Eastward the tracks bent left in a wide curve, and a good part of Fullington's newest industry with

8

them. By putting his cheek to the pane and peering sidewise, Kent obtained a view of the upper segment of the ragged horn of smoke rolling away under the steady pressure of the wind. The fire was clearly beyond the next plant to Fullchem, but it couldn't be much beyond. A straggle of figures had got out on the railroad tracks and were hopping ties or trotting along the cinders toward the scene of action. Watching their lines of convergence, Kent could guess with some accuracy at the location of the blaze. He thought suddenly of the latest real-estate acquisition of Fullchem. The Engineering Vice President had put the deal through, in fact sold it to Stocky against Kent's judgment. It was odd how Stocky could sometimes be sold a bill of goods, how he could play favorites despite his eye on net income available for dividends. Denis Prouty was one of his soft spots. Kent had to remember that he owed his own promotion to Executive Engineer to the fact that Denis was losing his grip. Denis couldn't carry responsibility, couldn't make decisions. Depending more and more on Kent, he was always raising objections, wanting to call in outside consultants, postponing the vital and complaining when the unimportant wasn't carried out overnight. When no one could cover up for him any longer, Stocky kicked him upstairs as Engineering VP. Stocky had a sense of team loyalty. He wouldn't throw a man out on the street within three or four years of retirement and pension.

The run-down cluster of vacant buildings that Denis thought he had bought cheap—from a Jew outfit, as a matter of fact—would make an ideal fire hazard. The old plant was supposed to provide a new home for Fullchem's limited-sales products. Kent hadn't had time to put a crew in to clean out waste, hadn't even had time to make a thorough inspection, but he had insisted that Stocky cancel the insurance and place a new policy, at double the former amount, through Fullchem's own agent. Poor old Denis! It would pretty nearly finish him if Prouty's Purchase was going up in smoke.

Choices ran through Kent's mind. He could check the location by a telephone call, but wherever the fire might be, it was near enough to be interesting. He'd rather inspect for himself and see whether the boys in the red helmets had the situation under control. The impulse to personal action was gaining force when his door opened and Denis Prouty began speaking before Kent could turn his face from the pane.

"I don't want to interrupt, Cap," Denis said, "but I was looking around—say, what do you see out there? Some good-looking chick walking the ties?"

"They don't walk the ties any more," Kent said. "The tramps' union takes care of them."

Denis gave the appropriate smirk. "Well, listen, Cap. I was just looking around on the top floor of Vitamins. Stocky got a complaint about inadequate lighting up there. Came from the Grievance Committee. Jesus, these unions! Next thing they'll want is a free analysis by a head-shrinker, on company time, for every guy that doesn't pay his dues on schedule. Well, I think there's a pier up there that's out of plumb. You'd better take a look at it. We don't want the roof falling in."

"I'll have young Shepherdson make an inspection and report to you," Kent said.

Denis was dissatisfied. "Shep's all right. I know you think a lot of him, you've been training him, bringing him along and all that, but we can't give him too much responsibility around here yet. He's still green."

"I'd do it myself," Kent said, "but I was thinking of stepping out and taking a look at the fire."

"Fire?" Denis noticed for the first time the wail of sirens and the confused mutter of a mass event. Uncertainty and apprehension came into his face, which looked like a wedge of sallow cheese thatched by loose, yellowish hair. He came to the window beside Kent and peered out. "Jesus!" he said. "Where is it?"

"One of the things I want to find out," Kent said.

Denis looked again. "Jesus, it couldn't be—that would be just one thing more!" His right hand went up to his forehead and brushed away the tarnished lock that fell toward his eye. His left hand went to his pocket and extracted a bottle bearing the company label. He unscrewed the cap, tipped two pills into his palm, and conveyed them to his mouth. His eyes pleaded vaguely, not really taking in what might be happening or what actual problems it would create, merely begging, "Don't let this, whatever it is, happen to me." He became belatedly conscious of his performance with the pills. "What a day," he said. "Can't take a breath without feeling like a sword-swallower whose act has gone wrong. Nervous stomach, the doctor calls it. Personally, I think I've got a cancer." He laughed unsuccessfully.

"I'm going out to take a look," Kent said.

"Yeah, someone ought to." Relief appeared in Denis's face. "I'd go myself, but this damned stomach— If anyone asks where you are, Cap, I'll say I sent you to report. Jesus, I hope it isn't— that would be just one more thing."

Kent moved toward the door. "Take it easy till we know, Denis," he said over his shoulder. "Anyway, don't forget we've doubled the insurance."

Poor old Denis. His wife was getting herself analyzed, without any prospect of an end to either the therapy or the cost; his youngest kid had been thrown out of three schools; and if he didn't actually believe he had cancer, he was just as raddled as if the doctor had told him the worst.

After crossing the hall, Kent opened the door of his assistant's office. Young Shepherdson bent over his desk, his face intent. "Shep," Kent said, "Denis is worried about a pier up on the top floor of Vitamins. He thinks it's out of plumb. Go up and tap a pier with a hammer and report to Denis that everything's all right."

Shepherdson grinned discreetly. "Want me to drop what I'm doing, or can it wait?" he asked.

"Let's do what we can to make Denis feel better in the morning," Kent said. "He may need to. I'm going out to take a look at the fire."

"Fire?" Shepherdson half rose from his chair. He wouldn't have heard the sirens. He had an internal office with steam pipes that clanked and throbbed. He would fare better in the new building, despite the lop in estimates.

"Not in the plant," Kent said, "but near enough to call for a look. "There's no way of telling from here, but it must be close to Prouty's Purchase."

He didn't like to allude to Denis's vulnerabilities in front of a subordinate, but you had to have a mutual understanding with a man you were training to step into your own shoes when the time came to shed them. Shepherdson's look showed that he could discount personal equations; he was already thinking of the actual problems that would result if the new plant for limited-sales products went up in smoke before it was even occupied. You judged a man by slight responses of that sort, and Kent liked Shep's responses.

The highway along the front of the building would be impossibly jammed. Kent decided to use the back entrance, along the railroad, though it meant going down three flights of stairs that brought out the worst in what by courtesy was called his football knee. It had taken Abby a long time to accept the euphemism. The effects of a sprung cartilage in football had pretty well worn off, he had to admit, when a car full of kids had tried to pass him on a straight stretch of road where he was making time driving home from a fishing trip. It was the kids who had to give way when the race reached the turn at the end of the stretch, but the brat of a driver lost control and made contact with Kent's car. He could hardly blame Abby for putting him in the dog house for an unusually long time after that, but something in him rose against her judgment all the same. Put any of those kids in front of Cap Warner with a football in the old days, preferably the biggest and the fastest, and Cap could have brought him down with a tackle that would have jarred his back teeth. The bigger they are the harder they fall. Perhaps that was kid stuff, as Abby seemed to think, but if a man didn't have some of it in him he'd turn out no better than Denis Prouty. He could have put up a better story to Abby if a cop hadn't been following the kids all the time. The company fixer practically had to buy up the mortgage on the clerk of court's house to keep the name of Warner off the docket.

Stepping through the door that faced the railroad, Kent saw one of his maintenance crew standing a few strides away beside a pick-up truck, his face turned to watch the coils of flame that now, like spikes of fever in a ragged throat, writhed through the smoke. "Get in and drive me over there, Mike," Kent said.

"Didn't see you, Mr. Warner," Mike said, swinging around. "That's quite a blaze. Three alarms, they tell me. Lucky the wind ain't this way."

"I want to check up on it," Kent said. "Let's get going."

"I got this leak to fix in this hydrant," Mike said uncertainly.

"It doesn't seem to amount to much," Kent said. "If anyone looks for you, I'll say your grandmother died and you had to go to the ball game."

Mike grinned. He put the wrench he was holding in a tool box on the truck and took the driver's seat. Kent used his arms to haul himself up the high step on his side. The truck rattled on the rutted dirt track.

"How are those loan payments coming, Mike?" Kent asked.

"Christ, Mr. Warner, I haven't torn up a ticket on the horses in two years. When I wanted to raise the devil in me, I used to know where to find him, but they've turned me into that steady a family man, he hasn't got a nook to roost in any more."

"You may not see much of your paycheck after deductions," Kent said, "but you're better off than you were with the loan sharks. You've got a house, and your daughter's been through business college and got a job with the company."

"I meant to thank you for that, Mr. Warner," Kent said. "The wife and I certainly appreciate—"

"I'm glad things are on the up," Kent said.

Mike gave him a sheepish glance. "Katy and the wife look at it that way," he said. "Sometimes I'd rather be drunk in the doghouse."

Kent laughed. He'd had enough experience of the doghouse himself to feel a bond of sympathy.

The truck lurched and bounced over pockets of mud until it reached the fence at the back extremity of the plant. The gate stood open, and the gate of the next plant across the road. "Keep going," Kent said, and Mike drove through, holding to the strip along the railroad. Badger Extrusion Machinery looked deserted. Everyone must be hanging out the east windows, or perhaps the work force had been dismissed to get home as best they could. The smoke, increasingly laced with flame, boiled almost overhead. Kent could see lines of hose looping across the nearer railroad tracks, and a long freighter stalled behind them, headed by its blunt-nosed Diesel, waiting to pull out of the yards. Kids in blue jeans were shinnying over the fence from the tracks. The truck passed the final building of Badger Extrusion, and Mike jumped the brakes as if he suddenly found himself on the brink of hellfire.

The first view settled the main point. Prouty's Purchase was going up in combustion, climbing the sky in a blast of evil-looking smoke through which flame lashed like the flicks of bullwhips. The odd thing was to see not merely one but all five of the old brick structures equally burning. The fire must have spread through the interconnecting tunnel system under ground, which Kent had half explored during the one hasty inspection he'd been able to make. Old light and power wires hung from the ceilings of the wood-studded shafts, and God knows what piles of waste had accumulated in corners he hadn't had a chance to investigate. Well, he'd have to cross-examine the watchman, determine a cause if possible, though weeks might pass before the rubble could be cleared enough for a guess. The first problem for the company would be to collect the insurance, or as much as they could chivvy from the adjusters.

For a moment Kent allowed Mike to idle his motor while they took in the scene. A couple of hose lines had been hitched up to hydrants in Badger Extrusion, and a pumping engine had taken position a few yards inside the lot. Kids ringed it ten deep, pestering the brace of firemen in charge, wincing away when the wind allowed a backlash of heat to work upstream from the fire. The real crowd was massed along the southern extremity, on the far side of the highway. Their wedged bodies made a shifting conglomerate through the refracting heat waves, like a mob of trees under water.

In the building nearest the truck, a muffled sound and an explosive uprush of sparks, like a swarm of gilded gnats, marked the collapse of a section of roof. Liberated smoke poured in doubled volume through the gap. Upper windows cleared and glowed with vibrating strands of pure, bright flame. It wouldn't

14

be long before the walls gave way too. Probably nothing would be gained by hanging around and waiting for them to collapse. Of course this was the upwind side, Kent reminded himself. The fire was on Fullchem property. If it was going to spread, it would spread downwind, to the east. No harm in taking in the whole situation. "Drive up the street to the right," Kent said, "and see whether we can swing around front. I want to get a look from the other angle."

Mike looked doubtfully at the hose lines they would have to cross in the street.

"This pick-up is light," Kent said. "It won't make a dent in those lines with the pressure they have in them."

Mike put the truck in gear. The front tires were bumping over the first hose when a fireman on the pumping engine yelled and jumped from the rear step. At the same time a police whistle pealed from somewhere behind the fire apparatus, and a cop rounded its hood at a trot. "Keep going, Mike," Kent said. "We haven't heard a thing." Mike kept going, but as the truck pushed up the side street toward the highway, its progress was more frequently interrupted. One young cop proved especially stubborn. He seemed to want to hustle them both off in the paddywagon forthwith.

"I'm Kent Warner, Officer, engineer for Fullchem," Kent said. "We own this property, and I want to see what's going on."

A glint of recognition appeared in the cop's eye. Kent couldn't remember him, but very likely the company fixer would know who he was. "You'll have to leave your car here," he said. "I'll keep an eye on it for you."

"Thanks," Kent said. "I'll let Mr. Hoague stay in charge, and I'll walk around by myself."

He lowered himself from the truck, good knee first. A man in a loose-hanging topcoat stepped forward from behind the cop. He had a notebook in his hand and took a pencil from behind his ear. "I heard you say—" he began.

"Sorry, I don't know a thing," Kent told him. "I just came over when I heard the alarm. Maybe you can tell me how this started."

Disgruntled, the man put his pencil over his ear again, and Kent turned his back. In order to work around to the front of the burning plant, he had to keep fairly close to the highway, where the crowd massed, bulging against police restraint. Hose lines paralleled each other more closely here. Knots of firemen stood about pumping engines and rescue trucks. Kent stepped over lines, worked forward, explained, until he got to a point midway along the frontage, where he could see the plan of attack. The big central building, safely isolated in the middle of the lot, was being allowed to burn itself out. The main forces were concentrated along the eastern boundary, whose outlying buildings were being saturated with whatever hose the chief could bring to bear. Arcs of spray made an almost continuous curtain, and though it had little effect on the immediate blaze, it minimized whatever threat the fire offered of spreading. Kent's eye picked out the extension ladder angling far up from the long base of its truck. In a crow's nest at the top of the aluminum webbing a couple of firemen in black sou'westers, like two dark berries on a silver stem, trained a nozzle toward the fire. A long arch of water looped out from them and splayed into the pit of flame. Kent thought of the wheeze about the man who asked the anthropologist what was that object he had on the mantelpiece. A phallic symbol, said the anthropologist. Oh, is that it? Well, you know what it *looks* like. If a fireman could throw a stream like that, no wonder little boys wanted to be firemen when they grew up. Or no wonder they used to, because if they wanted to nowadays, it would be because a fireman is on the city payroll, the taxpayer's money, and can sit around the station all day watching the ball game or the Westerns on TV until he's interrupted by an alarm. As Kent watched, a shift of wind or a freak boil of heat swung a thick eddy of smoke toward the extension ladder. The men in the crow's-nest disappeared, enveloped in a brown curtain of murk. The curtain cleared, and there they were again, still directing their looping stream toward its target.

Kent became conscious of movement to his left. Emerging from behind a fire engine a few steps away from him came four men, slightly bent, gingerly carrying some burden. Others, a cop, a couple of firemen, a youngster who might be an intern or orderly, followed them. They were bearing a stretcher, heading for an ambulance parked a few yards off. A blanket reduced the victim on the stretcher to a series of vaguely human bulges. Probably a fireman had been trapped by smoke, but it was possible that the day watchman employed by the company had been caught when the blaze broke out. He would have a family to be taken care of, and he might be a source of information about the cause of the fire. Kent was about to step forward and make inquiries, but before he could get his legs in motion an eruption boiled out from the crowd along the highway. Noise rose on the air, like the opening strains of a riot. Kent turned to look. A wedge of figures came catcalling and capering across the street, the laggards grabbing at the forerunners and struggling for the lead. Beer cans described parabolas above their heads. Behind them a scattering of cops, grim-faced and also on the run, converged on their heels, and behind the cops came more of the crowd, breaking through the gap in the thin cordon.

College kids. Fraternity brothers from Rowley. They didn't see the stretcher that the bearers were sliding into the back door of the ambulance. They swept around the vehicle in a divided stream, heading for the fire engine at Kent's left, God knows what crazy notion in their heads. They swarmed up and over it with fatuously earnest faces. One scrambled into the driver's seat and began poking around the ignition and clutch, as if he meant to kidnap it and take it for a joyride. Another climbed on a tank or equipment box behind the cab, struck a pose, and opened a prodigiously large and oddly rhomboidal mouth as if to begin a declamation. Cops and firemen reached the beleaguered apparatus almost simultaneously with the students. Their zeal might be whetted by the rising wail of the ambulance, trying to move out through the crush, but no doubt the ancient feud of town and gown was provocation enough. A blue bulk appeared with jack-in-the-box abruptness beside the incipient orator, and a brief, one-sided wrestling match ensued. The boy's body jackknifed backwards over the brass railing of the fire truck. He put forth a spasm of heroic effort as he fell and took the cop with him, but the cop got up and the boy lay twitching and groaning. Another boy started climbing over the rail of the fire truck, evidently with escape in mind. A cop put a hand down his collar from behind and jerked. The boy's face convulsed and went red. By reflex he hooked his elbow backward and caught the bridge of the cop's nose. When the nightstick hit him, his face softened and relaxed with an innocent, an almost blissful resignation. That face—it belonged to a boy Kent had seen more than once. Broad at the top, narrowing down to a thin jaw and a trout mouth. Of course. Young Herman Stockwell, Herman, Jr., the boss's son.

Time was when Kent wouldn't have minded diving into a good ruckus on his own and taking a swing or two at the gendarmerie, but he was too old for all that now, and with his trick knee he'd be down and trampled on before he could pick out a jaw to use as a target. The fire, he judged, was under control. He couldn't take any useful part in the three-way struggle now going on among the cops, the Rowley brethren, and the street toughs who had broken from the crowd and joined the scramble. They were the real menace, gang-fighters, kicking and kneeing, probably some of them with knives. The cops were trying to restore order generally, but when they had a choice their preferred victims were obviously the disciples of learning. The only thing saving the brethren from Rowley was that paddywagons were coming up and taking them forcibly aboard. Kent's cue was to get back to the office. He ought to let Stocky know that his kid would be on the police blotter, ought to make sure that Stocky set the company fixer to work on the case. Young Herman could put up a better story to his dean at Rowley if he wasn't handicapped by charges on the docket. Colleges were harder to fix than police courts. Stocky had tried to plant the kid at Yale and Princeton and a dozen places that might have put some polish on him, but they'd all turned him down. Stocky couldn't understand it. Weren't they begging for money all the time?

Kent turned and headed back toward Mike and his waiting truck. Young Herman might have taken more of a crack on the head than his skull could stand. The boy might be hurt, but that was unlikely. He'd come to with an egg on his cranium, an egg that would be sore for a week, but he wouldn't be permanently damaged. As for the fire, it would burn itself out in a few hours. Kent was glad, all the same, that he'd decided on a personal inspection.

The office building breathed an air of musty vacancy when Kent got back. For a moment he wondered whether Stocky himself might have gone home, as it seemed all the lesser executives had, but as soon as the elevator grill slid back and disgorged him at the top floor, he was relieved of any doubt about Stocky's personal presence on the scene. Stocky must have left his door open; he was audibly chewing someone's ear. It was nothing unusual for him to blow his top; he would blow it if, at an inopportune moment, an executive sneezed three rooms away. As a rule he wasn't hard to bring to reason; treat him with a mixture of firmness and fact, and he'd cool off fast and begin to estimate the situation at its real worth. Whoever confronted him at the moment, though, obviously didn't know how to cool him off. "Bill of goods," Kent heard. "Goddamn fire hazard, no precautions, no responsibility—" When Stocky got worked up, his voice would break into a sort of spasmodic bleat, like an offended sheep. As Kent reached the office door, the bleat identified the object of its current outrage. "All right, Prouty, you'd better get out of here and think things over. It would be a good thing for your position in this outfit if you showed a little judgment now and then, a little guts. What I want in an executive around here, an executive ought to be on the ball, see? Using his judgment, see?"

Kent couldn't remember when Stocky had ever called his Engineering VP anything but Denis. The first-name joviality of the lunch hour had vanished. Poor old Denis clearly needed to be taken off the hook. Kent put a hand against the door-jamb and looked in. "I'm glad you're still here, Mr. Stockwell," he said. "I'd like to report, if you have a minute."

Stocky seemed to turn from Denis with relief, but the startlingly blue eyes he brought to bear on Kent carried a message of glaciated suspicion. "I was wondering when you'd show up," he said. "Come in, Warner."

As Kent stepped forward, Denis passed him, bled white, making for the door. He barely met Kent's eye with a look of appeal and of gratitude for his release.

The better to vent his indignation, Stocky was pacing the floor, crossing and recrossing in front of the portrait of himself that hung above the old-fashioned glassed-in cabinets behind his desk. The subject seemed to have inspired the artist to use his brush aggressively, and the result was at least an emphatic likeness, from the blue eyes to the trout mouth. Stocky had thrown his London-made topcoat across his chair, and his hat rested on it upside down. "Well, what about it, Warner?" he demanded. "What have we got left?"

"A heap of rubble," Kent said. "Some sawtoothed walls that will have to be knocked down and carted away."

Stocky started in again on Denis, on accident prevention, on the standards of judgment expected of Fullchem executives, on the painful destiny of anyone who sold him a bill of goods. Kent refrained from even obliquely saying 'I told you so.' "I don't know what Denis could have done in the way of prevention," he said. "As soon as it's possible, I want to see whether we can establish a cause."

"Damned right," Stocky said. "And when you say soon you'd better mean soon." He glared as though Kent himself could be mysteriously responsible for the undetermined cause.

"Another thing, Mr. Stockwell," Kent said. "We may have a more valuable property without those old brick morgues than with them, especially if we can get the adjusters to come through. The cause may have a lot to do with the insurance."

"You're telling me?" Stocky said, but his pacing came to an abrupt halt. The fishlike arc of his lower lip relaxed a little, and shrewdness came into his eyes. He picked up his topcoat and hat and tossed them toward the desk. The coat began to slide and the hat to roll. Kent retrieved them while Stocky sat down in his chair and pulled an ashtray toward him. "You haven't called for bids yet on the new office building?" he said.

"I have a little more work to do on plans," Kent said. "I was figuring to ask for bids tomorrow or the day after."

"Lay off for a while. Wait till I give you the word. I don't know, Warner. This property Denis stuck us with, values are going up around here, it's a good site. We might sell it, maybe we could put up the new office building there, maybe rig up this dump we're in for limited-sales production. I don't know."

Kent felt his new building slipping away from him, leaving a hollow inside him as big as the Grand Canyon. He reminded himself that Stocky was merely postponing the project; after selling it to the Directors, he could hardly cancel it out of hand. He saw the sense in what Stocky was proposing, but he had already begun to imagine designing still another new building for limited-sales products on the scorched site of Prouty's Purchase. He mentioned the difficulties and costs of remodeling the old office structure for manufacturing use.

"That's your problem," Stocky said. "I want plans and estimates right away. If it looks good, we'll put it up to the Directors." He stirred in his chair and made a motion toward his coat and hat, but Kent hadn't yet broken the news about Young Herman. That would take diplomacy. Begin with the scrap; nothing like a little preparatory comedy to soften a blow.

Stocky listened to the preliminaries impatiently, as if suspecting a diversion, but his mouth screwed itself into a sour grin. Eventually Kent had to come out with the fact that he'd recognized Young Herman, and the kid was in trouble with the constabulary. That was the end of good humor. Stocky's top threatened to blow right through the ceiling. He got up from his chair, paced the rug, goddamned the police, goddamned education, goddamned Young Herman. Then he turned on Kent. "What were you doing, Warner, while they were beating him up? Enjoying the show?"

"What could one man do against that howling mob?" Kent asked.

"You were on the spot. You're an officer of this company, and wherever there's an executive of this company, he's a responsible officer on the spot, wherever he is. His responsibility is to be smart and act for the interests—" It dawned on Stocky that his line of thought was leading him into difficulties. "Goddamn it," he said.

Hit the man who's off balance before he can recover. Kent had learned the maxim in sports and relearned it in business. "All right, Stocky," he said, "so I should have hopped a plane for Washington then and there and taken the case to the Supreme Court on a writ of *habeas corpus*. The trouble was, I didn't see any planes and I didn't see anyone passing out writs. I thought the best thing I could do was get back here and tell you so that you can put Joe to work on it."

The mention of the fixer's name had the desired effect. The glacial blue of Stocky's eyes thawed, and the corners of his mouth rose a little. "Don't get riled, Cap," he said. "I should have thought of that myself instead of chewing you. I'll get in touch with Joe if I have to have him paged in a whorehouse." The bleat in his voice turned suddenly pathetic, the hurt instead of the indignant sheep. "I don't know why that kid Herman does the things he does to me. I've done everything for him, given him everything he's ever asked for, and do I get any gratitude? He's just like all the rest of his generation. Don't want to work, think it's vulgar to make money, but they like to spend it as if it came free, like air out of a line at a filling station. Against American business and American know-how. Don't want to do anything constructive. All they want is to drive foreign-made sports cars and get girls in trouble."

"Both at the same time, preferably," Kent said.

A joke might be hazardous diplomacy at the moment, but Stocky took it pretty well. He grinned faintly and relaxed in his chair.

"We all have our troubles with kids," Kent said. "Parents can't win."

"You never spoke a truer word, but I don't know why you should say it. You and Abby did all right with Ruth and Randy."

Stocky's voice contained a thread of envy, an admission of failure in one direction, though a failure he could no more understand than he could take in the laws of physics. He was trying to be decent. Kent only wished he hadn't so casually mentioned Randy. He couldn't tell from Stocky's tone whether Stocky remembered that they didn't have Randy any more, that whether they had done all right with him or whether they hadn't, the books had been closed on Randy's account, closed for good.

Kent felt a sudden downward pressure of fatigue, a sinking of energy. "If that's all, Stocky, I think I'll head for home," he said.

"I'll be getting out of here myself," Stocky said, "as soon as I can locate Joe."

Kent made his way to the elevator and back to his office. The afternoon hadn't given him time to call Abby and explain that he would be late for dinner. He dialed, and Abby answered at once. She must have been hovering near the telephone, waiting for his voice. She told him she had seen the smoke over the industrial district and worried about him, but as a matter of fact he wouldn't be late after all. Ruth had called to say that she and Brainerd were driving up for a visit, and he could still get home in time to carve a hot roast.

"Are they bringing the kids?"

"The grandchildren," Abby said. It was her way of distinguishing, partly to mollify him, between Ruth's own children and the boy Ruth inherited when she married a widower.

"Is it just a visit, or do they have a problem?"

"Ruth said they have something important to talk over with us."

"That means a bill before the evening is done."

"Cappie! You sound as though you didn't want to see your own daughter and grandchildren."

"I do. I just hope the price tag won't be too high."

"You're tired," Abby said. "I can tell by your voice. Are you sure you're all right?"

"Nothing wrong but the ravages of the years."

"Nonsense. You start home and we'll be waiting for you."

Kent replaced the telephone and thought briefly of his son-in-law. Brainerd's virtues had to be measured on a different scale from those that he felt had any affinity with himself. He certainly didn't want to dislike the guy, but he couldn't help wondering why Ruth, with all the available males in the world she might have chosen from, put her finger on the one she did.

23

Not only a widower who had already given one hostage to fortune, but a social-service worker, the sort of character money wouldn't stick to if you glued it on. Kent could understand the desire to help the human race; but if that was a man's ambition, why didn't he qualify as a surgeon and make a pile for himself and his family while doing good at the same time? Brainerd Hitchens. A nickname would help, but nothing could be done with Brainerd, and Kent's one or two efforts to establish Hitch as a convenient handle had been met by stolid passive resistance.

Kent looked at his desk, where the plans for his new office building still lay spread. He could see the blue abstracts turning into steel and aluminum and concrete and glass, the design he had conceived. He picked them up and shut them in a drawer, thinking that he wouldn't be asking for bids tomorrow or the next day, thinking that if the place ever got built, he would take Randy on a tour of it. No, that was exactly what he couldn't do. The building might someday be built, but Randy would never see it.

∘ ∘ *2* ∘ ∘

As Kent swung north along the river drive and then west toward the residential section, the fire began to jostle for a place in his mental reservoir of anecdote. The drunken mob howling past the ambulance, the attempt to capture the fire engine, Young Herman's blissful face when the nightstick clipped him: here were all the elements of a yarn that only needed time to mellow and an audience to listen.

The curve of his own street brought the house into view. He saw the children's car parked at the curb. He had sent them a check for the down payment on it only two or three months past, but already it wore the long-suffering look of an article of family use. Kent made out, piled hugger-mugger on the shelf at the back, an old blanket, a box of tissue, a small toilet seat, a sprawled Teddy bear. They would be waiting for him inside, Ruth and Brainerd and young Kent and young Randy.

In the hall he almost stumbled over a mound of suitcases and children's gear. The chief obstacle was a folding playpen with its mattress; caps, mittens, and zipper suits rayed out from the central bivouac. He heard voices in the study. Ruth and Abby were trying to exchange news by talking at the same time, the boys were yelling for attention and being told not to knock things over. Kent had to appear in the doorway before they knew he had come home. Ruth saw him first. She tried to get up too quickly from her chair and had to steady herself by putting a hand on the center table. Somehow Kent had let it escape his mind that she was within a month or two of adding a third grandchild to the family. He wondered whether she really had to emphasize the point by the toreador pants, if that was the term for them, and the short, rather beaten-up-looking jacket she had chosen to wear. She had to bend well forward to kiss him, and when she straightened he felt as though he had been bumped in the middle by a warm basketball. He had to steady his own balance while he shook hands with Brainerd; young Kent was trying to swing on his football knee. Randy had barely reached the toddling stage; he couldn't make himself as much of an impediment, but he did his best. Abby got her turn at him at last. She put her lips to his cheek, then recoiled, looking shocked. "You taste of soot," she said, "and you simply reek of smoke. If you wash and change quickly, you can have a drink before dinner."

"I need no urging," Kent said. "Brainerd knows where the liquor cabinet is. Perhaps he'll set up a tray, and we can all slake our thirst."

Brainerd's big face seemed to open in surprise and doubt at this suggestion. Then it focused judicially, and he said, "Why, yes, of course. I'll be glad to."

Kent made his way upstairs, but when he came out of the bedroom after changing and started down again, he found himself pinned back by a counter movement. Young Kent was charging up as fast as he could work his legs. Behind him Ruth was boosting Randy step by step; behind them Brainerd, one arm bearing a suitcase, the other trying to compress the play-pen and its mattress into a manageable burden, was advancing to challenge the ascent. "Don't bump into Grandpa," Ruth called. "Remember his leg." Young Kent dodged past, his face earnest with effort. An edge of the mattress, doubled under Brainerd's elbow, worked free and unrolled itself. Brainerd stepped on it. The whole mattress leaped out from under his arm, the playpen swung open on its hinges and rapped him sharply on the shin. He muttered briefly and stood surveying the tangle as if it posed a problem for prolonged study. "You remind me of the wheeze about the parson who couldn't take the Lord's name in vain when he dubbed a golf shot," Kent said. "He just spat, and where he spat the grass never grew." Brainerd grinned sheepishly and propped the pen against the wall so that Kent could pass.

He went back to the study and noticed with satisfaction that the bar wagon, suitably stocked, had been wheeled into posi-tion beside his customary chair. The stool on which he propped his leg had been pushed into place, too. That must have been Abby's work, but Abby herself was missing. She must have gone to the kitchen to supervise preparations for dinner. Kent sat down and poured himself a highball. The accumulated fatigue of the day, the emptiness of the room, took sudden hold on him. He looked about for something to distract his mind.

The room was full of reminders of place and past. The place was Amity, the past the years during which he was growing up in Amity, in small-town upper New England, practically rural New England, so closely were town and country inter-fused. The center table that bulked too large for comfort in the small study had come down from Grandmother Randall. The big circle of its elaborately inlaid top squatted on a stout, fluted column that splayed out into claw feet. On it, beneath a standing lamp, stood a reminder of a more recent past. It was a photograph of Randy in the year when he would have gradu-ated from college—the real Randy, as Kent's mind continued to think of him, not the grandson whose title to the name never seemed quite so valid. Kent remembered the letter Ruth had written when her second was on the way. If it proved to be a boy, she said, she was going to name him Randy. Abby cried at that, one of the few times she had failed to keep a stiff upper lip since Randy's death.

Kent's eyes met the eyes in the photograph, young, expectant, inexperienced. He turned away and looked elsewhere. In a corner of the room rose the old whatnot, the étagère, as Grandma Randall called it. A ridiculous object to keep; once a month, at least, he and Abby decided to get rid of it. On its third shelf stood an enlarged snapshot of an eight-point buck, the first Kent had ever shot. It swung from a tree, its black tongue stiff between its mild jaws. On either side of its muzzle stood Kent himself at sixteen and his old man, their rifles crooked in their arms.

As Kent looked back on those early days in Amity, it seemed to him that he had never known what it was to be tired. The only moment of exhaustion was the moment when he slid into bed and sank at once into a lassitude as intense as his day-long exertion. The memory of Amity was the memory of extravagant physical resources extravagantly spent. It often reduced itself to a memory of running, of thighs happily pumping from one locus of effort to another. After his high-school classes, in Octobers long past, he would shift into football togs and trot, or perhaps pedal his bicycle, a mile and a half to the field at the edge of town. There till twilight he would scrimmage, blocking, tackling, ball-carrying with a savage love for the shock of opposing shoulders and of turf already crusty with frost. After practice, he would jog home for supper, his legs still resilient. In the evening he'd be off half the time to sit around with the gang in some girl's parlor, eating burned fudge, and he'd have enough sand left in his legs to run home to bed. On holidays he'd tramp with his old man into the country that stretched right up to Amity's back door. Major, the droop-lidded, slack-jowled, splayfooted old hound, veteran of many a fox run, would pad after them and with luck put his nose on a fresh trail. They would listen to him baying over the ridges and argue which way the fox would run. Then each would take an agreed post on a wood road somewhere, waiting for a chance shot at a streak of red fur stretched in the air for a split second. In winter the gang would be coasting or skating by moonlight, while the snow squeaked under the runners or the ice went off like pistol shots in the cracking cold. In spring he'd turn out for baseball and find time to go fishing. Always his image of himself, as he looked back on it in Amity, was an image in motion. Sundays were the only days of enforced and unendurable inactivity. Come rain, snow, or ninety-in-the-shade heat, Sundays meant the long prayer and the hour-and-a-quarter sermon in the First Congregational Church. Grandma Randall was inflexible about that. Hymns on the blood of the Lamb and the Rock of Ages at least taught him part singing, and paid dividends later when he could claim to be a better than average barbershop tenor.

It wouldn't be fair to Amity, though, to give it credit only for the physical activity it encouraged. It called for mental activity too. Amity High School in those days offered an education. It wasn't afraid to flunk the thick-headed, and it wasn't afraid of drill. Kent recalled the math teacher who used to walk around the classroom, looking over shoulders, interrupting study to demand an algebraic formula. If it wasn't forthcoming, he'd lift a kid out of his seat by the scruff and hold him there till it was. Kent got all the math he needed, right there in Amity, to start with an advantage over half his engineering class. When he saw that German would be a help too, he got that, though the time was right after World War I and he had to persuade the principal to form a special group under a retired teacher who'd been ostracized when the atrocity stories were in full cry.

Sometimes, in Amity, effort seemed its own fulfillment. Of course a measure of success or failure was always in sight: you tried to win the game, you tried to master the algebra. Yet the days when the fish wouldn't bite, when the fox wouldn't show himself flashing across a span of wood road, couldn't be counted days of loss. It was a good life to know the streams where the trout lay with their noses toward white water, whether they reached the frying pan or not; a good life to know the feel of a gunstock at the shoulder, even if the shot missed. You tried to win because if you didn't you weren't respecting yourself or your opponent. To give and take, though, to respect the opposition even when the opposition kicked you in the kidneys or pushed your face in the mud —that had its weight, perhaps really as important as the score at the end of the ninth inning or the second half.

The same balance held later on, in business. There, of course, the score became money. Unintentionally Amity taught that lesson in addition to its others. You might have it drummed into you at the First Congregational Church that if a man asked for your cloak you ought to give him your coat, too; but while in restrospect Amity might look a bit like Eden before the serpent got in, it didn't perceptibly advance the kingdom of heaven. Amity respected financial standing. To do well, in the town's eyes, meant to have a good job, to be moving up and taking your family with you on the scale of mundane comforts, freedom from worry and pennypinching and the dread of dependence. Goals and satisfactions! What became of them as the years went by? Where now was the zest of those remembered days, that inexhaustible fund of energy that renewed itself in the act of being spent?

Kent took a swallow of his highball. He heard a door open, heard footsteps crossing the hall toward the study. He looked up hopefully and was rewarded when Abby appeared in the doorway. "Everyone went off and left me," Kent said, "like a shipwrecked mariner."

"Poor old deserted Cappie!" She put out a hand as she passed him on the way to her chair, and he allowed his cheek to be patted. "I just went to the kitchen for a minute to see how dinner is doing."

Her face was flushed from the heat of the stove, a strand of hair was out of place, and her eyes were pinched and reddened. "Sit down and let things take care of themselves for a minute," Kent said.

"As if they would!"

"Shall I mix you a drink?"

"A little one. The children will be down right away, and dinner is almost ready."

"The children, all two and a half of them. When does it become three?"

"You shouldn't have to ask," Abby chided.

"I have my own production schedules to remember," Kent said. "I'm reminded of the wheeze about the old married man in the army. They asked him how he kept his wife from two-timing him between leaves. He said he kept her barefoot in the winter and pregnant in summer."

"Cappie! You're insinuating nice things about your own daughter!"

"I'm not insinuating anything. I was just reminded of a wheeze. Brainerd doesn't quite keep her barefoot, but he fills the rest of the prescription."

"You ought to think more about his good qualities. He has a fine mind, and he's trying to do something for the world. He isn't limited by material values. And Ruth loves him."

"I hope so. She's in a family way often enough."

"You want a woman to be either a doll or a household drudge. You wish children came out from under cabbage leaves. You didn't like me when I was pregnant."

"I wanted you to get over it."

"There's only one of a woman's functions you can bear to think about, and you don't like the consequences of that."

"I hope I don't get to the point where I can only think about it."

Abby smiled in spite of herself and let him have the last word. She had to, Kent told himself, feeling his spirits lift, feeling the warmth of whisky diffusing through his capillaries. Noises of opening doors and emerging footsteps came from upstairs. Ruth's voice said sharply, *"Don't* slide down the banister!" They all came trooping into the study. Ruth had changed into a dress designed to make her impending maternity less obtrusive. Kent felt vaguely that she might have done better, but at least it was an improvement on the toreador pants, and she had tucked a scarf around her neck so that her throat looked less like a plucked chicken. Brainerd's big visage looked solemnly good-natured above his heavy shoulders. Collectively they constituted his family, Kent told himself. They were what his years with Abby had given and had left.

They finished the roast, the browned potatoes and the eggplant, the salad and the rolls, and even made a considerable inroad on two pies, acknowledgments of the special occasion. Kent offered brandy, and Brainerd surprised him by accepting. Ruth shepherded young Randy from the table, his eyes puffed with sleep, and then came back to help Abby clean up. At last they all gathered in the study again, where the problem arose of persuading young Kent to go to bed. He agreed on condition that his grandfather would tell him a story.

"I can't tell bedtime stories," Kent said. "I can only tell true stories."

"When was the last time you told the truth and nothing but?" Abby demanded.

"It's a standard I never depart from, except for a few innocent embellishments."

"Innocent!" Abby said. "Your embellishments drove your Grandmother Randall to an early grave. You used to deceive her right and left about the mischief you were up to."

"Poor old girl," Kent said. "She only lived to be ninety."

"Eighty-seven," Abby corrected. "You've begun embellishing already."

"A fairly ripe age. Wasn't it the bard himself who said, 'The readiness is all'?"

"She was ready for her reward after bringing you up," Abby said. "Where would you have been if she hadn't stepped in after your mother died and kept you at least a little in line?"

"I'd be in jail for fraud, murder, and adultery."

Ruth looked on with mild indulgence while they played out their match, but kidding was one of the endowments that must have been out of stock when Brainerd's equipment was packed. His face hung open as though he expected violence to begin at any moment.

Kent finally agreed, in lieu of a story, to exhibit the mysteries of cat's cradle. He got young Kent stowed under covers and quieted, switched off the light above the boy's bed, and went back to the study. After making his way around the center table, he sat down in his chair again, extended his leg, and glanced at the glass-topped stand beside him. The image of a highball took form on the vacant surface, tawny warmth mellowing itself on melting cubes of ice. Too early; they'd have to take up the business of the evening, whatever it proved to be, before he could allow himself a nightcap.

"We drove up on short notice, Daddy," Ruth said, "because we felt—because something has come to a head. We can't avoid it any more. We wanted to talk it over with you."

"You know me," Kent said, "just a grubber in the vulgar scramble for profits. But I'm your old man. If I can help in any way—"

"You've done so much for us already," Brainerd said, "I wouldn't feel justified in letting Ruth bring this matter up, except that ultimately it affects—"

"It's about Franklin," Ruth said.

Franklin. Brainerd's child by his first wife. Kent tried to stifle his distaste. It was certainly remarkable what a man could be called on to do, in this case not even for his own daughter, his own grandchildren. He ought to be providing for his years of retirement with Abby; he ought to be building up an estate that would educate Ruth's two—no, three, and likely enough more after that. But of course, if Franklin needed expensive medical treatment or surgery—

"Is it his school?" Abby asked.

"We don't want to protect him more than he should be protected," Ruth said. "We don't want him to grow up prejudiced or feeling superior to children who don't have his background. But we don't have the right to deprive him of advantages, either. If you only knew what it's like! He isn't learning anything, he isn't making friends, he has nervous headaches, and terrible nightmares when he ought to be sleeping."

She went on to draw the portrait of a big-city school which was daily becoming more and more of a racial and economic melting pot. Listening, Kent felt as though she were recreating newspaper scareheads for him: vacant-lot rumbles, extortion schemes, dope peddling, collapse of authority, an educational and moral wasteland. Amity offered no parallel.

"It should be our problem," Brainerd said. "I wouldn't let Ruth mention it, except, as I was trying to point out, it affects Kent and Randall too. Franklin is disturbed to such an extent—"

"He feels alone and different," Ruth said. "It makes him resent Kent and Randy, and that's the worst possible thing for all of them."

Kent could see her position. She had to assume the rôle of mother to Franklin; she had to make them all feel, as much as she could, equally her own. He wished the situation could be different, but there it was.

"Where could you put him if you took him out of public school?" Abby asked.

A good private day school was available, it seemed, near enough so that Franklin could get back and forth. They had even been offered a small scholarship for him, but on their budget they couldn't accept it without a supplement.

"What are you waiting for?" Kent said. "Take the scholarship as soon as they'll let him in, and I'll make up the difference." He was tempted to add that they might consider some family planning for the future, but he restrained himself.

They would have gone on thanking him indefinitely if he hadn't put an end to it by proposing a nightcap. No one wanted to join him in a drink, but they'd keep him company while he had one himself. He went to the liquor cabinet, feeling virtuous enough to pour himself a liberal allowance. When he came back Brainerd said that at his new school Franklin would be exposed to sports as he hadn't before. He thought the opportunity might be good for the boy, but he hoped athletic competition wouldn't be emphasized to excess.

"The iron law of life," Kent said. After undertaking to subsidize Franklin's education, he was willing to indulge himself in a familiar litany that relieved his feelings. "Competition. Nature red in tooth and claw. The struggle for existence. Survival of the fittest. Keep one jump ahead of the other guy, or he'll jump on your ribs when you're down."

Ruth smiled at him. "You're not half so savage as you like to sound, Daddy. You roar like a lion, but you act like a lamb. I don't believe you ever jumped on a man's ribs when he was down."

"I've pushed his face in the mud many a time when a man was down on the football field."

"I don't believe it. I don't see why."

"When a man has to dig turf out of his eyes and nose, his wind is short and he can't see so well for two or three plays. That helps win games, if he's a member of the opposition."

"Do you always have to win? Does somebody always have to lose?"

"Or to ask another question," Brainerd said, "isn't sport supposed to be played by the rules? Is dirty—are illegal tactics part of it?"

They were challenging him; they were skeptical, Kent saw, they thought—what was Abby's word? They thought he was embellishing. Well, he'd let them have their fun. "It's give and take," he said. "I've had a rib kicked in myself, but I never held it against the guy that did it. I remember a guard on the team in Amity. I can see him to this day, Bull Chandler, the big, lazy ape. He used to slouch through a few plays, not even bothering to get his shoulders down for the charge. Just when his opposite number decided he was in for an easy afternoon and came in low and hard, Bull would bring his hands down and his knee up. After that Bull would be facing a substitute."

"I should think you wouldn't have allowed him on the team," Ruth said.

"We were a small school," Kent said, "and met a lot of tough opposition. We had to win by guile when we couldn't win by brute force. I remember when I used to pitch for the Amity High ball team. One game in particular—" He saw the glance that Ruth exchanged with Abby. "I may have told this one before," he said, "but I don't believe Brainerd has heard it."

"I'd like to," Brainerd said.

"You will," Abby told him. "Go ahead, Cappie, play the game again."

"In those days the high-school team was the town team. When we played a home game the whole town turned out, ready to scalp the opposition if it looked as though they might win, and when we played away the town tagged along to balance the local crowd that was ready to scalp us."

Kent addressed himself to Brainerd's face, which was looking at him in pendulous expectation, but through it his eyes began to see again the etched details of that far-off day of contest. He saw the dust and brightness of the June weather, the faces of the team, high-school kids, all scattered now, all lost track of, more than one of them dead. His fingertips bit delicately on the stitching of a baseball, feeling for the familiar grip from which he used to deliver his drop. He could stand batters on their heads with that pitch; it was called a sinker now, but then it was a drop, and a pitcher who could throw one was worth his weight in gold.

"We had a big game coming up one Saturday with an academy up the river from Amity. They were a bunch of hicks, but tough and scrappy, free hitters when they got up to the plate. Give them one they could get hold of, and they'd slug it into the next county. We'd beaten them the year before, and we knew they'd be laying for us with everything but pitchforks."

The day, if he had allowed it to, would have relived itself minute by minute in Kent's mind. He saw himself, Cap Warner, climbing with the rest of the team aboard the decrepit yellow railroad coach; he felt the agony of the old car as it lurched and grated up the branch line that followed the river. He saw the pinochle game conducted by a cluster of faithful townsmen at the head of the car; he saw his old man sitting upright at the back beside a deacon of the First Congregational Church. Rich material to sacrifice, but skip the preliminaries; get the audience to the ball game. No, begin with the trolley that was waiting at the railroad station to take them to the academy field on the far side of town across the river. He'd never forget his first sight of that trolley, an old-fashioned number, open at the sides, or it would have been open if it hadn't been completely boarded up except for a bare slit through which the motorman could see the rails ahead.

"Why was it boarded up?" Brainerd asked.

35

"We soon found out. We swung into Main Street, stopping every ten yards while the motorman clanked the bell with his foot and swore himself blue. Clods, brickbats, rotten eggs, everything but cobblestones beat a tattoo on the boards as we went by, while the multitude outside howled and reviled us."

"You always claimed before," Abby said, "that they picked up the cannon balls from the green in front of the Town Hall and threw them too."

"Did I forget the cannon balls? Thanks for reminding me," Kent said. "Well, the trolley line stopped at the bridge across the river. We had to tramp the last quarter of a mile, lugging our equipment in the dust and heat, escorted by the local constituency yelling profane catcalls and now and then bouncing a piece of turf off someone's neck.

"When we got to the field, the opposition pitcher was limbering up his arm. I recognized him right away, because he'd umpired for school games I worked in and given me pointers. He was an old pro. He'd pitched a dozen years or so for the Philadelphia Athletics. They'd be giving him ten or fifteen bucks for the afternoon's work. As a matter of fact, a couple of scouts from the Boston Braves had looked me over and made offers, but my old man wouldn't let me listen."

"Is that true, Daddy?" Ruth asked.

"True as Holy Writ. Ask your mother. Well, the umpire called play before we were half warmed up. The umpire was a priest, a big Irishman with a nose like a wad of red pebbles stuck in putty. If he had some close decisions to make, there wasn't any doubt which side he'd make them for. I saw right away that we'd be lucky to score against their pitcher, especially with His Holiness calling balls and strikes. All I could do was try to keep the opposition from getting on base. I threw curves, curves, curves all afternoon, and that's murder on a pitcher's arm. By divine intervention, we got one lucky run, and it held all the way down through the eighth inning and the first half of the ninth. Score, one to nothing, our favor, when they came up for their last turn at the plate.

"By that time I was through. I wobbled out to the mound

and tried a few warm-up pitches, and I knew my hour had struck. My fast ball had no hop, my curve wouldn't break, my change-up fell in the dirt before it even reached the plate. My arm was a toothache."

Kent paused, and Ruth said, "Go on, Daddy. Tell how you won anyway."

"Up comes their first batter and gets a resounding single through the box that almost takes my head off on the way by. The tying run on first base. The crowd sense the kill and begin to howl like hyenas. The next batter, by the grace of God, hits a little pop foul and is out. The crowd groan and consign him to everlasting perdition. The next guy gets a hit. The tying run on second, the winning run on first, and only one out. The crowd revive and yell like savages getting ready to throw a missionary in the pot. I look at the next batter, and I know it's a hopeless cause, but I get the signal from the catcher, go through my motion, heave the ball toward the plate, and pray. I hear the clean, sweet sound as the fat of the wood meets the ball, and I know it's over. A magnificent drive to right field. Ten feet one side or the other, and it would have gone for a triple and won the game. But somehow our luck held. The ball went straight for our right fielder's shoetops. He staggered forward, fell on his knees, got his hands on it, and somehow hung on. Two out. One more, and we have the game. The crowd reach a state of suicidal despair. They've been robbed, cheated, hornswoggled. They call down imprecations from on high and follow up the imprecations with cabbages and ripe fruit.

"Meanwhile the ball comes back to the infield, and our gang throw it around a bit, killing time to give my arm a rest. I walk over to our first baseman, and when someone tosses him the ball I stand up close, talking to him. In those days the hidden-ball play hadn't been ruled illegal. While the crowd howled and gibbered, he pretended to hand the ball to me, but he palmed it in his glove instead. I walked back to the mound and turned to His Holiness, the umpire. I stuck my chest in his belly and put my glove under his jaw and I said to him under my breath, 'Our first baseman has the ball, and he's going to tag

37

the runner when he takes a lead, and you're going to see it and call him out.' Sure enough, I put my foot on the mound, I get the catcher's signal, I begin my motion. The runner takes a lead off the bag, the first baseman tags him and holds up the ball in full view. I have my glove under the umpire's jaw again. 'Out!' says His Holiness and jerks his thumb. It was the game, but it was a costly victory."

"What happened?" Brainerd asked.

"We ran. The crowd boiled out on the field, primed for rape and murder, and we ran. Everybody grabbed the nearest glove or bat and took off. We ran till we had no legs, no lungs, no heart, with the crowd at our heels, baying for blood. We ran a quarter of a mile to the river and across the bridge and into the boarded-up trolley, and if the crowd hadn't got tired of the pursuit and begun taking it out on their own team instead of us, we'd be running yet."

"You enjoy replaying that game in your mind more than you ever did while it was going on," Abby said.

"Didn't you ever *lose* a game, Daddy?" Ruth asked.

"Now and then," Kent admitted, "but it's the victories you remember. A kindly law blots the defeats out of mind."

"And makes the victories ten times as big as life," Abby said.

She was welcome to the last word this time if she wanted it. Their faces showed they hadn't been suffering; they just couldn't bring themselves to admit as much.

Kent examined his glass and saw that it was still half full. He was entitled to wet his whistle after finishing his yarn; a workman was worthy of his hire. He allowed himself a generous swallow, and when he looked up, Ruth was getting to her feet, explaining that she and Brainerd needed sleep after a long hard drive. Abby went with them to the door, asking whether they were sure they had everything they needed. Then she came back and seated herself across from him again, stooping to rumple his hair on the way by. "Good old generous Cappie," she said.

"It's just the first step in a chain reaction," Kent said. "Three of Ruth's coming along to be educated, if it stops there, and everything I hand out now is taken out of what you and Ruth ought to have when I'm no longer around."

"You'll be around for a long while yet, please God."

"The years are catching up with me."

"Nonsense. You're in the prime of your powers. Besides, it may not be as bad as you expect. It won't be long before Brainerd moves into a bigger position, I'm sure. Ruth says he's just had another article accepted by one of the leading social-service journals."

Kent chose not to express his skepticism about Brainerd as a provider. Another thought was pushing forward in his mind. "Ruth looks as though the cat dragged her in," he said.

"She's tired, naturally. Who wouldn't be, in her condition, after that long drive?"

"Her neck is scrawny."

"You're oversensitive to the fact that she's giving us another grandchild."

"Isn't there some beauty course for expectant mothers that she could take? Or suppose I added two or three hundred to what the school will cost, couldn't she get herself up differently?"

Abby looked at him dazedly for a moment. Then her mouth trembled, and finally she laughed. "If consistency is for little minds, you have a great big one," she said. "Why don't you turn me into a doll? I'm the woman you have to see every day."

"You can have anything you want," Kent said, "as long as you promise not to change."

Abby turned away, concealing her expression. Then she faced him again and said, "Ruth can always use additions to her wardrobe if you want to give them to her."

"I'll write the check. You tell her what to do with it."

"I'll try," Abby said.

She remembered something she meant to attend to in the kitchen. Solitude closed in again, and with it fatigue and a lowering of spirit. He felt his eyes being pulled toward Grandma Randall's table, where the picture of Randy stood just within the circle of illumination from the standing lamp.

Abby had photographs of Randy in ski clothes, but she kept them out of view, shut away in drawers. In the picture on the table Randy was wearing a light summer jacket and khakis, and his shirt was open beneath his straight chin, beneath the face that everyone called the spit of Kent's own. Randy was good on skis, but no law on earth or above it protected the best against accident. Notching down a trail on a week-end in the mountains, Randy had swerved and tried to stop when a college crony ahead of him spilled. Randy hadn't made it; he went out of control himself and wound up against a tree. The hospital staff said it wouldn't have made any difference if the ski patrol had got him down sooner. Nothing could have undone the blow his head had taken. Kent accepted their word, but for a considerable time he had dreamed recurrently of scrambling and floundering, on powerless legs, through drifts without purchase, up the side of an impossibly steep and zenith-high mountain, crowned with blazing white, desperately trying to find an indefinite something it was necessary to reach in a hurry. At last, in a climactic recurrence, the dream melted at the end into a vision of Randy lying on the white-padded aluminum examination table, rolled on its rubber wheels, as it actually had been, into a bare anteroom of the hospital. A shadow at his side in the dream became Abby. They looked down at the face on the table and were convinced of what they had already been told in words. After that, if the first symptoms of the dream began, Kent seemed able to control its progress. He would roll over deliberately, wake, and remember its appropriate end. Well, that was that.

Kent took a last swallow of his highball. The liquor sat rancidly on his tongue. He was glad when Abby came back from the kitchen and asked him whether he wasn't ready to sign off and go to bed.

∘ ∘ 3 ∘ ∘

Kent had got well into his morning's work when Denis Prouty bobbed in for one of his unpredictable visits. Denis seemed to have made a remarkable overnight recovery. He was no longer the victim hacked white by Stocky's rough-edged blade; he even affected to be jaunty.

"Well, Cap," he said, "now that we know the worst, when do we sweep up the ashes?"

"I've called the only wrecker in town who's equipped to do the job," Kent said, "but it's a big one. It will take time."

"It's big all right." Denis's eyes dilated with a sort of awed pride at the magnitude of the problem his purchase had created. "Maybe we ought to get bids from some out-of-town firms? Maybe we ought to get advice?"

"I guess we can get rid of a pile of rubble without advice, Denis," Kent said. "Right now I've got a photographer over there taking pictures. Before we move a brick, we want to get the extent of loss on the record so the adjusters can't accuse us of faking the facts."

"Pictures. That's good, Cap. You're on the ball. The insurance, that's the thing that's going to settle whether we get out of this with any skin on our ass."

'Our,' Denis said; he must know that the threatened area of skin was his own, but he was hopefully trying to spread his risk.

"Do you think we're in for trouble, Cap?" he went on. "We had to push our agent pretty hard to get him to accept our valuation, and I don't know what sort of case he's going to put up to the adjusters."

For once Denis had a point. Kent could see trouble shaping up himself. The timing of the fire was bad, right on the heels of the new policy. No one could accuse Fullington Chemical and Pharmaceutical Corporation of burning down the barn for the insurance, like a farmer without a potato in the pot. All the same, the adjusters would fight for every nickel, and the coincidence wouldn't look favorable. "One of the things I want to do if we can is establish a cause," Kent said, "though as a matter of fact, cause unknown might help us more."

"How do you figure that?" Denis asked. "Stocky wants the cause cleared up right away."

"I have it on the pad to see the watchman this morning," Kent said. "I want to get his story before anyone else does, before the rumor factory starts to work. You notice the papers said 'fire of unknown origin.' They've checked with the fire chief, and so have I. He isn't planning any investigation and doesn't know anything we don't. We want to find a cause if we can, but if we can't, the adjusters can't raise any question of negligence. If they can't show that—"

"I see your point," Denis said, "but Stocky—"

"Let me talk with Tim O'Brian and find out what he has to offer," Kent said. "I'll check with you and Stocky later."

"Okay, Cap. Do that, and keep on the ball."

Denis went out, his face momentarily serene. He could worry about the trivial for a while, telling himself that he'd done his bit by the important and wouldn't have to confront it again for several hours. Kent began thinking how he would handle his cross-examination of Tim O'Brian.

He was glad he had called Tim from home before setting out for the plant that morning, to make sure that the night watchman would stay put and hold himself available for questioning. When he had come down the corridor to his office at the start of the day, Kent had found a delegation waiting for him from the union Grievance Committee. "We understand, Mr. Warner, you've fired Tim O'Brian, and the union can't put up with that." A lot of talk about seniority rules, and a lot of parading of contract provisions under his nose. He had to waste a quarter of an hour persuading them that he hadn't fired Tim, that nobody had or would. They knew as much all along, of course; they were just showing that the Grievance Committee kept active and alert.

What had put the idea in their heads, though? It was natural enough that Tim hadn't been heard of since the fire. He had probably reported for work, discovered that his occupation was going up in a holocaust, and taken himself home again to worry, afraid he might be held responsible. He might have called up the union himself as a precaution.

Tim was a mild, wizened little Irishman, steady in his habits by report, not given to drinking beyond a mug of beer now and then. The image of Tim brought up its counterpart, the lump under a blanket Kent had seen carried by on a stretcher just before the fight around the fire engine began. Tim had been luckier than his opposite number, the day watchman. A couple of freight clerks at Badger Extrusion had known Paul Zyblocki and surmised, when they noticed the first bloom of smoke, that he might be making his rounds. They got him out, but no respirators had been able to revive him.

Kent had planned to summon Tim O'Brian to the office, but he began to think it might be better to visit him on his own premises. A summons might put him in a funk; he might lose his head or lie so that no one could get the facts from him. The thing to do was to set him at ease, to make him feel he was helping the company; and the way to do that was to talk with him under the security of his own roof. The Grievance Committee had to be reckoned with, also. In thirty seconds they'd know whether Tim was on the lot, and they'd waylay him and make trouble. Kent asked his secretary to call the O'Brians' number; it would be well to warn them that he was on his way.

Tim's address led to a narrow side block a few corners from the municipal park at the center of town. The street cut a defile between flats of frame, stucco, and brick. Kent found a gap in the line of parked cars into which he could just wedge his own. When he got out he set his eyes on a shabby wooden three-decker, but no, Tim's number conducted him to a much more substantial apartment building of scrolled yellow brick, which rose to an eminence of six flights. No doubt Tim and his wife occupied quarters in the basement. Tim probably janitored the building during his afternoon hours. Wrong again: the name and number plate indicated a first-floor apartment. Kent pressed the button and let himself in when the buzzer sounded. At once a vigorous female voice began to welcome and guide him down the corridor.

"This way, Mr. Warner. We're at the back, just under the stairs. I'd have turned on the light, but the bulb has gone, and Tim hasn't had time to get his stepladder and put in a new one. Tim, here's Mr. Warner. I said to Tim when you called, I said, 'Mr. Warner is a wonderful man to work for, Tim. Here he is coming to see you himself, instead of asking you to go over to the office after all the worry you've had about the fire.' Wasn't it awful, Mr. Warner? About that poor day watchman—I never can say those Polish names! We can none of us tell when our hour will come, isn't that the truth?"

Confronting her now at the door of her apartment, Kent agreed it was the truth. He had a blurred, somewhat overpowering impression of a big, vigorously handsome face opposing him at close range, of a mass of black hair, of a pair of exposed forearms either one of which could have picked Tim up in a spoon.

"Come in, Mr. Warner. I've got a bit of coffee boiling on the stove. Tim, Mr. Warner's here. I'll just go see that it's hot. Cream and sugar, Mr. Warner?"

Kent said that he liked his coffee black and followed her into the apartment. She vanished into the kitchen, her skirts describing rapid arcs to left and right as she walked. Tim still failed to appear, though Kent detected hesitant movements in the adjacent room. His eye had a moment to survey the O'Brian parlor while he waited. It was generously large, or might have been, but it crowded on the visitor with a mob of objects, a heavy old-fashioned desk, several ornate tables, chairs adapted to large figures and small, a TV set of spacious screen. On the mantel stood a head of Christ, painted in electrically vivid colors and framed in gilt. From its crown of extravagantly long thorns, drops of blood fell like cranberries. The Holy Mother stood nearby in glazed earthenware. On desk and tables appeared photographs, no doubt of the O'Brian progeny, but so many pictures, taken at such various ages, as to defy a guess at the number of individuals represented. Kent had time to distinguish a girl in white veil and confirmation dress, a young priest, an Air Force sergeant, and a Little Leaguer in baseball uniform winding up to pitch. Then Mrs. O'Brian returned with coffee for three, and Tim entered diffidently from another door, timing his arrival to fall in behind her.

"There, Mr. Warner. Sit down and let me give you a cup. Tim, pull up a table so he won't have to hold it in his lap, and perhaps you'd like a slice of nutbread, Mr. Warner? I was

44

baking it just yesterday afternoon. I might have been taking it out of the oven the very minute when that poor Paul what's-his-name—" The whites of Mrs. O'Brian's eyes, rolling upward, implied that however unfathomable the coincidences of life might be, they were providentially governed, and invoked the mercy of the Holy Mother on the soul of Paul Zyblocki.

Kent insinuated himself into a chair, pinned between the desk and a heavy table. "This is a fine place you have," he said. "Have you been here long?"

Tim glanced guardedly at his spouse and seemed to receive a permissive glance in return. "Since Maggie came into the property," he said.

Maggie allowed herself a shade of complacency. "My uncle left the building when he died, Mr. Warner. Of course there was a mortgage, and we had to work hard to meet the payments, but the boys and girls, when they started to work themselves, always brought home part of their pay. They're good boys and girls, and we've never lost one of them, thanks be to God."

It wasn't hard to imagine the boys and girls putting their paychecks in Maggie's maternal palm. Janitorial in status? The O'Brians were capitalists. At least Maggie was—a *rentier* if not an entrepreneur. Kent decided to take the short way to business. He said he'd been surprised to find some of Tim's friends at the plant worried for fear Tim would be laid off. Tim would know better than that himself, wouldn't he?

Tim squirmed a little and hoped no one had made trouble for Mr. Warner. He'd only called up a friend in the union and asked him, just as a friend, whether there was anything he ought to do. He didn't think any harm would come of that. Kent said no harm had been done, but he hoped Tim was satisfied that the company would keep him on the payroll.

"It's good of you to come over and tell us, Mr. Warner," Maggie said. "I told Tim myself he wouldn't have anything to worry about with you in charge."

Kent saw that it was going to be hard to detach Maggie from the conversation. Both she and Tim were suspicious and afraid, afraid that Tim would somehow be held responsible,

45

that he might be asked to perjure himself, afraid of God knows what. Suppose, Kent said finally, a fire should break out in this very building. He hoped nothing of the sort would ever happen, but if it did, Maggie and Tim would make every effort to discover the cause, not in order to blame anyone, but because you never could tell what might come up in an insurance case. Tim could help the company greatly by confiding whatever he knew. This appeal to the instincts of the *rentier* took effect. "You men," Maggie said, "want to settle your business, and you don't want a woman sticking her nose in it." She gathered up the coffee and nutbread and retreated to the kitchen.

Without the support of his commanding officer, Tim became more than ever a lone private in dread of ambush. He couldn't understand Kent's minute interest in the details of his watchman's rounds. His plaintive look implied that Kent should have a mind above such small potatoes. Kent had to drag every step from him, and even so the account remained blank, nothing seen, heard, observed to suggest a cause of the fire.

"Tim," Kent asked in a final probing effort, "did you ever look into the tunnel system that connected the buildings underground?"

Tim had never received any instructions to do so.

"I'm not saying you should have, Tim. I'm just asking whether you ever did."

Tim knew about the tunnels. He couldn't help finding the doors to them when he patrolled the cellars. Had he ever walked through them on his rounds? Well, Mr. Warner would understand that when the weather was mean it was a lot easier to use the tunnels than to fight his way from building to building above ground, through the mud and the midnight wind. Of course; no harm in that. But was the light system working, or could he make his way by flashlight? The Holy Mother was Tim's witness, what with the rubbish and the broken timbers, he couldn't trust himself down in those black holes with nothing but a flashlight.

Well, no doubt on the night before the fire he made his rounds through the tunnels. The weather was mean enough then, the tail of a three-day southeaster.

No, he'd made his rounds above ground that night.

Why?

The chair in which Tim sat appeared to grow uncomforta-ble. He shifted his weight, and his short arms pulled at his coat as if it were binding him. His eyes went toward the kitchen with a cornered look. Light but perceptible sounds from behind the not quite closed door suggested that, while Maggie had withdrawn her presence, she might well be keep-ing herself within earshot.

Why hadn't he gone through the tunnels that night? He didn't think it mattered, so he hadn't mentioned it to anybody, but he did turn on the tunnel lights, only as soon as he threw the switch, the fuse blew. So he put on his hat and coat and boots and made his rounds through the rain, and it was blowing and coming down that fearful you might think it was Noah's flood.

That was all that happened? He blew a fuse? He didn't have any extra fuses handy?

Well, he did have some extras, as it happened.

Did he try another? More than one?

He didn't think it made any difference. He did try the ones he had, but each time he put a fuse in, it blew, so he gave up and went out into the rain, the way he said.

A picture of Tim's operations formed in Kent's mind, the subdued little Irishman, with his sandy face, his freckled but-tons of cheekbones, his mouth like a pouch with its drawstring pulled tight, patiently feeding fuses into their sockets to no avail until he resigned himself and slumped out into the weather. The first fuse wouldn't matter; Tim was right about that. It would merely report and nullify a short circuit. But the second and the third and any beyond that! Suppose a break in the tunnel wall somewhere outside the main building, where Tim would start. Suppose a washout occurred during the rain, and a trickle of water seeped through the break into the tunnel, wetting the frayed insulation on the old light wires. There was your short circuit, all set up and ready to function! Each time Tim screwed in a fuse, a current would wing through the wire to the moist spot, and enough heat would build up to ignite any adjacent fuel. A little waste caught

47

on a beam around the wire, a spark falling to a pile of litter on the floor—any amount of inflammable trash would be handy. It would begin to smolder. For the rest of the night and most of the next day the slow combustion would eat its way through the tunnel system. Paul Zyblocki would smell it during the afternoon. He might go down cellar and open a tunnel door to see what was happening. The smoke might well burst around him like an explosion. Smoke could bewilder and overcome a man before he knew what was happening. Paul would blunder to the stairs and make his way up. Then he would pass out, the small pockets of his human lungs oxygen-starved, and the fire would find the draft and air it needed to purge itself into flame.

There you had a cause. The reconstruction spelled possibility, even probability, but of course it didn't spell certainty. It left plenty of room for a plea of cause unknown, and cause unknown looked more attractive than ever. The important thing at the moment would be to keep Tim from talking. It wouldn't do to have the story of those successive fuses providing material for the rumor factory at the plant.

Kent considered what he could do to keep the drawstring pulled tight on Tim's mouth. The chances looked favorable. Tim didn't booze it up with cronies at the bar, and it seemed likely that Maggie would help to keep him discreet. The kitchen was remarkably silent. An expectancy screwed up to the breathless point seemed to reach out from it, waiting for what Kent would say. He tried to speak distinctly without raising his voice. Tim couldn't be held responsible for the fire; the cause might well remain entirely unknown, in fact that was Kent's best judgment. Just one little piece of advice, though: if a fuse ever blew in the apartment building and its successor followed suit, Tim had better quit right there and call an electrician.

Tim squirmed in his chair, and his watery eyes ran over with questions he didn't dare ask. He might be thinking of Paul Zyblocki, and if so the unstated thought had best be left to nag his mind inarticulately. "The reason for keeping quiet," Kent said, "is that you never know about insurance. You try to protect yourself, but you may have to go to court to collect on your policy. Now I hope that won't happen, but if it should, and if your story got around the plant or anywhere, you might be called as a witness, Tim, and there's no knowing how you might be cross-examined by some smart lawyer."

Kent watched to see the effect of the shot, and he thought it had gone home. Tim seemed to grow smaller in his chair, and paled under his freckles. Kent heard a moist exhalation from the kitchen. "Say good-by to Mrs. O'Brian for me, and thank her for the coffee, will you, Tim?" Kent asked, and he managed to make his exit without confronting Maggie again in person.

Stocky was not alone when Kent presented himself to make his report. Denis Prouty sat by the desk, his knees crossed, the upper shin swaying in short, rapid strokes, though Stocky didn't seem to be chewing Denis's ear at the moment.

"Well, where have *you* been, Cap?" Stocky demanded. "Down in Georgia playing golf with Ike?"

"I said when we couldn't find you around the plant—" Denis began, but Stocky cut him an impatient look.

Kent explained his motives for interviewing Tim O'Brian on the home front.

"Well, where do we stand?" Stocky asked. "What did you find out?"

Kent described his cross-examination.

"So what! He blew a lot of fuses," Stocky said. "Where does that leave us?"

It was as hard to explain physical causation to Stocky as it would have been to Tim, but Kent tried to sketch the possibilities.

"Goddamn it, I don't like it," Stocky said. "It looks as though they might have an angle, negligence or some God-damned thing."

"I'm telling you and Denis how I'd reconstruct what happened," Kent said, "but I'm not telling anyone else. If we can keep Tim quiet, I think we can argue it's a case of cause unknown."

49

"The way I see it," Denis put in, "that may be better than if we could establish the cause."

Denis avoided Kent's eye. Stocky cut him another uncomplimentary look, but Stocky was beginning to get the point, as he usually did when it was made for him. Kent said he thought that if the company's claim for losses was well presented, the adjusters would have a hard time making the question of cause an obstacle to settlement. Nothing could be learned from Paul Zyblocki, who hadn't got out alive. As for Tim, he had an unimpeachable character record, and if he kept his mouth shut about what he didn't need to say, he could simply furnish a report that he'd observed nothing out of order on the night of his last rounds before the fire.

Stocky's eyes glinted. "All right, Cap, that's the way we'll play it. You're going to follow this insurance deal all the way through. You," he added as though by afterthought, "and Denis."

The assignment wasn't one that Kent coveted; he wanted to be an engineer, wanted to begin putting up his new office building. He'd done his bit by the insurance problem, and what did he know about that kind of thing anyway? Still, he felt himself edging closer to the decisions of management, and he couldn't complain if Stocky showed confidence in his judgment outside the purely technical sphere. "If we get a good settlement," Kent asked, "does that affect the building program?"

Stocky grinned with a mixture of sympathy and resistance. "You want to get going on the new office, don't you, Cap? Sorry. That waits. We've got to see whether this shack can be revamped for limited-sales. I want to bring that up at the next Directors' meeting. I want a report right away."

"Okay, Stocky, I'll get to work," Kent said.

"Anything I can do to help," Denis said, "let me know."

Denis got up, and Kent started to follow, but Stocky motioned him to keep his chair. "One more thing, Cap," he said. "It won't take but a minute."

Kent sat down again, surprised. It was unusual for Stocky to launch anything he had in mind on an apologetic note.

Time was his to command. Denis went out with an uneasy look over his shoulder. When the door closed, Stocky seemed at a loss to begin. He spoke vaguely of an expanding future, rich with incentives and rewards, which obviously wasn't what he meant to talk about. One of the things that would come up at the next Directors' meeting was the question of revising executive salaries. They wouldn't be revised downward; that was for sure. He wanted Cap to know.

Kent said the news was welcome and put in a word for young Shepherdson. Shep would be bought off by a competitor if he wasn't recognized at his value.

Stocky looked momentarily disgruntled but agreed that Shep's case ought to be considered. At last he brought himself to the point. "You have a brother-in-law at Rowley. Professor of something, isn't he?"

"Arthur Scheuer?" Kent said. "He's a Professor of Biology. We call ourselves brothers-in-law, though strictly we aren't. Arthur married Abby's kid sister, Rachel."

"What does he do for a living? Teach the boys how to cut up frogs to see what makes them tick?"

Kent allowed himself to smile. "He's more of a big shot than that. His specialty is genetics, and he's supposed to have something of a scientific reputation. Books, honorary degrees, that kind of thing. As a matter of fact, he's trained two or three of the young longhairs who make new products for us here in the lab."

Stocky's expression did not suggest that he had been much illuminated by this information. He looked a trifle disappointed. He said, "If your brother-in-law is in the scientific line, he probably won't even know this guy over there that Herman thinks is a tin god on wheels."

"A faculty member?" Kent asked.

Stocky's expression became plaintive; the bleat of bewilderment and pathos made itself heard in his voice. "Education!" he said. "Goddamn it, what does it do to the boys, Cap? Take me. Didn't even finish high school, but I hacked my way up, I'm doing something constructive and making some dough besides, if I say it myself. Now every little bastard has to have a college degree and a starting salary of seven, eight grand just because he's got a sheepskin, even if he doesn't know how to wipe his own ass with it. Well, they talk about opportunities, and I don't want to stand in the way of Herman having what I didn't have, but what does higher education do to him? Know what kind of a fool idea he's got in his head now?"

"I'm afraid I don't," Kent said.

Stocky's distress became so acute that he couldn't articulate. His throat tightened as if he were trying to swallow a baseball. "The kid thinks he wants to be—" Stocky had to pause again before forcing out the final distasteful words. "Wants to be a creative writer. Creative! What's that, Cap? You and I think we're doing something constructive around here, but what's this creative business? What does it mean?"

The word was one that did not come readily to Kent himself, though he hardly felt Stocky's aversion to it. He could think of no answer at the moment that would alleviate Stocky's discomfort. Stocky saved him the necessity of speaking.

"Well, they have this guy at Rowley, writer in residence, or something like that they call him. He's a writer. Writes novels, by what Herman says. When Herman comes home, which isn't often, he hasn't a word to say about anything except how this guy is a creative artist and the greatest thing since Shakespeare wrote *Gulliver's Travels*. I thought maybe your brother-in-law might know him, might have some dope on how this kind of thing figures in a college set-up. Young Herman, I can't get him to put his mind on anything he could use, economics, accounting, practical stuff like that. Writers, they're off my beat, but by what I hear—well, Goddamn it, I'm no prude, but you can't even pick up a good war yarn these days without it's full of sex and worse. I'd just like to know what gives with this guy Herman thinks is such a hot shot."

Kent felt himself dragged from one novel commission to another, from insurance claims to private intelligence service. The second commission he thought he could pass off lightly. "As a matter of fact," he said, "Abby and I haven't seen

Arthur and Rachel since the fall term opened up at Rowley. We'll be getting together soon, and I can at least find out whether Arthur knows the man you're interested in."

"Do that," Stocky said, and appeared relieved even by a gesture that would probably be fruitless.

Reminded, unexpectedly and out of context, of the man who had married Abby's sister, Kent found himself still thinking of Arthur Scheuer when he reached his office; not of the present Arthur, the geneticist of established and comfortable distinction, but of the shy, self-contained boy who had grown up a couple of years behind Kent himself in Amity. The Arthur of those days could have made himself into a halfback or a shortstop; he was lithe and well coordinated and had a burnish of outdoors about him, but he disliked the mud and sweat and body contact of football and the long moments in baseball with nothing to do except stand around waiting for action. Not all the blandishments or appeals to school spirit that Cap Warner and his teammates could bring to bear would induce Arthur to come out for sports. Arthur's family maintained a similar detachment from the life of their neighbors. The Scheuers weren't known to be members of any church. They were of German derivation, and in Amity the prejudices of the First World War were slow to fade out. The name would have been no handicap if the Scheuers had cared to mix with the Randalls, Rumfords, Amsdens, Larkins, Warners, Kellys of Amity; but if they didn't, their alienation was hardly surprising.

Kent didn't have much use for Arthur in those days. All through high school they might hardly have crossed paths to any purpose if it hadn't been for one unexpected encounter. Kent had gone for a tramp by himself into the country one Saturday in late summer. He took along his twenty-two on the off chance of meeting a fox; at worst he could keep his marksman's eye in practice by picking off a squirrel. He must have tramped five or six miles over ridges where the chestnut burrs were pushing out their quills and the beech nuts beginning to ripen, before he came down a

53

wooded slope and out into a meadow where someone long ago had cleared a farm. The land was rapidly going back to brush, but patches of run-out hay still intervened among the clumps of sweet fern, the gray birches, the seedling scrub-oak. In the midst of such a patch, Kent perceived a sunlit figure standing motionless, tilted slightly forward, peering down at something in the grass at his feet. Kent came quietly up behind. Arthur was so intent that he wasn't aware of an intruder until Kent was at his heels and could see what Arthur was looking at. Two green-snakes had woven themselves a little pillar of hay stalks, and halfway up this twisted column, three or four inches above ground, they had implicated themselves tightly with each other in a knot of coils. As Kent's eye began to distinguish details, he made out two heads and necks looping downward and outward in opposite directions from the central knot; loose ends of serpent seemed in fact to ravel out every which way, while the involved mid-coils were drawn so tight that the lighter green of the bellies had paled until it looked like the whites of eyes. From one of the heads, with its minute, impersonal, elongated bead of an eye, a gentle yet intense rhythmic motion passed down the neck and along the spine.

Kent felt a spasm of revulsion. He found a stick in the grass and picked it up with an impulse to smash into the knot of coils or at least poke it and see what would happen. As he stooped, Arthur noticed him. He put out his hand and lightly touched Kent's arm. Kent felt himself restrained, he could hardly say how or why. "They're copulating," Arthur said.

Kent knew about copulation; he didn't know the word, but under the circumstances it was self-clarifying. Funny, he'd never thought that snakes—they just laid eggs that you came on now and then in pockets of moldy bark. For Christ's sake, imagine! They were just like dogs and cats and male and female in general. Well, naturally, when you stopped to consider.

In Amity you picked up your knowledge of that kind of thing by back-alley education. You got no help from your old man, who, if he alluded to the subject at all, spoke in hor-

54

tatory euphemisms. You got no help from school, and of course none from the First Congregational Church. Kent gave Arthur a look. The sort of interest Arthur was taking in the spectacle had an odd quality about it. Certainly it wasn't a back-alley interest. Kent had the feeling that Arthur wasn't quite human. Amity gave much, but it didn't provide such terms as detachment or pure curiosity or craving for knowledge as such. Kent came to feel in retrospect that Arthur had given him his first glimpse of the property of mind that went into science, a property very different in degree if not in kind from his own relation to engineering. Kent wanted to get things right; he wanted to know what would work and what wouldn't; he wanted to keep abreast of the latest methods and advances; he could make his own fresh applications now and then as an industrial designer; but he needed a practical problem as incentive, and it wouldn't have occurred to him to devote his life to theoretical research regardless of whether any application ever ensued or not. For a kid in Amity, Arthur had achieved quite a fusion of field observation and book knowledge; as the years went by he swung further and further over on the theoretical side, until he liked to say he wasn't even a scientist any more, he was a philosopher who'd missed his calling. In any case, he was the man who married Abby's sister. It was just as well none of them could foresee at the time what would come of that.

∘ ∘ *4* ∘ ∘

The October afternoon was drawing to a close, darkening Arthur Scheuer's office in the Biology Building. The office had been a seminar room when Arthur acquired it; he still used it for his own graduate seminar, but since it wasn't a lab adapted to experimentation, he saw no need to keep it austere. It was comfortably large, and he had taken the trouble to furnish it with an Oriental rug beneath the seminar table, tiers of bookshelves between the windows, and a watercolor or two on available wall space. Now and then he thought he detected a glint in the eyes of colleagues, as though they were sniffing at these appurtenances, looking on them as affectations, but Arthur refused to be deterred.

He glanced up at the windows and switched on his desk lamp. Janice had already pulled the cord of the overhead light above the table. "This is a hard one to answer, Janice," Arthur said, picking up the last of the letters he wanted to dispose of before letting his secretary go.

"The poor girl," Janice said, raising her eyes briefly from the shorthand notebook braced on her knee. "I can imagine how she must feel."

"I've never had an appeal for advice of this sort since I began teaching," Arthur said. "At my years, I'm insulated from the personal problems of students. The generations come and go, I see them as rows of pencils taking notes, the lab staff grades their experiments and exams, and that's that. I don't mind being protected, I confess, but this letter makes me feel how remote a man can become without realizing it."

"The girl who wrote it didn't think you were impossibly remote," Janice said. "You must have made an impression on her."

"Well, I'll have to send her an answer," Arthur said.

He didn't need to look at the letter again to recall it almost sentence by sentence. If the girl only knew what nerve she had unwittingly touched in her former teacher! Dear Professor Scheuer: Of course you won't remember me—of course he didn't. Did she secretly hope that among the hundreds who yearly sifted through his lecture room she had miraculously left behind some impression of her unique identity? You won't remember, but three years ago I took your course in Evolution and Genetics. I hardly ever spoke to you, but you seemed so understanding, even in your lectures—that's why I'm taking the liberty—

The girl's problem was commonplace enough to a geneticist. She married; a child was born and lived only a few days. They didn't want her to see it; everyone told her not to, but she insisted. All she could bring herself to say was that the baby hadn't been *right*. Her husband thought they should try again right away. Her gynecologist said what happened the first time didn't mean the next child would be abnormal, and it would be best for her if they went ahead and everything turned out well, as they could reasonably expect it would. The girl herself, though, was troubled. She admitted wanting a child very much, but she remembered things that Arthur had pointed out in his lectures. She'd meant to keep her notes on his course, but somehow she'd mislaid them. The old folk saying that lightning doesn't strike twice in the same place— hadn't he said that it didn't apply genetically? That if something went wrong, the lightning was more likely to strike the same couple again than just any couple starting fresh? Weren't there curves that showed how the chances rose for given hereditary conditions? The girl wanted to be *sure*. Could Arthur give her any advice, or tell her what to read?

The girl might not have learned much, nor learned it very well, but here she was at a point where mind, the fruits of research impelled by curiosity, intersected with the shocks of personal life, and she was trying to use mind, trying to use her education, to the best of her lights. Arthur shouldn't find it hard to encourage her. He cleared his throat and said, "I know just what I'll have to tell this girl, but the words won't come. I don't know why it should be so difficult."

That was being less than candid; he did know why he was finding his answer difficult. The letter made him feel transparent, as though his life were hung up on a fluorescent scroll in his chest cavity, so that anyone who looked at him could read it. How had he managed to stand before a lecture room full of undergraduates three times a week year after year, talking genetics? Just because they remained strangers? He glanced at his clock: almost five. As his eyes let the dial hands glide out of focus, the whole round face, with its highlights reflected from the desk lamp, seemed to give him a look at once blank and knowing, as if it too had seen through him.

"I tell you what, Janice," he said. "It's about quitting time. "I'll be alone this evening. I'll take this home with me and type out an answer myself."

"I'll be glad to stay if you want to finish it, Arthur."

"No, you go along. I expect Claudia will be calling for me any minute. She said she'd drive me home after she finishes with her job."

"You must be proud to have a niece like Claudia," Janice said, already folding her shorthand book and getting up from her chair. "She looks more beautiful every time I see her."

"I sometimes have the same impression myself," Arthur said, "but I try to maintain a reasonable agnosticism about it."

Janice took her coat from a hanger in the corner of the room, shook her graying hair, and put on her hat. In the corridor outside Arthur's office, a sound of footsteps approached. They couldn't be Claudia's; no one but Lamson Crocket could produce, on the uncarpeted floor of the Biology Building, just that series of sharp percussions. Why couldn't the man wear rubber heels, like the rest of the human race? Arthur hoped against the weight of probability that Lamson wouldn't wheel in the door for one of his enigmatic visits, but his fibrous little figure appeared just as Janice was gathering up her handbag and gloves. Lamson dodged around her and looked sourly at her back as she said good night and went out. Arthur was aware that his command of a full-time secretary gave an occasion of envy to colleagues less fortunate. He owed the luxury to his large undergraduate lecture course, Biological Sciences 3, Introduction to Evolution and Genetics, which required more staff work and bookkeeping than he could be expected to handle without Janice.

Lamson took the long way around the room, circling the seminar table, compulsively touching stacks of books, charts, and papers with a nervous fingertip as he passed. "One of the things we need around here," he said abruptly, halting at a talking distance from Arthur's chair, "is more secretarial help."

Arthur didn't enjoy disliking colleagues. He made an effort not to dislike Lamson Crocket, but he had to admit that the man could create an effect of rasping discomfort. Lately he wondered whether he could detect some obscure change in Lamson's manner toward him, some gloating edge to his sarcasm, some air of knowing a thing or two that Arthur didn't. "If you get your Project going," Arthur said, "no doubt extra secretarial help will come with it."

"A lot of things will be different when we get the Project under way."

Now what did Lamson mean by that? Arthur told himself that he had no objection to Lamson's Project as such, though he didn't care to become immersed in it himself. Let Lamson sink himself as deeply as he wanted in a plan for team-research into space-age biology and medicine, even to the exclusion of everything else; but when he tried to drag the whole department with him in his obsession, Arthur begged leave to dissent. Crocket's Craze, Arthur privately called the Project, though each time he used the phrase in his thoughts he tried to remind himself that it might not be altogether just. He did think he was fair in foreseeing that if the Project swept the whole department it would mean an almost total dependence on government subsidies; and it would also mean a loss of concern for Biology as a whole, a loss of a comprehensive and philosophical way of looking at the subject. Yet of course the age of space was coming on, like it or not, and research into it was part of the immense adventure in the Baconian advancement of knowledge on which the survival of a population already overcrowding the planet would depend.

Lamson evidently didn't mean to take up Arthur's mildly offered opening about the Project. His mind made a grasshopper leap to something else. "Well," he said, "I see you've lost your fair-haired boy."

It took Arthur a moment to see that Lamson referred to a promising assistant, who had left abruptly in mid-term for a more lucrative job in the laboratories at Fullchem. Crocket must know that the loss, and especially its manner and timing, inconvenienced and disappointed Arthur considerably. He must know, too, that Arthur would resent the charge that he tried to make disciples and favorites of his younger staff. Well, it was Lamson's way; he probably thought he was kidding. "If he'd been a white-haired boy," Arthur said, "I'd have tried harder to keep him. His life is his own."

"You'll replace him. That gives you another nice little appointment plum."

"I'll have to replace him. I wish I didn't. I don't know that necessary staff appointments are plums, in a political sense."

"How many do you have mopping up for you now?"

"In Bi Sci 3? Twelve," Arthur said, "for about three hundred students, lab work, exams, and discussion sections."

"Quite a block of patronage."

Lamson's tone made Arthur look at him closely. He was astonished at what he saw. Lamson's left cheek was turned toward him, and in its pinched, sallow cavity a small green nerve, like a tiny caterpillar, twitched biliously. Arthur was unused to personal dislike or hostility. He suddenly seemed to find himself confronted with it in an acute form. The impression was overwhelming. He thought of the Project, and then he thought of the Committee on the Revision of Departmental Offerings. He was himself a member of the Committee; he had no reason to expect hostility from that quarter. But Lamson was a member too. Lamson was using the Committee to further his Project, or trying to; would he also use it to shoot Arthur's course out from under him, unless Arthur agreed to a trade, swinging his support to all that Lamson wanted from his Project?

Arthur despised himself for his suspicion, and no sooner thought of it than the thought seemed to him absurd. Human nature didn't act, except in books, from deliberate and sustained Machiavellianism; it was too impulsive and unstable, even in its enmities and its malice. "I don't mind being kidded, Lamson," Arthur said, "but I wouldn't like it at all if I were really considered a patronage hog." For an instant he was pleased with himself; he had said the thing at once firm and pacific. Then he felt less certain. His temper rose. If Lamson actually meant what he had insinuated, Arthur should simply have told him to go to hell. As it was, he'd let Lamson put an idea in his head that wouldn't easily be displaced. Lamson the Machiavellian Iago, Arthur Scheuer the suggestible Moor. That was too funny. There couldn't be anything in it.

"Don't take it hard, old man," Lamson said. "No one could seriously suggest that vested interests have any place around our shop, could he?"

This time no nerve quivered in his cheek. He laughed briefly; he'd even offered something like an apology. Or had he? His question hung in the air with an ambiguity that almost seemed calculated. And Lamson had insinuated another phrase into the talk, 'vested interests.' "I certainly trust no one could," Arthur said. "This course of mine, Bi Sci 3, it wasn't my proposal in the first place, you know. The Department wanted a new introductory course that would appeal, if possible, to students in any field. They asked me to try it. That was about ten years ago, before you joined us. Part of the idea was to provide junior teaching opportunities, and hence my staff of assistants. I've had the impression the Department wanted me to keep on with the course, because I didn't know any other member had a relish for this particular job. Of course the Department could call it off if it chose to."

There, that ought to show any reasonable man that Arthur didn't go in for vested interests or patronage for the sake of position. But hadn't he protested too much? And if the Department merely intimated a wish, would he really give up his course with no hard feelings or hurt pride? It came over him sharply that he didn't want to give it up. It meant a lot more to him than simply one part of his teaching assignment; his feelings toward it were creative. It was a book that he wrote serially, term after term, modifying, bringing in new knowledge as knowledge grew, a book he wrote by his own active presence, not merely setting down typed symbols in private. Through the course, though, he hoped to work his way toward a final printed and published book that would constitute his legacy to any who might read. These were things he couldn't say to Lamson. By that very fact Lamson had put him needlessly on the defensive.

Lamson's mind made another of its grasshopper leaps. He picked up a book from the seminar table and appeared to sniff at it. "What's this?" he demanded. "*All Men Are Islands*, by Malcolm Islay. How does that fit into the philosophy of evolution?"

"Islay, if you've happened to notice," Arthur said, "is our Writer in Residence for this year. I fell in with him one day at lunch at the Faculty Club, and that led to an exchange of books. *All Men Are Islands* is the collected volume of his short stories."

"What does he mean? You might as well say all men are watermelons, or all men are flypaper."

Arthur laughed. "You can't expect the language of literature to be the same as the language of science, though I sometimes think the two aren't so far apart as we suppose. Metaphor has a place in both. What's our model of the DNA molecule except a sort of metaphor worked out in wire and plastic instead of words? Islay, I suspect, is reversing the fashionable tag from Donne, to the effect that no man is an island to himself. Perhaps the suggestion came from his own name—Islay is an island in the Hebrides, as I reminded myself by looking it up."

"Literature," Lamson said. "How do you find time for it?"

"I wish I could find more."

"Is this Islay teaching you to write novels?"

"He would have had to start thirty-five years ago, as he's doing with the students he has here now."

Lamson's eye swung sardonically toward Arthur's two volumes of essays, addressed to laymen, wedged in their corner of the bookshelves. Arthur was prepared to hear him suggest that he had already tarred his hand with fiction, but if Lamson had the idea, he kept it to himself. He turned about abruptly and set his progress toward the door. As he passed the bookshelf, he dragged a compulsive nail along a row of books, as a boy trails a stick along the pickets of a fence. "Well, nice to see you, Arthur," he said from the doorway. "See you tomorrow in the Committee." The click of his heels receded down the corridor.

Arthur looked up himself at the titles of his two collections of essays. How could anyone see a menace in such a bundle of mannerisms as Lamson Crocket? *Evolution and the Human Spirit*, by Arthur Comfort Scheuer. *Genetics and Ultimate Purpose*, by Arthur Comfort Scheuer. That little green hostile nerve twitching in the man's cheek. Something was eating him, but it would be absurd to worry about it. What could be keeping Claudia? If she meant to drive him home, she should have appeared ten minutes ago. She'd probably lost track of time helping some graduate student with a report in Anthropology. As a secretary, Claudia was too generously interested in personnel.

Arthur Comfort Scheuer. Three lines of type on the spine of each book. Why not just Arthur, or A. C.? Comfort was a ridiculous name at best, an aberrant Puritan gene that by some accident got into the Scheuer heredity. Don't think about aberrant genes now. Time enough for that when you take that girl's letter home to answer tonight. Perhaps, when he got to the final book he wanted to write, he would drop the Comfort. But no, he liked the formality and the rhythm of the full name, pretentious or not. It went somehow with the style he aimed at, the style that reviewers praised him for. Clear, elegant, and racy all at once, they said, or some of them did. The praise might not mean much coming from reviewers inured to the trade jargon, but Islay praised him too. Of course Islay wasn't given to understatement, at least in conversation; he was extravagant and impulsive. Arthur didn't know why the two of them had seemed to hit it off so well at first sight. Odd, what a capacity the man had to break down barriers, especially when he made such a play of the notion that all lives run on unbridgeable parallels and no human being ever pierces through to the reality of another. Almost at once Arthur had felt Islay's mottled eyes lancing into him as if they could read at sight that scroll hung up in his chest. More strangely still, Arthur caught himself almost wishing that Islay could read it, or that he could break through his own reserve and lay himself bare. Unthinkable notion! Islay would put him in a novel with the mocking undertone that played beneath the ingratiating surface of his work.

Islay's praise was pleasant, at any rate. Not only had he read Arthur's two books, he'd tried to cope with some of his technical articles, as well. "You've read a lot," Islay said. "My kind of reading, I mean. I didn't know you scientists ever came out of the lab long enough to look at a poem."

"I don't know why we should shut each other out of our different ways of trying to deal with the scheme of things."

"That poem of Arnold's you quote somewhere," Islay said.

"If I'd remembered it, I would have used it as an epigraph."
His voice, deep and roughened at the edges, rang out unself-
consciously through the dining room of the Faculty Club
and caused an amused turning of heads. Arthur heard the lines
in double intonation, part Islay's voice, part the more remote
and abstract voice he had caught long ago from the printed
page:

> Yes, in the sea of life enisled,
> With echoing straits between us thrown,
> Dotting the shoreless, watery wild,
> We mortal millions live alone.

"There's more to the poem, you know," Arthur said.
"There's the stanza in which the nightingales divinely sing,
and at least make their notes audible from shore to shore."

"You mean a writer should burble like a nightingale," Islay
said. "No, it's illusion. Nothing but the noises come across.
People hear each other's noises and think they're communi-
cating, but they're just kidding themselves."

"How is it we both respond to Arnold's poem the same
way, then?"

"How do we know it's the same way?"

"But if you can't understand others," Arthur persisted,
"how can you write for them, and if they can't understand
you, how can they read you? Some part of the evidence seems
to go against your view, Malcolm."

"Oh, they're all grist for my mill," Islay said. "Mutual understanding isn't necessary. A writer is an egotist. All life is a
grindstone for his little ax. He has no life of his own except
what he creates in his writing, and that's done from appearances. 'This great stage presenteth naught but shows,' if we're
going to quote poetry at each other. I give people an image
made up out of what I can see, and they fill up the outline
with what they imagine they feel inside themselves, and then
they think that's what I meant. Every man knows he's Hamlet, but no two men agree what Hamlet is."

The loose, particolored skin of Islay's face began to twitch
and slide this way and that in patches. Arthur watched, fascinated and amused, until the whole mobile play settled into
an expression almost solipsistic in its absorption. Islay had

withdrawn so completely from his surroundings that the room in the Faculty Club might as well have ceased to exist. Then the expression undid itself by an elaborate counter-play, and with a triumphant glint of eye, Islay was back at the table again. "I could make a story out of that," he said. "There's an idea there. Two men, each convinced he's Hamlet, only each has an absolutely different conception of Hamlet's character. One sees him as the delicate intellectual with an over-refined superego, too good for this world, the glass of fashion and the mold of form, fresh out of Wittenberg with a *summa cum laude*. 'O cursèd spite that ever I was born,' and so on. Sprinkle with Freud to taste. The other sees him as Prince of Denmark, a standard medieval revenger, with a veneer of courtier's graces cribbed from Castiglione and a touch of affected melancholy to please the sophisticates at Eliza's court. What keeps him from revenge is the simple fact that a monarchy is apt to be pretty well guarded, and, aside from hitting the bottle too freely, Claudius is no dumber than any monarch who doesn't like a real or pretended madman around. Well, they get to arguing with each other, these two men do, each insisting he's Hamlet and the other is just a boor who doesn't understand. They get so bitter they kill each other, or one kills his rival. Hamlet kills Hamlet, which is just what he does in the play, with all the self-contradictions he's supposed to have and the bungling he does. The revenger kills the self-pitying intellectual. No, the irony is better the other way around. The cursèd spite boy kills the revenger. That's what's happened in the history of criticism, isn't it? A lot of details to work out yet, but it's an idea."

Arthur could envision the story as taking respectable rank in the Islay canon. It would certainly be a thoroughly characteristic performance. He said he hoped it would get written, and then he was led to make a confession. "I'm glad you read *Genetics and Ultimate Purpose*. I'm flattered, but I don't want it to be my last go at the subject," Arthur said. "I'd like to write an extension or a restatement—a completely new book, really, trying to state a position I don't think I succeeded in stating."

Islay's look studied him as he himself would study a clone

of paramecia. "You want to put the spooks in," Islay said. "You want to get God into the last chapter."

"I'm afraid there's no danger of that," Arthur said. He felt slightly annoyed, and at the same time put on his mettle.

"You aren't satisfied to be a scientist," Islay told him. "I can see that. You set up all the gods, the great trinity of Darwin, Mendel, and DeVries, and then the newest and the oldest, Chance—a latecomer to the Trinity, like the Virgin. You lay out all the building blocks, genes, mutation, probability, and show they're the stones out of which the human madhouse is constructed. You can't say as a scientist that they leave any room for a teleology that would do us any good, but you can't bear to let it go at that. You still want the universe to be a gleam in the divine eye. You want it to be on the side of moral responsibility and the good life and peace on earth, whereas it doesn't give a damn. What you really show is that it's a flip of the coin whether a man comes out of his mother's womb a Mongolian idiot or an Einstein."

"The flip isn't that simple," Arthur said. "You haven't read me closely enough, Malcolm, if you put it as baldly as that. Unfortunately the chances seem to favor the idiot more than the Einstein." He didn't feel that he'd answered well at the moment. Malcolm's random shot had made him wince, and Malcolm, talking from intuition, could talk a lot faster. But after all, the exchange had only left him with his book to write; he was grateful to Malcolm for increasing his impatience to get at it.

Arthur looked at his clock. Claudia was half an hour late by now. He picked up the letter he was taking home to answer and put it in his brief case. He heard footsteps in the corridor. Claudia at last. He got up and crossed the room to take his coat from its hanger. He was settling it on his shoulders and turning toward the door when a short, unfamiliar figure appeared there, a girl, obviously an undergraduate, looking at him uncertainly. "Professor Scheuer?" she asked.

"What can I do for you?"

"I know it's late. I won't take a minute of your time. I just wanted to ask one question."

"If it's only one question, come in," Arthur said.

As she came forward, Arthur noticed that she was rather smartly dressed and moderately attractive. "I'm from the Rowley *Register*," she announced.

A lady reporter from the undergraduate daily. Arthur shared a degree of faculty suspicion about the accuracy and motives of campus journalists. "What does the *Register* want?" he asked.

"I just wanted to ask whether it's true— Well, we heard you might be giving up Bi Sci 3 next year, and I wondered whether you had a statement you'd care to make."

Arthur saw the small green nerve twitching in the hollow of Lamson Crocket's cheek. He spoke more sharply than he intended. "What gave the *Register* that idea?"

"Well, we heard—I asked the Department Chairman, and he told me I'd better come straight to you."

Why hadn't the Chairman simply denied the rumor out of hand? Was he being intimidated by Lamson? Of course the girl might not be reporting him truthfully, but what was going on behind Arthur's back? He felt a twinge not only of anger, but of confusion and fear, fear of trouble, fear of nastiness, fear of his own ability to deal with his situation. "You can tell the *Register*," Arthur said, "that I plan to keep on giving the course as usual. I have no intention of giving it up."

The girl looked startled; he must have let some of his feelings color his tone. She folded up the notebook she had taken from her purse. "I'm glad," she said. "That is, I took the course last year myself. I didn't do too well, but I thought your lectures were terribly stimulating."

"Well, thank you," Arthur said. He might have wondered to what effect his lectures had stimulated her, but he had more important considerations to think about. Standing at the door, his coat on, his hand half consciously twirling his hat, he did not hear Claudia come down the corridor until she was almost near enough to touch him.

Arthur straightened in his chair, summoning his energy to deal with the letter he had brought home with him. His desk lamp glared hypnotically at the empty sheet in his typewriter. His solitude made him sharply aware of the vacancy of the rooms he could feel familiarly grouped upstairs and down about his second-floor study.

He reminded himself that he had nothing to fear from the emptiness of the house. Time was when the dread of coming home and finding his quarters vacant, in a sense it still made him wince to think of, had been real and valid. Now his solitude only meant that Rachel was rehearsing with the Civic Orchestra. Fullington was anything but prolific in viola players, and when Rachel proved adaptable to the instrument, though her first love was the violin, she had promptly been installed at the first viola desk. A phrase from the Brahms symphony the orchestra was working up came into Arthur's mind, and he imagined her bowing it with the rest of her section under the conductor's awkwardly caressing beat, in her dark eyes the innocent zeal of which study and practice had never robbed her.

He tried to bring his mind back to the letter. A sentence of sympathy at the start. No doubt the girl and her husband had eliminated any possibility of injury or infection during pregnancy. She knew about the effects of German measles, for example, during the first two months. A phenocopy could often mimic a genotype—no, don't make the language technical. You're answering a letter, not giving a lecture. End by telling her about the still new profession of genetic counseling. Point out that she is within reach of one of the small number of good clinics, attached to a teaching hospital.

Arthur's fingers began typing words in the wake of his thought, but they came reluctantly, and he wasn't displeased when the telephone called him downstairs. "Kent," Arthur said, "glad to hear from you." Kent pointed out that the

Scheuers and the Warners hadn't put in an evening together since college opened. What about a date for dinner at the Warners', depending on Rachel's musical commitments? "I'll ask her when she comes home tonight," Arthur promised. Kent had another reason for calling. Had Arthur run across a writer of some sort who was supposed to be teaching the boys and girls at Rowley to be literary geniuses? Old Stocky's kid Herman seemed to think this guy was the greatest thing since the twelve apostles, but Stocky was afraid he might be turning Herman in the wrong direction. Kent just wanted to report whatever Arthur felt like saying, anything or nothing. Arthur *had* met Malcolm Islay; he wanted to invite Malcolm to the house and give Rachel and Claudia a chance to meet him too. Why not transfer the dinner to the Scheuers', where Kent and Abby could see Malcolm for themselves? They'd enjoy it. Kent said that was more than he'd bargained for, but if Arthur wanted—Kent rang off with a message for Claudia: tell your niece she grows more beautiful all the time.

As he climbed the stairs to his study again, it occurred to Arthur that the dinner could be expanded. Malcolm had said he'd like to entertain his class for an unpedagogical evening some time, but, living in a small off-campus apartment, he had no place to do it. Why not let Malcolm invite his students in after dinner? Claudia could ask some of her set too. He'd have to consult Rachel, but it would make the sort of evening they both preferred, a mixture of elements rather than the same round of shop-talking faculty faces. Kent would have a good time; it would be surprising if he didn't find occasion to display his talents as a raconteur, and Arthur suspected that Malcolm would be amused if not impressed.

Arthur resumed his place at his desk and looked at the letter he had begun to type. He was dissatisfied; he pulled the sheet impatiently from the machine and substituted a fresh one. His mind was resisting the task before him; it was all tangents, grasshoppering like Lamson Crocket's. The green quiver of enmity in Lamson's cheek, the girl from the *Register;* what did they add up to? In a comparable situation, Kent would act at once to find out. That's what he ought to be do-

ing, instead of shilly-shallying with a letter that had accidentally revived a crisis in his own past.

The strangeness of life could overpower a man at times.
Yet suppose, Arthur thought, suppose we could imagine a vast
chart, inconceivably vast, a sort of graph sheet commensurate with the sum of things, on which every contingency
of human life could be plotted. Then nothing would seem
strange. We could assign probable frequencies to every outlandish coincidence, every preposterous incongruity in human affairs. They would all look necessary and normal. Such
a chart would be discouraging; it would confirm the line of
thought that held change to be an illusion, it would confirm
the predominance of the One beneath the Many. Of course
change wasn't an illusion; it had occurred—the evolution of
organisms of incredible variety, for example, both surviving
and extinct. Yet if he himself could stare for a while at such
a universal graph, it would cease to seem strange that his life
should be interwoven with Kent's and Abby's and Rachel's,
that Amity had summoned them all into existence and begun
the web of their improbable relations.

The household in which Rachel and Abby grew up was at
least out of the ordinary. Their mother was never visible; it
was generally taken for granted that she was dead. Mr. Rumford, by the time Arthur got to know the clan, was drooping
his life out under wrinkled lids; he had the face of a senile
New England mandarin. He was thought wealthy, but his
death revealed that he had eked out to nothing the funds left
from an antiquated carriage works. Arthur recalled that when
with no small trepidation he shouted into the old man's better
ear his desire to marry Rachel, the folded eyelids had stretched
and opened, a look of indecent gratitude had warmed and
brightened the dull pupils, and an aged claw had come forward to shake his hand with unseemly cordiality. Kent told
him the same thing had happened when he put in his bid for
Abby. "The old buzzard spent the whole last years of his life,"
he said, "worrying about the girls. They couldn't be working
girls. They were ladies. By the time he'd put Abby through
college and Rachel through music school, he hardly had

enough left to eat. He was so glad to have them taken off his hands he could have cried."

The real beginning for Arthur took place on a December night during his next-to-last year of high school. The skating pond had frozen clear, as black as if the spaces between the stars had congealed into a glacial sheet. Arthur had taken his skates, expecting to tour the ice a few times by himself before the zero wind made itself unbearable. Why was it that at the ordinarily gregarious age he had been self-contained and withdrawn? Was it his German derivation in a Yankee town, or did he carry a gene for the trait 'lone-wolf'? At any rate, he couldn't maintain his isolation on that particular evening. Couples began to swarm on the ice. It was vacation; Kent had come home from engineering school, Abby from college. The high-school crowd turned out in force. Reunions took place. A pile of old railroad ties blazed under the embankment where the track passed close to shore. Much to-do went on over the lacing of girls' skates, while the girls held down their skirts, which were considerably longer than they would be in a couple of years. Now and then a hand grew careless and a skirt riffled out in the wind, to be recaptured with a squeal. They may all have been islands, dotting the shoreless wild, but it would have been hard to think so as they waltzed, cracked the whip, invited collisions and accidents, and tumbled in bi-sexual heaps on the ice. Arthur could recall his shyness and embarrassment at that time of his life. If he'd had to pair with any particular girl, he would have fled. As it was, he let himself be swept into the contagion. The impersonality of the frolic made his assimilation easier. He stayed while the cold sank down the scale, while the wind bit more savagely. The half-moon passed its meridian and started down its western arc. The thickening ice exploded in pinging cracks. When the skating broke up, Arthur didn't know how to detach himself. He was swept along with the rest of the crowd, back to the Rumford house.

Once inside the lighted parlor, the sexes divided. Abby, as hostess, vanished with two or three other girls into the kitchen. Boys in threes and fours began to talk hockey and basketball. Girls put their heads together and turned elaborately oblivious backs toward the male population. But the segregation had its limits. Arthur noticed that Kent and one of his former football cronies had been cornered on the sofa by a pair of girls who in their high-school days had been considered 'fast.' In those years, in Amity, being fast probably represented a peak of innocence American society would never recapture.

When Abby and her helpers returned from the kitchen with a jug of boiling-hot cocoa, the party amalgamated again. Boys were drafted to pass cookies and mugs and marshmallows. Knees and shoulders touched on chairs, on sofas, on the floor. Familiarities were exchanged, tousling of heads, poking of ribs. Degrees of ticklishness were established. A female voice, excited by its own forwardness, proposed that each of the girls describe in turn the kind of man she would marry.

Arthur found himself standing awkwardly isolated in the lee of a sofa, suffering from a violent desire to escape. He shouldn't have come into the parlor with this swarm of aliens; he should have gone home and gone to bed after the skating. The impulse to escape turned into a panic. He *had* to get out unnoticed. The kitchen; that was the way. He could slip across the room as if to put his mug down on the glass-fronted mahogany bookshelves near the corridor through which Abby had come and gone. Then no one would pay any attention if he just kept going into the kitchen. There must be a back door; he could find it and sneak quietly out.

The first part of his plan succeeded smoothly. He set down his mug and turned to survey the room. No one was watching. He opened the door and stepped quickly through, only to find himself in a corridor where he almost collided with a couple who were carrying familiarities to a point considerably in advance of the general mores of Amity. They sprang apart, and Arthur confusedly perceived that the male was Bull Chandler, the football player. Bull evidently felt called on to look belligerent, and he did. The girl looked flushed and indignant. "Arthur Scheuer, what are you doing here?" she demanded.

"I didn't know anyone—I didn't mean to interrupt," Arthur said. He edged around them to go on down the corridor. Bull seemed briefly to consider breaking his neck for him, but if he had the impulse, it wasn't strong enough to produce action. The girl muttered something about collecting bugs, what else does he do, and Bull's guffaws practically pushed Arthur down the rest of the corridor and through the swing door into the kitchen.

Before his eyes could find the hoped-for escape, he became aware that again he wasn't alone. A voice said, "Oh!" A girl stood by the stove, her left hand holding a thick cookbook, her right a wooden spoon poised like a conductor's baton before the down-beat. She had turned her head and was looking at him in startled inquiry. Through his daze he recognized her as Abby's sister, Rachel. He hadn't noticed her either at the skating pond or later, when the party trooped into the house. "Excuse me," Arthur said, and sought for words to explain his plight, only to find that it was unexplainable.

Fortunately she seemed intent on accounting for her own presence. "I—I thought they might all like some fudge," she said, "so I came out here—there's an awful lot of them, though, and I've never tried to make it alone before."

She looked at him appealingly. Perhaps he felt in her a shyness comparable to his own; perhaps he detected that she too had wanted to escape from the gregariousness of the parlor. At any rate, he was moved to say, miserably enough, "Maybe I could help."

She seemed to gain confidence. "Well, I could try you out," she said, and so he found himself alone with a girl in a kitchen, helping her make fudge, buttering pans, measuring out sugar, scoring the finished product with a knife so that it would break in neat squares. By steps he couldn't retrace, he forgot the crowd in the front room, he forgot Bull Chandler, he became conscious of Rachel as an existence of flesh and blood that surprisingly enough he had never distinctly seen or acknowledged before. She was unmistakably Abby's sister, but despite the family resemblance, she looked very different. Her face was built on the same vertical lines, high and narrow, but to Arthur it gave a sense of quite another kind of life. Her hair was dark to the point of blackness, her cheeks had a deeper, a more smoldering color than Abby's, her eyes were wider and brighter. His memory couldn't chart the progress of the evening, nor retrace the degrees by which they got on a comfortable footing with each other. He didn't recall that they said very much. What he remembered permanently was a moment that later on he came to think of as one of the slight but important bridges over which his life had passed. She happened to be standing near him; for the duration of the moment they suspended whatever they were doing and simply stood, motionless and close. They didn't touch, but a message seemed to cross the gap between them, as wordless as the choreographic communications of bees. It was like the opening, or at least unlocking, of a door somewhere in some unseen passage.

Eventually the evening came to an end. He was on his way home, alternately running and walking. When he ran, icicles of breath burned right through the bottom of his lungs; when he slowed to a walk, the tips of his ears tingled in freezing granules. But he was only partly conscious of the cold. He was possessed inside by the glow of some new element in his experience, which his mind was trying to help him understand. His mind found no way of telling him, though, until he suddenly stopped on the prosaic winter street. The revelation was about to occur. He stood waiting for it, oblivious to everything else. His mind gave him the picture of Rachel standing by the stove with her cookbook and wooden spoon, and with the picture came words: Well, there's something to count on, I have something to count on. For a moment the pronouncement seemed wonderfully lucid and certain. Then he came to, saw that he was standing opposite a neighbor's frozen lawn and lightless house, saw the dark gable biting a wedge from the star-fretted winter night. He shivered and went on home to bed.

In those days, in Amity, young couples were slower in coming to the point than later generations of human pairs. Means of support, position in the world, were expected to precede marriage, and indulgence wasn't. Yet as he looked back on his own relation with Rachel, Arthur could almost be surprised that it hadn't expired from neglect or want of nourishment. The feeling expressed by the words *something to count on* remained with him, but he carried it around in the privacy of his mind, sometimes pretended to himself that he was bored with it, almost asked it to go away and let him alone. He wondered from time to time in later years whether it might ever have been possible for him to forget Rachel, to marry some other woman. If he had—but no, for all that happened, he could never wish it had been someone else.

The next confirming incident he could recall didn't occur till spring. He looked out through the window of the family parlor and saw Rachel, in a summer dress, going by outside with a violin case under her arm. She stopped, lifting and turning her head toward the open windows of the house. In a room that overlooked the tree-shadowed back yard Arthur's father was playing a Beethoven sonata on his own violin, an heirloom which had emigrated with the first Scheuer to come to America. Arthur's mother played the accompaniment on the Chickering grand piano acquired in Boston. Arthur got up from his book by the window and hurried to the door, hoping that Rachel hadn't gone on. She was still there, motionless, her head lifted toward the music. "Hi, Rachel," Arthur said, partly descending the steps of the porch.

"Who's playing?" she asked.

"It's my father. Why don't you come in and listen, if you like it?"

"I don't know whether I ought to," she said uncertainly.

"You could play with him. He likes to play duets."

"I'm not nearly good enough. What is it he's playing?"

"Beethoven. He plays Beethoven all the time."

With some hesitation, Rachel came up the walk and climbed the steps. She put her violin case on a chair on the porch. "Don't tell him I play," she pleaded.

Arthur led her into the music room. Her entrance did not interrupt the performers. Arthur's mother smiled at her between chords, and his father's jowl, crowded against the violin, wrinkled benevolently. There was time enough for introductions when the sonata came to an end. Rachel stayed a long time; the occasion marked her initiation into a realm of music beyond the horizon of Amity. It took weeks before she confessed that she was learning the violin herself, and more than that before she would join Arthur's father and mother in a trio, but musical afternoons with them no doubt had a lot to do with her eventually going to conservatory rather than college.

Years later, after they were married, Rachel told him that when she casually alluded to that first visit to the Scheuers, Abby put her through quite an inquisition. She had actually gone alone into a boy's house? What had they done? She was sure Arthur's father and mother had been there every minute? Rachel laughed, but she didn't resent the memory. Abby had played both the maternal and paternal roles in the Rumford household. Abby was the practical and responsible one, holding the reins with a steady and conscientious hand. It was just as well, as it turned out, that Rachel had an older sister of Abby's character to lean on.

Part of Arthur's mind began to heave itself up in revolt against any further reliving of the history of his marriage. He was harrowing himself needlessly; why go through it all again? He snatched at diversions: Lamson Crocket, the letter beside his typewriter, still unanswered; but the letter was the very provocation that had jogged him off on his excursion through his past. The current was too urgently set; he would have to let it run its course.

Rachel's firstborn. Just as the girl said in her letter, the baby wasn't *right*, so far from right that it had small chance of surviving. Arthur made it privately clear that he wanted no exceptional efforts made to prolong its survival. He told Rachel himself when within a few days the imperfect organism ceased to function. Meanwhile he began to think. He asked Rachel about her mother, and was surprised at how little she knew, even more surprised how little Abby knew when he found occasion to question her. Abby wouldn't even have known when her mother died if she hadn't accidentally found a letter among old Mr. Rumford's effects. The date was far more recent than any of them had imagined. Abby could barely remember her mother, Rachel not at all. Their father had scarcely mentioned her, treated her as in effect dead, though she was surviving in an institution as they grew up. Few details could be learned. The facts of record amounted to little more than dates of admission and ultimate departure.

Arthur had to find a way of intimating to Rachel that another child might constitute a risk they ought not to assume. The effect appalled him. He was cautious enough to begin vaguely: they would have to think where this disappointment left them, what to do about the future, and so on. It was some time before his point began to dawn on Rachel. "What do you mean? You keep driving at something, but you won't come out and say what it is." By the time she got that far, she must have known what was in his mind, but she had to force him to express it. And so he did, no doubt more bluntly and less considerately than he intended. Rachel's lips whitened; she turned her face down and away, so that he saw only the long chin and the deep, black sheen of hair. To his horror, a tear fell large and tangible on the rug. He had stepped off into profound and troubled waters with such abruptness that he was struggling in the current before he knew it was beneath him.

For a time she fought back fiercely. It was an accident, she maintained. The same happened to lots of people, and they went on and had normal children later. The doctor told her she ought to have another child right away. Look at Abby's and Kent's children. If there's something wrong with the *family*, why doesn't it show in them? You think it's *me*, she said bitterly.

That gave him a cue. It was only reasonable, he said, to consider what they knew about Rachel's mother, which was little enough. But Rachel was quite right: he might be just as guilty as she was, or they might be guilty in combination, except that guilt was a totally irrelevant notion. No one can be responsible for his heredity; he can only be responsible for what he does with it. Wasn't that true?

Perhaps he had made a mistake in using the word guilt, even for the purpose of dismissing it. Guilt can possibly be exorcised from the mind by sufficient reasons, but it won't so easily let go of the emotions. He came to fear that it had sunk profoundly into Rachel's emotional life, yet he couldn't be sure it wasn't a different feeling that disturbed her, a feeling not so much that she was guilty herself, in her own person, as that she was tainted in *his* eyes, that he regarded her as an unclean vessel. He wondered how he could appeal against that.

Abby at first allied herself with Rachel in opposition to him. It was natural that Rachel should confide in her, and understandable in human nature that she should sympathize to the point of indignation. Very likely she felt herself under indirect attack. At any rate, the form her disapproval toward Arthur took could still unhappily amuse him when he remembered those past years. He was being high-minded, she told him; she could see that, but she thought he failed to see what he was doing to Rachel. He was being too intellectual about it all. In effect she was saying 'Teacher' to him, and a man can always be put in the wrong just by being called 'teacher.'

In one kind of instruction Rachel was better prepared than he could have anticipated. Some months after the small Episcopal church in Amity had joined them in the holy estate of matrimony, blessed by our Lord and commended by St. Paul, she had told him about her back-alley education. He laughed at the phrase, a little surprised that she knew it. Abby had tried to tell her about boys, she said, but Abby's ideas were vague and alarmist. They didn't get beyond a few simple don'ts for beginners, and it never became very clear what the don'ts were designed to protect against. For a while, at the Conservatory, Rachel had roomed with a bouncy Italian girl who later studied abroad and became a well-known soprano. She had plenty of back-alley education to pass on, Rachel said. She had the advantage over Abby; she was experienced and explicit. She was cheerfully tolerant of Rachel's prudishness, as she called it, but she did think Rachel ought to know a few things, and, though shocked at the time, Rachel was grateful to her. Arthur wondered what some of the things were that the Italian girl divulged. Well, one of them was all about— well, contraceptives. Wasn't she a Catholic, Arthur asked? Didn't she go to confession? Rachel didn't know how she squared the things she did with the Church, but hadn't any doubt she did them.

So there was one part of her back-alley education that Rachel learned to apply, but while it solved one problem, it created others. Arthur couldn't believe that the mere use of contraceptives accounted for her emotional transformation. No, the trouble lay deeper. It lay, he surmised, in what she thought he was doing to her. He was depriving her of her functions of motherhood and continuing to use her for his own physical relief. Was that it? Their encounters grew less frequent and less satisfactory. Often she did not share. Arthur would wake in the night and hear, from the dark interval between their beds, the sound of sobs convulsing a sleepless house of flesh, and no word, no touch, no form of tenderness he could think to exercise had power to appease her.

Then she seemed to take a turn for the better. Her neglected violin sounded through the house again as she resumed her daily hours of practice. She joined an informal chamber group of gifted amateurs, and played with them a night each week. After one of these evenings she came home especially, if a little tensely, animated. Her wide-set dark eyes bloomed with light. She shook her black hair and put her hand on his arm in an unusually demonstrative gesture. They sat and talked and even drank a mild highball together. When they went upstairs, he had the sense that she was ready to share and meant him to know it. He was aroused, and she was responsive. In his impatience, he had forgotten to turn out a hall light. He could see her face on the pillow below him, flushed with deep and rapid breathing. She smiled up at him. She said in a hoarse whisper, "It'll be all right. You'll see it will." He was able to wonder even at that moment whether she had made a choice, taken it on herself to omit what were called precautions, but his desire was too far advanced for hesitation.

This time the gene, or the combination of genes, did its work with kindly finality and promptness. It is always better when the bad gene is lethal; then it passes out of the genetic currency. Rachel was convinced, at last, when a spontaneous abortion occurred, or she was too disheartened to oppose his view any longer. The days followed when he was afraid to unlock his door and let himself in when he came home from his day's work, dreading that the depression into which she sank, the withdrawal from him, from all purposeful relation with the world, would have found the means to make an end of itself. It was then he discovered in full force the virtues of the Abbys and the Kents in human society. The solid virtues, Arthur told himself; without Abby and Kent, he doubted whether Rachel could ever have survived, and certainly he could never have got any work done or made any progress in his profession for a long time.

The rôle of teacher might be invidious, but for a while Arthur felt constrained to try what it could do. Surely it would help if Rachel understood. Surely, if she gained some knowledge of how human heredity operated, she would forgive—forgive him, forgive herself, forgive a world in which chance and determinism collaborated in ways that defied common observation. So he tried to explain. He introduced her to a new and forbidding vocabulary. Mendelian ratios, mutation, the fertilization sweepstakes, as someone had called it—which sperm happens to reach the waiting egg. He drew simplified diagrams and tables of probability, a tadpole for a sperm, an oval for an egg, black and white cylinders for alleles of the same gene. Of course you mustn't think they *look* like this, but the way they work can be represented so. He supposed he grew eager. He supposed he treated her as if she were a pupil. She tried, but she would look at the tadpole and the oval with an expression that he finally learned to interpret as asking, 'You and me?' The worst of it was that she accepted him as omniscient. She never quite believed him when he said, "Of course there's a lot we don't know." The teacher is authority, and he is also the man whose view of things is never quite human. He came to understand himself better for his mistake with her. Trying to teach, he was thrusting his ego on her; he was, in a strange way, fulfilling himself, working his way out of his own part of their ordeal by intellectualizing it. That couldn't be Rachel's way. Deep in her emotions, in her woman's mode of responding to life, she couldn't forgive him for being able to look with detached scrutiny at the 'you' and 'me' of things. He saw the difference between them, and saw that it was deep; the best he could do was keep it scarred over by never referring directly to his work.

If teaching didn't help, something else might. He told Rachel they could adopt a child, more than one if she wanted. He regained a lot of credit with Abby for the suggestion, and at times it seemed on the point of working out. Rachel would emerge from her torpor, would seem to open a chink and let in a ray of hope and desire. Then she would take fright; no, no, she couldn't do it. Arthur was at a loss for any other expedient to recommend. As it turned out, he wasn't compelled to.

He felt as though he had survived the critical years of his life all over again. Perhaps now he could dispose of the letter he still hadn't answered. Words began to come. He was halfway through his reply when he heard the sound of someone opening the front door. It seemed early for Rachel to be coming home from rehearsal. "Uncle Arthur?" a voice called.

"Claudia," he said, "I'm up here in the study."

He heard her steps climbing the stairs, heard her voice speaking to an accompanying tread that somehow sounded masculine. Then she appeared in the doorway, and behind her, his eyes looking over her shoulder, rapidly and with open interest taking in Arthur himself, his bookshelves, the appurtenances of his study, a tallish, well-set-up young man whose face was unfamiliar.

"This is Jim Prescott, Uncle Arthur," Claudia said. "He's just come to work in the Anthropology Lab."

Arthur got up to shake hands, and Prescott met his grip easily and firmly.

"What are you doing in Claudia's lab?" Arthur asked.

"I was lucky enough to get a foundation fellowship for a year," Prescott said, "that gives me a chance to go where I like and see what I want."

"And Rowley has enough in Anthropology to detain you for a while?"

Prescott grinned. "You may not have the department that Harvard has, or Wisconsin," he said, "but you have a couple of special collections even they can't duplicate. I expect I'll be detained quite a while."

Arthur thought he managed to strike just the right tone, quick and frank without being smart or patronizing.

"We only have a minute, Uncle Arthur," Claudia said. "You've put in a whole evening alone, and I thought you might want to come with us and see the late show of that French movie that's just here for three days. It's supposed to be terribly funny and satiric. You could leave a note for Rachel if we don't get back before she does."

"You tempt me," Arthur said. He was tempted not so much because of the movie as because she had asked him, especially with a young man in tow. "I guess I'd better not. I have a troublesome letter to answer, and I'm just making headway with it."

"Couldn't you put it off?"

"I'd better not. I want to get it out of my mind tonight."

"I ought to be working myself," Prescott said, "but your niece has talked me into a night of debauch. We'd really like to have you come along."

"I guess the facilities for debauch in Fullington are limited enough so that you can explore them safely," Arthur said. "I'll delegate my share to you."

After they had gone, Arthur reflected that Kent was right about Claudia. She was remarkably beautiful. Or was she? Actual beauty was rare; perhaps Claudia was just a well-made, handsome girl in the bloom of youth. The test of beauty would come later, with increasing maturity, though Arthur didn't think that Claudia, at twenty-three, was young for her years. The new young man who was trailing her: he had something prepossessing about him, with his high, flat forehead, his flat cheekbones, his slightly pinched, inquiring eyes, his small mouth that smiled readily.

Claudia had saved Rachel in the end. When Arthur's brother was killed with his wife in a bus accident, Rachel became a foster mother despite herself. She was badly frightened at first, but a simple sense of duty stood her in good stead. "Why, of course, we must take her, but I—you'll have to help, Arthur. A baby—" Arthur couldn't see how, between them, they'd escaped spoiling Claudia. Perhaps Rachel's timidity protected her from making mistakes others would have committed. She hadn't known how to interfere with Claudia's natural development; she never got over wondering at the ruggedly healthy infant chance had delivered to their care.

Arthur sighed; he hoped he'd washed the past out of his system for a while. He finished his letter rapidly, found a stamp, and was just getting up to put the envelope on the telephone table for mailing next day when he heard the front door open again. He went down into the hall, where Rachel was taking off her scarf and coat. She smiled at him and asked, "Were you bored all by yourself the whole evening?"

"I had a difficult letter to answer and finally got it done," he said. "Claudia dropped in with a new young man. They tried to persuade me to see a French film, but I stuck to duty."

"A new young man? What was he like? Where does he come from? What was his name?"

Arthur laughed. "His name is Jim Prescott, his first appearance is likable, and he's on a research grant here in the museum. That's all the vital statistics I ferreted out."

"I hope Claudia will bring him around and let us see him."

Arthur thought it likely she would. He spoke of the dinner he'd arranged with Kent, and his notion of expanding it to include Islay's class. Rachel had no objection if he wanted to do it that way.

"How did the rehearsal go?" he asked.

"Well, I thought," Rachel said, "except for that abysmal thing at the end we're playing as a concession to modernism.

It has a whole two measures and a half where the violas have to play F-sharp against F in the oboe. It makes me want to scream."

She picked up her viola case, opened it, and took out the instrument. "I have to get that horrid F-sharp out of my ears," she said, lifting the viola into position, plucking and tuning with crisp motions of her fingers and wrist. Then she picked up her bow and began to play the rich lines of the theme from the Brahms symphony. It vibrated sinuously out in thick, warm tendrils of sound. Arthur looked at her as she stood bowing there in the hall. The soft, deep pile of her black hair was salted now in equal measure with gray. Nothing could set off more perfectly her wide-set dark eyes, the narrow structure of her face, the smoldering color of her dark skin. Her expression showed the innocent zeal beneath the competence with which she played. She would always keep something of the devoted amateur, something of the girl who stopped on the street outside the house in Amity and stood listening when she first heard a Beethoven sonata. No, Arthur told himself, he never could have let Rachel go. Despite all that had happened, he was still glad it hadn't been someone else.

○ ○ *6* ○ ○

For some uncomfortable moments at the start, Arthur feared that the evening would prove a failure. Mixing the elements was a good general principle, but perhaps they could be too violently mixed for profitable interchange. The trouble began when Islay arrived early. Arthur was washing when he heard the throaty acceleration of a motor turn the corner and swing into the block. He peeked out between the bathroom curtains as a rakish sports car pulled up to the curb. Islay unfolded his loose-jointed figure from the seat and stood on the pavement, looking for the number of the house. Arthur hurried to the bedroom, where Rachel was considering what earrings would go best with her costume. "Malcolm is here," he told her.

"Oh, Arthur! And you're not ready. What shall I do?" She turned toward him a face of comic dismay. She liked company when she could play her part in it unobtrusively, but she was still subject to fits of shyness with strangers.

"Keep him going till I get down. I won't be a minute."

"Hurry, then. Don't leave me alone with him."

When Arthur came down, he found them at the extreme rear end of the living room, what he and Rachel called the music end. Islay was saying that Rowley students ate at an unconscionably early hour; he'd got to thinking that the whole community had contracted this uncivilized habit. Rachel assured him it didn't make a bit of difference—Arthur had been kept at his office—it didn't make a bit of difference at all.

Islay was sitting in an easy chair near the piano. Rachel sat on the bench, half turned toward the keys, within touching distance of her violin and viola in their cases on top. She put out a hand as Arthur came in and rested it against the violin, as though reassuring herself by the contact. When she felt shy, she was capable of looking unapproachable and frozen, her chin and shoulders lifted, her dark eyes burning painfully under her heavy mass of pepper-and-salt hair.

Arthur made his own apologies; then he began to feel at a loss himself. They had got Malcolm into the house, now what did they do with him? Arthur had no trouble talking with him alone, but mediating between Malcolm and Rachel's diffidence was another problem.

"You must be a musical family," Islay said, "with a concert grand and two violins."

"The violin was my father's," Arthur said. "It came over from Germany before my time. Then there's Rachel's viola. She does all the playing. I just enjoy it."

"I'm afraid the piano is neglected," Rachel said. Then, as no one else spoke, she added, "We don't have any children, children of our own, just our niece Claudia, who doesn't play."

Arthur looked at her in surprise; it wasn't like her to mention this fact about them. He wondered what impression Malcolm was forming. "Rachel began as a violinist," he said, "but she's learned the viola to help our up-and-coming Civic Orchestra. It's something of a feat to transfer from one instrument to the other."

"I can imagine it is," Malcolm said.

"If you'll excuse me, I'll go set the cocktail tray, and we can have a drink. I won't be a minute," Arthur said, with an apologetic glance at Rachel. He stocked his tray and carried it back as promptly as he could, and by then the two of them were getting on more congenially. Islay had taken the obvious cue and was plying her with questions about music. Did she write music herself as well as performing? Oh, no, she lacked the talent. While she was studying harmony and counterpoint, she'd written a few little pieces for violin and piano. She even began a quartet one time, but the problems were too much for her, and she'd never finished more than half the first movement. Well, how did a musical idea come into her head? What was a musical idea, anyway? Rachel was spared the difficulty of answering. The doorbell rang. Arthur handed Malcolm the martini he had just mixed and went to admit Kent and Abby.

Kent was visibly tired; he looked as though he'd rather be at home, his leg propped up, the financial pages of *The New York Times* across his knees. A drink or two could be expected to revive his social energy. Meanwhile Abby was trying to protect him and be polite to Islay. "Cappie has had a hard day," she said. "The office hasn't treated him right, and neither has the stock market. Will anyone mind if he props his leg up? Where's your little stool, Rachel?" Arthur found the stool, and Kent somewhat sheepishly extended his leg on it. Malcolm's face chopped up and down sardonically as he observed these manifestations of solicitude. Abby turned her attention to him. She said it must be a privilege for Rowley students to work with him, and a privilege for him to share his experience with young people. The words were well meant; Malcolm might have passed them off, but they caught him on the wrong side. "I don't know anything about that," he said. "I haven't any sense of mission. I guess I came here because I thought I might get a new slant, and I can't write at home. I always have to be away somewhere."

Abby looked dampened, but she tried again. "You have a family?" she asked.

"Beth, my wife. Two boys."

It was the shortest answer to a question that Arthur had yet heard Malcolm make.

"A family isn't a help?" Abby asked, her chin jutting out slightly.

"Nothing helps a writer except someone who can read his stuff and see what he's trying to do."

The talk might have floundered if Claudia hadn't made her entrance at that moment. The cocktail dress she had put on was demurely cut, but the fashions of the year were tight and brief, and Claudia would have had to drape herself in a circus tent to minimize her attractiveness. Her effect was never lost on Kent, and it obviously wasn't going to be lost on Islay. Kent tried to get up from his chair, but she touched his shoulder and said, "Don't get up for me, Uncle Kent." Then she was shaking hands with Islay, telling him that she was reading his books when she could steal them from Uncle Arthur.

"If you like them," Islay said, "I'll get copies of my whole output and autograph them for you."

"All I can offer," Kent said, "is the tribute of age to beauty."

Claudia turned to Abby. "Is Uncle Kent feeling his age tonight?" she asked.

"He's feeling his youth," Abby said. "He wants to go galloping off across the pasture like a colt again."

"What I can't understand," Kent said, "is why you waste yourself on the headhunters and the bushmen."

Arthur saw Malcolm's puzzled look; evidently Claudia saw it too. "He's talking about my job at the anthropology lab," she said. "He likes to pretend there's nothing there but totem poles and stone hatchets. As a matter of fact, we have some quite good human specimens besides."

"Mummified and shut up in glass cases," Kent said.

"You wouldn't think so if you saw them. Some may be coming around later in the evening, and you can judge for yourself, Uncle Kent."

Islay asked her whether she was a student of anthropology. No, she was just doing secretarial work and odd jobs around the lab, learning a little as she went along. He persisted with questions, and she couldn't divert attention from herself until they sat down to dinner. Then she asked Kent about the progress of his new building, and he said it was just a castle in the air. When it would get into construction depended on the whims of Old Stocky, and anyone who could anticipate those ought to set up as a weather prophet.

Old Stocky, Islay said, savoring the name on his tongue; who was he? The big boss, Kent explained; something of a character. Decent enough to get along with, if you stood up to him, and he usually made the right decisions, no one knew how; but he had his picturesque side. Kent sketched a vignette or two: Stocky chewing an executive's ear. Stocky on the golf course on a Sunday morning, butchering the turf, swearing at his clubs, cursing when he lost a ten-cent syndicate. "Stocky is a type you don't see much any more," Kent summed up, "a leftover from rugged American individualism. Tough, competitive, uneducated. When I first went to work, I wanted to be a consulting engineer, in business for myself. I soon found that kind of thing was on the way out just as I was coming in. I've done nothing but work for management that didn't know a law of physics from a sick cow's tit—if you'll pardon the expression, my dear." Kent bowed to Claudia.

"She's used to your expressions," Abby said. "You haven't spared her."

"I remember the first technical report I wrote at Fullchem," Kent said. "I used the word *adsorb*. It came back from Stocky with *ab*sorb penciled in, and a note telling me to get on the ball if I meant to stay in this outfit."

"What did you do?" Claudia asked.

"I learned how to mix diplomacy with firmness, and I learned it in a hurry."

"It's been hard at times," Abby said, "but you've done plenty of constructive work, despite the obstacles. Cappie has been written up nationally for the buildings he's designed," she told Islay.

Malcolm wanted to hear about the buildings. Kent demurred, but then he said there was one project he liked to remember, the first for which he'd been noticed in the industrial journals. The problem was to put a new roof on a manufacturing building without interrupting production. You couldn't take away the old roof until the new one was in place.

"I'm not an engineer," Malcolm said, "but it seems to me you're describing the impossible. Have they repealed the law that says two bodies can't occupy the same space at the same time?"

Kent smiled. He admitted that the job had its complexities. The building was asymmetrical on account of the shape of the lot, and it was full of vats that boiled for long periods at tremendous heat. The two things together made it quite a job to figure the allowances for expansion and contraction with changes of temperature. Once he got the notion of suspending the new roof from external girders, though, everything fell into line. When the girders were in position, it was easy enough to hang slabs of cement-embedded tile from them. Then it was just a question of taking the old roof out from under the new one and throwing it away. They didn't lose a day's production, but Kent lost some sleep wondering when a staging would collapse and drop a hunky with a barrow of rubbish into a boiling vat. Did anything like that happen? No, Kent said; they got by without an accident.

Arthur was pleased by the admiration in Malcolm's eye. "Well, I thought industry was nothing but Madison Avenue hornswoggling people into buying what they don't need and didn't know they wanted," Malcolm said. "I see it can have a creative side too."

"Most of our effort is just trying to sell a few more million gross of tranquilizers than the competition," Kent said. "We don't even use the word 'creative' in our shop. We aren't creative the way you writers and artists are. I couldn't even write a story about a lost dog for the local paper. All I do is push pieces of matter around, take some steel and cement from one place and put them in another."

89

"It seems to me pushing matter around for a purpose can be creative enough," Arthur said. "That's what the original Creator did when he gave plan to an earth that was without form and void, set evolution going, and started chemistry manufacturing all sorts of species. Can any creation take place, even in the realm of idea, that doesn't at some point produce a physical change, an artifact, a tangible form, or perhaps a change of behavior? Malcolm's imagination wouldn't get far unless he could put it in books, and a book is an artifact that can be packaged and sold. It goes back to a couple of man's greatest artifacts—spoken and written language."

"There speaks the scientist who's a poet *manqué*," Malcolm said, "or a theologian without a church."

"Don't accuse me of theology," Arthur said. "My point is, we all want our share in creativity, don't we, and up to our limits, we can claim it?"

"I don't want to hog the word for writers or artists or anyone in particular," Malcolm said. "But I'll tell you what we all have in common. It's technical problems. I couldn't solve Mr. Warner's or Arthur's, and you couldn't solve mine, but the fun of the game is working out the technical solution for the problem you face. That's the fun your original Creator, old Yahweh-First-Person, the Ancient of Days, got out of dividing the firmament above from the waters beneath. I'll bet he had a hell of a time doing that. In fact that's why he invented Hell, as a technical solution of the problem of dividing the sheep from the goats. Personally, I don't admire his technique."

Malcolm grinned with self-satisfaction, but while Arthur was amused, he didn't like to rest the nature of creativity on the solution of technical problems. Beyond that lay the question of the created object itself, its value for use or delight— a world, a building, a system of thought, a discovery in science, a concerto. He wanted to pursue the theme, but Kent was looking triumphantly across the table at Abby and saying, "See? All my life I've thought I was just a slave to management, and now I find I've been a creative artist without knowing it!" As he spoke, Rachel's dessert was borne in from the pantry, and a chorus of tribute arose to it. Looking at the lighted tongues of brandy writhing up sea-green and sea-blue from the platter, Arthur thought that perhaps Cherries Jubilee could take at least humble rank as a creative achievement. He could congratulate himself at any rate that the mixture of elements had begun to work.

When the meal came to an end, they reassembled in the living room for the second cycle of the evening. Claudia's younger set began arriving, Jim Prescott among them, interspersed with the still younger members of Islay's class. Jewish features were recognizable here and there, and one very small, very black Negro. Arthur caught an apprehensive look from Rachel, and he knew what she meant. A heterogeneous population was taken for granted at Rowley, but it wasn't among the executives of Fullchem. Arthur tried to make his return glance reassuring. Kent might have his prejudices, or think he had; they were habits picked up from his associations more than reflections of his actual nature. Amity had hardly known a Jew or a Negro, but Fullchem had at least one Jewish vice-president, of whom Kent always spoke with respect, and in any case, he was man of the world enough to take a human being as he found him. An instant of contrast occurred when the Negro was introduced to Kent and they shook hands, the soft, bituminous cheeks, with their dusty bloom like black plums, confronting Kent's fair, clear-textured skin and compact firmness of feature. Kent out-topped the boy by a good inch; athlete that he had been, he owed his prowess to his spring of muscle and efficient energy, not to height or bulk.

Kent introduced Young Herman Stockwell, but after shaking hands with Arthur and Rachel and saying a brief "Glad to meet you," Young Herman retreated hastily to the side of a slight tubular girl dressed in a black sweater and skirt and black ribbed stockings. Between skirt and stockings appeared a pair of white knees that were more like elbows. Her face, Arthur thought, might have looked well featured, but it had a hard time showing between wings of black hair arranged as nearly as possible to conceal either eye. The girl maneuvered herself to a position directly in front of Islay, where he was pulling up a chair beside Kent and Abby in the lee of the piano. She sat down on the floor, and Young Herman wedged himself in next to her, while the rest of Islay's class disposed themselves in a loose half-moon at his feet. Claudia and her set formed a sitting and standing fringe of listeners on the periphery.

"How do you think a writer gets the experience he needs for his work, Mr. Islay?" the dark girl asked.

"It isn't his experience that counts, it's his ideas," Islay said. "Experience is what happens to you when you aren't looking for it and don't want it."

Kent laughed. "That's the way it is in business, all right," he said.

The dark girl looked at him reprovingly and returned to her theme. "Shouldn't a writer have all the experience possible?" she persisted.

"You mean a writer should be a Faust," Islay said, "take all knowledge and all sensation for his province. He should commit a few murders and adulteries, rob a bank, get shot but not killed in battle, and so on down the list, just to see how it feels. Personally I don't think it's practicable. It doesn't leave enough time for writing."

The answer evoked laughter, but the girl was undeterred. "Then what do you think is the relation between writing and life?" she asked.

Islay's face went through one of its elaborate shifts of expression, settling into a system of puckers that made it impossible to tell how serious and how ironic he meant to be. "People live, writers write. There's no more profound mistake than thinking that literature and life are identical. Life has to be imagined before we know what it is, and then it isn't the same thing. The people who live can't imagine their lives, and the people who imagine them don't live them."

"But if a writer doesn't live—" the dark girl began. She struggled a moment, then managed to say, "How does he know about life?"

A voice behind her snickered, but Islay answered patiently. "A writer is a parasite," he said. "A parasite feeds on his host without knowing anything about his host's life. Am I getting my biology straight, Arthur?"

"Sound enough so far," Arthur said.

"A writer," Islay went on, warming to his theme, "is a man walking down the street thinking how he would describe himself as a man walking down the street. Or better, thinking about the technical problem of presenting himself as he see-saws along with all his illusions while life goes by unknown on the sidewalk. If he stops trying to present himself and starts making up other people's lives for them, he makes them up the way they *ought* to be, the way they *must* be artistically. So he doesn't live, in the sense of living you seem to mean. He imagines life. It's *how* he imagines that counts."

The girl was ready with another question, her thin chest rising, but a fresh voice intervened. The Negro rolled up the whites of his eyes and said, "Sir, I remember in Proust—that is, he says somewhere, he speaks of making up a character by taking an ear from one man or woman and a voice from another and various things from—well, from any number. Do you ever start from an actual character, someone you know?"

"Good question," Islay said. "You're trying to trap me. If I take characters from life, I must be in some relation to life. It isn't quite that simple, though. Sure, you can take a strut from one man and a slouch from another and a nervous cough from a third. You can go beyond that. Everybody knows the type who always leaves you picking up the tab in the restaurant or paying the cab driver at the end of the ride. You can ask yourself why, and you can invent an unhappy childhood for him. He was insecure, his mother and father were divorced, he was shunted from one home to another, he never had anything he could call his own, he gets to the point where he can't bear to part with his nail parings. You might accidentally be right, but don't forget you're inventing the whole thing, making it up out of imagination. You haven't lived his life for him. You don't know. A novelist is someone who wonders why people act as they do, and he doesn't know, so he imagines an explanation, and that's his novel."

"Hasn't a lot of fiction been written about actual people?" the Negro asked.

"Yes," Islay said, smiling, "but that's just the point, it's fiction."

"I think the question is interesting," the dark girl said, "I mean about writing and experience, because—well, I've been reading a critical essay about your work, sir, and while it praises your technique, it says you're so—so obsessed by irony you don't know what a human emotion is. I wondered what you'd say about that?"

The question was brash, but Arthur wasn't prepared for the extent of its effect. Knotting and sliding, Malcolm's face betrayed a degree of disturbance that threatened to be painful. "You can ask me that," he said, "when you find out what a human emotion is yourself."

Too bad he had to make his retort personal, Arthur thought. He seemed to provoke a divided response: scowls and averted eyes, also titters and leers at the dark girl. Arthur was about to intervene with a question of his own—what about plausibility? How is fiction *true*? Surely Malcolm didn't think it *untrue*?—but Young Herman took the onus of diversion on himself. "Sir," he said, "I've seen you driving around in a Mercedes. That's what I call living it up!"

This time the response was uninhibited and uniform. Everyone laughed. Even Malcolm couldn't help grinning. It was partly that Young Herman spoke with utter ingenuousness, partly that his diversion was so completely unexpected it discharged any lightning that hadn't yet struck, and relieved the atmosphere. If he really meant to rescue his friend the dark girl, though, he didn't seem to earn thanks. Arthur observed that she cut him an ungrateful look and said something in his ear that made his triangular face flush and puff up oddly. She was probably dismissing him from the intellectual life for good.

When the laughter petered out, Islay asked Rachel if she wouldn't play for them. Arthur observed her reluctance; she believed in a firm separation between music and talk. She pleaded the want of an accompanist, but Claudia said, "Jim will play for you, Aunt Rachel."

"I'm awfully rusty," Prescott said, "but perhaps I can stumble along if you don't expect too much."

Rachel still hesitated, but she was overcome by a chorus of

94

invitation. She found a Bach sonata, propped it on the piano rack in front of Prescott, and turned to the rondo. "Shall we try this?" she asked. Prescott grinned and said, "You aren't going to break me in gently, are you?" He played a few bars of the accompaniment. "Faster," Rachel said. "Like this," and she illustrated.

While the music was in progress, Arthur went unobtrusively to the pantry and stocked a side table at the less musical end of the living room with milk, Coca-Cola, beer, whisky, crackers and cheese, ham and rye bread. As he came back toward the circle of listeners, the rondo was entering the complications of its last contrasting episode. Prescott found the going more difficult. He floundered and finally gave up altogether, letting Rachel's violin sing on unaccompanied, while she twisted her eyes at him reproachfully. He came in again with the last return of the theme, and they finished triumphantly together.

The audience begged for an encore, but Rachel stoutly refused. While she was putting her violin back in its case, Arthur became aware of a contretemps going on between Young Herman and the dark girl. He tried to put an arm across her shoulder. She squirmed away, gave him a look of spectral distaste, and said something that made his face mottle and swell. He got up, detaching himself from the group on the floor that had swung about to face the piano. For a moment Arthur thought he was going to make his way down the length of the room and out of the house without more ado, but the refreshment table caught his eye, and he made for it. Arthur forgot him in a new and different burst of music. Someone had found a book of rounds and madrigals; an *a cappella* choir was forming around the piano. Some very competent fa-la-lahing occurred. Mozart's nightingales melodiously sang, their voices pursuing each other in mock-sentimental canon. Campion's weather-beaten sail bent willingly to shore. The silver swan leaned her breast against the reedy bank and chanted her death-note. The choir wrangled amiably for favorites. With a hoarse, inaccurate, eloquent baritone, Islay joined in spasmodically. Kent unpropped his knee and hovered on the fringe of the group, his face hungry for participation. In a pause he suggested something less highbrow so that everyone could contribute. The choir humored him. Another accompanist appeared, who had at his disposal the complete stock of common chords and modulations. Daisy took her seat on a bicycle built for two, the saints came marching in, everybody worked on the railroad, the old mill stream received its tribute of nostalgia. The Negro produced from his slight figure a natural tenor of astonishing volume, high, vibrant, and sugared.

During an interval between numbers, Arthur was about to suggest that the refreshment table was ready for patronage, but he became aware of sounds of a different and ominous character from the region where it stood. He thought of Young Herman and decided it would be well to investigate. Partly concealed by a tall glass-front desk against the wall, a hunched figure, its back to the company, leaned forward on a chair in a dejected attitude, elbow on knee, head resting on hand. Arthur approached and noticed that a bottle of whisky on the table had been liberally depleted. The figure on the chair remained oblivious to anything but its own internal ordeal. It heaved forward convulsively, then sank miserably back. Arthur moved so that he faced the boy; he wondered what to say or do. The lavatory is just across the hall. Here, I'll show you. It was hard to make out, though, whether Herman's distress was more physical or more emotional.

Arthur was about to speak when he noticed Claudia and Jim Prescott coming to his aid. "How about a breath of fresh air?" Prescott asked. "Come on, a little walk in the open will make things better." He took Herman under one elbow and heaved gently. Herman let himself be hauled to his feet and turned toward the door. After a step or two his combative instincts asserted themselves. He yanked away, muttering that he didn't need anyone's hands on him, and lurched ahead independently. To Arthur's surprise, he managed to find the knob on the door and open it at a single try. He crossed the porch and got down the steps without mishap. Then he began angling across the lawn and taking from his pocket what seemed to be the keys of his car.

"He can't drive in that condition," Claudia said. "Don't let him."

"You think measures are called for?" Prescott asked. He shrugged with distaste but set out in pursuit. He overtook Herman at the sidewalk, and for a moment Arthur wondered whether a scuffle would break out. Perhaps Herman had enough remaining sense to see that he would be overmatched. At any rate, he returned the keys to his pocket and began to walk back and forth along the street with Prescott.

"He'll be all right," Claudia said. "Jim has him under control."

"It looks as though he has," Arthur agreed.

"I'll put some coffee on," Claudia said, loud enough so that Prescott looked up and waved to show his approval.

Claudia went toward the kitchen to start the coffee, and Arthur returned to his guests. By the time Claudia came back to the living room, refreshments had been well distributed. The chorus had diminished to a faithful half-dozen. They attained a final climactic chord, which the Negro tenor intensified by a beatific note of wonderful reedy altitude. Kent raised his highball glass in tribute. "I haven't heard a note like that since John McCormack sang 'Mother Machree,'" he said. "Barbershop harmony! There's nothing like it to purge the spirit!"

"Speaking of barbershops, Uncle Kent," Claudia said, "tell about the time you had to get a haircut in a hurry."

"You don't want to hear that yarn," Kent said. "It has nothing to commend it but gospel truth, and you've heard me tell it a dozen times."

"Mr. Islay would like to hear it, and so would everyone else."

"Well, if you insist."

Kent seated himself, propped up his knee, wet his whistle from his highball glass, and embarked on the preliminaries of the haircut saga: the fishing trip to a remote part of the state, the telegram announcing the death of an engineering classmate and asking Kent to be a pallbearer, a telegram that reached him only on the night before the funeral; the hasty packing at sunrise, the glance into the mirror of his car, the shock of seeing that his hair looked like John the Baptist's, the discovery in the first town he drove through that this was the day when all barbershops closed. Despair, frustration! At last a single shop open for business, a cobwebbed third floor cell in a Godforsaken four-corners village. Grimy implements and greasy bottles on the counter. A yellow, fly-blown mirror opposite the chair. The infinite leisure of the proprietor, who woke reluctantly from a nap and unfolded himself like six feet of carpenter's rule. Kent was driving through, was he? Seems though folks driving through was always hell-bent to get somewheres else. Never could see, himself, what was the tarnation hurry about a funeral, long's they got the corpse in the ground before it pocked.

Kent was swinging into the accent. He managed it pretty well, Arthur thought; of course it was the accent heard around Amity when he and Kent were growing up. The yarn was one of Kent's repertory pieces, but old-timers at the board could always watch its effect on newcomers. Jim Prescott, entering quietly from the hall, stopped and drew up his shoulders, estimating the new turn the evening had taken. His eyes puckered and his small mouth began to grin. The Negro, who looked as though he had never stepped three feet off a city pavement, appeared puzzled at first. Then moisture formed at his eyes, and he had to hold back a giggle.

Kent made snipping motions in the air, to indicate that when the barber finally took up a pair of scissors, he used them only to punctuate his recital. So Kent was going to a funeral, was he? Puts me in mind of a buryin we had around here, long about the time the ground thawed. Well, maybe twan't thawed, quite. Seems though there was still ice a foot down where the sun hadn't struck in yet. If it hadn't thawed all the way, though, it was beginnin to soften up some.

Kent protested that at any other time he'd like nothing better than to hear about the burying, but just then he was really in a hurry. Protest overruled. Like I was tellin, we had this feller, lived at the corners here, must a been nigh on sixty. Well, maybe not quite sixty; maybe fifty-six, fifty-seven.

Come to think, though, the year he fell in the millpond and nigh drownded, he was five then, that was the same year we had the flood, and that was fifty-three years ago to the dollar last spring. Well, sir, this feller was kinda sizable, might have gone, say, two hundred pound. Well, maybe not quite that much; maybe a hundred ninety-six, ninety-seven. Come to think, though, he was fillin out the year he died. Don't know how much of it you could rightly call his own weight. He had the bloat terrible. Doctor used to drain off this here fluid three quarts at a time. Well, maybe not three quarts, but enough to make a good run of sap. He had the asthmy, too, and he had heart trouble and a double hernium. Them herniums, mister, I'm tellin you they was an awful drag on him. Doctor said one time if he had anythin more wrong with him it would kill him. Goes to show the doctor was pretty near right for once.

A friend of Claudia's choked in the background of the listening group. She put her hands over her face. Then she controlled herself and said, "Go on, please." Kent settled to his work again.

Well, when Dolph—that's the feller I'm tellin you about—when he up and died, why, Rena, that's his wife, she asks me would I shave him and make him fittin for the funeral. I and Rena and Dolph been good friends, so I says I'll shave him, though I want to tell you, when I as a licenseed barber shave a stiff, I get three dollars for the job, but if the undertaker does it, he collects five. Don't seem fair nor right, but like I said, Rena and I been friends, so I agrees to do it for three. Well, the undertaker claims it's his right to shave him and take his five dollars. If I was a skinflint like that, I'd shave my grandmother's wooden leg and burn the parins for kindlin, but I says shave him and welcome, and I wash my hands of the whole thing. Only thing is, it aint so easy to shave a stiff as you might think. You take now, and you nick the skin just one little bit, just one little bit—

Kent paused to make a motion of nicking, as delicate as an engraver picking a superfluous dot from a half-tone plate.

You nick the skin, and that nick will run, just like a run in one of these nylon stockins. Well, the undertaker, he starts workin on Dolph, and pretty soon he nicks him. When he seen what he done, he don't dare go no further with the job. So he comes to me and wants me to finish it, but all he's willin to put up is my reglar charge as a licenseed barber, that's three dollars. He still stands to make two dollars for carvin Dolph up so's he aint fittin for his own funeral. Don't seem fair nor right, but like I said, I and Dolph been friends, so I said I'd do the job if an pervided he'd get someone to hold Dolph's head while I shaved him.

He goes over to the winder—we was in his shop, ground floor rear, where he keeps his collateral—and yells outside. I hear a lawnmower stop, and the big, ganglin kid that cuts the grass comes in. The kid was scared right away, soon's he heard what was wanted of him, but I got him steadied down and holdin Dolph's head right well for a green hand. Everythin would a been all right if he hadn't got to moonin, the way these kids do, but all of a sudden he jiggled that head, and I nicked the good side. Well, sir, when the kid seen that nick run, he let out a gargle and then he let go his holt on Dolph altogether. Dolph, he was kind of braced on one shoulder so's to bring his cheek up, and when the kid took his hands off, he flopped over, and one of them arms of his swung out stiff as a turkey's claw and practicly reached into that kid's pants pockets for the change he was savin to take his girl to the pitchers. Well, sir, if I ever see anyone take off, I seen it then. The kid, he didn't wait to open the screen door. He took it right along with him, hangin from one foot, sash and all. He took the porch railin, too. It was rotten anyways. It was worth them two dollars I lost to see that boy makin time. He come down on the petunia bed and acrost the length of it in three jumps, and then he started for the road, and if he hadn't been runnin blind so's he tripped on the lawnmower and knocked his wind out, he'd be runnin yet.

In the chorus of responses that followed Kent's yarn, Arthur caught Jim Prescott's eye, and they went out in the hall together. "How is our young friend Herman Stockwell?" Arthur asked.

"He's in the kitchen drinking a cup of coffee. I said I'd convey his thanks and good-bys. He doesn't want to make another appearance."

"Is he in condition to drive?"

"The critical event took place under your neighbor's lilac bush," Prescott said. "It was thorough. That plus coffee will fix him well enough."

"Was it too much whisky, or was it our sepulchral sister in black?"

"I'd say a mixture of both, combined with Islay," Prescott said judicially. "Everything he counted on got together to let him down. The poor kid is fouled up inside. He kept saying, 'Why do they all think they're so much better than I am?' "

"Too bad," Arthur said. "I hope he finds a girl who's better suited to him, or something to put him on a different tack."

"There are lots of ways of getting fouled up," Prescott said. "I've discovered a couple myself."

Arthur was startled by the seriousness of his tone. It was hardly a moment for confidences, though, and Prescott apparently didn't want to say more. "Well, you did a helpful job tonight," Arthur said. "Thanks for coming to the rescue."

They went back into the living room, where Kent was winding up an encore. Arthur recognized it, and began listening to it as a study in liturgical tradition, in consecrated phrases, as fixed as Homeric epithets. "My fast ball had no hop, my curve wouldn't break, my change-up fell in the dirt before it even reached the plate. My arm—" Yes; my arm was a toothache. The climactic phrase was prescribed, but Arthur felt a shock of innovation. "My arm felt like the crucifixion," Kent said. You could argue for one reading or the other, but it was rather as though the priest had suddenly altered the established wording of the collect.

Kent finished with the classic coda: if it hadn't been for such and such, we'd be running yet. Abby rose, and said, "Come along, Cappie, it's past your bedtime." The party was raveling out. There was much getting up from the floor, much circulating about Rachel, much saying of good nights. Arthur noticed Islay and Kent talking in the hall while Abby got her coat. He couldn't hear what they were saying, but they appeared to interest each other.

It was well after midnight by the time Arthur had helped Rachel carry loaded ashtrays and stale-smelling glasses to the kitchen, where they could be dealt with by the cleaning woman in the morning. He sent Rachel to bed and continued puttering and tidying around the pantry for a few minutes by himself. Usually Claudia would be at hand to help on such occasions, but for once she must have deserted and gone up to bed. When Arthur came out into the hall, a strong draft was blowing in through the front door, and the porch light was still on. Surprised, he went to lock the door and turn off the switch, but as he reached the sill, he became aware of two figures on the porch. They were standing very straight, confronting each other across a gap, one by the right-hand post of the porch, the other by the left. So that accounted for Claudia's desertion! She and Jim Prescott were staring at each other with a kind of charged fixation. She noticed Arthur's presence in the doorway, turned, smiled, gave a shiver in the keen October air, and said, "I'm cold. It's time to go in." Prescott shivered in turn, spoke a last thanks for the evening, a good night to Claudia, and went down the steps.

Claudia moved unhurriedly along the hall as Arthur closed the door and followed her. "Uncle Kent is such fun," she said, "and isn't Malcolm Islay fascinating?"

"I thought you'd find him so," Arthur said.

"He doesn't have any idea how human he is, how vulnerable, with all his talk about how his work has nothing to do with life."

Claudia stood silent for a moment at the bottom of the stairs, a foot one step up, an arm and hand extended to rest on the banister. It seemed to Arthur that her quality of youthful abundance and bloom had never been more manifest. He could hardly believe that her mind was exclusively occupied by Islay and Kent; she very likely wouldn't speak of what she was chiefly thinking of. She withdrew her hand from the banister and said, "Good night, Uncle Arthur. It was a wonderful party."

"Wonderful enough to leave me exhausted, anyway," Arthur said. "I'm not altogether sorry it's over."

Claudia smiled. "Perhaps it isn't. Did you hear Malcolm Islay telling Uncle Kent, while they were saying good-by, that he'd like to see the inside of Fullchem sometime, and Uncle Kent saying he'd be welcome any time he wanted to come?"

"I thought they began hitting it off, after a dubious start," Arthur said, "but I didn't take that in."

Perhaps, among the diverse elements the evening had brought together, some strands would continue to interact.

PART TWO

○ ○

Maker and Undoer

oo ⁄ oo

The December morning was so cold that Kent did not think to take off his coat until he left the elevator and started down the corridor toward his office. As he reached the doorway, he could see Isabel sorting his mail at his desk. The room was so dark that she had turned on the ceiling light. The window-pane, offering a view of the railroad yards and the city crowded in diminishing perspective on both banks of the river, revealed a dusting of snow along the tracks. The sky hung in a seamless overcast that momentarily threatened a further fall.

"Winter has us by the neck already," Kent said.

Isabel smiled unconcernedly. "I don't mind the cold," she said.

She was tolerably well padded, as a matter of fact, and despite her spinsterhood she had a maternally frowzy aspect that gave no indication of her intelligence and efficiency.

"How are all your nephews and nieces?"

"Half of them are laid up with the sniffles," Isabel said. "Otherwise they're fine."

"I hope you did something over the week-end besides wipe noses."

"I like to see clean noses," Isabel said. The telephone rang, and she picked up the receiver. "Mr. Stockwell wants to see you at eleven about the insurance claim," she said.

"Dig out the documents and have them ready for me, will you?" Eleven. For the second time he'd have to cancel a date with Pete Blanchard. Reluctantly he asked Isabel to dial Pete for him. Pete would begin to wonder whether his outfit had lost standing with Fullchem, and that would be regrettable, on grounds of both friendship and business. Blanchard Tool and Die Company, Pete's own creation, made special-purpose machines and manufacturing devices at high standards of workmanship and low costs. Equipment designed by Pete's draftsmen had more than once enabled Kent to save money for Fullchem and increase the efficiency of its operations.

While he waited for Isabel to get through with the call, Kent glanced at the correspondence neatly arranged on his desk. Uppermost on the pile he recognized the letterhead of Fullchem's branch plant in New Jersey. It was high time New Jersey answered his inquiries into their maintenance costs and requests for additional budget. If the answer wasn't satisfactory, he'd have to go down there and make an investigation on the spot. Perhaps he could delegate the job to young Shepherdson. It would enlarge Shep's knowledge of Fullchem and give him a chance to show his value.

Isabel handed him the receiver, and a voice said, "Cap?"

"Pete. How are you, old man?"

"A jump ahead of the sheriff. What's up?"

"We're having rotten luck getting together," Kent said. "Stocky has called a conference for eleven."

"Tell him to go to hell," Pete said.

"You're President of your own company. I'm only a hired hand," Kent said.

Pete grunted at the other end of the wire. "I know how it is, Cap, but I've been wondering what the score is with Fullchem. I wouldn't want anything to go wrong over there. If you have any complaints—"

"The score is par all the way. No complaints. What about Wednesday lunch? I'll have to shift a couple of things, but I can do it."

"Me too," Pete said. "I guess I can work it. I've got something here I want to show you. It's a brand-new gadget that one of our shop geniuses dreamed up. I think it will save you money, and I want to sell it to you."

"We're always ready to buy in order to save. Make it Wednesday, then, and I'm sorry about today. In fact I feel like the guy when the privy blew up under him." Kent slid a look toward Isabel, which she repaid with tolerant unconcern. "The paper said he'd been seriously discommoded."

Kent rang off while Pete was still making appropriate noises, and his mind came back to the letter from New Jersey. Picking it up, he saw at once that its tenor was anything but satisfactory. "About this," he said, "I want to see Shep right away. Tell him to step across the hall, will you?"

Isabel went out, and Kent looked at the next exhibit on his desk. It was a quarterly statement to stockholders by one of Fullchem's most formidable rivals. Isabel had circled an item on page five, reporting research progress with a new product, an asphalt that could be sprayed on arid land to retain moisture and give seeds a marked advantage during germination. Isabel didn't miss any tricks. A couple of years past, the Fullchem labs had developed a closely similar compound. Kent produced an exhaustive cost and manufacturing analysis, routed the document up to Stocky, and never heard of it again. He had filed and almost forgotten his own copy. The project, Kent remembered, came up at a turbulent period. Stocky's advertising manager had suddenly resigned and gone to a competitor, taking with him a lot of ideas the company was just beginning to develop. Stocky blew his top not once but many times over this perfidy, and in the crisis of reorganization he was in no mood for questions about a report on which he had presumably made his own decision.

Isabel returned with Shepherdson, and Kent said, "If there aren't any gaskets popping right this minute, sit down, will you, Shep?"

"Everything is screwed down tight as far as I know," Shepherdson said.

"Isabel, get me the file on New Jersey since about September, when they started complaining about the new equipment we authorized them to put in." Isabel vanished toward her inner office, and Kent said, "How much do you know about our New Jersey operation, Shep?"

"Not much. I've noticed their upkeep charges are pretty

well out of whack with what we expect up here, and they seem to be reporting trouble all the time."

"Too much trouble. I think one of us will have to make an on-the-spot inspection. I don't know what my schedule is going to be, with the insurance deal coming up. I want you to find out what you can from the files we have here and be ready to pack your bags—"

Kent stopped. Without the preliminary of a knock, Denis Prouty appeared from the corridor, coming into the office with his nervously furtive gait. At the same moment Isabel returned from her inner room, her left hand bearing a stout correspondence folder.

"Hi, Cap. Hi, Isabel," Denis said. He looked suspiciously at Shepherdson, who shifted in his chair as if uncertain whether to get up and said, "Good morning, Mr. Prouty."

Denis nodded, glanced at the three of them in turn, and said, "Well, I don't want to interrupt anything, but there's a little matter I have to talk over with Cap."

"Tell you what, Shep. Take the folder along, and this letter that just came this morning, and see what you make of them," Kent said. "I'll drop in on you later."

Shepherdson carried off the folder while Isabel went discreetly back to her office. Denis walked over to the window and surveyed the black and white railroad tracks and the gray lid of the sky, from which flakes were beginning to fall. "Goddamned winter," he said. "Here it is, only the first week of December—I don't see how I can last out another one. Every year the colds get worse and hang on longer. I've tried everything this or any other goddamned company makes— sprays, injections, anti-histamines—nothing works."

"The day they lick the common cold, the Black Plague will come back. It has to be something," Kent said.

"Aren't you right, though." Denis turned from the window and seated himself in the chair vacated by Shepherdson.

Kent wished he would show what he had on his mind. It wasn't a morning when he wanted to waste time kidding with Denis, but especially on Mondays Denis could be counted on to pop in promptly. He liked to check up on how everyone had spent the week-end. His own domestic rigors made it hard for him to join the poker or bridge games, the bowling matches, or the films of big-game hunting at the City Club, and so he was always afraid some shift of relations had occurred behind his back, or some piece of vital information leaked out that he ought to know.

"What are you putting Shep up to this time?" Denis asked suspiciously.

"I want him to read the file on New Jersey," Kent said. "All he can learn about the company is to the good."

"Well, sure, if you don't bring him along too fast."

"The young come along fast if they're good," Kent said.

"Okay, Cap, he's your man. Of course you've talked Stocky into cutting him in on profit-sharing already—"

"Incentive, Denis," Kent said. "If we don't reward him, one of our competitors will. He has a kid, another on the way. You can't keep the tortoise moving unless you dangle a meal in front of his nose."

Denis fidgeted in his chair, brushing back the lock that fell toward his eye. Then he seemed to come abruptly to his point. It wasn't curiosity about the week-end, after all. "Have you seen the Old Man this morning?" he asked.

"Stocky? No."

"You will. He wants us both at eleven."

Kent leaned forward and wrote the hour on his calendar, where he had already scratched out the name of Pete Blanchard.

"It's about the insurance deal," Denis said. "This is one thing we've got to get right, Cap. We can't afford to get hooked. A lot depends on what kind of settlement we pull off."

Kent had no trouble agreeing. You couldn't predict, but if Stocky was pleased with the settlement, he might even authorize Kent to go ahead with the new office building. He could almost tangibly feel his plans through the closed drawer of his desk, like a dollar in a kid's pocket burning a hole to be spent at the circus. Of course the new building wasn't what Denis had in mind. His eyes fixed appealingly on Kent's, and their message was easy enough to read: *You've* got to wangle a deal that won't leave *me* on the hook. "I'll be up at eleven," Kent said.

"Better wear your shin guards," Denis said. "Stocky is kicking out at everything in sight this morning, whether it's padded or not." His face twitched, and his hand went nervously toward the pocket where he kept his bottle of pills. He controlled himself, bringing his palm away empty. "Jesus, Cap, what's going on? Stocky hasn't missed a chance to chew someone's ear for a month now. Something is eating him that I can't figure out. Have you noticed—well, anything out of the way, in how he's been acting, I mean?"

"No," Kent said. In the act of speaking, he wondered whether he hadn't detected some sort of elusive change in Stocky during the weeks past. A sense of difference, he almost thought, had been registering itself quietly at the back of his mind; it hadn't come to the surface until Denis raised the question. Stocky may have chewed Denis's ear more frequently; otherwise it seemed to Kent that his temper had been if anything more equable than it was ordinarily. Stocky hadn't slowed down; his decisions were always capricious, but they hadn't lost their shrewdness. It was just that two or three times Stocky seemed, only for an instant, to lose contact. A look came over him fleetingly as though he saw something that wasn't there in the room, something more important than anything present. The expression would pass almost before it could be noticed, and Stocky would be back in the thick of things again, bleating and carrying on in his usual style.

"Well, I hope you're right," Denis said. He got up, hesitated as if about to speak again, and said finally, "See you at eleven."

Kent watched his back vanish into the corridor. Poor old Denis. Stocky had been riding him pretty steadily, that was the real trouble, and Denis couldn't admit that it was his own fault. He had to invent something wrong with Stocky to save his self-respect.

Kent crossed the hall to Shepherdson's office. Shep's back leaned intently over his desk. He seemed to have worked his way almost half through the New Jersey file. At his right hand lay a page of neatly digested notes. "What do you make of it, Shep?" Kent asked.

"Well," Shepherdson said, "it's hard to tell at this distance, but as far as I've gone, I can't see that the complaints are legitimate. You've given them a renovated plant within the year, and a lot of high-cost new equipment. They're reporting upkeep and repairs about three or four per cent on the average above what we do here, and claiming some of the new stuff is already obsolete. It looks as though they ought to be getting better performance."

"My thought exactly," Kent said.

He leaned over the desk while Shepherdson singled out items with his pencil point and put them to rapid analysis. They discussed and compared, and Kent said, "Someone will have to go down there and make a check. Think you can do it, Shep?"

"I'd like to try. I ought to be able to find where the bugs are, but—well, suppose they're not in the equipment but in the personnel? I'm pretty junior, and if they get the idea some young pipsqueak is nosing in—"

"I'll see you have all the authority you need," Kent said. "Of course, if there are soft spots in the personnel, you don't say anything about that down there. Your commission is to see everything there is to see. If you can help, good. If we need to make staff changes, you come back and report."

"I'll keep my eyes open," Shepherdson said. "When do you want me to start?"

"Whatever's cooking, I don't want it to cool. Why don't you head for New Jersey tomorrow night and show up at the plant bright and early Wednesday morning?"

Shepherdson looked momentarily glum. "Marge is due at the hospital almost any day," he said, "with our second. But we'll manage somehow. These things don't always come off on schedule, anyway."

Kent sympathized with him, but a man had to make sacrifices in a business career, and he was offering Shep an opportunity for which Shep would live to thank him. He made a mental note to ask Abby to keep in touch with Shep's wife in case of an emergency while he was away.

"I'd like to thank you for cutting me in on the profit-sharing plan," Shepherdson said. "If you hadn't backed me—"

"I hope it will amount to something. The company has been making progress, as a matter of fact, even though it's a recession year."

"I've noticed that," Shepherdson said, smiling faintly.

Kent crossed the hall to his office again. He put through a call to New Jersey and was hardly surprised when the branch manager resented the prospect of an inspection. He couldn't see why his letter hadn't completely satisfied—he didn't understand why a young assistant engineer—Kent said Mr. Shepherdson would be his personal representative, and of course he would be treated accordingly. The manager got the point. They would meet Mr. Shepherdson at his hotel at nine o'clock Wednesday, and he could see everything the plant had to show.

The call finished, Kent glanced at his watch. Half past ten already. He had to see his chief of maintenance, he had to see the union Grievance Committee. They wanted a new and more conveniently situated drinking fountain in the shipping rooms and a new lavatory in Vitamins. For once Kent thought they had a case, at least about the antiquated lavatory in Vitamins, which hardly met the current city building code. He tried to explain that he was sympathetic, but he would have to put a provision for the new facilities in the budget for the coming fiscal year. At three minutes of eleven, Isabel handed him the insurance claims report, and he took it with him toward the elevator.

In the top-floor corridor, on his way to Stocky's quarters, he passed the room where Denis officially avoided his work. Denis must have been lying in wait, not wanting to confront Stocky alone and unprotected, for he emerged and fell into step. Kent knocked at the presidential door, and at Stocky's "Come in," rather like the bark of a seal, they entered. Kent could see no sign of alteration. They confronted the familiar shoulders, hunched heavily forward toward the desk, the familiar trout mouth, the surprisingly blue eyes look-ing out from a triangular face. The same old Stocky. From the wall behind him, above the glassed-in cabinet, his facsim-ile reinforced his physical presence, the same mouth, the same eyes, the same double-breasted gray coat. Only the red neck-tie struck an incongruous note of difference.

Stocky nodded at Denis, waving his arm to indicate chairs. Kent and Denis each drew one forward to seat himself. "How's everything, Cap?" Stocky asked. "We haven't played a rub-ber of bridge in a dog's age."

"Any time you want," Kent said.

"Abby well? Ruth well? She's expecting, isn't she?"

"It's a habit with the young. If someone didn't do it, we wouldn't be here."

Stocky grinned sourly. "Sure, you have to keep the ball rolling," he admitted. "Well, let's get down to cases. I've got a letter here from our insurance agent. The underwriters acknowledge the claims and all that, but they don't commit themselves to a wooden nickel. All they talk about is setting up a procedure." Stocky picked up the letter from his desk and tapped its folded edge on the wood. "I don't like their attitude. It begins to look as if we might have to go to a show-down."

"What's the procedure?" Kent asked.

"They've appointed a board of adjusters to take up the claims and scheduled a meeting in New York. They say—well, listen to this." Unfolding the letter, Stocky held it in front of him and began to read. "'Are in receipt of your table of claims'—let's see—'beg to inform you the underwriting companies have designated a board of adjusters to consider in detail . . . would appreciate information from you'—well, they say they expect the company will want to be represented, and they want to know who's authorized to sign."

"You mean for Fullchem?" Denis asked.

Stocky's face made faint mouthing movements, as if he would have enjoyed chewing Denis's ear again, but he con-trolled himself. "You got it, Denis," he said. "Fast work."

Denis looked flustered, and Kent said, "If they're going to

be sticky about the claims, it may be all to the good to have a meeting where we can size up the opposition."

"It may be," Stocky admitted, "but that depends on how smart you boys are. That's where you two come in. I'm counting on you."

Denis made an effort to straighten in his chair and look aggressive, but while he raised himself an inch, he appeared to shrink in the act. "You and Cap," Stocky said, glaring at him, "go down to New York—let's see, Thursday the fourteenth—and sit in on this hearing, and if the board can't see reason, it's up to you to show the bastards where to get off. I want a settlement out of this, and I want a good one."

"We'll do our best for you," Denis said, "won't we, Cap?"

Stocky cut him a boding look but again controlled himself. "Now, here's the marching orders," he said. "Better get 'em straight. Denis is authorized to sign for the company, *if* you get a decent settlement, and I don't mean any half-assed settlement, either. We aren't in this for peanuts. But you don't sign unless Cap agrees, get that? You've both got to see it the same way, and that means Cap has got to be satisfied you've squeezed the last dime you can get out of the deal. How's that, have you got it straight?"

Denis looked as though his nervous stomach was giving him trouble. He was seeing his name on a settlement; that was his real agony. Once he put his signature on a document, he was committed, he was responsible; and if Stocky thought they ought to have done better— You could read Denis's misery in his eyes. "Wouldn't it be better if we both signed?" he asked.

Stocky looked seriously irked. "Any executive around here, I authorize him to sign, his signature is enough. You're a senior officer of this company, Denis. You're a Vice President, though by God I wonder sometimes—"

"I think we can handle this board between us," Kent said.

"If that's the way you want it, Stocky—I mean about signing," Denis said. "Of course Cap has done most of the figuring on these claims, and I'll rely a good deal on his judgment."

"You'd better use some judgment of your own, if you have any. I want two heads in on this proposition," Stocky said, "and I don't want both of them on the same neck."

Denis winced, and Stocky looked pleased with himself. "Well," he said, "any question either of you has got in mind, now's the time to bring it up."

"I can't think of anything," Kent said, "until we've had a look at this board."

"There's one thing," Denis said. "I still think—well, that item for amortization, I don't see how we're going to get away with that."

Kent saw the color begin to mount in Stocky's neck. If it went on climbing, it would reach his ears, and when it got to a certain point, Stocky's top would blow. "We aren't going to get away with it," Kent said. "That's just a bit of psychological warfare. Maybe I didn't make myself clear about it." He knew, and Stocky knew, that the point had been explained to Denis with painful clearness, but the thing was to keep that ominous mottled hue that still hovered an inch above Stocky's collar from climbing any higher. "It's the old political tactic," Kent said. "If you want to get your platform through a hostile committee, put in some planks they can knock out right away. Then they concede more than they have to on the points that count, or they don't watch the rest of the items so carefully. They knock out the amortization, we say we're just trying to give a complete business picture, and that's part of the picture."

"How about it, Denis? Get it now?" Stocky asked.

"I get the idea all right," Denis said. "I don't know how it will work out." His face brightened suddenly. "Wouldn't it be a good thought at this point," he asked, "to go over the items once more in detail—I mean, if we're going to start scrapping with this board next week—"

The mottled hue reached the base of Stocky's ears and went on rising. Denis's head on a platter wouldn't appease him now. "For Christ's sake, Prouty, what in the hell do you want to start going over items now for—*now*, for Christ's sake?"

"I only thought—maybe one more review—" Denis said.

Stocky's voice rose to a paroxysm. "What time of day do you think it is around here, anyway, Prouty? You've been over this claims report. You're supposed to have had something to do with it, you're responsible for these items, goddamn it. If you didn't like 'em, why in the hell didn't you say so while they were in the works? This is a hell of a time —I've been over this thing with you myself till I'm— I'm *sick*—"

Suddenly Kent saw what Denis had been getting at earlier in the day. Have you noticed anything wrong about Stocky? The startling blue eyes went vacant, or not so much vacant as focused on something altogether irrelevant to the room where they sat and the business that had brought them together. This time the expression was not fleeting. It stayed, and then it began to twist and stiffen. Kent might not be watching Stocky suffer a stroke, but he saw where and how Stocky *would* have a stroke at some hour to come, saw the right-hand corner of the mouth go slack, saw the seam run up the cheek beside it, a seam that would one day freeze into a paralyzed crust. Kent's reflexes brought him up out of his chair, but Stocky wasn't falling or even slumping. His figure somehow kept its balance. Kent heard an odd noise behind him and turned. With a shaking finger Denis was trying to dial at one of Stocky's phones. Denis's leg trembled so that his kneecap drummed against the desk.

A thick, unlocalized voice said, "What were we talking about?" Stocky was recovering himself. His face was relaxing, his blue eyes were coming to focus on the room again. "What do you think you're doing, Prouty?" he asked. "You want to make a call, why don't you use your own line?"

"I was trying to get—" Denis said. "Listen, Stocky, you aren't up to par today. You need—"

"None of your damned business what I need. I get these spells—I'm acting on doctor's orders, when I get a chance to around here." He glared balefully at Denis. "Put that phone back."

The receiver rattled as Denis restored it to its cradle. The

thing to do was to get Denis out of the room. He was a dangerous provocation.

"Well, Denis, we have our orders. Let's go," Kent said.

Denis was hard to budge, and they had to wait for a final
admonition from Stocky. "It's up to you boys now. And one
other thing. I don't want a goddamned word said about
anything that's happened in this room. You think you saw
something, you *didn't* see it, see?"

"You can count on us," Kent assured him.

"You'd better mean it," Stocky said.

By practically treading on Denis's feet, Kent got him headed
around and in motion toward the corridor. They walked the
dozen steps to Denis's office before Denis could contain himself no longer. "Jesus, Cap," he said and put his hand convulsively on Kent's arm.

"Take it easy, Denis," Kent said. "We don't know how bad
things are yet."

Denis gave him a despairing look. "Listen, Cap, I—do you
suppose we could go out and lunch somewhere? I need a
drink, if I can keep it down on this stomach I have, and there
are some things I'd like to talk to you about. I don't know,
though, maybe I ought to stick around." He glanced back at
Stocky's door.

Kent looked into Denis's office and saw that it was vacant.
His secretary seemed to be shut safely in her adjoining room.
Kent stepped inside, and Denis followed. "I don't think you
ought to stick around, Denis," Kent said. "Let's face it.
Stocky has got into the habit of jumping on you, and when
you're handy he gets excited and works himself up. Why don't
you lie low till we bring back some good news about this insurance deal?"

"You may be right, Cap," Denis said. "I don't seem to know
how—I've tried, but nothing I do—" He faltered and
shifted his ground. "What do you say to lunch?"

Kent hadn't the heart to refuse. He consulted his watch
and said, "Give me half an hour, then drop by and pick me
up."

"I'll do that," Denis said, looking as though he were wondering what to do with himself in the meanwhile.

Snow was falling as they drove to an uptown restaurant off the usual beat for Fullchem executives. An inch of it squeaked underfoot as they walked from the parking lot. They found a booth in a corner where they could expect privacy, and Denis decided that his stomach would tolerate a martini or two. His eyes grew humid as he moaned about his deteriorating relations with Stocky. Jesus, Cap, if anything should happen to Stocky!

Kent had already begun to do his own thinking about that possibility and was surprised to discover how much regret he felt at the prospect. As a young engineer, he'd sweated under Stocky's arrogance and ignorance, and at the same time admired his shrewdness and success. Stocky had been the boss, to be studied, placated, persuaded; Kent had learned how to handle him and had taken it for granted that this was the limit of his personal feeling about him. But when you lived through decisions and crises and explosions with a man, you developed more of a bond with him than you were aware of until the bond was threatened. Not that Stocky was in the grave yet, or necessarily on the edge of it; he might go on crowing and blustering and keeping profits on the increase for years yet. Still, it was obvious that he couldn't last forever, and that any crisis might be the last.

As Denis keened over his martinis and then over his sirloin smothered in onions, Kent began to see more clearly than before the assiduity of Denis's campaign to curry favor with Stocky. Denis had been keeping a watchful eye on the boss for a long time, hanging around the presidential secretaries, trying to pry information from them, trying to protect Stocky, to soothe and mollify him, to play the mother hen. That was why Stocky chewed his ear so often. Denis would have done better to keep out of the way, just sit in his office and let himself lose his grip quietly and inconspicuously. Denis knew, and Stocky knew, that Kent had been covering for him. If Denis had accepted the situation, they all would have understood each other and got along. Instead, Denis kept himself underfoot, and now he was saddled with responsibility for signing the insurance settlement. Stocky was giving him an unwanted chance, perhaps a final chance, to demonstrate that he had a value.

"I don't know, Cap, but I think it's happened before, one of these attacks, I mean."

"What gives you that idea?"

"Not in the office," Denis said. "I've suspected something was wrong, but I don't think anything has happened at the plant till this morning."

"At home?" Kent said. "When was it?"

"Back in October, the week-end his daughter came home. You know how she always hairs him up."

"I've only seen her once or twice," Kent said. "She struck me as tougher than old leather and fast enough to win the Derby."

"Yeah, well, I guess she was talking about a divorce—it would be her third—and Stocky told her it was time to settle down. I guess they had quite a talk. That was the same week-end you boys took him over to Willawicket for a round of golf. He didn't show up at the office for two days after that, remember? Jesus, Cap, what did you boys do to him? I called the house, and they said he had a cold, but I thought I was getting the run-around, and I never could get him to say anything about that golf match. What went on, anyway?"

Kent remembered that late October week-end well enough. Stocky suddenly decided that the Fullington Country Club was a slum. He wanted Kent to get up a Sunday foursome at Willawicket. Kent wasn't a member, and neither was Stocky, but Kent said he knew some members and thought he could get the foursome registered as guests. Oh, no; Stocky wouldn't play as a guest. Just let them know he was willing to be a member as of Sunday. Kent suggested that the club had the reputation of being conservative to the point of being stuffy. He'd see that Stocky's name was proposed and seconded right away, and election would follow as a matter of routine, but it might take a little time. Stocky pointed out in his most emphatic bleat that he didn't ask to join clubs; they invited him to join. Kent managed to keep the question of membership diplomatically out of view, and on Sunday the foursome duly drove the thirty-odd miles to Willawicket as guests.

"It isn't much of a yarn," Kent said. "Stocky insisted on dollar syndicates. Ten cents is about my scale, but he could call the turn. Well, at the eleventh hole no one had won a syndicate yet. It's a par three hole, and Stocky was lying pretty with a measly little putt for a clear win. That's thirty-three bucks practically in his pocket. As a matter of fact he was so near the hole he asked for a gimme, and he was sore as blazes when nobody would concede."

"Did he miss it?" Denis asked.

"Just as he swung his putter back to tap it in, a crow flew out of an alley in the trees behind the green. He caught a look at Stocky's rear elevation and cawed profanely. Stocky scuffed the heel of his putter in the grass, and the ball never reached the hole."

"Tough," Denis said. "Still—"

"Stocky hadn't finished consigning the game of golf and everything connected with it to perdition when one of the guys looked over his shoulder and allowed that we'd better run for shelter. Sure enough, a black cloud, black as the inside of a church at midnight, had been building up to westward while we concentrated on the match. It was coming on fast, but with seven more chances to clean up a syndicate, Stocky didn't propose to quit. He made some remarks about intestinal fortitude and sportsmanship, and we headed for the next tee. The squall caught us halfway there. The temperature dropped ten degrees before you could wink, the air was full of leaves and twigs and sleet flying level. We took off for the clubhouse by the shortest route and spent the rest of the afternoon playing the nineteenth hole. Then nothing would do but we had to stay for dinner and play poker afterwards. He didn't have any better luck at poker than golf."

"Quite a day," Denis said. "I can see why he never said anything about it."

Kent's mind was giving him uneasy twinges, though there

was nothing he could have done about the expedition at any point. Still, if Denis had actually seen the quarter-mile scuttle to the clubhouse, with Kent himself bringing up the rear on his bad leg and Stocky wallowing along a few strides ahead; if Denis had seen the blue chatter of Stocky's teeth, seen how his tropical sport shirt was plastered to his torso till the nipples stood out as far as the fat on his belly, seen the highballs he drank and the dinner he ate, followed by more highballs and poker till midnight before the cold ride back to Fullington —no wonder Stocky never referred to Willawicket. The question of membership didn't come up again.

Kent looked across the table at Denis. "Are we ready to reward the waitress for ignoring us and get back to the shop?"

Reluctantly, Denis put his napkin on the table and prepared to go.

The weather had cleared and the cold sharpened when Kent drove home at dusk. The four inches of snow that had fallen shut the house in snugly for the winter night. He felt a pleasant pressure from the budget of news he had to talk over with Abby at dinner.

"It will make a big difference, won't it," Abby said, "if anything happens to Stocky?"

"Plenty of difference."

"How will it affect you?"

"I don't see that I'll have anything to worry about if I keep performing up to standard. We'll have a period of readjustment, and that always means trouble, but it ought not to be worse than that."

"A new president may recognize you for what you're worth."

"Oh, he'll thank me for saving the company money, but the guys who increase sales and expand the business will go on getting the big rewards."

"Who'll be in the running? Is Fred Abramson still in line?"

"I'd expect one of the Vice Presidents to be moved up, and Fred has always looked like the winner. He's the one I'd bet on if we have an office sweepstakes."

"Would the Directors elect him?"

"Fred has his points, even if his father was a rabbi and he came up through sales and advertising. He's a team player, and he always consults and takes everything into account before making a decision. He'll never have Stocky's spark. And don't count Stocky out yet. If Denis lets him alone, he may keep the company growing for another five years." Kent described his lunch with Denis and mentioned Denis's suspicion that something had happened to Stocky after the ill-fated week-end at Willawicket.

"I was afraid you were going to have a stroke yourself," Abby said, "when you got home at two in the morning."

"The Lord wants to save me for hanging. He isn't going to let me off with a stroke."

"You can't tell what will happen if you drink too much and play poker till all hours and then drive under the influence."

"I didn't drive, and besides, I was just a helpless victim. There was nothing I could do about the situation at all."

"I don't believe the driver was in any better condition than you were. And in all that rain and fog—"

"You put me in the doghouse for a week after I got back," Kent said. "Don't start all over again. The law says you can't put a man in the doghouse twice for the same offense."

"You put yourself in the doghouse when you do things like that. I want to save you for my old age, Cappie, and I don't think you ought to get into situations you can't control."

Kent thought of answers, but perhaps, if he kept still for a minute or two, Abby would shift to another subject. His tactics were successful.

"When you go to New York about the insurance," she said, "you can visit Ruth and Brainerd."

"Well, this will be strictly business, and I may have to hot-foot it right back with a report. It depends on how the hearing goes."

"You can surely spare an hour or so for your own daughter, with the baby coming any time now. I wish Ruth had let me stay with her, but I suppose I'd just be in the way in that tiny house."

"Why not let the baby come first, and when it's got past

looking uncooked I'll pay a visit and give it my blessing?"

Abby looked at him patiently. "You're a case, Cappie," she said.

∘ ∘ *2* ∘ ∘

"Four for twenty-three," Kent said, laying down his card beside the cribbage board on the one-legged table the porter had hooked into the wall of the roomette.

Denis cursed as the old Pullman, the sole surviving overnight car on the run to New York, lurched violently on a curve. "We should have waited and taken a plane in the morning," he said. "Well, I've got to pair you for twenty-seven, and if you have another of those little bastards—" He put down the four of diamonds.

"You didn't really expect me not to?" Kent said, playing the four of clubs. "Too risky at this time of year. The planes might be grounded all day. That's thirty-one for two and three of a kind for six." He pegged eight holes and then, after Denis played, another for last card.

"Some people have all the luck," Denis said.

Kent spread his hand. "Game and rubber without counting the crib," he said. He made no move to reshuffle the deck. They ought to quit and turn in if they wanted to keep their heads clear for the board of adjusters in the morning. Denis looked glum, but he didn't suggest another rubber. Kent folded the cribbage board and put it back in its calfskin case. He congratulated himself on bringing it along. Without some diversion, he would have had to listen defenseless to the uninterrupted flow of Denis's ailments and woes.

Denis took an inhalator from his pocket and applied it to each nostril in turn. He tested his breathing and looked discouraged by the results. Restoring the inhalator, he extracted a bottle of aspirin. From its place on the floor between his feet, he lifted an already depleted fifth of whisky, offering it to Kent.

"No thanks," Kent said. "I've had my quota."

Denis added a shot to the dregs in his glass, poured an inch of water on top, and washed down two aspirin tablets. "I ought to take this cold to bed and head it off, if I could sleep on the goddamn train."

"It mightn't be a bad idea to get some sleep," Kent said. "We want to be ready for the opposition tomorrow." He glanced at his watch to reinforce his point. Half past eleven.

"Yeah, well, we've got to knock off sometime," Denis said reluctantly. "I could sleep just as well standing up in a hammock full of rocks."

"With the medication you've taken, you'll drop off like a babe in arms," Kent said.

Denis took out his inhalator again. He applied it and puckered as though he felt a sneeze on the way. He was a long time bringing it to a climax, but he finally succeeded and looked at Kent through eyes in which the veins were beginning to redden. "Jesus, Cap, if I don't feel any better than this in the morning—" He picked up his glass and shivered slightly as he took another swallow.

"You'll be all right," Kent said. "Just remember we have a job to do."

Denis drained his tumbler and examined the walls of the roomette as if searching for some last defense against a night of solitude and insomnia. Finally he reconciled himself to the inevitable. He got up, saying, "Well, get your beauty sleep, Cap. God knows I won't." He pulled the curtains aside and vanished into the corridor.

Kent didn't sleep well on trains himself, if the truth were known, but he dozed enough so that in the morning the porter had to wake him half an hour before 125th Street. He looked at his watch. The train was for once on time. He and Denis could check in at the hotel where they had reserved rooms in case a single day didn't complete their business, and they could eat breakfast in comfort.

Denis hadn't put in an appearance by the time Kent packed his bag and gave it to the porter. Kent tapped at Denis's door. A croak responded from inside, then the door slid part way back, and a subhuman figure revealed itself. Denis had dressed, but he hadn't shaved; a sallow fuzz blurred the outline of his face. For some reason he had already put on his hat and pulled the brim down over his forehead, and he was in the act of struggling into his overcoat. One elbow stuck out at an uncouth angle beyond the edge of the door, giving him the aspect of an ill-tended scarecrow. His bleared eyes looked wooden in their sockets.

"We're rolling into Grand Central," Kent said. "How do you feel?"

Denis uttered an inarticulate sound, which Kent translated as "Rotten." He pinched his Adam's apple between thumb and finger, as if to say that laryngitis made him unable to speak.

During the taxi-ride to the hotel, Denis maintained silence except for the constricted wheeze that came through his nose and half-opened mouth. Once or twice he seemed to forget himself and breathe more naturally, but his nose was running for certain. They stopped first at Denis's room, and Kent said, "I'll stow my bag in my quarters and then come by for you and we can get a bite of breakfast. Some juice and coffee will perk you up."

Denis was already eying the bed. "No use," he said hoarsely. "Can't make it. Stomach sick, chest full of rock wool. Sorry, Cap. I'm hitting the sack." He turned away and struggled through a paroxysm of coughing, how genuine Kent found it hard to judge. Then he turned about again. "Size 'em up, Cap. Come back right away and lemme know what you get. May be able to sign my name if they make it good." He sat down on the bed and avoided Kent's eye.

Well, there you had it. Denis was throwing in the sponge. Denis had his troubles, but you reached a limit of sympathy for a man who funked out in a crisis. "All right, Denis, I'll see what I can do," Kent said and turned on his heel.

Behind him, Denis's voice barked out, suddenly clear and natural. "Give 'em hell, Cap. Get us a settlement." Then he seemed to realize his lapse and added sepulchrally, "Wish I could be there."

Kent had no course but to leave him to his misery. He might be faking the nature of it, but as misery, it was real.

The board of adjusters had already assembled when Kent announced his presence to a secretary and was admitted. The room where its members sat made an impression Kent found unflattering to the corporate resources of Fullchem. One wall consisted of a temporary plywood partition, an ineffective barrier against the noises of an active office building. The place had no rug, but it offered at least some of the appurtenances of a directors' room, a heavy polished table, leather-backed chairs, a scratch pad and a supply of pencils at each occupied seat.

Kent saw that he was going to be outnumbered six to one; he'd better get everything right, and the point at which to begin was the matter of names. Business bargaining might be tough, a kind of horse-trading supposedly governed by nothing but the profit motive, but it could make a difference to call a man by his name at the right time. Chairman: McIntosh, a tall, pinched Scotchman with a big fist that looked as though it wouldn't let go of a sixpence if you burned it with a hot iron. He introduced himself without getting up and peered at Kent with suspicion. "You represent the Fullington—you represent the company?" he asked, glancing at his notes. "I thought there were going to be two of you, let's see, Mr. Prouty and Mr. Warner."

"My associate, Mr. Prouty, came down with a vicious cold on the train," Kent said. "He didn't want to inflict it on you gentlemen, so he stayed at his hotel, within reach by phone."

"Very considerate of him, I'm sure," the Chairman said. "I take it, Mr. Warner, you're authorized, since Mr. Prouty can't be with us, to sign an agreement for the company?"

Kent sat down uninvited in a chair at the end of the table, from which he could see all the two lines of faces at once. He put his brief case deliberately on the floor, unsnapped its catch, and began drawing out papers. "Mr. Prouty is authorized to sign," he said. "If we reach a satisfactory agreement, as I've no doubt we will, I can take it to him and he can sign before we leave New York, if you like."

The Chairman grunted. "I suppose we'll have to go ahead without him," he said. "Well, you'll want to know who we are." He named the members of the board rapidly, Fiedler on his left, Hampstead on his right, LaGrange, Bellini, Hofstetter across the table. Kent looked them in the eye in turn. They did not offer to rise or shake hands. Hofstetter was the name that would give him trouble if he had to use it; he pronounced it to himself twice over.

"I guess we all know what we're here for," McIntosh said. "I might briefly review the case just as a reminder." He launched on a needlessly exhaustive recapitulation of the fire, its date, the resulting claims, copies of which lay before the members of the board, the purpose of the present session, which was to discuss the claims and reach a settlement if possible. Kent heard him out patiently. "So I now declare the meeting open," McIntosh finished.

The man on his right cleared his throat and said, "I'd like to ask Mr. Warner—" He broke off and looked at his notes. Hempstead, Kent reminded himself. A shriveled little paring of a man in a seedy gray coat and a white shirt that pinched his neck. "Let's see, your position is—you're an engineer, is that right?"

"Right, Mr. Hempstead," Kent said. "Executive Engineer for Fullchem."

"What was the cause, would you say, of this fire?"

"I wish I knew, Mr. Hempstead. I'm afraid we have to put it down as cause unknown. I think you'll find that point pretty thoroughly treated in our covering letter. Do you have it there for reference? If not, I have a copy."

"It would be your business," Hempstead said, disregarding Kent's question, "to determine the cause if it were possible?"

"If it were possible, yes."

"I'd like to know what efforts you made. How is this board going to be sure that negligence didn't enter in?"

"Gentlemen," Kent said, taking pains to smile, "a company such as Fullchem doesn't operate on negligence. If we did, we couldn't stay in business against our competitors. We wouldn't make profits, and I think if you look at our annual reports—"

"All the same," Hempstead persisted, "you can tell us what you did, how you tried to establish a cause."

"All we have to go on," Kent said, "is the report of the watchman for the night preceding the fire. The rest of the story is buried in the ruins." He expatiated a little on the good record of Tim O'Brian as a watchman. He didn't think Tim had told anyone of the succession of blown fuses, and he could remind himself that, as a cause, they amounted only to a probability at best. All sorts of unknowns might have started the fire or helped to spread it. Paul Zyblocki, on his rounds by day, might have violated rules by smoking a cigarette and might have flipped the butt into a tunnel to conceal his infraction.

Hempstead seemed about to go on, and he could ask questions that would call for careful handling: just who, for example, talked with the night watchman? You, Mr. Warner? Kent was weighing tactics to meet the threat if it came when an irritable voice spoke up on his right, from beyond La-Grange and Bellini. "Mr. Warner, you tell us you're an engineer, but you don't even have a theory about how this fire began? Now I've had some training as an engineer myself—"

Kent looked directly at the speaker. He mustn't let his quick, provisional estimate of the board harden prematurely, but it was time he showed them a piece of his own mettle, and if he produced the desired effect it might foreclose any further discussion of cause or negligence. This time he didn't bother to smile as he answered. "Mr. Hofstetter, as an engineer I don't toy with theories. It's my job to know the facts, when there are any, and when there aren't, I don't try to pass off theories instead."

The shot was risky, but it seemed to go home. Hofstetter colored; he was ruffled all right, but he was also cowed. Kent waited passively through a moment of general silence until Bellini spoke. Bellini was a different specimen from his fellow board members. His brown suit looked recently tailored, and if his shirt and tie were on the loud side, he had the style to make the most of them. The eyes in his smooth, darkly polished face were shrewd and hard. "Mr. Chairman," he said, "I'm looking at the item for amortization in these claims. I'd like to move that we strike it out."

"Second that," said LaGrange.

"Mr. Chairman, I'd like to put in a word," Kent said. "It seems to me pretty early in these proceedings to strike out an item by formal vote, especially without discussing it."

"It's an obviously unallowable claim," Bellini said, smiling. "I'm sure Mr. Warner knows it is."

"If the board considers it unallowable, and makes the reasons clear, I'll be glad to take the word back to my associate, Mr. Prouty, and I'm sure the company will be reasonable. I might say we're trying to give a complete business picture here, and amortization is a pertinent fact."

"How did you get this figure?" Bellini asked.

"I don't understand your question," Kent said. "It's the figure on the company books."

"Well, you had these buildings. You must have used them for something. What were you doing over there?"

"At the time of the fire they were vacant."

"Well, what were you going to do with them?"

Kent repressed a smile as the possible purpose of the question begun to show through. Competitors were always trying to learn whatever they could about each other's businesses. If the public knew what went on in the way of industrial espionage! Even negative information might have some value. If Fullchem had intended to use the old buildings for its limited-sales products, then it hadn't intended to use them for something else. "The fire naturally changed our plans," Kent said. "Anyway, they represent a management decision that I wouldn't be at liberty to divulge."

"Mr. Chairman, I've made a motion," Bellini said.

"Second it," LaGrange said again.

"I don't think a motion is necessary," Kent said. Perhaps it wasn't worth fighting a vote on a point only put in for tactical value, but he had a feeling that the less this board left behind it by way of record, the better for the outcome. "I'll take the responsibility for saying that the amortization figure isn't part of the claim. It's part of a conscientious effort to give the whole business picture."

"I think the record ought to show—" La Grange said.

"You don't need a formal vote on what I've agreed to waive," Kent said.

McIntosh looked at Bellini, who said, "All right, as long as it's clear Mr. Warner has definitely withdrawn the amortization angle."

Kent had won his point, but the contest had confirmed his estimate of the board. As the questioning went on, he felt further confirmed, and he began to see more and more clearly what he would have to do.

Fiedler was next. Mr. Warner, you have here a chart where you've indicated various buildings by number. Now what would you say is the salvage value of building number one? Mr. Fiedler, you have our photographs. You'll see there's nothing left of building number one but a heap of rubble. It cost the company money to cart it away. Well, would you give us the salvage value of building number two, which seems to have been destroyed less completely? Mr. Fiedler, it's true the photograph shows part of a wall standing, but it had to be knocked down and hauled off as rubbish. Well, was there any machinery or equipment in any of these buildings that had a salvage value? Nothing whatever, Mr. Fiedler.

After beating down Fiedler on salvage, he had to contend with other lines of inquiry, all picayune, all avoiding the issue of settlement. The trouble was with the composition of the board itself. Cheeseparers, nickel-and-dime mentalities, small-time operators who could just about keep their collars white, except for Bellini, whose collar was salmon pink. They had no appreciation of the standing of Fullchem, they didn't live in scale with the size of the interests they were dealing with. He wouldn't mind haggling with them till hell froze over if they were getting anywhere with the issues, but from the board as it sat, the company could expect nothing but a stalemate leading to an expensive lawsuit. In a pause, Kent picked up his brief case and got to his feet. "Mr. Chairman," he said, "I think we're wasting each other's time. I don't see that the climate of this board is favorable to a settlement the company could accept."

McIntosh looked startled and abashed. The other faces about the table matched him in expression. Hofstetter's jaw fell open, and he seemed about to speak, but Kent didn't propose to give him the opportunity. "I'm glad to have met you all, gentlemen," he said. "Good day." No one broke silence as he went out through a secretary's cubicle and into the corridor toward the elevators.

It shouldn't take more than ten minutes to reach Dave Cronkhite's office by taxi. As insurance agent for Fullchem, Dave didn't handle the company's policies for nothing; he knew when he had a good thing, and it was time he showed his value to the company in return. Dave might be more amenable if someone from higher management called on him; Kent knew him only on a casual first-name basis, but time was important, and the line to take with Dave was so obvious that Kent felt confident he could carry it out. A good thing, after all, that Denis was tucked away in his hotel room, nursing his hypochondria. Denis would have stood an hour on one foot and an hour on the other, moaning and wringing his hands about what Stocky would or wouldn't authorize them to do.

The secretary was awfully sorry, but Mr. Cronkhite was in conference. As a matter of fact he'd be tied up most of the day. Did Mr. Warner have an appointment? Just tell Mr. Cronkhite that Mr. Warner had dropped in on immediate and urgent business about Fullchem. The secretary looked doubtful. Kent took off his coat and seated himself in a chair directly beside Dave's office door. The secretary knocked and went in. Kent heard three or four sentences exchanged, and not long after the girl had emerged Dave himself ushered out a visitor. They pumped hands and swore not to let so much time go by before they saw each other again. Kent got up and posted himself between Dave and his office door. Dave turned and affected pleasure and surprise. "Cap Warner," he said, offering his hand. "You should have told me you were going to be in town. I wouldn't have got so tied up."

"Didn't we write you that Prouty and I would be coming down?"

"Now that you remind me—things have been humming around here so I haven't had a free minute. Where's Prouty?"

Kent turned, walked into Dave's office ahead of him, and seated himself in the visitor's chair by the desk. "Denis is laid up in his hotel room with a raging flu," he said.

Dave smiled, but his expression didn't welcome the news. Denis, Dave might well think, would be easier to deal with than Kent intended to be. "Well, let's see," Dave said. "You've been meeting with the board of adjusters, right? How did it go?"

"It didn't go," Kent said. "I walked out on it."

"Walked out? How come?"

"It's a hostile board."

"Hostile? Well, Cap, I don't know about that. Of course I don't appoint them, but the companies involved have all been in business—I don't see—"

"It's a hostile board," Kent said again. "You're our agent, Dave. We want to get a settlement without going to court. We expect you to work for us."

Cronkhite laughed uneasily. "What can I do?" he asked. "Taking your word for it that it's a hostile—that you don't like their attitude, still, I can't dictate—"

"I was trying to think," Kent said. "What's the total face value of the policies you handle for us?"

Cronkhite's face colored. "I don't want anyone to think I don't appreciate Fullchem's business," he said. "It's an important account."

"With the plans we have for the future, it won't get any less so," Kent said. "We've always been satisfied with the way you handled it."

Dave caught the look Kent gave him with the words. He paled and shifted on his butt. "What's really the matter with the board?" he asked.

"The personnel, all and sundry," Kent said. "Small operators. They don't show any appreciation of what they're dealing with. I haggled with them for a couple of hours, and we didn't get around to accepting a single item."

"Well," Cronkhite said, his face knotting, "I don't know

what I can promise. I can't appoint— Where are you going to be, Cap?"

"I'll be wherever you want to reach me. At the hotel, if that's all right."

"I'll see what I can do," Cronkhite said. "Give me till tomorrow morning, will you? I'll call you up first thing."

"I'll be there," Kent said. "Make it good, Dave."

He went out, feeling that Dave would make it as good as he could. Dave understood competition; he wouldn't lose Fullchem as a client if he could help it, no matter what strings he had to pull.

At the hotel, Kent tapped on Denis's door. Denis opened it promptly, his face expectant. He'd spruced himself up past all belief. He was shaved, his clothes were in order, and except for an inflamed and overworked nose, he hardly showed symptoms even of a cold in the head. "God, Cap, I might almost have come with you. Cold took a turn for the better. No use, though. You can't negotiate when you're threatened with the trots. It ruins your bargaining position." Kent accorded him the expected laugh, and Denis said, "How's it going? Are we on the way to a settlement?"

Kent would have liked to keep him in ignorance, but he hardly thought he could stretch his discretion that far. He explained the situation as concisely as he could, and Denis immediately relapsed into a bad state of jitters. They'd disregarded instructions, they ought to have called Stocky direct, what was Stocky going to say when he heard—? "I'm going to call Stocky myself," Kent said, "but I'm going to have a bite of lunch first. It's late and I'm starved."

"Well, you be sure and let him know how it was with me," Denis said. "Tell him I was flat out the whole morning." Then he thought he might be able to join Kent for lunch; after all, he hadn't had any breakfast, and he was feeling steadier where it counted.

Denis's appetite proved equal to a steak and a slice of apple pie, but by the time Kent was ready to call Stocky, Denis had worked himself into a lather of apprehension. He wanted to hang over Kent's ear, but Kent made much of the awkwardness of a three-way telephone conversation and secreted himself in his room. He had his own misgivings, but Stocky wasn't without a sense of the dramatic, and Kent thought he could make a palatable yarn out of the board meeting and the pressure he had put on Dave Cronkhite. A plywood partition. No rug. A hostile board. Gentlemen, as an engineer I don't toy with theories. Gentlemen, what is the salvage value of a heap of rubble? Gentlemen, I didn't come here to divulge company secrets. Gentlemen, good day.

Stocky grunted and grated and bleated through the wire, but he got the points as Kent made them, and while he threatened and bullied about exceeding instructions, he approved the use of judgment on the spot as the situation called for it. "One more thing," Kent said. "Would it be all right for Denis to take the night train back and keep out of the office till he's got over his flu?"

"I get it, Cap," Stocky said. "Okay, I'll authorize that."

"Can I make it an order?"

"Order him to go to hell while you're about it."

Kent gave Denis his own version of the order and announced that he wanted to put in an hour or so jotting down notes and reminders while they were fresh in his mind. Denis didn't want to be deserted, but Kent escaped to his room again, where he put through another telephone call. Hadn't Abby said he simply must look in on Ruth while he was so near at hand? He could at least see whether she was at home and in any state for a visit.

The commuters' local discharged him after a half-hour's run, and a taxi set him down in front of the small frame house that Ruth and Brainerd rented. It stood in a respectable but seedy area between residential suburb and a patch of urban blight where Brainerd found an arena for field work. Kent could remember living cheerfully in quarters not much superior when he and Abby were beginning family life; he only wished he could see more tangible prospects for Ruth and Brainerd to improve their status.

Ruth met him at the door and managed to put her face to

his for a filial kiss, although he was afraid she would dislodge the baby in the act of doing it. He didn't see how she got around, pushing that burden in front of her. She said it was lovely to see him; she couldn't think of a nicer surprise than his telephone call. Brainerd had to go to an important social-service dinner and meeting. She was afraid Kent would find it a dull evening, but it would be ever so much nicer for her than sitting with the neighbor who had offered to come in. Kent asked whether he couldn't save her a lot of work in the kitchen by taking her and the grandchildren out to dinner somewhere, but she laughed and said she'd let him take her out another time, under different circumstances, and anyway she had everything planned and was glad she could give him a home meal in her own house. It turned out she had even procured a pint of Scotch from the couple next door. She sat him down with it while she bestirred herself in the kitchen.

His highball became an object of interest to young Kent and Randy.

"Why do you drink that?" young Kent wanted to know.

"It's a grown-up drink."

"Will I drink it when I grow up?"

"I shouldn't be surprised."

"Why don't Mummy and Daddy drink it?"

"They do sometimes."

"But not as much as you do."

Kent decided to concede a round. The boy thrust a finger into the glass and sucked it. He made a nauseated face and hopped around the room, uttering exaggerated sounds of revulsion. Young Randy poked at the glass in imitation of his brother, but Kent lifted it out of reach as Ruth came in to announce dinner.

Establishing a lifetime precedent, Kent offered to help wash dishes, but Ruth said he could help more by getting the boys to bed. As he chivvied them up the stairs, he heard the explosive pop of the gas heater coming on. Ruth must have one of the last copper boilers in captivity that had to be lit by hand.

With some difficulty, Kent diverted questions about when

the baby would come out from inside mummy, and got on the more congenial topic of wild life and its habits—bears, foxes, owls. When he came downstairs again, mission accomplished, Ruth was ready to sit down and talk with him about Abby, about the prospects for his building, about the insurance meeting. Kent wondered why Franklin put in no appearance. It seemed that, for reasons Kent didn't quite understand, Franklin was being boarded with a friendly master at his new school until the household was back to normal again.

Rather suddenly, Ruth announced that she was tired. "I'm sorry to cave in this way, Daddy, but if you don't mind too much, I'm going to take a bath and lie down upstairs. Do you mind too much waiting till Brainerd gets home?"

"Of course not," Kent said.

"I'll turn the heater off on my way up. Perhaps you'd like to look at some of Brainerd's articles. He wouldn't let me show them to you if he were here. He's shy about putting himself forward, but he's making a name for himself. They're right there in that folder in the bookcase."

The articles hardly made an exhilarating prospect. He would have preferred a good combat novel or an account of Grant's Vicksburg campaign, but he took down the folder and settled himself with it in a chair. Title: "Problems of Rôle Formation among Gang-Oriented Adolescents." No thanks. "Conceptions of Sexual Behavioral Norms in the Mental Attitudes of Field Workers." He could leave that to the headshrinkers. Upstairs he could hear Ruth's bath water begin to run. "Some Impacts on Community Patterns of Relocation as an Aspect of Urban Renewal." That was a mouthful too, but it suggested at least a remote bearing on the world he himself understood. He began to read. The language made hard slogging, but by translating it, where he could, into his own terms, Kent found himself unexpectedly interested. Problem: You want to give a city a face-lifting, so you start clearing out a slum. That means land-taking, and immediately the realtor gains an advantage. Eminent domain assembles for him in one big tract, at low cost, a lot of parcels of land it would ruin him to put together one by one. Then the builder puts up his housing, and with construction materials and wages what they are, the cost per room goes up one, two, three hundred per cent. The widows and orphans and down-and-outs that lived in the slum—

"Daddy?" said a voice from upstairs. It sounded small and apologetic. He could hear no other sound in the house at all. Ruth must have finished her tub and gone to bed. "What is it?" Kent said.

"I hate to bother you, but would you mind making a phone call for me?"

"Of course not. What about?"

"Well, it's just the nurse. Her name and number are written down on a pad."

"The nurse?"

"I just thought it would be a good idea to find out if she's at home."

"What do you want a nurse for?"

"I don't. I just want to find out—"

"Look here, is it time you went to the hospital?"

"I'm not going to a hospital, and it isn't time. I just thought—"

"Not going to a hospital?" What did the crazy child think she was doing? Why hadn't he been aware of her plans? Had Abby told him when he wasn't listening, or had Ruth kept them both in the dark?

"The hospital here isn't very good," she said, "and if I went into New York I'd have to reserve a room and probably wait a week while nothing happened. It would cost a lot, and besides, there's no one to take care of the children."

"Damn the cost," Kent said, "and why didn't you slip the kids up to us?"

"It's all arranged, Daddy," Ruth said. Kent wasn't encountering her stubborn streak for the first time. "The doctor and the nurse are ready on call, but I thought it would be a good idea—"

"All right." Kent found the name and number and made the call. The nurse had gone to the movies and probably wouldn't be back for an hour or more.

"Oh," Ruth said. "Well, you go on reading, if you can bear to wait till Brainerd comes. You know where the rest of the whisky is."

It was thoughtful of her to remind him. Kent made himself a highball and sat down to resume his reading. Brainerd's vocabulary was a cipher you had to decode, but he was making the point that when people are thrown out of a slum they have nowhere to go but a worse one. Even so, they weren't just kicked out and made to move. They may have been living in a ghetto, but when you scattered them you did more than disrupt so many families or individuals. You broke up their institutions too. They had their schools, their churches, they knew the cops who patrolled their own streets and could tip them off when their kids were heading for trouble. You couldn't pick up all this mass of linkages, in which everyone figured from the storekeeper to the undertaker, and set it down intact in a new place. What happened was a net increase in disorg—

"Daddy?"

"Yes?" Kent said.

"I'm sorry. I seem to be an awful nuisance tonight, but right by the telephone, beside the nurse, the doctor's number is written down."

"The doctor?"

"If you wouldn't mind, you could call and make sure he's at home, just in case."

"Just in case?"

"There's nothing to worry about, but I'd like to know—"

"I'll give him a buzz," Kent said.

A woman answered his call. Under questioning, she identified herself as the baby-sitter. Her voice hadn't been in the melting pot very long, but at least she didn't sound like a high-school kid. The doctor and his wife had gone out for an evening of bridge, leaving a number where he could be reached if necessary.

"Oh," Ruth said. "He isn't at home."

"Shall I call back and say it's an emergency?"

"Oh, no, there's no need for that."

"You're sure you're all right?"

"Perfectly."

She seemed to mean it. Kent found the paragraph where he had stopped reading and picked up the thread. Among the cohesive agencies in a blight area, small businesses were important. The corner food shop, especially; the proprietor of a little delicatessen unintentionally performed a community service over and above the profit motive. He gave credit, of course, if he had the margin to afford it, but he also supplemented church and school and provided a substitute for club or forum. Not only eggs and milk, cheese and rye bread, salami and pickles changed hands in his store; information and opinion were swapped, whose child is sick, who's out of a job, who's who in ward politics. Land-takings that drove the small shopkeeper from his corner not only deprived him of his established business but broke one more of the links that kept a community functioning against odds.

Brainerd had not only analyzed relocation in general; he had done a lot of legwork, tracking down victims, getting case histories. Kent felt his respect rise in spite of himself. Still, he knew plenty of hard-luck stories; he didn't think he lacked sympathy for hard luck. The point was, you could help a man who was able to help himself. The kind of mass sympathy Brainerd felt for the whole swarm of the helpless and the dependent, the cranks and the down-and-outers who would be totally sunk if government or charity didn't spoon-feed them—

"Daddy?"

"Right here," Kent said.

"I think you'd better have them call the doctor at that number where he can be reached. I think—" Her voice failed. After a moment Kent thought he heard her release her breath. "I think things have started."

Kent lowered his propped-up leg and stood. The situation hadn't been set up right at all. Ruth ought to be safe in a hospital this very minute, with nurses and doctors rallying around to take care of her. Nurse at the movies, doctor playing bridge; it was bad executive planning, damned bad. "I'd better get a cab and take you to the local hospital," he said. "The doctor can meet you there."

Ruth giggled. "What would you do, Daddy, if it came in the taxi?"

"If it's that bad, I'll call the ambulance."

Ruth laughed again. "Everything's all right. Just call the doctor's house."

The trouble with women. You couldn't get them to plan sensibly, and then in a crisis they were either completely helpless or completely stubborn. Kent picked up the phone, and again the voice of the baby-sitter answered. "I'm calling for Mrs. Hitchens again," Kent said. "Has the doctor come home yet?"

"What you think? You think I'm still here if doctor come home?"

"This is an emergency," Kent said. "I want you to call the number he left, or let me have it."

"What I shall say is the emergency?"

"It's Mrs. Hitchens."

"Mrs. Hitchens, she is then an emergency?"

"Listen," Kent said. How should he put it to get his point across? She's in labor? No knowing what the woman would make of that. "She's having a baby."

"Doctor must know she is having a baby without I call him while he plays bridge."

"It's on the way," Kent said. "Can't you get that?"

"She is now in labor?"

"Yes."

"She is having the pains?"

"Yes."

"How often the pains are coming?"

There were days and times when it didn't do to go by instructions or wait for them; a man had to act on immediate judgment. "One a minute," Kent said.

He heard a grunt and a gasp at the other end of the wire. "I call doctor right away." The phone clicked and the connection broke. He guessed he could trust her to dial; he hoped she hadn't mislaid the number. While he was at the phone he called the nurse again and left instructions that she wasn't to lose a minute after getting home. Was there anything he himself could do to help? Hot water, he thought; hot water always seemed to be in demand on these occasions. He went to the kitchen, found a kettle, and set it over a burner. On his way back he called upstairs, "Are you all right?"

"All right, Daddy. Don't worry."

She didn't sound frightened or even unduly excited. Nothing to do but wait for the troops to arrive and take over. He settled himself in his chair and picked up Brainerd's folder again. From time to time he heard Ruth stirring in the bedroom. Now and then she seemed to hang on to her breath, if you could judge by the subdued gasp with which she let it out. He wondered whether he shouldn't insist on calling an ambulance, but she'd only show her stubbornness if he suggested it, and probably she knew what she was doing.

Eventually a car drew up outside with a squeal of brakes. Footsteps came at a run up the walk and the porch steps. "Have you got hot water ready?" the doctor asked as Kent let him in. He looked alarmingly young, practically unfledged, but at least he wasn't wasting time. He was already throwing his coat over the banister and starting up the stairs.

"I've put a kettle on the stove," Kent said with satisfaction.

"Kettle! I'll need lots of it, lots," the doctor said.

"In this house, mister, if you want lots of hot water, you light the old copper boiler and wait."

The doctor had already reached the second floor; the shot was wasted on him. Kent lit the heater in the kitchen. The doorbell rang violently, and, when he answered, a woman who must be the nurse brushed unceremoniously past him and panted toward the stairs. A lot of activity seemed to be going on between bedroom and bathroom. In the midst of the hurly-burly, Brainerd blundered innocently through the door. He stood bewildered in the hall, listening to the commotion, and when Kent explained, his jaw hung open, even more nonplused. "Baby coming?" he said, as if it were his first intimation of the event. Then a course of action occurred to him. He made for the stairs in his turn, but the nurse met him and shooed him back. He came into the living room, sat, immediately got up again, toured the premises in heavy strides, apologized for his absence, and, when he heard a smothered cry from the bedroom, looked as though the court had just sentenced him to hanging. If he had only learned how to drink he could have poured himself a stiff one and relaxed while the Marines held the beachhead. Fortunately Kent didn't have to put up with him for long. The doctor had hardly got to work, it seemed, when a thin, outraged squall made itself heard in the bedroom. Half an hour later he and Brainerd gained the upper floor, and the nurse was asking, "How do we like our new little daughter and granddaughter?"

"Ask me in sixteen years," Kent said. "She isn't a glamour girl yet."

The nurse laughed and then affected indignation. "We're just a perfect little baby," she said, bending over what looked to Kent like the upper end of a red worm, at the same time stringy and bloated, with brief appendages ending in tiny fists and a face of senile dissatisfaction with the world into which it had been ejected.

Kent began to think about getting back to his hotel. If he got a cab quickly, he could just make the last commuters' train. The confusion of the household was sufficient so that he could write a check to Ruth on the sly and leave it on the dining-room table to be discovered next day. He wouldn't wake Abby up with a call at this time of night. The first order of business after he got some sleep would be to ring her from the hotel and claim his credit as an obstetrical engineer. After all, he'd managed the business tolerably well. His timing had been perfect.

Abby was more alarmed and concerned in the morning than he thought his report warranted. "The poor, dear, foolish child," she said. "Are you sure they're both all right?" As far as Kent knew, they were. The doctor hadn't given any grounds for apprehension. Dave Cronkhite called on schedule and said he thought he'd made progress, despite the fact that Kent had given him a tough assignment. In fact, if Kent would let the situation ride until summoned again, Dave thought he would meet an entirely new board, different in membership, different in attitude. Quite a day, yesterday. In sixteen hours or thereabouts he had taken over when Denis quit, got rid of a hostile insurance board, thrown a productive scare into Dave Cronkhite, and practically delivered a baby. He could call it a day's work.

Arthur had got used to the hostility, even contempt, he received from Lamson Crocket. The whole Department, Arthur thought, was in the same boat; everyone in turn felt the lash of Lamson's sarcasm. No doubt the drops of acid he deposited ought not to do more than raise mild skin blisters that smarted for a while but did not damage any central tissue, yet perhaps they all submitted to Lamson too easily, Arthur included.

The Committee on Departmental Offerings was the arena where he couldn't escape Lamson's antagonism. As the fall passed into winter and the snow set in early, Arthur was more and more nettled and obscurely alarmed by what happened in its weekly sessions. The Department had set up the Committee at Lamson's own suggestion. They would perform a service and set an example, Lamson maintained, by subjecting their whole program to a candid self-scrutiny, trying to modernize it and strengthen it in both content and teaching method. If Lamson's motives were suspiciously high-minded, they were hard to oppose. Arthur didn't see how the Committee could do worse than waste time, and, without enthusiasm, he accepted membership. The trouble was that, when the meetings got under way, Lamson used them to campaign for his Project at the expense of everything else in sight. It began to seem that his chief target in the existing program was Arthur's own course, Bi Sci 3. Lamson didn't attack openly; he sniped. He made increasingly frequent use of the phrase 'vested interest.' Of course he didn't mean to suggest that anything of the sort would be consciously tolerated; he wasn't imputing motives to anyone; but there ought not to be any hesitation about taking a hard look at everything the Department was doing. If Arthur lifted his eyes at the end of one of these tirades, he could usually count on meeting Lamson's relentless little pupils sardonically fixed on him.

Arthur tried to laugh off his feeling that Lamson had it in for him personally and for his course. What had Lamson to gain by trying to undermine Bi Sci 3? Arthur's budget for secretary and assistants wouldn't make a drop in the bucket of Lamson's Project. He was letting Lamson disturb his mind, his work, his whole life out of all proportion or reason. The phrase 'vested interest' was at the root of his discomfort. He felt such a distaste for the words that he couldn't bring himself to acknowledge their existence in connection with his own work or character. The result was that as he sat in his place at the Committee table, Arthur began to feel a curious sense of isolation. Most of the Committee, he thought, were putting up a patient, massive resistance to Lamson by methods for which academicians have an ingrained aptitude, the methods of delay, qualification, subdivision of the question, reference to committees within the Committee for further study. He even felt that a number of his colleagues would have fought his individual battle for him if he were only more active in fighting it for himself. In the midst of one of Lamson's attacks by insinuation he would catch an eye looking at him expectantly. Here's your chance, it would say; stick up for yourself, Arthur. Challenge him, and you'll gain support. Baffled by some obscure disability, Arthur would remain silent. The eye would drop; the moment would pass. Lamson would gloat as if he had won a round in an undefined contest.

A dozen weeks of the term had already gone by. Christmas was impending. He'd survived eight meetings of the Committee, at which he couldn't see that anything had been accomplished but wrangling; couldn't he cut the one at which he would be due in another five minutes, the last before the New Year? No, Arthur told himself, it was an obligation, however irksome; he tried to be formally conscientious about obligations. It was the student body who had the privilege of being irresponsible. Still, he'd noticed posters announcing a public lecture by Islay at the Committee hour. He felt a strong curiosity to see Malcolm perform. He was bored to the point of misery by the prospect of the Committee. He told himself that his head ached; it almost did, and he was certainly so out of sorts that he would say nothing again or be goaded into betraying his distaste and resentment.

He was still in a state of indecision when he left his office and encountered Lamson Crocket in the corridor, walking toward the Committee room. He realized suddenly that he was carrying his overcoat and hat. To his chagrin, Lamson noticed the incriminating evidence. "The Committee isn't hot enough for you?" he asked jovially.

"I just picked these up by habit," Arthur said. "Or perhaps my unconscious picked them up as a protest against committees."

"About most of them, I'd agree," Lamson said. "This one I take seriously."

"Is any particularly serious or novel business coming up this afternoon?" Arthur asked.

"You haven't done your homework. Didn't you get the minutes and agenda?"

"I've been getting them faithfully since September. To tell the truth, I don't see that they show anything much accomplished. They aren't exactly exciting to read."

"Not like Islay's novels."

"No," Arthur said, wondering whether Lamson could see into his skull or whether his intended defection was written on his face.

"I'll refresh you," Lamson said. "We're going to finish considering the report on cooperation with the Physics Department, especially how we might team up with them in the Project."

"How much considering is there left to do? We all know what they think."

Lamson surveyed him for a moment with an enigmatic expression in his ferret eyes. "If you want to skip out, I'll tell the Chairman," he said.

"Give the Chairman my regrets and tell him it's one of

those end-of-the-semester days when I'm done in and half under the weather," Arthur said. "I wouldn't be of any use if I came."

"I'll convey the message," Lamson said. "I hope you'll feel better in the morning."

Arthur slipped late into a back-row seat in the nearly filled lecture hall. He was a long way from the stage and lectern. Malcolm's tall, loosely bound figure and mobile face looked remote and diminished at the far end of the elongated room. His expressive voice lost much of its timbre as it traveled through the intervening space. Arthur felt as though he were outside the perimeter of radiation. He might almost as well have bored himself at the Committee, but he waited to shake Malcolm's hand at the end of the lecture. Malcolm seemed surprised and grateful that he had taken the trouble to come, and Arthur felt in better spirits as he left the hall and embarked on his walk homeward.

Fresh snow covered the small space of turf in front of the Administration Building. Snow caught in the corners of stone window ledges and softened the twilight bulk of slated gables and roofs. Halfway across the winter rectangle, Arthur heard his name called. He stopped and turned. His colleague and fellow Committee member, Pritchard, was bustling to overtake him. A plant ecologist, and a more than competent one; a self-contained man, who spoke little except when excited about his narrow but fanatically pursued interests. Pritchard came up quickly, without slackening his gait until he was directly opposite Arthur, stopping at that point as if he had bumped into an obstacle. "You weren't at the Committee meeting," he said.

"I'll make a confession of weakness," Arthur said. "I'm so fed up I thought for once I'd take a cut."

Pritchard looked at him oddly. Then he began to walk on, talking with a sort of rapid, level determination. Arthur fell into step.

"I'm having nothing to do with it, you understand that," Pritchard said. "I never lift a hand in departmental politics. But you ought to know, Arthur—perhaps you do, but you don't seem to—you ought to know Crocket and his hench-men have their knives out for you."

So; it was coming out into the open. Arthur felt a mixture of depression and relief. "You don't take me altogether by surprise," he said. "I'm aware Lamson doesn't view me with favor, but I rather thought he didn't view any of us with fa-vor."

"I don't know that there's anything personal in it," Pritch-ard said. "Or rather I don't think a man gets mad at his neighbor and then tries to do him out of something. He starts trying to do him out of something and then gets mad at him because that's what he's trying to do. Lamson is trying to do do you out of Bi Sci 3, Arthur. You'd better understand that."

"Why?" Arthur asked. "My budget won't finance his Proj-ect. He'll need government money for that, lots of it—mega-bucks, as he would say."

"I don't know why. I don't know the man's motives. He may just be offering a trade. He'll let up on Bi Sci 3 if you come out in support of his Project. Your support would be worth having. Your judgment counts over in the Adminis-tration Building, for one thing, where the President sits."

"I don't intend to be bought," Arthur said. "I'm not against Lamson's Project as such. That is, I don't care what kind of work he wants to do or how fanatically he does it as long as he'll grant me the same privilege. I don't think his Project ought to swallow the whole Department, to the exclusion of everything—"

"Agreed," Pritchard said. "I haven't interfered with Lamson, and I haven't played his game, or anyone's game. All I want to do is my own work and let him do his. I could do my work anywhere I could find flora to do it on, from here to Lapland. I just happen to be doing it at Rowley. A little more of Lam-son's Project, and I'll be ready to go to Lapland instead."

"You talk about Lamson's henchmen," Arthur said. "How much of a following has he developed?"

"You know the young appointees he's brought in by get-ting himself put on the Appointments Committee. Some senior members will go along if you don't speak up for yourself, Arthur, not because they agree with Lamson or have anything against you, but because he has them cowed with his tongue."

They had reached the corner of a dormitory, where an iron bracket thrust out from stone to support a bulb housed in a coach lamp. Pritchard stopped abruptly. The light came on and fixed them in a cone of illumination. As Pritchard stood looking at him expectantly, Arthur suddenly perceived the extent of the service he had tried to perform. He had overcome reticence and forced himself to give Arthur a warning and tell him to stand up for himself. "Thanks for speaking," Arthur said. "I'm glad to have this out in the open. It's much better that way. I count it a friendly act on your part, and I appreciate it."

"I just thought you ought to know," Pritchard said gruffly and set off at an angle to Arthur's homeward route.

It occurred to Arthur, as he resumed his walk, that he'd neglected to ask Pritchard an important question: What happened at the meeting I skipped this afternoon, or what was said? Lamson must have shown his hand in some way, Arthur felt sure, and he hadn't been there to receive the attack or strike a return blow. He could almost hear the tone of insult in Lamson's voice, and for a moment his body heat rose and burned and he couldn't see clearly. The normal response of anger; he recognized it for what it was and reminded himself that he didn't know what Lamson had said, didn't actually know he had said anything. Again, it might be that his own absence hadn't mattered, after all. Very likely Lamson took advantage of it to bring his attack into the open, and that was all to the good, far better than continued sniping from cover and innuendoes that couldn't even be acknowledged. Now, Arthur told himself, he'd have to decide what to do in retaliation. No, not in retaliation; it wasn't vengeance he wanted, he hoped he had more dignity than that; just in vindication of his own position.

What to do: the thought was clear, simple, and inevitable, yet nothing seemed to follow from it except a sense of confusion and pure astonishment at his own position. Arthur

Scheuer, a quiet, studious temperament, who felt himself liked and respected, who got on pleasantly with people, had an enemy, a bitter and determined one, it seemed. The discovery was startling. Of course, as Pritchard said, Lamson's viciousness might not be personal at bottom. His purpose didn't spring from initial spite; his spite was the product of his purpose. A shrewd analysis, but in the upshot it all amounted to the same thing.

What to do? Suddenly Arthur saw why his mind had been confused, why he had sat silent for so long under Lamson's insinuations. The nub of Lamson's campaign of slander was plain enough: it was the charge of vested interest. That was a difficult accusation to answer. The very charge silenced the man accused. What could he say? Just up and deny it? Ways existed by which a man could be put in the wrong without effective means of appeal. Call him teacher, and if he protests that the epithet doesn't remove him from the sphere of common humanity, he meets a derisive flicker of the eye and a quiet dismissal. Tax him with vested interest, and if he indignantly repudiates the charge he only confirms the indictment.

The irony of the dilemma was so neat that Arthur was almost ready to smile. But he felt that Lamson's attack contained an even more insidious element that he hadn't yet sifted out. Could it be, was it possible—let's see, how long had he been giving Bi Sci 3? A dozen years. It did occupy a favored position in a way, and not all members of the Department thought that evolution and genetics made the wisest topics for a large introductory course taken by a good many students who weren't majoring in science, as well as the hard core who were. Arthur disagreed, but still— Was Lamson right, or partly right? Had the course, had he himself, insensibly developed into something of a vested interest?

Arthur stopped walking and took note of his surroundings. He was at the edge of the traffic artery. He'd have to wait his turn to cross when the light changed. He felt suddenly a little weak. He put the palm of his gloved hand against the post of the traffic light, wanting for some reason to feel the resistance of the ribbed metal. Lamson was undermining him from within as well as without. He had performed an act of mental infiltration; he was destroying his victim by internal subversion. Had he been clever enough, Machiavellian enough to foresee how sensitive Arthur would be to the particular charge he chose for his weapon? Or did he just blunder into tactics that happened to be fatally well adapted to his foe?

The light changed, and Arthur crossed. What to do? He wouldn't trade; he'd give up his course before he'd do that. And he could give it up by his own volition. The thought occurred to him for the first time as a serious possibility, but at once his sense of his own integrity rose in bitter opposition to it. Just yield under Lamson's pressure? Too ignominious, too downright pusillanimous. Pritchard's words came into his mind: I could do my work wherever I could find flora to do it on; . . . a little more of Lamson's Project, and I'll be ready to go to Lapland. The one statement contained a bit of bravado, perhaps, and the other was a joke. All the same— Was he himself really contemplating another possibility, Arthur wondered, the possibility of going somewhere else? He wasn't so unrecognized that he couldn't go elsewhere and do well if he wanted to. The idea of resignation glittered briefly in his mind. It would be the clean way out. But would it? Wouldn't it rather mean a tame acceptance of defeat, even a practical confession that Lamson's indictment was well founded?

If he was going to entertain any serious thoughts of resigning, he ought to tell Rachel. Perhaps he ought to let her know what was going on, in any case. The trouble was that he had to move guardedly with Rachel where his work was concerned. He had erred with her once before by trying to instruct her in his professional subject when it thrust itself into their lives. She had nothing against academic life; on the contrary, Arthur sometimes thought she regarded his professorship with undue awe, but she had built up an emotional block against the very idea of genetics. They had a tacit understanding that this was exclusively his province, and he never spoke of it with her. He couldn't very well explain what Lamson was up to without mentioning Bi Sci 3, and that was exactly the dangerous ground. The thought sprang into his mind that Rachel wouldn't be altogether displeased if he were deprived of the course Lamson wanted to take from him. Oh, she'd be disappointed for his sake; she'd side with him and understand how he felt, but wouldn't she be secretly relieved? Once again, going up the steps to his own door, Arthur felt an odd sensation, as though his legs were losing their strength. He seemed to be facing more complications than he knew what to do with.

When he opened the door, he found the hall lighted, and he could see light upstairs, but the living room was dark. He called her name; the answer came from unexpectedly nearby. She was standing just inside the living room, by the glass-fronted cabinet desk. "You startled me," Arthur said. "I thought you must be upstairs. Why don't you turn on a light?"

"I was thinking," she said. "I didn't even notice it was dark."

Her voice was not quite itself. Arthur pressed the light-button with his finger and turned to face her. Always dark and rich, her coloring seemed to be heightened and deepened, and the flesh had puffed up a little beneath her eyes. "Is something the matter?" Arthur asked.

"You got a letter," she said and impulsively thrust toward him a small gray envelope, already slit open. The handwriting of the address looked young and feminine. It conveyed no sense of recognition.

"I'm awfully sorry," Rachel said. "I just came home from playing with the quartet, and I picked up the mail and started reading this one before I noticed it was yours. I thought it was an invitation to something or other."

"It doesn't matter," Arthur said. "I haven't any skeletons in the cupboard."

She gave a start, as if the expression had touched an exposed nerve. Arthur drew the letter from the envelope and looked at the opening lines. An unknown someone thanking Professor Scheuer for his kind answer and his helpful advice.

"I'm sorry, Arthur," Rachel said. "I started reading before

I thought, and when I saw what it was about, I couldn't stop. I just had to read it all through. It was stupid of me. I don't ordinarily do such things."

"It doesn't matter," Arthur repeated automatically. He was trying to collect the sense of the letter. His eye took in the phrase 'genetic counseling,' and he began to understand. "I remember now," he said. "It must have been a couple of months ago, I mean when this girl first wrote. I found it—I had an extremely hard time answering. It took me a whole evening, but she's done what I suggested, I think she's in good hands. We can forget her, can't we?"

"Do many of your students write to you for that kind of advice?"

"No, this is a unique case," Arthur said. "I couldn't throw her letter away, could I? She was entitled to the best judgment I could give her, wasn't she? Now it's done and we can forget."

"How can I forget when you still teach about it?"

Arthur felt himself go sick with helplessness. Once, before he had learned to steer clear of his professional interests with her, she had said to him, 'I always feel as though you got up there on the platform and lectured about *us*.' It was of no use to explain that he taught a subject, he didn't teach 'us,' that he would have taught and tried to advance the subject regardless of any misadventures they suffered or escaped. Knowledge is impersonal, he'd like to say; it has to be, by its nature. But he couldn't say so; what he could say to any effect, he didn't see.

They heard footsteps crossing the porch to the front door. With an effort Rachel recovered something like her normal voice. "That must be Claudia coming in," she said. She turned and walked toward the back of the room, where she would be out of sight. Claudia hailed Arthur briefly as she passed through the hall on her way upstairs to ready herself for dinner. Rachel turned about, wiping her eyes with her handkerchief, and approached him again. "I'm sorry, Arthur," she said. "I won't be silly again, I promise. It was just that when I read that letter, everything came back."

Arthur bent down and touched her hair with his lips, and she accepted the pacifying gesture. They made a constrained group, though, when they sat down to dinner. Even Claudia had little to say for herself. She was abstracted, and some of her bloom seemed to have been rubbed off. Arthur dredged for safe and neutral topics, but he was preoccupied enough himself to find the effort considerable. He asked Rachel about her afternoon of music. She had enjoyed it, but it didn't lead to prolonged talk. Finally Claudia rallied enough to ask, "Was the Committee meeting any better this afternoon, Uncle Arthur, or was it the same awful bore?"

"I committed a mortal sin," Arthur said. "I played hooky."

"You did?"

"I went to Malcolm's lecture instead."

"I begged an hour off and went too," Claudia said. "I thought he was quite brilliant, didn't you?"

"Perhaps I sat too far back. Perhaps I wasn't in the mood," Arthur said, "but I thought he made a mistake reading from a typescript and trying to make a formal academic performance of it."

Claudia looked a little let down, and Arthur said, "I didn't see you there. Did you go with Jim Prescott?"

To his surprise, Claudia flushed and answered with unaccustomed shortness, "No. I was alone."

"Is Jim out of favor?" Arthur asked and immediately regretted the question. He had too much on his own mind to think what he was saying. Claudia's face tightened and paled; he could hardly remember seeing her so disturbed. "Please, Uncle Arthur," she said, "I'm sorry, but would you mind if we changed the subject?"

After dinner Claudia excused herself and went up to her room. She had brought home some work to finish, she said, as the price of leaving the lab early. For a while her typewriter made itself audible, but work couldn't have occupied her for long. The tapping of the keys fell silent. Arthur seated himself in his usual chair near the piano and tried to immerse his mind in an article reporting experimental studies on the primordia of guinea pigs. The day had been such that he let himself be unduly gratified by the respect with which early investigations of his own were mentioned in the bibliography. He became aware of a tension in Rachel, seated near him; he looked up and encountered her eyes fixed on him with painful expectancy and reproach. He noticed that her hands were trembling quietly in her lap.

"What is it?" he asked, leaning forward in his chair, ready to rise and go to her. "What's wrong?"

"How can you sit reading when she's so upset?"

He needed a moment to bring his mind into connection with hers. "Claudia?"

"Haven't you noticed? Haven't you seen she hasn't been herself for days? Didn't you see tonight at dinner?"

Arthur relaxed somewhat in his chair. Upset, yes; but he doubted whether Claudia was in a state that warranted quite such concern. "I asked her a question that rubbed her the wrong way," he said. "I'm sorry for that. I've had an unpleasant afternoon, or I would have known better."

"It's that Jim Prescott," Rachel said. "I don't know whether they've quarreled, or whether she cares for him and he isn't serious about her, or what."

"If they're serious, a few tiffs and tensions wouldn't be abnormal," Arthur said. "I think Claudia is stable enough to survive anything of that sort. After all, it's her first real affair, if it is an affair."

"What do you know about him, Arthur?"

"Prescott? Nothing, except that he strikes me as very likable, and he ought to be good in his field to hold the grant he does."

"Can't you find out? There must be people you could ask, people in his department."

"Conduct an FBI investigation?" Arthur said. "I can't see myself doing that."

"You could talk to Claudia. You're much better at talking with her than I am."

"I don't see why you say so at all."

"I'd be so upset I'd only upset her more. She's unhappy, Arthur."

Her tone implied that unhappiness might be the common lot of common humanity, but that an unhappy Claudia was unthinkable.

∘∘ 4 ∘∘

For the second evening in a row Claudia climbed the stairs to her room on the pretense of work to finish. The eyes of Rachel and Arthur silently disbelieved her. She wished she could have told them why she wasn't behaving like herself, but, for a whole lot of reasons, that was impossible.

Her room needed putting to rights, or she persuaded herself it did. She smoothed a wrinkle in the blanket cover of her bed, rearranged the pillows, took down a hanger she had hooked over the top of her door to allow a slip and a pair of stockings to dry, and put them away in her bureau. She emptied a deposit of cigarette ash in the waste basket, crumpled a paper tissue and moistened it with tongue and finger, wiped and replaced the ashtray. What to do next? She could look into the state of her spring wardrobe. She went to her cupboard, took out dresses and suits and skirts to see what hems would have to be raised, what could be worn again, what would have to be discarded. Then it struck her as ridiculous to be worrying, ten days before Christmas, about her spring clothes.

Did she have a book on hand interesting enough to distract her? On top of her shelves lay the draft of a monograph Jim had been working on all term. She had offered to type it for him in final form, since his battered portable, nicknamed Jumping Jesus, had a habit of skipping spaces in mid-word. After what Jim had told her that evening a week past, she found it an ordeal to type out his page after page of professional anthropology, but she would keep her word and finish the job all the same. She could do half a dozen pages right now. Arthur and Rachel would hear the keys and think she'd meant what she said about work. No, not right now; she wasn't equal to looking at a sentence of anthropology now.

Poor Arthur, poor Rachel! They were wonderful people. She knew more about them than they gave her credit for. She couldn't remember how early she had begun to feel the pressure in the household of a secret she wasn't supposed to share. She could remember asking at some time, with paralyzing effect on Rachel, why she didn't have brothers and sisters. She wouldn't have thought, then, of questioning Arthur; he moved through her childhood as a gentle but somewhat austere and unapproachable figure. After a certain amount of nagging, her Aunt Abby had let her understand that she would have had two cousins to grow up with if—Abby went into formidable language about the purpose that guided everything and was wise in ways that human beings couldn't always take in. Claudia supposed the answer must have intensified her desire to penetrate the secret. She would have forgotten it if everyone hadn't screened it in mystery. Later, as college drew closer, she got on different terms with Arthur. She talked with him more nearly as an equal and gained some understanding of his work. She thought of becoming a well-known biologist herself. She didn't know quite what prompted her to put two and two together—some clue Arthur probably hadn't any idea he'd given her, since he wouldn't realize the extent of her curiosity about her missing cousins—but she pinned Abby down to confirming what she'd begun to suspect. The knowledge gave her a sharper sense of what she meant to Arthur and Rachel. It scared her a little and made her feel responsible to them. Perhaps knowing that they weren't her actual parents had saved her from a lot of useless adolescent rebellion.

She ought to be making a noise on her typewriter for their benefit. She could answer Helena's letter inviting her to New York for the holidays. That was the solution! With relief she put a sheet of stationery in her machine and began to type. She would love to come to New York for part of her vacation. It would be mean to leave Uncle Arthur and Aunt Rachel alone over Christmas Day itself, but the chance to see

Helena again and really get to know her husband came at just the right time.

A few lines disposed of the invitation. Claudia went on, trying to gossip about her job and the personalities it threw her in with, but Jim Prescott kept thrusting himself between the lines. After a page or two, the effort to keep him out became too great. She finished the letter, sealed and stamped it, and thought of taking it out to the corner box, but she didn't want to face questions downstairs.

What could she do with herself before going to bed? As recently as a week ago she would have had no problem. She would be going out with Jim to a late movie or a session of talk over beer or highballs at someone's apartment. Even if she had been reading alone at home, she would have been perfectly content with her own resources. Then that evening Jim's apartment—she still didn't understand just how it affected her, how it *ought* to affect her, or how to deal with it.

She had known with utter certainty what Jim was going to say after they climbed the stairs to his cramped kitchen-and-bedroom suite. Jim didn't make the signs difficult to read. He was going to tell her that he loved her and ask her to marry him. She was ready to respond. She had enjoyed her life as a girl, but she'd been a girl long enough. She was ready to be a woman. But chiefly, of course, she was ready to respond to Jim. She liked everything about him, his little ways of doing things, his sense of humor, his ease with people. Toward Jim she felt as she hadn't in like degree toward any other man: she wanted to touch him, to take his face between her hands or rub her palm over the close-cropped hair on the back of his head. And Jim—the word was stupidly inadequate, but she made it mean more by giving it emphasis—Jim was a thoroughly *decent* human being. He was generous and tolerant, yet he was a driving worker with a sharp mind.

Jim had asked her to share a meal he proposed to cook with his own hands. "You may not believe it," he said, "but cooking is high on my list of accomplishments. I have a steak in my matchbox refrigerator, and I can toss a salad with the best chef in Paris. Or you can toss the salad, if you really know how to make a French dressing, which I doubt. It's a masculine art."

"If I can't make a better French dressing than you, I'll—"

"You'll what?"

"Never mind what, but you can toss the salad yourself, you're so confident."

"I have a fundamental humility," Jim said, "but I never allow it to interfere with my confidence."

He showed his decisiveness around the museum, as a matter of fact, and his easy handling of the boy who'd got drunk at the party was another indication. Claudia supposed she could love a man who was constitutionally incapable of making up his mind, if she just happened to love him, but vacillation would be terribly exasperating. It was nice to know that Jim could make decisions.

They climbed the three flights in the remodeled sprawling frame house where he had found a hideout he preferred to Rowley's graduate dormitory. She preceded him into the room, put her gloves in the pocket of her coat, tossed her coat, scarf, and hat on the bed, and looked possessively around his bachelor cell. She had vaguely expected a male clutter of clothes, books, and God knows what, and imagined herself tidying up for him with a few deft strokes, but the room was neat, spare, and dustless.

"If you want to wash up, the bathroom is right over there," Jim said. "I've put out a clean towel."

"Thanks. You keep everything in its place and spotless, don't you? Do you clean and sweep for yourself?"

"Except when Mrs. O'Grady comes in once a week and whisks the dust I overlook under the rug."

Claudia laughed and went toward the door he had indicated.

"Don't swing a cat in there," Jim said, "or you'll break the window and knock everything I own on the floor."

The bathroom was tiny enough, but Jim had laid out the clean towel he spoke of, large, rough-ribbed, and masculine. As she dried her hands on it, Claudia inspected the room. Jim couldn't possibly cramp himself into the funny old half-tub squatting on its iron claw feet. He would use the shower, whose white curtains hung from a metal hoop. Behind those curtains he would stand naked, while water poured down over his skull, over his hair that just curled at the ends, over his flat cheeks and little triangular eyes, which would be pressed shut, over his wedge of chin and his small humorous mouth, over his broad shoulders and his chest and all the rest of him. On a glass shelf above the basin, aligned with military precision, stood his electric razor, a bottle of bay rum, a tin of powder, a deodorant stick. The cord for the razor hung from a light fixture.

When Claudia came out, she heard him bustling in the kitchen. He appeared in the doorway with a tray and a highball. "I'll leave you this for company," he said, "while I shake out the lettuce and butter the steak. There isn't room for two of us around my little sink and counter."

Claudia accepted the tumbler and stood holding it in her hand. "I'll wait till you're ready to join me," she said.

"Please make yourself at home." He went back to the kitchen, where his voice continued. "I'm afraid this dump hasn't much to attract the eye. The truth is I've lived a suitcase life ever since I was in my late teens. It means more to me than you can imagine to see a family again, you and your uncle and aunt, in a house that contains such things as music and taste and decent comforts."

"Tell me about your family, Jim. You've told me some, but tell me more."

"Highly respectable," Jim said. "No blots on the scutcheon that I know about. But after my mother's death— It was from her, incidentally, I got whatever I can do in a limited and neglected way with the piano. I had dreams for a while of being a musical genius, but I guess I was just trying to keep some sort of link with the past. I gave it up when I reached college and got seriously interested in anthropology."

"I wondered how you learned to play so well," Claudia said. "But what about the suitcase life?"

While they talked her eyes were taking in everything the room offered to sight, the hideous yellow-oak desk, the varnished bureau, the dead-white table at the foot of the bed, the two straight chairs that matched the table in their leprous pallor. In the corner opposite the bathroom, a screen painted with flamboyant roses concealed a nook of some sort, probably a substitute for a cupboard.

"My father didn't last long after my mother," Jim's voice was saying. "Anyway, when she died, I went off to school and then college. From then on I've hung my hat in a cubicle in a dorm, or a rented room like this, or whatever hole I could find on jobs in the summer."

"Jim, what a time you've had! I didn't know—I'd say how sorry I am if that did any good."

"I was just giving the facts," Jim said. "I didn't mean to sound like an orphan of the storm pleading for a sympathetic tear."

He might pass it off lightly, Claudia thought, but he must have been starved at times for the affections and securities that she had taken for granted. She felt a sudden panicky sense of her own inexperience. Never mind; she wasn't a baby for all that! She would make it up to Jim for the ways he had been defrauded in the past.

Claudia went over to the screen in the corner—it was only a step—moved the nearest panel quietly, and peeped behind. Jim's clothes: a suit, a tweed coat, pairs of trousers, all suspended with impeccable neatness on a bar beneath a shelf. Behind the clothes a blue denim laundry bag dangled limply, like a fat, dismembered torso.

Jim was speaking of an older brother, his only immediate relative, who was a partner in an advertising firm on the West Coast. Claudia raised her eyes to the shelf and saw standing on top of it a large photograph framed in maroon tooled leather. She might have noticed the upper edge of it protruding over the screen if she hadn't been so anxious to peak behind. She moved the screen panel a little more and stood on tiptoe for a better view. Jim's mother? If she had married young and died when Jim was in his teens—but the woman was trying to look younger than she was. Her neck showed her age, and if she wanted to leave so much of herself on view below the neck, she might have found a more becoming dress. Her features were attractive, in a way, but she used too much make-up, and her expression, the big, wide-set eyes, the wide mouth, half open in what was meant for a dazzling smile—Claudia couldn't fit the picture in with Jim at all.

"He helped a lot with school and college expenses," Jim was saying. "It was damned decent of him, because he didn't share my interests. We aren't the same breed of cat."

"You must still meet and see each other, don't you?" Claudia asked.

"Our ways don't often cross," Jim said. "Perhaps it's partly my fault, but actually—"

She became aware that his voice had ceased speaking. She turned about. He was standing in the doorway, a drink in his hand, looking at her. "You've discovered Magda," he said.

His tone startled her more than being caught in a small act of spying. He seemed all at once utterly crestfallen and uncertain. "I didn't mean to snoop, Jim," she said. "You told me to make myself at home. I hope you don't mind. Who is she? Someone else in your family?"

He took a hesitant step into the room, lifted his glass, looked at it as though surprised to find it in his hand, then lowered it again. "I was going to tell you about her later," he said, "after we'd had a drink or two and tasted my delectable viands."

His attempt at lightness rang false. He hadn't simply meant to propose to her, after all; he had a more elaborate program, with complications, and she'd thrown it off balance. Claudia's feelings clouded and sank with undefined dread. "You don't have to tell me anything you don't want to, Jim."

"I just thought it might be better—I thought we could talk after we'd done justice to my steak and salad."

Claudia felt a twinge of impatience. "Are you so ravenous, Jim?" she asked.

"Not that ravenous, no," he said. "But you've got me in a position where I don't know what to do, what to put first."

"Let's eat your steak, then. That's what you want."

He still stood looking at her in hesitation. Then his air of decision abruptly came back. "No," he said. "I've started something I've got to finish. You shouldn't begin a story you don't mean to go through with." He took a swallow of his drink, went over to the shelf, seized the photograph, and placed it firmly in view on the desk. He reversed one of the straight chairs and straddled it, peering at her over its back with his chin on his hands. "Here goes," he said. "Try to understand, will you, Claudia? Because it isn't going to be easy—"

"Wait, Jim, please!" Claudia said. "Of course, if there's anything you want to tell me, and I can help by listening—but I don't want to *ask* for confidences. I—"

"It's very important to me that you should know about Magda," Jim said, his eyes studying her intently across the back of the chair.

"Then tell me, Jim."

So he told her. He started out simply enough. Magda was a department member at the university where he'd taken his A. B. and begun his graduate work. She was brilliant, completely at loose ends in her personal life, neurotic—that was the adjective that summed her up, he guessed. Claudia saw what was coming, but she saw it through such a glaze of incredulity that to her, as the revelation went on, it seemed at first wildly unreal. Jim blamed himself for being a young fool, for being drawn in. He didn't say more against Magda than he could help, but he did make it clear she had reached out for him and snared him, fastened him to her by everything a woman could use to get what she wanted. Jim said—he flushed and looked not only sheepish but despite himself a little smug —he said he supposed he'd been flattered at the start. He didn't find out for some time that he was merely the latest in a string of young men Magda had run through. The only credit he gave himself was that he'd seen fairly quickly how impossible the relation was and broken it off. That was hard; he'd felt like a beast doing it, but it was fundamentally how he came to get his traveling grant. He'd done that by his own efforts, without using her as a reference or even telling her his intentions. He meant the grant to indicate that the break was final, and Magda

164

understood all too well. She wrote him a letter that was un-printable. It was more than that, it was un*speak*able. He hoped it gave her some satisfaction, Jim said, because all in all, he had it coming to him.

Claudia felt him looking at her, chin on hands, across the back of the chair, his revelation finished. She was called on to make some response, and there was none she could make. It was real, after all; it had happened. It wasn't a story he'd invent against himself. He'd actually been getting in and out of bed with that—that neck, the woman who could wear that dress, a woman old enough, almost—well, Jim's mother couldn't possibly have looked like the photograph, but— It wouldn't have mattered if he'd kept a dozen mistresses, only he might have robbed the cradle instead of the grave. Oh, of course, the woman wasn't at death's door, far from it. She could still be considered attractive, Claudia supposed; some people would think so, Jim must have. But that was the very point it was hard to take in. Just the thought of them together, Jim and Magda, made her feel creepy-crawly, and she simply couldn't fit the facts in with *Jim*. She'd thought she knew so well, so certainly, what he was like; now she was anything but sure.

When she could find nothing to say, Jim spoke again. "Nobody knows the worst about himself, but I've told you the worst about me that I'm conscious of."

"Oh, Jim, what do you want me to say?" she asked. "I don't want to blame or judge. I—" She stopped; she really didn't know what to say, didn't want to be called on to say anything at all.

"I blame myself, but it's finished, done, kaput," Jim said. "You understand that, don't you?"

"You've kept her picture." The words came out automatically, and she at once felt she had been petulant and foolish. Somehow she had to gain time, though; everything in her had to be readjusted, and it couldn't happen just on the instant.

"Up to now I have," Jim said. "I don't quite know why. It's usually tucked away in the bottom of my baggage. Two or three times I've taken it out and looked at it, I suppose partly as a way of looking at myself. I was going to get rid of it to-night, but I thought, maybe, after we'd talked, you might want to see what she was like, just once. I'll tear it up now." He got to his feet, swung the chair about to face the desk, and reached toward the photograph.

"No," Claudia said. "Don't, not on my account. She—she's been an important part of your life. You'd be sorry."

He suffered one of his moments of uncertainty. "I could chuck it in the wastebasket now," he said, "and it would leave no scar as far as I'm concerned, but symbolically it seems like throwing *her* on the rubbish heap, and no human being deserves that—not even me." His face made a wry smile of appeal. "She shouldn't have occurred, but she did, and I guess I can't look back on the whole thing as *total* loss. With all her destructiveness, she was a rewarding person to know in some ways."

"Rewarding?" Claudia had to struggle to keep from laughing at that. If she had let it loose, it would have been a laugh of bitterness.

"Don't hold me responsible for the complexities and ambivalences of human relations and everything else in a complex world," Jim said. "It's quite possible for a person to be a menace, destructive as hell, and rewarding at the same time. I'm trying to be honest, Claudia. I thought honesty would count with you. It hasn't been apple pie, it's been humble pie, but I'm telling you the truth."

She saw that she had disappointed him, that he had expected a response from her that she wasn't capable of giving, certainly not yet. What had he expected? I'm glad you told me, Jim. I know you've told the truth. Now it's all out and finished, and it doesn't matter in the least, and we can just forget it. Something like that? He *had* told the truth; the whole truth, the *meaning* of his part in it? "I do value honesty, Jim," she said. "I always think people should be honest with each other." It was as far as she could go.

"Then be honest with me," Jim said. "You're holding back, somehow. What is it? Because— Oh God, Claudia, this is what

I meant to put first, but it must stick out all over me anyway. I love you. I didn't love Magda. That was just an affair, a foolish and embarrassing one that's all over and battened down under hatches in the past. I know the difference now. I want to marry you. I was going to ask—"

"Jim," she said and felt a depth of misery rise around her and engulf her. He had spoken the words that all along she had known he meant to speak, and at just the moment when he had destroyed her capacity to give them the welcome, full and frank, she had meant to give. "Jim, not now. The only honest thing I can say is that right now I can't—can't say anything. Oh, Jim, I think I'd better go home!" She got up and reached for her coat where it lay across the foot of his bed.

"No, Claudia, don't go." He made the words an appeal she couldn't resist, and of course it was cowardly just to run out on the situation. "It's too late for you to get dinner at home," Jim went on lamely. "Unless you'd rather I took you out somewhere? I haven't started the steak yet."

She could have laughed at the mention of the steak again. "If you really want me to stay," she said.

Jim busied himself with the steak, and, while it was broiling, handed her through the doorway the makings of the salad. She set up operations on a card table in the living room. She had never struggled through a meal in such wretched constraint. Their knees almost touched under the table, and the walls of the tiny room seemed to cramp them together above as well as beneath the unsteady surface. Magda, though Jim had turned her photograph face-down under the papers on his desk, crawled like ectoplasm into every corner. Claudia forced herself to sit through coffee before announcing that she really must be getting home.

"Before you go—" Jim began, and hesitated. She met his look across the uncleared card table.

"Yes, Jim?" She remembered that she loved him, or had loved him. Did she still? She couldn't say no, but the feeling, if it still had a place in her, waited in complete abeyance.

"What hurdles do I jump?"

"Oh, Jim, I'm not going to set hurdles for you to jump."

"I may not be Prince Charming in person, but I think I'm a half-decent sort. I know how to try hard, and I'd do my best."

"I'm not a princess."

"Then what's holding us up?"

"Oh, Jim, I need a chance to straighten things out in my head. I need time."

"That's reasonable," he said reluctantly. "Take all the time you need, honey, only remember no one has forever."

He was trying to be considerate to her, but he was impatient; he wanted her to square things with herself faster than she could.

"I see something is wrong deeper under the surface than— I see this has been harder for you to take than I thought it would be, Claudia. I'm sorry for that."

He wanted to know how she felt, and she wasn't clear enough about it herself to tell him. Her hands came together in her lap under the table, and her fingers tangled with one another in a hot clasp.

"I've been a fool," Jim said. "I've made a—an untidy misstep. I don't want to excuse it, but—you're enough of an anthropologist by now to know that everyone has to be initiated, and the ceremonies aren't always tidy. The question is, are they—am I forgivable? Aren't I? Ain't I? Am I not?"

Claudia laughed, but it was a superficial reflex. Of itself her voice blurted out, "Why couldn't you have told me you slept with—with girls, any number of girls, or had a dozen illegitimate children?" She flushed painfully; he'd think she was a fool for fair. To her surprise, his face turned positively grave. He sat looking at her with an expression of utmost thoughtfulness. "I see," he said at last. "I see how it looks from the world you live in. Yours has been a different world from mine, Claudia, though it seems to me we could effect a successful merger. But from your perspective it looks awfully —murky, would that say it? This affair with a woman who should have been married and bringing up children for fifteen years by the time I met her. *I* look murky, don't I? What I've done is to step into your world and foul it up. I'm truly sorry for that, Claudia. I'll do penance for that. I'll tell you what," Jim said, his voice intensifying, his face taking on a look that alarmed her by its almost fanatical resolution, "I'll pass any fitness test I can think of. I'll make amends. You'll see. I give myself credit for some strength of purpose when I get going. You've asked for time, and I'll give you time. In the meanwhile—"

"In the meanwhile?"

"You won't cut me on the street?"

"Of course not, Jim." Claudia tried to laugh. "We'll go on being friends, won't we?"

He looked disheartened at that, but he accepted her implication. Claudia got up, and he helped her on with her coat. As she went toward the door, his hands came down on her shoulders, turning her about. She faced him, and he drew her closer. "Once," he said, "before we start being friends. Because I want you to remember I love you, and I'm deadly serious." She felt his hands at the small of her back, felt the rigidity of his collarbone against hers as he pressed his lips in her hair behind her ear. Her suspended feelings revived in sudden force. For an instant she wanted to throw off her heavy lambskin-lined coat and let him begin over again, nearer to flesh and bone. She pushed against him lightly with her hands, and he let her go.

In the days that followed, she had set to work at once trying to understand, to put herself to rights and decide how she felt about Jim and what his affair with Magda meant about his character. And here she was, alone in her room again this minute, still at the task. It seemed so—so *unnecessary* for Jim to get involved with that—that middle-aged neurotic. It seemed incestuous. Was it the kind of life he had led, a suitcase life as he called it? Was he looking for his mother? Did he have an Oedipus complex? Ugh! She found it hard to believe that of Jim; and in any case, Claudia told herself, he'd hardly choose *me* as a mother substitute! No, the whole thing must have been *physical;* yet that wouldn't do, either. Jim had made that clear. Magda was rewarding—that was one word she hadn't succeeded in forgiving, for all his boasted honesty.

What was it, then? Perhaps an older woman could have a fascination for a younger man. The thought was new to Claudia, and discouraging. The fascination of experience, something that she herself lacked! It meant that Magda couldn't be kept framed in a picture, offstage, relegated to the past. It made her a rival. How could anyone starting off fresh, with everything to learn, hope to deal with her on equal terms? Jim might say he was done with her, but he wouldn't forget; he couldn't.

Jim had given her up, though. Claudia supposed he could have got involved blindly. She supposed Magda might have seemed a flattering opportunity, as he said, to a younger man, at first. But she hung on; that was obvious from the letter he'd told about her writing to him when he made the break. Once involved, of course, he found that he was trapped. He must have been humiliated, must have gone through a kind of slavery it was really repulsive to think about. He must have *suffered*. Why couldn't she have understood that, Claudia asked herself, and made the response he expected? Instead, she had failed him, and she wondered whether she hadn't failed herself. He'd asked her, in effect, for maturity, and she'd taken the whole thing as if she were a child.

What made her inadequate? She'd never considered herself hopelessly unsophisticated, certainly not a prude. She began to think of her years at college. Perhaps she hadn't used them as she might have. She remembered her Uncle Kent saying once that in his day a man was expected to learn how to drink at college. It seemed as though another requirement had since been added to the curriculum: boys and girls were supposed to learn how to sleep together, if they hadn't already. She was putting it a little absurdly, of course, but there was enough pressure in that direction so that it was hardly more than conformity to succumb. She began to remember cases she had known about at first hand, pregnancies that led to marriage or didn't, two or three suicides, the girl who had innocently enough gone to a boy's room on ordinary sign-in privileges and been assaulted as a reward. Claudia had been in the dormitory when the girl got back, and it was pitiable and horrid.

Somehow she had kept herself out of the emotional and physical affairs that went on around her. Why? She didn't think it was self-righteousness. Dates never came hard, and other girls made her a confidante, professing envy of her ability to keep aloof. She really didn't think they meant to imply she was smug or morally upstage when they called her poised and mature, when they asked how she kept from getting emotionally involved, not even when a group of dormitory friends paid her the backhanded tribute of voting her the old-fashioned girl most likely to succeed.

She could hardly think of a girl, except for the minority of Catholics, who viewed the question as a matter of moral or religious principle. She didn't herself. Her best friend, Helena, had for at least a college year slept with the man she later married, and while she felt that Helena had been lucky, she certainly didn't feel superior to her. She couldn't see that Helena's marriage was anything but right and stable. It was just that she had never let herself get in a position where she had to make Helena's choice, and to tell the truth, she hoped she never would. But why was that?

The best she could tell herself was that she had some feeling of taste or fastidiousness that held her back, yet she didn't quite like her image when it presented itself in that way. Was there something secretly timid or cold or sanctimonious about her that she had never recognized? Had she caught some kind of straight-laced attitude toward things from Arthur and Rachel? She certainly didn't want to blame them; but could it be a drawback to have had a protected childhood, to have gone along smoothly and without a lot of adolescent conflict? It occurred to her that she'd always enjoyed being herself, Claudia Scheuer. Jim, she realized, had broken in on her, not simply with a disappointment and a problem, but with a challenge to discontent and self-questioning. Would it have been better if she had acquired some experience, fallen violently in love with an older man at fifteen, experimented with emotional or physical affairs at college? Meaning by 'better,' of course, would she now be better able to understand Jim?

But if Jim loved her, he would have to love her for what

she was. That was the only kind of mature love people could give each other, wasn't it? Of course it meant a lot of growing and changing and learning on both sides. Jim's words came back to her: I may not be Prince Charming in person, but I think I'm a half-decent sort. She didn't want a Prince Charming, so she believed; but, without knowing it, could she have nourished an image of herself as the princess, *virgo intacta*, waiting for the equally unblemished prince to wake her and initiate her at once into a life without any horrid complications? The thought was ludicrously out of keeping with her sense of herself; could it contain a minim of truth? Perhaps her expectations had been just too simply romantic. If so, she could forgive herself that. All she had to do was to grow up and understand that things were going to be harder and more *real* than she'd foreseen. That wouldn't be too difficult. If that was the challenge, she could prove herself equal to it, she knew she could.

She seemed to have reached a moment of illumination. She seemed to understand herself better, and Jim better, and without having to renounce what she felt she essentially was. But the moment lasted only a moment. Its fugitive illumination slipped back into a cloud of distaste. If only Jim had confessed any sort of scrape or even disgrace except Magda! She couldn't all at once get over Magda; she'd simply have to take more time and do more thinking. "Take all the time you need, honey, as long as you remember that no one has forever." The words rang a little fatefully in her ears, but she couldn't pretend to have settled the issue as yet.

She became conscious that the doorbell was ringing downstairs. Who could be calling at this time of night? She heard voices and steps and her name being called. "Yes, Uncle Arthur?"

"Here's a gentleman with a present for you. It's Malcom Islay."

She got up and surveyed herself in the mirror. She powdered her face and considered the dress she had put on for dinner. It would do, but she added a garnet pin at the shoulder. She went down, wondering why Malcom Islay should be bringing her a present.

Half a dozen books teetered in an uneven pile on the living-room table. "I promised you these when I first came to dinner," Islay said. "One or two items are still missing, but it's so near Christmas I thought I'd bring what I could scrape up. Consider the whole household included."

She opened the books one by one, each inscribed and autographed. She tried to put adequate thanks into her voice. They all sat down at Arthur's urging; then he vanished into the pantry to provide hospitality. Claudia mentioned Islay's lecture, and he professed to be flattered by her coming to it. She recalled a point or two he had made, and he expatiated on them a little. When Arthur supplied him with a drink, Claudia sat back and let them do the talking. She didn't feel up to carrying her part; Rachel also was silent. Islay asked about the progress of Arthur's book, and Arthur said that for various reasons he'd encountered too much psychological interference during the term to make any real headway with it. Presently Rachel asked Islay about his holiday plans. Would he be going back to join his family?

"Beth has ordered me to," Islay said, his face working itself into a grin.

"Will you have your boys with you?"

"I'll have to buy them presents, if I can think of anything they won't bash each other's heads in with."

Claudia heard herself announcing that she meant to visit her college friend Helena in New York for a few days during vacation. She saw the surprise in Arthur's face and Rachel's. "I'll come back on Christmas Eve at the latest," she said.

Did she have transportation? Islay would be delighted to drop her off in the city on his way to Maryland. "My one bourgeois indulgence is my Mercedes," he said. "I'm a good driver. I respect a well-built car as I do a well-written book."

Claudia said she would love to be a passenger: it would make the trip ever so much more interesting. Poor Arthur, poor Rachel! They looked so taken aback. She'd make it right with them as soon as Islay left. She began to look forward to the New York visit, to the ride in the Mercedes. Any change, any new experience, would help her to settle her mind.

5

As she fitted herself into the seat of the Mercedes, Claudia suffered a moment of trepidation. What on earth would she talk about with Islay during the hours of driving that lay ahead? She couldn't help taking in his frank look of admiration as he opened the door and stood aside for her to climb in, and when he settled himself at the wheel she became conscious of their proximity in the low-slung car. The seats were like adjacent hammocks. Did he have an X-ray eye? Would that long-fingered, mottled right hand reach out and pat her benevolently on the knee? She arranged her lambskin coat more tightly over her legs and tucked it in beneath her. Then she decided she was being silly; she didn't have anything of that sort to worry about. He might admire, but his way of looking at her was *mental*, as though she were an object of study rather than possible advances.

The problem of conversation didn't come up immediately. Islay was vindicating his claims of skill as a driver. They passed the Rowley campus almost before she knew they were underway, and as they turned down the river drive he judged the lights and overtook cars with discreet efficiency. They surmounted the bridge by the hospital and maneuvered briskly along the highway through the industrial section. Claudia pointed out the immense sign, supported by metal webbing, above her Uncle Kent's factory, FULLINGTON CHEMICAL AND PHARMACEUTICAL CORPORATION, and underneath it the superfluous and only less spectacular legend, PHARMACEUTICALS. Islay grinned and said he was glad she had called his attention to the display. It reminded him that he'd meant to accept Kent's invitation to a tour of the place. Then he was silent while they gained the fringes of open country and began to roll southward.

"It's awfully kind of you to take me along like this, Mr. Islay," Claudia said.

174

"The privilege is all mine," Islay said. "Call me Malcolm, won't you? After all, we're going to be on fairly intimate terms for a while in this buggy. It's about as intimate as bundling, isn't it, to mention an old New England custom?"

Claudia laughed. At the same time she wondered whether she would have to revise her conclusions about him. "I don't think this would be a very good place to put it in practice," she said.

Islay gave her an amused look. "It just crossed my mind as a Puritan oddity," he said. "When I'm in a region, I like to get the feel of it. New England is—was—a fearful and wonderful invention of the devil. It isn't all over yet, is it? Your Uncle Arthur is an example."

"But he isn't," Claudia protested. "We came from Germany. We weren't Puritans."

"New England reserve, the New England shell," Islay said, squeezing a throaty burst from the Mercedes to pass a big trailer truck. "That's what I mean."

"Do you think Uncle Arthur has a shell? It never occurred to me. I suppose we're all—well, a little reticent sometimes, but I didn't think we were abnormal."

"Understand me," Islay said. "I'm very much taken with your Uncle Arthur. He's made the year for me—the term—at Rowley."

"I'm glad," Claudia said. "I know he thinks a lot of you."

"But as for having a shell—do you know what he said to me recently? I've had the idea from the first that Arthur is a man with a secret. I thought he was almost going to break down and come out with it. I was saying I was surprised to find a scientist who saw anything in my books, and he said, 'There's been enough irony in my life so that I can appreciate an ironist.' Now what did he mean by that? What was the irony in his life?"

Claudia began to feel uncomfortable. Islay—Malcolm—was prying. She could almost suspect him of subject-hunting for his work. She resented something chilly, something that lacked feeling, in his tone of amused curiosity. She looked out the window at the knolls of snow, the clumps of leafless trees, the roadside stands, boarded up for winter, that fled backward as they passed. "I really have no idea," she said.

"Arthur and Rachel are lucky to have you for a niece," Malcolm said. "You mean a lot to them, I can see that."

"I'm very lucky to have them."

"Did they bring you up from the start?"

Claudia wished he would stop prying into the family history. She tried to think of a way of diverting him; meanwhile, she could hardly refuse to answer. "I don't remember my real father and mother at all. They were killed in an accident when I was less than a year old."

"So that, to all intents and purposes, you've been Arthur's and Rachel's child," Malcolm said. "They didn't have children of their own, did they?"

Claudia felt herself growing really angry and offended. She could see his mind at work on a theory; his face was chewing at it with its odd lateral and up-and-down movements. He might at least not try to worm information from her. If a man had no reticence himself, he might at least respect the reticences that others wanted to preserve.

"I would have had two older cousins, if they'd lived to grow up," Claudia said. "I don't know much about it, because Arthur and Rachel aren't the sort to talk about such things, and of course I don't question them." That should give him a hint that he'd pushed his inquisition far enough!

Islay looked taken back, but evidently it wasn't on account of her hint. "You've upset my ideas completely," he said. "I had it all worked out that childlessness—I know that means a lot to some people. What happened to them—your cousins, I mean?"

"It's really a subject I don't care—don't want to talk about," Claudia said.

He trained on her a look of astonished curiosity. She felt embarrassment, anger, and pure confusion warm her skin. She must have spoken primly or sounded rude. And she'd said just the wrong thing, too. By making a mystery of it, she might well have given him a clue to the truth. She had to remember that she was his guest, or passenger, and he was a man

176

of actually international distinction. "You may be right, Malcolm," she said, forcing herself to laugh. "Perhaps we do have shells. Perhaps I have one myself."

His face chewed on that for a while, then he said, with a sort of humorous resignation, "Well, I see I've committed a trespass. What do you do to trespassers in New England, burn them at the stake or merely drown them in the ducking stool?"

He spoke so disarmingly that she felt her discomfort cool. Perhaps she had got over the hurdle harmlessly, after all. "I don't know much about it," she said. "I'm not so New Englandish as all that, but I think we go to law and sue each other."

He laughed outright; in fact he laughed with almost superfluous heartiness. Then his face settled into a fixed concentration, so intense that she felt she had vanished from his consciousness. He still seemed alert to the road, but he appeared to be driving by the second-nature reflexes of trained experience rather than by immediate attention to what he was doing.

Claudia welcomed the relief. She took occasion to watch the winter landscape through which they were passing. At the moment it was a stretch of back country, a series of hills, not high enough to be called mountains, but abrupt and sharp, compelling the road to twist and climb on grades pocked by frost and glazed by packed snow, except for two black ruts in the middle. Slopes of pasture stretched white under gray sky. Patches of oak still kept their brown-paper leaves. Pinewoods rose dark from a milky base, each trunk like a separate hair, casting no shadow under the uniform cloud ceiling. Here and there a small wooden schoolhouse, paintless and weathered, shut tight for vacation, squatted disconsolately in the gray cold, or a square-towered church stood sullenly on a green or a knoll, its approaches not yet shoveled out for Sunday service. At the top of a rise they came into a snow flurry, though it wasn't properly a flurry, Claudia told herself, just a lazy, windless fall of polka-dot flakes with a lot of space between them. As they crossed the divide and reached the hollow beyond, a skating scene emerged into view, sped toward the car, enlarging as it approached, and hovered briefly opposite the window. It made a composition, with figures as numerous as in a Breughel: a pasture oval of ice backed by three fine elms and crowded with children of assorted ages, from tots bundled up so closely they could hardly flap their arms, to striplings in sweaters and windbreakers lunging at a puck with their hockey sticks. The front center of the small stage was occupied by a tableau of comic pathos, one very small boy who must have tumbled hard or succumbed to the misery of the cold. He was simply sitting on the ice, his legs straight out, his mouth an open circle of woe, his cheeks fuchsia red, the freezing trickle from his eyes and nose almost visible.

Claudia wished suddenly that Jim Prescott were with her in the car to share the sight. If they went by so fast that he couldn't take it in, she could describe it, and he would understand and say something amusing and sympathetic. At least he would if he were the Jim she thought she had known before the intrusion of Magda. Was that the essential Jim?

She felt a sudden difference in the motion of the car. The brakes took hold, the wheels began to sideslip. Then she felt the correction of the skid, and the Mercedes decelerated smoothly behind the tailgate of a trailer truck that was approaching a curve. She must have tightened in her seat or let a telltale breath escape her, because Malcolm turned reassuringly and said, "I had it under control. It isn't too good to get struck with an idea in the middle of driving, is it, though?"

Claudia said he drove like an expert; she guessed she'd been daydreaming and came to with a start. The slight incident seemed to break his concentration and turn him loquacious again. "You know," he said, "speaking of Arthur, your uncle. It's the writer in me that makes me try to figure him out. That's what I am, a writer. If I tried to be anything else, except maybe a chauffeur, I'd wind up on relief in six months."

"I can understand trying to understand people," Claudia said, "but—" She could hardly go on and say that invading their privacy or using them as guinea pigs might be another matter.

He disregarded her unfinished thought. "I guess you've

heard me say a writer is a parasite. He finds a host, or a succession of hosts, and feeds on them—not that he knows anything about what they are in themselves, really. He wonders why people are what they seem to be, and he doesn't know, so he invents a fable explaining them to himself. That's the art of fiction."

"Are you planning to put us all in a novel, Malcolm," Claudia asked, "as exhibits of New England repression, or something?"

"I don't write *romans à clef*," Malcolm said. "Don't worry. By the time a novelist gets through with a real character, he isn't real any more, for that matter—I mean real in the ordinary sense," he added hastily. "But a parasite has as much initial right to live as his host has, whether the parasite is a hookworm or a mistletoe. Arthur would support me there."

"I can't really believe you think of yourself as a hookworm," Claudia said, "or a mistletoe strangling an oak tree."

She didn't know how he might have answered if they hadn't at that moment reached the edge of a town. He slowed and kept his eyes on traffic. They tunneled under strings of municipal Christmas lights and cardboard Kris Kringles driving teams of cartoon reindeer. As the store-fronted street raveled out into country again, he asked, "Have you been reading my books?"

"Of course I have," Claudia said, "and I can't tell you how much I've been enjoying them."

"You really like my stuff?"

"I really do."

"But the irony," he said. "That's the only word the critics can seem to find for anything I turn out. I've been plastered with it so often it sometimes turns into a nonsense word on me. Ironic, irony, ironist. Bibbledy, babbledy, bubbledy. It's like a declension or a conjugation in a language you don't know."

Claudia laughed, but she saw that he was engaged with some problem that was serious to him. "I can see it would be tiresome," she said, "but still, it's there, isn't it, the—well, I'll try not to use the word again. The quality they speak of?"

"You don't mind it?"

"I enjoy it."

He seemed gratified, but he wasn't through worrying his problem. "Have you read that critical article about me that really takes me over the coals?" he asked.

"I'm afraid I haven't," Claudia said.

"I thought you might have looked it up. It's being talked about, I gather."

"I don't believe I'd like it, if it takes you over the coals," Claudia said. If he seemed insensitive to reticence, he was also an egotist, a self-confessed one. In his lecture he'd insisted that a writer had to be an egotist. He was a spider who spun his product out of himself. He had to feel important to himself, had to believe the filigree net he wove important, or the secretion it came from would dry up at the source. The gland would wither. If he lost his feeling of self-importance, he had to find someone who could restore it and keep him going. Somehow Malcolm made his egotism ingratiating, up to a point, at least. He was so frank and disarming about it. Hookworm, egotist—he seemed cheerfully indifferent to the image of himself that he projected. "What does the article say?" Claudia asked.

"Oh, the indictment is lethal. Irony isn't enough. I'm just a gimmick artist, a maker of contrivances that violate all the noble words—compassion, commitment, human dignity. I have no tragic sense because I only know how to mock. I don't create people, only figments that fit into ironic—goddamn the word!—patterns. I'm fundamentally bloodless and hostile to life. I don't know what a human emotion is."

"Well!" Claudia said. "Is that all?"

"It would be better for me if I got religion—that's another point. If I believed in something, a God of some sort, no matter how crazy the belief might be, I'd acquire—how did the little twerp put it? I'd acquire 'a sense of the tragic seriousness of human destiny.' "

"Anyone who wrote that about you," Claudia said, "must have lacked a sense of humor."

"You don't think there's anything in it?"

Claudia felt herself being pressed to the point of strain. She managed to say, "I think your critic is expecting you to be something you aren't, judging you by other writers who are fundamentally different."

"Go to the head of the class," Malcolm said, and for an instant it seemed as though his hand actually was going to reach out and pat her knee.

They were rolling through towns more frequently now. Another slowdown for traffic was necessary before they came to open road again. The road surface was bare. The stubble fields on either side poked through a thinner snow cover. The clouds were breaking overhead, and sunlight needled down here and there on weathercocks, on the texture of old barns, on patches of bright meadow.

"So you'd really dismiss the indictment and call me innocent, would you?" Malcolm said.

"I think the fun in your books is in the way you deal with —well, the incongruities and ridiculous things in what people do. I don't suppose—" Claudia hesitated, but she felt she was in for it and had to go on. "I don't feel as though you ask the reader to *share* the feelings of your characters, to suffer with them, as much as to *see* how tangled and absurd feelings and motives can be. I think you have a delightful sense of humor about that, and I don't know why anyone should ask for more."

Claudia hoped her effort would pacify him and put the topic to rest, but from the intentness of his face, she feared she would be called on for more. Now that he had brought up the charge himself, she began to think there actually was a slightly non-human element in his books, a sort of imperviousness to the fact that people could be hurt as much by a comic plight as by a tragic one.

They drove through a four-corners. They drove up a rise and down a rise. Malcolm said, "Well, I don't dismiss the indictment. The fact is, I've been running down. I've been coming to a stop, and if I can't keep writing, how do I live? What becomes of Beth and the boys? I may not amount to much as head of a household, but I don't want to see them grub and grind. I've got in a rut, I know there's a missing element in my stuff, it's time for a new Islay, but where do I find him? I don't swallow all that sentimental rot about compassion and commitment and believing in some religion you don't believe in on the theory that if you have a myth about life you must be taking it seriously. But I don't know—this article has got under my skin, I guess because it coincides with an internal crisis. I've written only one little short story since coming to Rowley. If anyone has a prescription, I'm damned near ready to try it. Damned near—why, I've even been reading Dante, this little critic boy recommended him, to see if the theologico-mythico view of things would do anything to my incurable frivolity."

Claudia laughed, but his voice had gathered heat; his urgency was genuine.

"Where do I turn? What do I do?" he asked. "What would *you* say?"

She heard the words in astonishment. The very eminent Malcolm Islay, much her elder, was asking her to solve a crisis in his life. "Why, Malcolm," she said, "I'm hardly the one— I should think Beth—Mrs. Islay—"

"Beth," he said. "Beth is a remarkable woman. She keeps me from falling apart, keeps the whole household together—well, on the mundane side, shall we say. I'm not at home much— can't write in a wallow of domesticity. I take a hotel room or go to New Mexico or wherever. I told her when she insisted on marrying me—"

Claudia must have made some uncontrollable sound. She encountered his look bent briefly toward her in a comic contortion of earnestness.

"She did, you know. I warned her repeatedly that I wasn't cut out for the rôle of paterfamilias, but she just said she'd decided to marry me, and since I must know it was inevitable, I might as well give in and accept her early as late."

Had the man no reserve at all? Actually his total want of inhibition had a liberating effect. She began to feel a little giddy. Malcolm seemed not to notice her state, or not to mind it.

"Well, she got her bargain," he said, "and she's stuck to it, though I should think from her point of view it's a shabby one. I haven't done my part at all—can't, if I'm going to do what I can do—yet I count on having her there all the time when I turn up. I don't know why she does it. I don't know why she wanted me in the first place."

"I don't think that's hard to see," Claudia said. "She must have been very much in love with you."

He looked at her as though she had really startled him, or perhaps, Claudia felt, as though she were a child and didn't know what she was saying. She couldn't tell.

"Love," he said. "That's another of the things my critic friend says I know nothing about. I've read the French moralists on the subject. What we love is the image of ourselves projected on someone else. That's what they say. It's an illusion produced by egotism. I see that, but I don't think it's the whole chapter. I think the root of it is possessiveness. We go after what we think we need and try to swallow it whole, and we call that love. What do *you* think?"

Claudia had reached the point where she saw no object in trying to defer or to keep to amenities. She might as well be bold and say what she thought. "I believe people have to learn to love each other for what they are. I supposed that was a kind of—well, a test of maturity about it."

She seemed to have amazed him to the point of incredulity. "And you think that's possible?" he asked.

"We can try to make it so." She felt her face grow warm, she would cling stubbornly to what she had said if he challenged it. She thought of Jim; she felt as though she had taken a step toward solving her own problem—if only she hadn't committed herself to something beyond human power. She was inexperienced, but she could learn and do as well as the next person.

Malcolm let her words pass unchallenged. He was silent a moment, then he said, "Well, you see, I can hardly expect Beth—you know, it isn't her fault, I wouldn't blame her for it, but she has an insidious faculty for making me feel inferior—morally inferior, if you know what I mean. She does a lot of things—oh, handling the boys, for instance—that I feel I ought to be doing, only she has the gift for it, and I haven't."

"Tell me about the boys," Claudia said. "What are their names?"

"Wallace and Bruce."

"What a wonderful pair of names for two little Islays!"

"It was Beth's idea. She thought we ought to perpetuate my Gaelic origins, though they're too remote to mean anything to me. I'm afraid I'm pretty remote from the boys, too. I sometimes think they look at me like an unexplained stranger when I occasionally turn up. They seem to spend their time fighting with each other. Beth can always make them shake hands and act like brothers, I don't know how."

His picture of the Islay household suddenly affected Claudia as anything but comic; it was purely depressing. Did he think New Englanders were queer, buttoned-up and reticent? He should strip the scales from his eyes and see how his own image looked as he spilled himself out with neither restraint nor any sense of how things looked to ordinary, normal feeling.

For escape, she looked out again at the landscape sliding past. They were well down into Connecticut by now. She began to be impatient for the end of the drive; she wanted to be relieved of Malcolm's rather formidable presence, to reach Helena's comfortably familiar and less challenging company, to see what Helena and her husband were like together, now that they had established themselves as a married pair. She might even find a chance to talk with Helena about her own situation. In general, of course; she wouldn't mention names or be specific. Well, it was too soon to get impatient yet.

Above a bare black stand of trees beyond a meadow they were passing, a flight of crows caught her eye. She couldn't count them, but she thought of the nursery rhyme—how did it end?

> Five crows silver,
> Six crows gold,
> Seven for a secret
> Never to be told.

No secrets for Malcolm! Yet after all, wasn't there something attractive about his complete, uninhibited candor? If he let his egotism and self-revelation pour out like a wide-open faucet, there was a kind of freedom in the performance, an absence of petty timidities, of any kind of stuffiness. It was a different way to live, Claudia told herself, a rather fascinating way. Perhaps it had its advantages. And certainly Malcolm had been flattering to her, asking—imagine it!—for her opinions and advice on his work and his future.

She felt the car begin to slow. They were approaching a minor crossroad; Malcolm appeared to be studying the town names and mileages on the signpost at the corner. To her surprise, he came to a complete stop. "I thought we were just about getting to the turn," he said. He looked at her and asked, "Do you have to reach New York at any particular time?"

What was he going to do or suggest now? Whatever it was, he implied delay. Her impatience mounted. "The friends I'm going to visit have asked some people in for drinks before dinner," she said. "I'll want time to get ready. Why, Malcolm?"

"I've had an impulse. After the way we've talked, there's someone you ought to see. My editor—well, she's a lot more than that. She has a greater flair for spotting a writer, seeing what he's trying to do—she has a gift of divination about it, like one of your up-country dowsers witching for water. She reads all my stuff. I couldn't get along without her."

"But Malcolm—"

"She lives just off to the left here—fifteen miles, the sign says. I was going to skip by incognito for once, but we'd stop for lunch somewhere, and you'd be impressed by her house and impressed by her."

"But Malcolm, I'm a total stranger, and you haven't said we're coming. You couldn't—we couldn't just descend on her that way, unannounced, for lunch. I'd be embarrassed to death."

"Not the slightest need to be," he said. "I'm always dropping in on her without warning. Rosamund—her name is Rosamund Temple—she's the wife of the lawyer who represents my publisher as counsel, and she reads for the firm. I'll deliver you in New York in plenty of time, and I don't care if I drive half the night."

"But we simply can't impose on her that way. I can't walk in as a stranger, just the way I am—"

He examined her with a look, and his face dismissed any objection based on just the way she was, bundled up in her lambskin coat. "You're letting yourself be ridden by conventions," he said.

"How do you know she'll be at home?" Claudia asked.

Malcolm's expression knotted and clouded. "She's always at home," he said. "It's never failed when I've stopped by. Trust my psychic intuition. Don't worry about inconveniencing her, either. Sam, her husband, is filthy rich, the big bourgeois oaf. Her house is something; you'll see. Besides," he added, as if the point were decisive, "I have a typescript I was going to mail her, but I can hand it to her direct."

He set his directional signal for a left turn and swung the car into the crossroad. Claudia felt herself helpless. Her embarrassment was extreme, but what could she do? What was Malcolm's relation with this woman, this Mrs. Temple, Rosamund? Was it strictly author and editor, nothing more? If anything more was involved, Claudia told herself, he surely wouldn't be taking her along as an exhibit. What about her own position? Would she look like a conquest? That was a silly notion, though; she was letting herself make too much of the whole business.

The Temples were filthy rich, were they? Claudia began to think how she was dressed. The tailored suit she was wearing would do as well as anything she could have put on, but the proper gloves and hat to go with it were packed away in her baggage. Of course she didn't know whether Mrs. Temple would turn out to be ultra chic or a Bohemian type or something utterly unpredictable, and Malcolm would only laugh at her if she asked. No doubt she'd at least be offered a chance to smarten up a bit.

They made an elbow turn around a red barn that thrust itself into a crook of the road; then the car dipped down toward black water sliding beneath ragged shelves of ice, rattled through a covered bridge, and climbed the far slope into a village. The perfection of its grouping around its open space of snow-covered green burst on Claudia and was gone before she could take it in. She could only catch glimpses of the leaded panes of fan windows above venerable doors, the subdued rose hue of mellowed brick chimneys, the delicacy against blue and white sky of a church spire as exquisite as any she had ever seen. They turned abruptly off on a dirt road, left the village behind, and drew up at what could well be the most venerable and flawless doorway of all. Malcolm handed her out and seemed bent on hustling her up the walk in a fit of eagerness, so that she had time only for the hastiest impressions of winter lawn and dormant garden stretching out toward the side and rear of the house, of plantings neatly boxed in burlap, of window frames and clapboards that under their impeccable shade of warm pink showed the texture of their age. Then Malcolm was thrusting out a long arm and finger to press the doorbell. His other hand held a brief case, no doubt containing the precious typescript.

For moments no response to the bell occurred. Psychic intuition had failed, Claudia began to think; she was going to be spared. The woman was out, and no one was going to answer. Malcolm seemed unperturbed; his faith was unshaken. Claudia did not hear a step beyond the square panels of the heavy door, but presently it opened, swinging soundlessly and slowly backward. Claudia found herself confronting a woman of full, fair face and just slightly pug nose, a woman whose rather tawny eyes appeared to focus deliberately, almost lazily, and whose hair looked as though it had somewhat thinned and faded, so that its color was a little indeterminate. The woman looked at her for a moment in mild but tolerant unrecognition; then Claudia was startled by Malcolm's voice just behind her left ear. "Rosamund!" he said in a voice she thought had a note of affected gallantry in it.

The unhurried eyes in the doorway shifted to Malcolm. They seemed to light with genuine pleasure, Claudia thought, but they remained completely cool.

"Malcolm! This is a coincidence. I was thinking of you just

this morning, wondering whether you wouldn't be driving home for the holidays."

"That's what I am doing," Malcolm said.

"Come in, both of you. Don't stand in the cold."

She moved slowly aside, holding the door, and Claudia advanced past her into the hall. Malcolm was making it as awkward for her as he could, leaving her still without introduction or credentials for her presence. She turned and watched as Rosamund closed the door and took a measured step or two away from it. Malcolm was standing in wait. He bent down toward her, and she offered him her cheek with a kind of serene indolence that was almost complacent. Malcolm did not have far to stoop. Rosamund held herself very straight and was built on rather generous proportions. Claudia was fascinated by the housecoat she was wearing—Chinese, it must be, heavily embroidered in gold thread. The primness of its straight collar and the vertical line where it met down the front made the best of a figure that was otherwise rather soft in its contours, actually thick through the hips, though Claudia noticed the beautifully delicate turn of hand and wrist. For some reason she had expected a considerably younger woman, of Malcolm's age or less, a kind of smart New York type with a quick-witted executive voice. Instead, Rosamund was definitely older than Malcolm, and she spoke in the same slow way she moved and used her eyes. The tones came out in what was almost a drawl, each syllable like a plumped-up pillow. The fascination of an older woman! For a moment Claudia was back in the thick of her problem.

Malcolm was introducing and explaining her at last. "I hope I'm not intruding, Mrs. Temple," she said. "Malcolm didn't tell me he was going to impose me on you this way. He didn't tell me anything until we were practically here." She turned an accusing look on him.

"Nonsense, child. You must feel perfectly at home. Malcolm is always bringing unexpected visitors, and I must say I can seldom quarrel with his taste. Malcolm, take her coat and hat. You must stay to lunch. We'll have it very informally in my morning room. Hang them up in the cupboard, and Claudia, dear, if you want to freshen up after driving, you'll find everything you need right through the bedroom at the head of the stairs. I'd come with you and lead the way, but I'm limited to a daily quota of stairs. It's very stupid, but I hope you'll excuse me."

She had to admit that Malcolm was right about the house and about the economic scale necessary to support it. Making her way upstairs, Claudia could only approve of everything she saw; she could hardly suppress a twinge or two of envy, in fact. The beautiful old curved banister, the prints on the walls, the books at every possible point, the curtains and coverlets in the bedroom she passed through, the bureaus and mirror and highboy and night-table—museum pieces on all sides, but they didn't suggest ostentation in the least; they suggested comfort and use and taste. And Rosamund! Imagine being called 'child' and addressed as 'Claudia, dear' at first sight and not minding it! There was something fascinating about her, no getting away from it! She was kind and withdrawn, genuine and yet detached at the same time. She couldn't be altogether as simple and straightforward as she seemed. She had an air of mystery about her somewhere. Her almost languid manner was on the verge of being an affectation, and yet it wasn't, quite. If she was allowed to climb the stairs only a certain number of times a day—and what was her age? Claudia wished she could see Rosamund's husband, Sam, the big bourgeois oaf, as Malcolm called him.

Claudia studied herself in the bathroom mirror. She ran a damp washrag over her face, combed and arranged her hair, applied lipstick and wiped it carefully, used a drop of perfume, smoothed her skirt, and adjusted the white fringes of cuff under the sleeves of her tailored jacket. When she came down, neither Malcolm nor Rosamund was visible. They weren't in the hall, they weren't in the living room next to it. She listened and made out voices at a distance, apparently off the far end of the living room. She walked toward them, past a fireplace big enough to roast an ox in, past old desks and highboys that glittered dully with butterfly fittings of brass, past drop-leaf tables and a butler's table, past the squat mass of a spinet piano. As she came within earshot of what they were saying, she hesitated. She grew conscious of the deep pile of the rug beneath her feet. They weren't aware of her approach. Malcolm's voice rose, its tones hoarse at the edges. "Goddamn it, maybe I don't know what I want, but I've got to have something. I'm grinding to a stop. I—"

Rosamund's interrupting voice was quieter, almost placid, but its intonations were so clearly molded that they came out with surprising distinctness. "There are just too many things you aren't thinking of, Malcolm." After its intervention, the voice sank. While she was deciding whether to retreat or advance, Claudia thought she heard the name 'Beth' and the words 'anchor' and 'absolutely at sea.' She had no line of retreat; she'd just have to go ahead and make an entrance, feeling as though the spotlights were trained on her embarrassment. Claudia cleared her throat and said, "May I come in?"

"Of course, dear." The invitation was entirely unperturbed. "We're right here in my morning room."

Claudia stepped forward to a sunporch blinding with the glare reflected through French windows from the snow-sealed garden outside. When her eyes adjusted, she saw that Rosamund had established herself on a chaise longue near the warmed panes. Malcolm slouched in a chair at an angle to her, rather in the attitude of a small boy in a sulk. He didn't get up; he hardly raised his eyes, but Claudia caught a look of gentle appraisal from Rosamund and was grateful for its obvious approval.

"Do pull up a chair for her, Malcolm," Rosamund said, and Malcolm, a little abashed, began unwinding his legs.

"Don't bother, please," Claudia said, drawing forward a wicker porch chair with a blue cushion bottom and seating herself.

"Malcolm has been telling me in his letters how much your —it's your uncle, isn't it?—has meant to him this year."

"If it wasn't for Arthur, I wouldn't have lasted," Malcolm said. "I'm not cut out for academic life."

"You'll find you've gained more from it than you think," Rosamund said.

"I've written nothing but one short story the whole time. Here," Malcolm said, lifting his brief case and presenting Rosamund with a typescript. "When you read it, see whether you find anything different—"

Rosamund laid the typescript beside her on the chaise longue. She turned to Claudia. "Has he showed it to you?"

"Oh, I've only read Malcolm in print," Claudia said.

Malcolm seemed to become aware of her presence again. "She swallowed my stuff, irony and all," he said. "Education hasn't spoiled her taste. She's a naturally perceptive reader."

"I can well imagine." Rosamund gave them both a glance of tranquil amusement that seemed totally free from malice. "Has his vanity been battening on you while you were driving down?" she asked.

"We talked about his work," Claudia said, "and agreed that it was good."

Rosamund laughed, just two or three subdued notes, as if more would have been a departure from her scrupulous composure. "I can just hear you agreeing at length about that," she said.

"All right, have your fun, both of you," Malcolm said. "Seriously, though, what I want you to tell me is whether you see anything new in this one, a different Islay pecking his way out of the shell. It's about two men—well, you know every man thinks he's Hamlet. I don't know about women, but men do. The trouble is, no two people agree on what Hamlet was—is. I have two men—"

"Don't tell me, Malcolm," Rosamund said. "Let me read it for myself."

"It's on the theme of human identity," Malcolm said stubbornly, "how we build up a sense of identity and struggle to preserve it when it's threatened. That's a human theme, if you ask me. The idea is obvious enough, once you see where it's going, so it can't be spoiled by telling a little about it. Each of these men thinks he's Hamlet, but they have directly opposite conceptions—"

"You mustn't give it away," Rosamund said. "Let me find out for myself. You've told too much already."

"It's the only thing I've done in months," Malcolm said miserably.

"You're in one of those periods of accidie that all writers go through. I've seen cases before."

"Where does that leave me? One case in a clinic. Sometime I'm going to make you give up the clinic and stick—"

"Now, Malcolm!" Rosamund turned to Claudia, her look inviting participation. "A doctor can't limit his practice to a single patient, can he? Or a lawyer to one client. Sam couldn't," she said, turning back to Malcolm.

"Sam gets one-man treatment. He has all the luck," Malcolm said.

Claudia felt the relief of change when a tray-bearing figure appeared soundlessly in the doorway, a small woman with a pinched face, her unflattering bosom softened by the ruffles of a maid's apron. "Do the honors, will you, Malcolm?" Rosamund said. "Just half a glass for me, and we'll have lunch as soon as you're ready, Ethel." With the entrance of sherry, the conversation took a different turn. Malcolm was led into a description of his classroom adventures; he became charming and amusing, even rather humble in his admission of inadequacies as a mentor to the young. They were finishing their glasses when the telephone rang, and Rosamund picked up an extension by her chaise longue. The tones of a vigorous male voice made themselves audible at the other end of the line. "Darling, I'm perfectly all right," Rosamund said. "It was nothing at all this morning." The male voice spoke again. "I'm on the sunporch, and we're just about to have lunch. Who's we? We, besides me, are Malcolm and a very charming traveling companion he's dropping off in New York on his way home." Rosamund listened a moment, then her eyes, gently sardonic, turned toward Malcolm. "He's the same mooncalf," she said into the telephone. Once more she looked at Malcolm. "Sam wants me to tell you Merry Christmas and mind your manners," she said.

Malcolm grinned reluctantly. "Tell him 'Same to you.'"

As Rosamund put the phone down, Ethel began removing the sherry. When she returned, it was to serve lunch. The lunch was delicious, Claudia thought, the clear, seasoned bouillon, the chafing dish of bacon and mushrooms, the salad, the fresh-made applesauce to go with coffee. It might not have been enough to satisfy Malcolm, but he had himself to thank. Once, while Malcolm was making good-natured if not very well-informed fun of the New England character—he got away from himself and his work for a while—she looked up and caught Rosamund off-guard. She was startled by what she saw, a strange expression, questioning, listening, for an instant almost haggard, as though Rosamund were paying careful attention to warning signals of some secret kind. She dismissed them, whatever they might be; she returned as if from a distance and asked Claudia, smiling, whether she thought New Englanders as odd as Malcolm made them out. Claudia said she didn't suppose any region had a monopoly on oddity; she felt suddenly as though her voice were too loud, as though her words were blows, that for all Rosamund's inclination to plumpness she was really as fragile as a glass bell; a breath might shatter her to pieces. Her air of languor, her exquisitely sustained indolence weren't a manner, they were a necessity; they required frightening control. Then Rosamund's voice went pleasantly and composedly on, and Claudia wondered about the reality of her momentary impression.

Lunch came to an end. Claudia climbed the stairs again to make ready for the final stretch of driving. When she came down, Rosamund was standing in the hall with Malcolm, who had already put on his overcoat and held his hat in hand. He helped Claudia into her lambskin, then turned to claim Rosamund's cheek. She offered it with the same detached receptivity, and, when she had been released, Claudia began to say her thanks. "Good-by, Mrs. Temple. It was ever so kind—"

"You must call me Rosamund."

"Good-by, Rosamund. I can't tell you how perfect everything was, the lunch, the house—"

"You're a dear child, and it was a pleasure to have you. I mustn't call you child, must I? If you're ever near this out-of-the-way corner again, do call on me. I'm always at home, as Malcolm knows, and I love to be visited."

She put her hand on Claudia's shoulder, and Claudia perceived that she too was being invited to accept a farewell kiss. Leaning forward, she felt herself drawn into a light, brief embrace that seemed to express a cool yet altogether genuine affection. She wished suddenly that she could bring Jim to this house, that Jim could see this woman, that she could present herself to Rosamund under other auspices than Malcolm's. Perhaps, someday, if she and Jim—she pictured the two of them driving down the dip of road past the red barn, driving through the covered bridge and the village to the Temple house, pictured Jim's finger pushing the bell instead of Malcolm's, Jim's face awaiting the slow recoil of the door.

Malcolm seemed in no mind for further delays when they climbed into the car and drove off. He was apparently anxious to finish the journey. Claudia was grateful; she wanted no more diversions, but she had lost the extremity of her impatience. They would be in plenty of time; it was just a question of sitting out the remaining miles.

"Rosamund is a remarkable woman," Claudia said. "You were so right about her, and I'm so glad, now, that I had a chance to meet her. She's so—so kind. She didn't *let* me feel like a stranger."

"Kind," Malcolm said. "I never thought of applying that word to her. I wouldn't deny it, of course, but people see different sides of each other, don't they?"

"I suppose it's her health that keeps her at home so much?"

Malcolm's face worked thoughtfully. "She's had a medical history. I don't know much about it. But she doesn't like the rat-race life Sam leads—fourteen hours a day at the office and millions hanging on a brief. She likes her house. Personally, I think it's a Yankee mausoleum, but you can see, if you care for that kind of thing—"

"Once, at lunch," Claudia said, "I had the impression—I wondered whether she was in pain."

The car jerked. Malcolm's foot released the accelerator as he turned to look at her, then pressed it down again. "Pain?" he said. "She has to take care of herself, but she's as—she goes along as evenly as a good motor."

Claudia told herself that he really ought to know better

194

than she did. He was an odd, fascinating, complicated character, though; he was self-obsessed and gifted and distinguished, and all that didn't keep him from having a problem, probably only intensified it. He had certainly made the ride interesting. She must take pains to thank him just as cordially as she knew how when he let her out at Helena's and went on, all the way to Maryland, alone.

◌ ◌ 6 ◌ ◌

Kent disliked to shave in the lurching old Pullman. Consulting his watch, he decided he had time to leave his bag at home, make himself presentable, scratch up some breakfast, and still reach his desk by ten. Even though he had the insurance settlement in his brief case, that would be early enough. Stocky seldom got to the office before ten these days. Doctor's orders, he said, implying that the orders were senseless and superfluous, but if he paid for them, he might as well get his money's worth.

From his taxi Kent stepped out into a warmth of January thaw that was almost like summer. Abby's azaleas and japonicas thrust up through pocked gray snow. The house, he observed, needed a paint job. No end to the expenses a man was put to during the years when he ought to be laying by an estate. The children, Ruth and Brainerd, would have to move into bigger quarters, now that a third grandchild had arrived, and they couldn't do it without help. Abby was already campaigning for that, though actually no campaign was needed; he saw the point himself. He thought of Abby, down there visiting the new grandchild, perhaps at this very moment routing Brainerd's ungainly bulk from the couch in the living room to which he had been dismissed while Abby shared the bedroom with Ruth.

Without Abby to cook him an egg, Kent would have to make do with what he could find, some juice from a can, or better half a grapefruit, if one happened to be already cut, perhaps a bowl of cereal. He could compensate at lunch. He picked up the *Times* from the doorstep as he went in. After shaving and putting on a clean shirt, he began a diligent search for the canister in which Abby kept the coffee. He noticed it too late, in full view on the kitchen table, after opening a fresh tin. He assembled a cereal bowl, a cup, milk and cream, and spread the *Times* at his left elbow. The world situation was bad all around the horizon. The country was giving itself away in aid to the underprivileged, without any return except that the Commies went right on making gains wherever you looked. The cost-of-living index had gone up again; escalator clauses would push wage scales up with it. His own investments, Kent saw, were keeping pace with the market; if it weren't for the capital-gains tax, he could sell out and do better than scrape by for the rest of his life, always excepting inflation.

He finished his cereal, put the milk and cream back in the icebox, and left his dishes on the table. Abby would be coming home in another forty-eight hours; meanwhile he could eat his dinners at the club and leave the clean-up problem for her. She'd never get over the shock if she went into the kitchen and found that he'd washed the dishes. Besides, it was time he got to the office.

Isabel looked at him expectantly as he hung up his coat and hat. She didn't ask point blank how the insurance negotiations had turned out; she asked instead about the new grandchild, but she was obviously watching his face for signs. He was about to tell her that he hadn't been outsmarted when he heard steps approaching his door. He thought of Denis Prouty, but when he looked up the heavy-shouldered, deliberate bulk of Fred Abramson appeared. "Come in, Fred," he invited, and Isabel withdrew to her inner room.

"How did it go, Cap?"

"We made a killing," Kent said. He was a little surprised by Fred's visit. Kent didn't report to him in the chain of command.

"Good," Fred said. "I won't ask about details now. Stocky

will want to see you as soon as he comes in, and I'll be there, but if you got a sizable settlement, he'll be pleased."

Fred still hadn't given a clue to the purpose of his call. Kent looked at him, trying to make a fresh estimate of the rather broad and pouchy features, the solid shoulders that slightly rumpled Fred's expensive and conservative tailoring. A good many people might not take Fred for a Jew if he didn't make a point of bringing up his origins on his own initiative. He didn't do so aggressively, Kent had to admit; he had no chip on his shoulder, but he tossed in a reminder whenever occasion offered, just to keep his credentials clear. He had a fund of Jewish stories which he was ready to tell, and he never seemed embarrassed by the ensuing laughter.

"Want to tell me the total?" Fred asked.

Kent mentioned it, and Fred whistled. "Stocky won't be pleased, he'll be tickled pink."

That would depend, Kent reflected, on which way the cat chose to jump. Stocky could see the settlement as a whole for what it was, or he could blast the liver and lights out of a subordinate for disregarding instructions again. Kent didn't care to confess his misgiving to Fred in advance; he preferred to wait and trust his knack of playing on Stocky's sense of the dramatic. Perhaps it would be just as well, though, if Fred were in the room. Fred was as good as a tranquilizer when Stocky's top threatened to blow.

"Stocky may not always show it," Fred was saying, "but he appreciates good work from the team. You know, other companies may be more lavish with benefits to management. I don't mind saying I'd like to see us treat ourselves a little more liberally." Fred smiled, his large features opening to include Kent in a party of legitimate self-interest. "I dare say we will. I think Stocky is coming round to a more modern outlook. But we're an outfit, all the same. We have a team, and we have a future."

Kent began to smell out the object of Fred's casual visit. What Fred meant to convey was that, if anything happened to Stocky, he couldn't help knowing that he was in line for the presidency. Don't worry, Fred was suggesting; no one has anything to lose if I take over. Fred was conducting a diplomatic mission in his own interest, spreading reassurance, quietly inviting allegiance and support. A smooth job.

"Prouty wasn't with you this trip, was he?" Fred asked.

"No," Kent said.

"I guess we all know why. It's no secret that you've been covering for Denis, Cap. It's another thing Stocky appreciates. What are we going to do with Denis? Can we kick him higher upstairs and keep him safe till he retires? Is there any upstairs to kick him to where he won't fall through and bring the ceiling with him?"

"Offhand, I don't know," Kent said.

"Well, give it some thought, will you, Cap? I haven't any ideas myself right now, but it's the only out I can see." Fred got up, then turned as he was on the point of reaching the door. "How's Shepherdson? That was a first-rate job he did in New Jersey."

"A good man," Kent said.

"We'll have to have a new manager down there. I suppose you want to keep Shep with you?"

"We can get a man in the market for New Jersey a lot easier than I can break in a new assistant."

"Maybe, but we've got to balance that against the value for Shep himself of some knocks in the field."

"That's a point, Fred, but he's too big for a branch operation, and New Jersey would close the road to him here."

"That's a point, too," Fred conceded. "You want him, don't you, Cap? Well, don't worry. All views will be considered." Again on the point of leaving, Fred stopped once more. "See you with the settlement when Stocky gets in," he said. "As the Jew told the clerk when he bought a prayer robe for his friend the rabbi, 'Wrap it up nice. It's a Christmas present.' "

As Fred vanished into the corridor, Kent almost reached for his little black reminder book of wheezes and stories. But no, he didn't run into enough occasions when he could use one of Fred's cracks.

He looked at his calendar for the day and noticed the entry: 11:30—Islay—show plant. He needed a moment to remember what the appointment was about. Islay—he was the writer Arthur and Rachel had invited to the house along with his class. Kent thought of the paperback collection of Islay's stories that Claudia had pressed on him. Islay could spin some amusing yarns, but too fantastic most of the time for Kent's taste. Well, he ought to be through with the insurance business in time to show Islay anything he wanted to see.

Kent turned to the mail and memos that Isabel had arranged on his desk. The pile contained another reminder, a news clipping this time, of the asphalt spray product one of Fullchem's big competitors was developing. Apparently it was almost at the production stage. Well, that was a fish that got away. You couldn't land them all. He was going through a routine departmental report when his telephone rang. Isabel opened her door to tell him that Mr. Stockwell had just come in and wanted him to report right away. Kent picked up the insurance settlement and headed down the corridor toward the elevator.

When he reached Stocky's office, Fred Abramson was standing behind the desk, his head partly obliterating the portrait beyond and above it, so that only one blue eye and one corner of the down-turned mouth peered out past the flesh of Fred's left ear. Stocky himself sat quietly at his desk, leaning forward a little, braced on folded hands, as if he had schooled himself to accept the best or the worst in the spirit recommended by doctor's orders. "How about it, Cap?" he said. "What have you got to offer? Fred tells me it's good."

"Here's the figure," Kent said, laying the agreement under Stocky's eye, the total neatly tabulated on the top sheet.

Fred Abramson said, "I tell Cap if he can bag them that size, we ought to send him out with gun and camera all the time."

Admiration, almost ungrudging, showed in Stocky's blue gaze. His mouth relaxed, its corners rising nearly to the horizontal. "I don't know but what Fred has a point. Figuring we put in the amortization for bluff, that's—well, for Christ's sake, it's *more* than we asked for." Stocky's face changed; he was beginning to look for the catch. "Can we make it stick?"

Kent was willing to let him find the catch for himself. "It

will stick," he said. "Dave Cronkhite lived up to his word. He got us an entirely new board, gentlemen of a different feather. We ought to remember it in Dave's favor."

"I've never met a gentleman yet," Fred said, "who'd give away money he didn't have to. You must have helped them loosen up, Cap. How did you do it?"

Stocky was turning the pages, beginning to focus on details. He scowled at an item disallowed or reduced here and there, but they were minor items. In view of the grand total, even Stocky couldn't boggle at them. Then he reached the final page, and, as his eye traveled quickly toward the bottom, the color suddenly rose in his neck. "What's this?" he demanded.

Kent knew what he was looking at. It was his own signature, Kent Warner, Executive Engineer, for the Fullington Chemical and Pharmaceutical Company.

"Goddamn it, Warner," Stocky said, "I didn't give you authority to sign for the company. Your orders were, by God, not to exceed instructions. I told you it was the company's decision to decide whether we sign or not." Stocky breathed deliberately; he was trying to keep himself in hand. "Now, look here, Cap. I know you've been doing a good job around here, and we're prepared to cut you in more on management, but we've got to have authority around here, we've got to see that orders—"

"Maybe Cap had his reasons," Fred Abramson said mildly. "Maybe he has something to say for himself."

Stocky's expression altered from the outraged to the glum. "You'd better make it good and make it fast."

"I'll make it as short as I can, Mr. Stockwell," Kent said, "but I'll have to ask you to picture the scene. In the first place, the surroundings were different. We had a rug on the floor, and a real room, not just a plywood compartment. And as I said, we had a new board, new faces all around, thanks to Dave Cronkhite. We all shook hands, told a few stories and exchanged a few wheezes, and then sat down around the table. Someone spoke up and said, 'Mr. Chairman, I see here an item which appears to be well substantiated. I move it be accepted.' Everyone said, 'Ay,' and the Chairman said, 'Voted.' So it goes, pretty nearly right down the line. 'I see here an item, I move it be accepted.' 'The Chair rules it's accepted.' Well, we get to the end, with the total as you have it there, and someone says, 'Mr. Warner, I assume you're authorized to sign for the company.' That was when I had to make my decision, Stocky, and I didn't bat an eyelash. I'd been keeping track as well as I could, and I noticed they'd gone so fast they overlooked one important item. Nobody moved to strike out the amortization, and there it was, included in the total. I grabbed the pen and signed, then and there. In fact I *prayed* my signature onto the sheet before I even reached for the pen."

Fred Abramson lifted his big chin and laughed. "Cap, you're a slick one!" he said.

Stocky hung between the resentment of flouted authority and admiration for a deal. After an effort he broke down and chuckled. "You do that in the army," he said, "they either give you a court martial or make you a general. Goddamn it, Cap, I guess we can't put you through a court martial."

"I figured you could always repudiate my signature," Kent said.

Fred laughed again, but Stocky didn't mean to be appeased without resistance. "You win this time, Cap, but you got to watch your step how you disregard instructions. I was going to tell you, if this deal came out all right, you could go ahead and get bids on the new office building, but Goddamn it, I authorize that, you'll start putting up the Pentagon and claim you got in a jam where orders didn't fit."

"I guess we can trust Cap," Fred said.

"Well, get going. Get your bids in. And another thing." Stocky glowered for emphasis. "I don't say that this is decided, but it looks as though we'd put up a new plant for limited-sales products on the fire location. Start figuring on that. I I don't know what we'll do with this slum we're in now. Maybe we'll let Denis burn it down for the insurance." He grunted with sour satisfaction.

"We'll find something for Denis to do," Fred said. "I've been talking with Cap about that. We'll come up with an idea."

"Tell him to dig himself a hole and pull it in after him."

"While Cap is putting on his general's uniform," Fred said, "I want to talk to you about a sales program that will take some outlay but ought to pay off."

Fred and Stocky were putting their heads together as Kent walked out. In the corridor he felt an almost irresistible impulse to share his elation. He thought of telegraphing Abby. It wasn't the insurance deal; that was all right in its way, one of those things a man was called on to do in a business life, a contest of wits in which the winnings went to the smart side. What he had really carried with him from Stocky's office was a building, not merely one building, but two. He was going to be constructive—creative, if he wanted to use the word they'd batted around the dinner table at Arthur's and Rachel's. He saw himself sitting across from Abby in the study at home; he was telling her that the building program had been authorized, trying to make little of it so that he wouldn't get a swelled head, knocking on wood to fend off bad luck. He saw himself standing, blueprints in hand, beside the contractor at the new office site, and Randy was at his elbow, listening while he pointed to girder frames and explained problems. No, he'd let himself fall into that trap again. It certainly took the starch out of his impulse to send a wire.

Turning in at his office door, Kent was conscious of a lanky figure rising from the chair by his desk and looking at him expectantly. Of course. He'd forgotten. It was Islay, waiting to be taken on his tour of the plant.

Equipment and operations that Kent usually counted on to impress visitors didn't seem to have much effect on Islay. He didn't appear to know what he was looking at. His face worked in patches, like the skin of a horse who can pinpoint a fly and twitch the square inch necessary to shake it off, but his eye didn't light. He wanted to see the suspended roof Kent had told him about, but there was no good vantage point from which to view it. He would have learned more from the plans if he had known how to read them. The packing machinery, with its files of containers turning squads right or squads left to be filled and sealed by automatic spigots and arms, left him looking depressed as much as anything. He thought the laboratories with their aproned personnel were about what anyone could see on television.

He began to respond when Kent took him through the employees' clinic. They watched a nurse treating a technician for an acid burn on his wrist. Kent put the victim through a quiz and got him to admit that he hadn't paid due respect to safety regulations. Islay hadn't realized, he said, the kinds of social services a modern corporation provides for its help. "You really take care of them, don't you?"

Kent said they probably saved money by it in the end. They avoided injury claims that might win extravagant verdicts, they avoided complaints from the Grievance Committee, they increased efficiency and production. Encouraged by Islay's interest in the clinic, Kent took him to the plant cafeteria for lunch. They found Shepherdson and sat down at a table with him. After lunch Kent suggested that they all three relax for a few minutes in the employees' lounging room just off the cafeteria.

Kent had found space for the room himself when the cafeteria was installed. It boasted tables, ashtrays, upholstered chairs, but its walls were still unfinished, just concrete slabs beneath the I-beams that supported the ceiling. Islay sat down and stretched out his long legs. Kent offered him a cigar, but he preferred his own cigarettes. Two or three of the advertising staff came in, and Kent introduced them. One, with a face that looked fresh out of college, evidently knew who Islay was. He asked whether Mr. Islay thought that writing advertising copy made a good preparation for writing a novel, and got rather a short answer. Mr. Islay didn't think so. There was no preparation for writing a novel. If you had it in you, then you wrote it; anything else you did or had to do was probably an obstacle.

The advertising crew began talking among themselves about a new insect repellent the company was about to market. The group threatened to split down the seams; it was time for someone to pull it together. Kent passed easily from insect repellents to hunting and fishing, and that put him in mind of a story with a moral: never go into the woods with anyone who can't hear. Kent's old man had taken him deer hunting once with George Westermark. Kent could see George yet, though he'd been sleeping half a generation now in the graveyard of the First Congregational Church in Amity. George was as deaf as his own headstone, but they let him tag along on the deer hunt anyway. George was to shape his course along a beech ridge, keeping to the crest, while Kent's old man would go into the spruce swamp at the foot on one side and Kent himself through the parallel swamp on the other. If either put up a buck, it would make for the ridge, and George, with an open view down both slopes, would get a shot. George nodded and smiled and hadn't heard a word either of them said. He plodded off, got tired of bowlegging it along the ridge, and took the path of least resistance right downhill toward the spruce swamp. When Kent's old man flushed a sizable bear, it took right off in a straight line through windfalls and tangles and came within a hair of running right over George, who was snoozing with his cap over his eyes in a patch of November sunlight just above the swamp. As for the rifle Kent's old man emptied when he got his one glimpse of the lurching black back, it sprayed slugs as thick as hornets around George's recumbent figure. They had to tell him what happened, or try to. He didn't even wake up till Kent's old man, in pursuit of the bear, stumbled over him and shook him by the shoulder.

Islay obviously liked a yarn at least more than he liked machinery. As for the advertising chief, when he wasn't thinking how to give money to the networks, he lived for his collection of guns. His face lit, and he said he had in his desk right now something special in the way of firearms. If they'd wait a minute, he'd like to show it to them. He went out, and Kent found no difficulty in covering the interval with further lore. The advertising chief was considerably out of breath when he came back. "Don't do anything with a gun until you're sure it isn't loaded," he said. "That's elementary. I broke open the chamber and inspected on the way downstairs. What I want you to notice is the action. It's sweet." He pointed the revolver at the floor, just off the foot of the youngster who had asked Islay about writing a novel. "See, it's as light as this," he said and squeezed the trigger. In the cement room the detonation that followed must have been as earsplitting as a thunderclap; Kent never could account for the fact that he didn't hear it. For an instant he knew only that the unexpected had happened. Then he did hear, everyone must have heard, the succession of wire-drawn pings that ricocheted from the concrete walls and the steel I-beams overhead. The knee of the youngster whose foot had almost occupied the line of fire gave a belated jerk. Islay's face hung open, asking blankly what was going on, was this a part of his planned tour? Young Shepherdson was rolling up his pant leg. Incredibly enough, a frayed hole appeared in the fabric, yet the skin wasn't broken underneath. A small mound of proud flesh was taking shape on it, but no blood spurted out. The face of the advertising chief sagged blue with incredulity and mortification. Shep was rolling down his pant leg again, gravely picking up from the floor a squashed pellet of lead.

Someone finally recovered voice enough to say, "He didn't know it was loaded," and the reaction of hysterical laughter set in. They all laughed except the fresh-out-of-college youngster and the chief. The youngster was looking murder—he'd taken a bad scare—and the chief was beginning to babble his disbelief and chagrin. "Jesus, I don't know how—I broke the chamber open on the way down—"

Kent became aware of a figure in the doorway, regarding with amazement the scene in the room, the revolver that dangled from the chief's wrist as if he wanted to drop it and couldn't let go, and at the same time trying to gain attention. It was Mike Hoague from the maintenance crew. Catching Kent's eye, Mike spoke, failing to make himself audible but obviously framing his lips to say. "Mr. Warner." Kent got up and went over to the door. The laughter continued behind him, but the kidding had begun, not without an edge of sarcasm and resentment. They weren't going to let the chief off without rubbing it into him that he might have killed someone. He had it coming to him. He'd done one of those things that are funny when no one gets hurt, but he shouldn't be trusted with a nursery pop-gun. "What is it, Mike?" Kent asked.

"I don't want to interrupt, Mr. Warner, but they've been looking for you all over the plant. I said I'd seen you in the cafeteria, so I thought I'd take a squint in here—"

"Who's looking?"

"Everybody, Mr. Warner. Your office, the big boss—Mr. Stockwell, I mean—"

"Is it an accident? Anything wrong with the plant?"

"Not as far as I know. Mr. Stockwell's office—"

"Thanks, Mike. I'll get to a phone. Take care of yourself."

Kent turned and made excuses, confiding Islay to Shepherdson's care. The nearest telephone would be in the dietitian's office. He made his way to it and used it. He got one of Stocky's secretaries, and the agitation in her voice suggested that Stocky's top might be lifting like a rocket from its launching pad.

Fred Abramson stood behind Stocky's desk as though he hadn't shifted his position since morning. Something else about Fred had changed, though. He kept his impassive composure, but the good nature had vanished from it. Somehow he looked more Jewish, as though his face had been pared down to essentials. A few steps to his right stood the Vice President who had charge of the development of new products, and a step or two from him the Director of Laboratories. The air crackled as though everyone had taken a grilling. The Director looked testy and defiant, as though he were telling himself that he was a scientist and didn't have to take treatment he didn't like from an ignorant boor. Stocky sat at his desk, immobile, the peak of his lower lip thrust sourly forward. "Well, Warner," he said, making an undisguised effort to breathe slowly and evenly, "where have you been? Fishing?"

"I had a date to take a visitor through the plant, Mr. Stockwell," Kent said. "Public relations."

Stocky's eye lit briefly with the zest of flaying a victim. "Why the hell didn't you leave a message where you could be reached? An executive in this company isn't where he can be reached, he ought to let someone know where they can reach him. That's a simple—" Stocky checked himself. His eyes dulled, he embarked on another course of controlled breathing.

"I'm sorry, Mr. Stockwell," Kent said. "Isabel could have got me in two minutes except when I took this visitor to lunch at the cafeteria. As soon as I got word, I came right up here to find out what you wanted."

"You'll find out. Now, what I want to know—I get this call from one of the Directors, Chairman of the Board as a matter of fact. He wants to know, he has sources on what the competition is doing, and when he asks me, by God, if we've gone to sleep on a thing up here—" Stocky broke off and ran a finger around the neckband of his shirt. "Doctor's orders. Can't get hot under the collar. You tell him, Fred."

Fred drew up his big shoulders a little. Kent felt his look, not hostile, not suspicious, not unduly excited, but watchfully prepared for any consequences. "Ever hear of a plastic spray," Fred asked, "for use in arid farming?"

"I've seen the claims that something along that line is close to production. Correct me if I'm wrong," Kent said, turning to the Lab Director, "but we did some research here about two years ago—"

"We did," the Director said crisply, his eyes focused on a point just off Stocky's right foot.

"What I want to know," Stocky said, "is what happened to it? Who's been keeping me in the dark around here? By God, here I get an inquiry from the Chairman of the Board—"

"Tell Mr. Warner what you've told us," Fred Abramson said to the Lab Director.

"I intend no implication about Mr. Warner." The Director kept his eyes sardonically fixed on Stocky's rug. "We made a research summary, and I understood it was to go to Mr. Warner for a study on production. I never heard of it again. I assumed it had been vetoed by—rejected for—well, for commercial reasons."

"I'm in the same position," said the Vice President in charge of new products. "I knew about it in the early stages, then it never came up in a conference that I can remember."

"Well, there we are," Stocky said. "You were supposed to

make a report, and it never got to me. By God, Warner, I don't mind putting it to you, it's a question how the competition got hold of this thing. I don't know the technical side, but they tell me this product may have a big future, and it's the same— it's practically identical with what our people were working on here. Now we've tracked this thing down to you, and there it stops. The question is—"

"Mr. Stockwell," Kent said, "I made a complete report at the time and sent it up to you through channels. Mr. Stockwell—" He was about to say that if Socky really meant to suggest that he had peddled the discovery himself or leaked company secrets, then Stocky ought to fire him on the spot, and he'd be glad to go, but Stocky cut in.

"You say you made a complete report. You say you sent it up to me. All right, how is it I never saw it? How is it, when the Chairman of the Board calls me up—"

"I don't know any more about that than these other gentlemen," Kent said. "I can get my copy from my own files, if you want."

He turned toward the door, but stopped when Stocky's voice squeaked to its full bleat. "Nobody leaves this room till I get to the bottom of this. Fred, you call his office and have —what the hell is his secretary's name? Have her bring this thing up—if it's there, if she isn't out taking someone on a public-relations tour."

Kent had a strong impulse to announce that he was a free citizen, to turn his back on the room and walk out; but a man didn't throw away a lifetime's work during the most lucrative years before retirement, didn't throw away two buildings that only a few hours before he'd been authorized to put up. In a minute Isabel would come up with his report, and he'd be holding the ace of trumps in his own hand. He'd get an apology from Stocky yet. Suddenly it occurred to him why, in all probability, his report had never reached its intended consumer. He felt a twinge of commiseration at the thought of the storm that would break over the ultimate victim, but it was too late now to forestall the catastrophe.

While Fred dialed, the Lab Director raised his eyes at last

and gave Stocky a long-suffering glance. "Will anyone object if I sit down?" he asked. He pulled a chair from under the table at the right of Stocky's desk, mopped with a spotless handkerchief the delicately boned temples under his nearly white hair, and seated himself, compressing his lips. No one else made any attempt to speak until Isabel knocked at the door and opened it, a little breathless, the report in her hand. She offered it to Kent, her eye meeting his with a slight air of 'I told you so.'

Kent was about to take the mimeographed document from her, but Stocky interrupted the motion. "Give it to me, right here," he said. Isabel colored, and Stocky conceded to amenity so far as to say, "Please."

"Thanks for bringing it up, Isabel," Kent said. "I think that's all Mr. Stockwell wants."

Stocky squared the report in front of him on his desk as Isabel went out. Kent visualized the type Stocky would be looking at. The top page in itself would contain the incriminating evidence: To Mr. Prouty, for the attention of Mr. Stockwell. Date. Signature: Kent Warner, Executive Engineer. Stocky left no doubt that he took in the significant name at first glance and drew the appropriate inference. He seemed to rise in his chair as if by levitation, or as if inflated by the mounting color in his neck. Evidently, though, the doctors had found some way to make their orders effective. He settled back, controlled himself, and began turning pages his eye dodging over technical analysis, reading steadily when he came to the end, where Kent had tabulated his recommendations: High priority urged, new equipment to be designed, cost estimates, market studies suggested.

"Prouty," Stocky's voice said hoarsely. "Someone get him here."

"Maybe it would be just as well if I took this up with Denis privately," Fred Abramson said. "I think I can get the story from him, and I don't know that we need—"

"Prouty. I want Prouty here." Stocky cut Fred a look implying that the Vice President next in line had better mind his orders like everyone else.

"I'll get him," Kent said. It might be possible at least to put Denis on guard, for Stocky's sake as much as his own.

"You've covered for him long enough," Stocky said. "Just get him in here, Fred, and don't try to pull anything."

Fred still hesitated. Then he shrugged slightly and put himself in motion. Kent almost hoped for delay, hoped that Denis would be off on one of his tours of evasion around the plant, but hardly more than seconds could have passed before Denis was coming into the room while Fred Abramson followed, his impassive face looking over Denis's shoulder.

It seemed as though Denis must have read the symptoms, caught the portents from the air, but he tried apparently to make his entrance causually jaunty. His eye even seemed to flicker with a glint of hope that Stocky was taking him back into his good graces. "You wanted something, Stocky?" he asked. He became conscious of the others in the room. "Well, quite a conference! What's going on?"

Stocky let the silence dilate while he breathed deeply and savagely. Then he thrust the report at Denis, who accepted it with an uncertain hand.

"Ever see this before?"

Denis examined the top page and whitened. He looked for an instant as though his legs might give way. "Why, sure," he said finally. "Yes, I did. About—let's see, the date's right here. Two years ago. It was when—"

"Ever give it to me?"

"Why, sure. It says here it's for your attention, so I must have. I'm trying to remember."

"Never got to me. Never saw it. You think if I'd seen it, I'd sit here with my hands under my butt while the competition goes ahead and develops this thing? Maybe *you* want to talk to the Chairman of the Board, maybe *you* want to explain—goddamn it, have you got anything to say?"

"I'm trying to think." Denis visibly conducted a struggle of some sort, but the stress was shaking him like a chill. "It was while—well, you know, just when the sales manager resigned and we had a big personnel problem. You remember the time. You had a lot of things bothering you, Stocky. You said yourself you didn't want to be bothered with a lot of secondary stuff, and maybe I thought the time wasn't right—you're always rubbing it in that you want executives to use judgment—"

In his extremity, Denis began to bluster, but the attempt was weak and late. He saw the impression he was making and stopped.

"Secondary stuff," Stocky said. "Judgment. Bother." A whimper of laughter came from him. "Yeah, that's what running this business is, just a bother. It's a bother to watch out for the interests and profits of this company. It's a bother to keep a jump ahead of the competition. That's funny! That's a good one!"

Kent wondered how long the inevitable tantrum could be postponed. Stocky's voice began to grate. The explosion was on the way.

"I'll tell you about your secondary stuff and your judgment and your bother, Prouty. I'll tell you what the hell you bothered to do about this report. You bothered to shove it under your ass and sit on it, and now—now—"

Everyone in the room must have seen what was coming; everyone must have been waiting for the final detonation. All the symptoms were present. Kent watched the color climbing Stocky's neck, heard the squeal in his voice working up to its ultimate pitch. But something happened to avert the climax. Perhaps it was doctor's orders, perhaps the very abjectness of Denis as he stood with his hangdog mouth slack and his knees ready to buckle. Stocky suddenly looked as though he had peered into the pit of uselessness and seen its bottom. He began to breathe in long, measured periods. He turned his eyes from Denis, put a hand across them, and said thickly, "Someone take him away. Someone get him out of here."

Fred Abramson touched Denis on the shoulder, relieved him of Kent's report, and walked with him to the door. "Are we at liberty to go now, Mr. Stockwell?" the Lab Director asked and, receiving no answer, conferred the liberty on himself. The other Vice President followed. Kent hesitated. It was hardly the time to extract the apology he felt was due to him, but Stocky might have a word of his own to say. While he stood undecided, Fred Abramson re-entered the room.

"Well, I guess your nose is clean about this, Cap," Stocky said.

Fred Abramson added his endorsement. "Cap's nose is usually clean. In fact, I haven't known it to need wiping yet."

"I don't mind being put on the spot," Kent said, "but when you insinuate, Mr. Stockwell, that I'd leak information to competitors, I'm not prepared to take it."

"Don't get riled, Cap. I had to get to the bottom of this thing, didn't I?"

"Do I understand the insinuation is withdrawn?"

"Of course it is," Fred Abramson said. "It never was made. In the heat of the moment, maybe Stocky said a word or two he didn't really mean the way you took them, that's all."

Kent looked at Stocky for confirmation, but Stocky might as well have been absent. His blue eyes had strayed altogether from the question at hand. He sat dejectedly in his chair, all the starch gone out of him. "You try to do the right thing," he said, "you try to keep on the ball yourself, you try to keep the outfit on the ball, you try to take care of a guy like Denis instead of throwing him out on the street, and he lets you down. He lets you down."

∘ ∘ *7* ∘ ∘

"This will be one of your rehearsal nights, won't it?" Arthur said, sipping his coffee, fixing the plan of the day in his mind. Claudia had already finished her egg and toast and gone upstairs to make ready for her job. He could prolong breakfast a few minutes and still allow time to go over his notes and work himself into the agreeable tension he needed for his ten-o'clock lecture. After that he would answer his mail with Janice, go over laboratory and thesis plans of students, lunch, and meet his graduate seminar. The day could be a pleasant one if only it didn't have to end with the first session of Lamson Crocket's Committee since the holidays. He thought gloomily of the Committee, thought gloomily how long it had been since he had done any really productive experimentation of his own. After a certain age, the knack for devising fruitful experiments declined. Philosophy set in. He couldn't regret that; he could only regret that life didn't seem to permit equal progress in both activities at once.

He wondered whether he had heard Rachel's answer to his question correctly. "It will be, if I go." Was that what she had said?

"Why, of course you'll go, Rachel. They'd be crippled without you. That is, unless there's something wrong. Is there?"

He looked at her across the table and was chagrined that he hadn't noticed how she was dressed. She usually came down to breakfast scrupulously smart and costumed for the day, but this morning she was wearing a wrapper. Its fur-bordered throat showed the lace fringe of her nightgown underneath. The skin beneath her eyes appeared granulated. To his dismay, they suddenly overflowed. She averted her face, ashamed of her weakness.

"I'm just foolishly upset," she said. "But I'm beginning to think it isn't worth while, the orchestra, I mean. I detest half the music we play, and besides—"

"What besides?"

"Just something that happened. It isn't worth telling about."

"But I want to hear. Tell me."

"The other evening, I—we were going through a new score, it's dedicated to our Herr Conductor himself. About half of it is for nothing but percussion and brass, but there's a viola passage, it's hideously tricky rhythm, and I made a false entrance and took half the section with me. Really we were all playing something different, no one knew quite what."

Arthur couldn't help laughing a little. "I can see it must have made an embarrassing moment," he said, "but just in rehearsal—"

"I wouldn't have minded so much if Herr Conductor hadn't

flown into a tantrum. He singled me out—made a whole speech about how the first viola desk must be acquainted with the simple operation of counting. One, two, three. Everyone sat absolutely still and listened. I felt a hundred pairs of eyes boring into me. I always hated big audiences anyway. I just want to play music I like with friends. I can't stand being made a public—"

"The conductor was a boor," Arthur said. "Still, do you really want to give up the orchestra? It's not only made astonishing progress, it's remarkably good and a tremendous credit to the city."

"Oh, I don't know. I guess I'm just in a state because—it isn't only the orchestra. I'm worried about Claudia."

"I thought she'd seemed much more like herself since coming back from New York."

"But she's so tense, Arthur. Can't you see it?"

"I think I see a little bit, but I don't know—"

"It's something to do with that Jim Prescott. I never have been very good at—being what I should be to her, and now that she's grown up, I feel so helpless."

"Now that she's grown up, she's responsible for herself," Arthur said, "and it seems to me she's as capable of that as we could ask."

"I wish you'd talk with her, Arthur."

"I'm not at all sure there's anything to talk about, and I don't see how I could bring the subject up, but if I get a chance, I'll try."

Rachel looked partly relieved. She had at least brought her worries out into the open, and that usually helped. Arthur wished he could do the same with his own; he was beginning to feel bottled and stoppered with his resentment and confusion over Lamson's Committee.

Walking to his lecture, Arthur found it hard to keep his mind on the topic he had to discuss. The impending Committee meeting gave a distasteful undertone, gray as the weather, to the whole day. The week had started with a January thaw; now the rotted snow had frozen to a granular crust, and the air was bitter again. It was a problem of endurance, Arthur told himself, endurance of the cutting edge of Lamson's offensiveness while the Committee ground through another session of stalemate. Unless, of course—and he could do it if he wanted to—unless Arthur took matters into his own hands, made a move of his own, tried to bring the ordeal to an end by forcing a decision at once. He had his move ready. It had taken him a long time, but he had thought out a line of action that he believed would be reasonable and effective. Perhaps this afternoon he would nerve himself to try a blow on his own behalf. He was letting Lamson exert altogether too much influence on his life. The thought of Lamson not only reminded him that he had slacked off as an experimenter, it kept him from pushing ahead with his book, and that was intolerable.

Lecture, mail, student conferences, lunch, graduate seminar; Arthur got through them all comfortably enough, but then the fatal hour of four o'clock unavoidably shook the antiquated Rowley bell tower. Arthur stepped through the Committee room door just as the secretary cleared his throat and began reading the minutes of the previous meeting, the session Arthur had cut. The secretary was one of the younger members of the Department, a Crocket man, Arthur halfheartedly suspected. He had a white neat chin and pink unscarred cheeks; he was clearheaded and crisp and serviceable. He looked up at one point, a brief glance over gold-rimmed bifocals, his only hint of departure from impersonal efficiency, to report that Professor Crocket, at the end of the meeting, held the Committee's terms of reference made it necessary to scrutinize all the offerings of the Department, without omission or favor, even such established and respected courses as Bi Sci 3, to take a leading example. Arthur's mind telescoped the ensuing phrases: new opportunities of the space age compelled review . . . priorities in a time of crisis . . . yesterday's innovations become today's vested interests. Within himself, Arthur felt the die cast, felt decision settle down on its base, or not so much decision as acceptance of the inevitable. For a moment his spirits rose with the elation of combat; then a revulsion of self-doubt and distaste set in.

Would there be any additions or corrections, the Chairman asked, to the minutes as read? Arthur assumed that none would be offered. He shifted his weight and was on the point of speaking when Lamson Crocket's voice forestalled him. Lamson moved the acceptance of the minutes but said he thought for natural reasons they failed to give full emphasis to one or two points in the report delivered by their colleague from the Physics Department at the meeting before the holidays. If the Committee would bear with him, he'd like to remind the members of some of the possibilities of cooperation in his proposed Project that the report had outlined.

Arthur settled back in his chair, hoping his attention would catch anything significant that Lamson might say, in the midst of his sharp-edged drone of recapitulation. He surveyed the room and the half-dozen faces in it besides his own. The secretary's head bent slightly forward from the straight incline of his back as his pale hand scribbled rapidly on his note pad. Pritchard sat across the table, fretfully absorbed in some internal problem. At the end the Chairman's white-thatched skull bulged at the temples, as if it had been molded around a tray set in above his ears. The room was rugless and bare. Its conference furniture presented nothing more enticing to view than glass ashtrays and varnished wood. Lamson was carrying on with his amplification of the report from Physics, exceeding any possible scope of the minutes, adding opinion and interpretation, adducing private conversations. Arthur's own voice surprised him when he intervened at what seemed a full stop in Lamson's run of words. "After all, Lamson, aren't we all familiar with the views of the physicists on your Project? Do we need to hear them again?"

Lamson looked startled and put out. The little green thread of bile quivered for an instant in the hollow of his cheek. "I suppose seniority confers the privilege of interrupting," he said.

Arthur felt himself flush. He mustn't lose control. "I'm sorry, Lamson," he said. "I didn't realize I was interrupting. I thought you'd finished a sentence."

"I'm developing a set of views."

"All right, I apologize," Arthur said, "though I rather

thought we were free to talk back and forth here without quite such formality. I do want to ask whether we need—"

"Mr. Chairman," Lamson said, "the report from Physics contained important points I was afraid might be overlooked, especially as my distinguished colleague was absent from the meeting when it was presented. I ask to be recognized."

The Chairman cleared his throat, wrinkled his white mustache, and looked flustered.

"I apologize for being absent too," Arthur said, "if it's necessary. But we have the report well covered in the minutes, and most of us know from personal talk what the Physics people think. This Committee has met almost every week since October without perceptibly—"

"If Professor Scheuer is determined to interrupt—"

"Oh, come off it, Lamson," Arthur said. "I think you're repeating what we all know, but if you judge otherwise, go ahead. Just say when you've finished, and then I want to say some things myself. I hope I haven't done more than my share of talking up to the moment."

"The Committee has appreciated your reticence," Lamson said.

Pritchard's voice intervened. "Arthur's right. In fact, Lamson, I think you're exaggerating the enthusiasm of the people in Physics."

"Would it help," the secretary asked, looking up smartly again over his bifocals, "if I simply amplified the minutes to include Professor Crocket's points? I could discuss them with him."

"Move they be approved as they stand," Pritchard said.

"I've already made a motion to that effect," Lamson reminded him. "I was trying to emphasize and supplement, but since I seem to have the weight of the Committee against me, I yield to Profess—to Arthur, who seems to feel what he wants to say is more important."

The Chairman pulled himself together enough to announce, "If I hear no objection, I will the rule the minutes stand approved." He looked expectantly at Arthur.

His occasion had struck, but Arthur found himself so exasperated and humiliated that he could hardly put his wits in order. He had got himself entangled in a ludicrous brawl over interruption and precedence, and he was smarting under the lash of Lamson's ill temper. He wanted to retaliate, but prolonging an undignified squabble would gain him nothing. He had to keep his gravity and his composure at all costs. "I'm sorry," he said, struggling with his voice. "I didn't mean to precipitate a—I'd be happy to let Lamson go on developing his views. I can wait."

"I'll reserve the right to come back to any point I think is being slighted," Lamson said.

"Very well, then, but I'm not going to talk about the report from Physics," Arthur said. "I want to raise the question of this Committee itself, whether it's getting anywhere." He wasn't expressing himself well; Lamson made the task inordinately difficult. He was having a hard time just forcing his mouth open and producing consecutive noises. Arthur leaned forward, braced his hands on the edge of the table, and tried again. "We started these sessions way back in October, as I think I remarked before, and frankly I can't see that we've made perceptible progress toward what I understand was our original object. I've come to think there's a reason for our— a reason for it. The reason is, we're attempting to deal with two things at once that ought to be kept separate. We began —this Committee was set up in the first place to review our offerings and see where we could strengthen them. What have we done? Practically nothing, as far as I can see, except consider Lamson's Project for a sort of crash program in space-age Biology. We all know Lamson's ideas by now. He has an ambitious plan, one that's urgent and necessary, if it's undertaken in the right way by the right people in the right place. Whether that place is Rowley I'm not at all sure. I point out, at least, that the Project far exceeds the resources of a single academic department. No matter where we cut or trimmed," Arthur said, trying to catch Lamson's eye directly, "we couldn't possibly start the kind of thing Lamson wants without additional personnel, money from government or foundation sources, money on a scale that doesn't exist around here. If we tried to do it by ourselves, those of us with different interests and I dare say different competence would simply be diverted into fields where we don't belong. Now what I want to propose—"

Arthur paused and surveyed the table. His audience was certainly expectant. He had to fight a bout of self-consciousness under the eyes directed on him.

"What I want to suggest is this. I propose this Committee split in two, or rather I'd like the Chairman to appoint two groups, one, headed by Lamson, to wait on our administration, consult with President Aiken about the possibilities of setting up the Project here. The other would take over the functions of this Committee and see whether we can improve our offerings as they stand."

Arthur stopped to estimate the effect he was making. He thought he detected a flicker of relief in the Chairman's tired patience. He thought Pritchard was passing a silent verdict of approval. The young secretary glanced briefly at Lamson, then twirled his momentarily idle pencil between thumb and finger, studying its eraser top with earnest concentration.

"Mr. Chairman," Lamson said, "what's being proposed is nothing less than the entire abdication—"

"Wait, Lamson," Arthur said. "It's my turn to object to interruption."

"You've said enough already to let us see—"

"If I'm not mistaken," Arthur said, riding down Lamson's voice with an effort, "there's been a latent issue among us here, one I judge was perhaps more than hinted at in the minutes of the last meeting. I can't help being aware that Bi Sci 3 enjoys a budget and staff most of our courses lack. Now, if the second committee or group I propose, the one to review offerings, feels that Bi Sci 3 has outlived its usefulness, ought to be superseded for any—" Arthur looked at Lamson and forced himself to pronounce the words he loathed. "Because it's one of those yesterday's innovations that become today's vested interests, then the committee in question ought to be free to take that view, and I'll be the last man to stand in the way. Only I shouldn't be a member of it, that's obvious. I can't and won't."

Arthur found himself breathing with difficulty. He wanted to say more. He wanted to look at the faces about him and make an appeal: Bi Sci 3 has served the Department and the subject well, you know it has. The Department originally asked me to undertake it; I didn't volunteer. Look at its enrollment over the years if you want to see whether it has worked well and meant something. Look at me and look at Lamson Crocket, and decide which one of us is really acting from motives of vested interest. The appeal wasn't one he could put into words. "All right, Lamson, I've finished," Arthur said.

Something of a hubbub followed his abrupt conclusion. The Chairman tried to bumble appreciation, confident that all present would want to join him, for Arthur's distinguished services. Pritchard sharply affirmed that Arthur's proposals made the only sense he'd heard since the Committee began sitting. Lamson Crocket struggled to gain recognition. "Mr. Chairman, Mr. Chairman!" Wearily the Chairman gave him a permissive eye.

"Mr. Chairman, I can't agree for a minute that the question of course offerings can be divorced from the Project. What's been suggested here is just a tactic of obstruction and delay, if it isn't a proposal that we simply abdicate our function. I want to elaborate on that, but first I have a point of personal privilege. I've been accused of making an insinuation about motives—vested interest. I make no insinuation about motives at all. We aren't called on to deal with motives, just with facts as we find them. Now, the fact is, Bi Sci 3 has a budget and patronage—I don't use the word invidiously, I'm just describing facts. It has resources, virtually under one man's control, that our other courses don't have. A committee to review offerings couldn't avoid taking a look at the facts. I'm glad to see Arthur agrees with me about that himself."

Lamson paused, and his face clenched for an instant as if he were cracking a nut in his teeth. Then he gave Arthur a smile that in another man might have been disarming. "Arthur, old boy, I should think you'd want to give up Bi Sci 3 yourself after all these years. Why don't you go back to experimenting and give us more work of the standard you did on the primordia of guinea pigs? Philosophy of evolution—you can say all they can take in about that in one lecture. Genetics—is that an undergraduate subject? You can't carry them through the ABC of it. Why don't you give up popular preaching and join the Biology Department again?"

Arthur could only stare back at Lamson's grin with a sense of unbelief and something like horror. What was in the man that he could try to eviscerate a fellow human being in the company of his associates? Vested interest, decline as an experimenter, popular preaching—Lamson had made the indictment complete. Why hadn't he gone right on, while he was about it, and found some way to allude to—the image of Rachel's face passed before Arthur's eye. Why had Lamson overlooked one vulnerable area? Just because he didn't know, Arthur told himself savagely; then he repressed the extravagant thought. Not even Lamson would do that, and he didn't need to; he'd done his work anyway.

Pritchard's voice addressed Lamson tartly. "You seem to forget one service Bi Sci 3 has performed. It sends up a surprising number of well-trained students to graduate school. I'm a specialist myself, and proud of it—a narrow one, as they say, with no hankering to be broader, but there's something about Arthur's approach—"

"I've no doubt Bi Sci 3 has performed services to the Department," Lamson said. "I don't consider we depend on a single course for qualified graduate students, though. Pride is out of my line. I suppose everyone has free choice of what he wants to be proud of."

By rallying to Arthur's support, Pritchard had only brought himself under the whip. He tightened his jaw and sat back in his chair, while Lamson went on at length to argue the inseparability of the Project from the whole biological curriculum.

"Would you really object," Pritchard asked, "if we made you head of a committee to wait on the President? It's going to come to that in the end."

"I would object," Lamson said. "It's a matter of timing. I don't want the administration in the picture till we have a united Department."

"How are you going to unite us," Pritchard demanded, "by character assassination?"

Lamson flushed at that and was silent in his turn.

"Mr. Chairman," Pritchard said, "I don't think the atmosphere is conducive to deliberation. I move we adjourn and put Arthur's proposals on the agenda for next time as the first order of business."

"I'll be compelled to oppose them," Lamson said.

"I've moved adjournment. I'm adjourning myself whether anyone else does or not," Pritchard announced. "Furthermore, I can't be here a week from today. I trust the Chairman will hold off for a fortnight." He got up, and the rest of the Committee accepted his example. To Arthur the relief was so welcome he could hardly believe it real. He made his way around the table as the Committee members converged on the door, and touched Pritchard's arm. "Thanks for the unavailing help," he said. "I take it kindly."

"We can go away and think about something clean for a while," Pritchard said.

"This business gets between me and my work," Arthur said.

"It will blow over. Things do."

Pritchard was in a hurry to get to his next occupation. Arthur followed him into the corridor, where he strode off rapidly, passing Lamson Crocket and the Committee secretary without speaking. Then, as the secretary took leave, Arthur found himself approaching Lamson, who was unlocking his office door. Lamson did not face about as Arthur drew up to him. If he meant to speak, he'd have to address Lamson's back. "Lamson," Arthur said, "what is it you have against me?"

Lamson turned and met his look. "Nothing at all."

Arthur surveyed him incredulously, and Lamson seemed to read his expression as calling for a further word. "I intend to fight until I get the Project set up," he said. "You'll come around, Arthur."

"It might be that some of us will fight back, at least to the extent of not allowing the whole Department to be swallowed up."

Lamson gave Arthur his closest view yet of the little green worm in the hollow of his cheek. "I'd advise you not to," he said.

It was extraordinary how paralyzing the man's effect could be. "Very well," Arthur said, "we'll all have to act as we think best."

Walking home after half an hour of fruitless effort to cope with a professional journal, Arthur felt his thoughts playing leap-frog over the same familiar field. How do you propose to unite us, by character assassination? He wished he could have said something as sharp as that himself. That shut Lamson up, for a minute or two at least. Popular preaching. Patronage. No imputation of motives. Well, as Pritchard said, things blow over. But not everything ought merely to blow over. Some things ought to be faced and resolved.

He had faced and resolved, hadn't he? Seized occasion, made his proposals, reasonable and fair ones, which as far as he could see might well go through. Yet the business wasn't that simple. Lamson had succeeded in tarring him, there was no escaping it. He might even have weakened his position. By showing awareness of a charge he detested, he'd done what he could to fix it in everyone's mind, and when a variety of minds get hold of a question, some take one view and some another.

What really would happen? He thought the Committee would agree to split. One group would wait on Aiken about the Project, the other would review course offerings. What would the second group do? They might drop a hint that Bi Sci 3 had outlived its value; that would be a dose he'd find it hard to swallow. They might just quietly sweep Lamson's charge under the rug, where it couldn't be aired again. If they did that, Arthur would be unable to complain and unable to live comfortably with himself. They might, of course, give Bi Sci 3 a resounding vote of confidence. He could take such a vote as a vindication; even so, he could never be sure they hadn't acted just to spare his feelings. Why couldn't he summon the courage to tell Rachel, or persuade himself, that they were going away for a year and not coming back?

Rachel was in the living room when Arthur let himself in. He saw that she was wearing one of the white blouses with long sleeves that she put on when she expected to play. Of course; he'd forgotten this was a rehearsal night. He ought to be glad she'd decided to keep faith with the orchestra, but he couldn't help a moment of irritation. She would go out and leave him alone with a set of emotions that had already depressed him enough. If he could only talk about them with someone who could see his position as he saw it—well, he must keep himself under control. He fended off her question about the day by saying it had been a Committee day but he had survived. Before long Claudia came in, and they sat down to dinner.

Claudia seemed more cheerful than she had been for weeks, Arthur thought. She spoke of her holiday ride to New York with Islay, filling in details she hadn't told them before, chiefly about Islay's editor, Mrs. Temple, and her house. For a time Arthur listened gratefully, with unforced interest. He glanced at Rachel, and she too seemed conscious of Claudia's improved spirits. Rachel talked more herself than she usually did, asking questions, trying to project herself into Claudia's life, it seemed, and make it her own. Then Arthur discovered that he was missing sentences, even failing to hear the voices on either side of him. He became aware of a silence, noticed that he was staring at the table surface, arrested fork in hand. When he raised his eyes, both Rachel and Claudia were looking at him intently. "Sorry," he said. "Did someone ask me something?"

"I just wondered whether anything was wrong," Rachel said. "You're so preoccupied tonight, Arthur."

"I guess I was woolgathering," he said, trying to laugh off his absence of mind. He brought his attention back to what they were talking about and kept it there successfully for a while. He didn't realize it had strayed again until Rachel said, "Arthur, what is it? You're miles away. Are you coming down with something?"

"I'm perfectly well," Arthur said. "I just have some busi-

224

ness on my mind that I can't seem to shake off. I'll tell you about it sometime, but let's not spoil dinner with it."

He managed to finish the meal without further lapses, at least none that excited comment. When Rachel put on her coat and scarf and picked up her viola case, he considered what he could do with himself for the evening. He could go up to his desk in the study and think about his book. No, he couldn't accomplish anything useful; the state of his mind would prevent that. Perhaps one or two of Malcolm's stories that he hadn't read yet would distract him for a few minutes. He went into the living room and established himself in his usual chair. He became conscious that Claudia had followed him. She sat down opposite, in Rachel's customary place, and he felt her looking at him as if with an invitation to talk. Here was his chance, obviously, to do as Rachel had asked, to find out whether anything was going on between her and Jim Prescott. How could he begin?

"Was the Committee particularly dreadful today?" Claudia asked.

She knew enough about him, he supposed, to account for his distraction at dinner as the effect of the Committee. "It's always an ordeal for me," he said. "As a matter of fact, it was even more of an ordeal this time. I dare say I make altogether too much of it."

"That odious Lamson Crocket," Claudia said. "You ought to squash him flat. Everyone is waiting for you to squash him."

"Why, what do you know about Lamson Crocket?" Arthur asked. "What do you mean, everyone is waiting—"

"Oh, it's common talk how he has his knives out for anyone who stands in his way, how he wants to take Bi Sci 3 away from you. Jim says—" Claudia paused and colored a little.

"Jim Prescott? What does he know about the Biology Department?"

"Jim tells me what he hears," Claudia said, "because he admires you enormously, and because—well, he knows I'm concerned. He doesn't go around gossiping generally."

"What does he hear? What's being said?" Arthur asked,

immediately regretting the question. Abhorrence rose in him for the scandal that must be going on, for his own invitation to his own niece to play informer.

"Mostly what I've told you already—that Lamson Crocket wants to get his Project so much he'll wreck the Department to do it, and he regards you as his chief obstacle, so he's trying to destroy your course. He's an odious little man, and you ought to step on him like a worm."

"Even granting that the epithet is a fair one," Arthur said, "I don't seem to have the talent for stepping on worms. It isn't an occupation that interests me. But I had no idea all this talk you speak of, no idea you knew—"

"It is going around," Claudia said. "Of course I don't hear it directly, only what Jim tells me."

"The less of it the better. I hope it's understood I have no part in it."

Claudia looked at him gravely. "Do we have shells, Uncle Arthur?" she asked.

"Shells? You mean—what do you mean?"

She laughed. "That was a funny question, right out of the blue, wasn't it? I was thinking of Malcolm. On the way to New York he accused you—all of us—of having shells. He was making fun of us as monsters of New England reserve. *He* certainly hasn't any! The things he told me about himself and his wife and his problems!"

Arthur was amused and felt his interest piqued. "I strike Malcolm as having a shell? I should have thought we were fairly uninhibited with each other. Some things, of course—"

"He tried to pump me about you," Claudia said. "Of course I wouldn't be pumped. I tried not to be."

"What was he trying to find out?"

"He thinks you're a man with a secret."

Arthur looked at her, startled. She surprised him by getting up from her chair, coming to him, kissing the top of his head. "You've never mentioned it, never told me about it, but I know. You and Rachel are wonderful people. You've been wonderful to me, always. You've had lots of courage, both of you."

Courage was not one of the virtues he thought he could claim in great measure; certainly, at the moment, he felt melted and almost dissolved by the weakness of being touched beyond his capacity to respond. "I hope you know what you've meant to us, Claudia," he succeeded in saying. "Our child—we think of you as our own."

She had gone back and sat down across from him again. Her eyes, frank, youthful, and direct, began to moisten. He fell back desperately on Lamson Crocket as a diversion. "I'm afraid it's true," he said, "that Lamson doesn't have much use for any of us, but what I can't see is why he should regard me as his chief obstacle."

"It's because you're respected and distinguished and fair-minded, and those are things that influence people."

"You make me blush," Arthur said. "But you know, the baffling thing—let's leave names out of it. There's a view that's been expressed, hinted at, that Bi Sci 3 has become a vested interest, and whether that's so or not—"

"But that's outrageous, Uncle Arthur, it's absurd."

"I'm glad you think so, but once a charge like that is made, it's awfully hard to answer. Any answer just confirms the charge." He looked at her hopefully to see whether his plight would be understood.

"But that's ridiculous! Everyone who knows you knows it would be impossible for you to—to play politics for the sake of position."

"All the same, it's odd how impossible it seems to deny it with any effect. Try denying it, and you merely strengthen the indictment."

"I think you're being oversensitive, Uncle Arthur, if you'll let me say so. All you need to do is tell that odious Lamson Crocket—tell him off, and everyone will be glad."

Arthur felt his spirits sink. Only a moment ago she had touched him deeply; they had seemed to go through an instant of intensest sympathy. But she wasn't going to *see* his dilemma as he saw it. Her failure was a bad omen. Would anyone ever perceive the irony of his position as he perceived it himself? Well, no doubt he was oversensitive; he ought to repress himself long enough to think of her, to carry out Rachel's commission. "Well," he said, "I'll have to work things out for myself as best I can. I'm glad you've spoken to me, Claudia, glad you've told me all you have. In return, could I ask you a question?"

"Of course, Uncle Arthur."

"Lately we've felt—Rachel has felt, especially—that you've been disturbed or unhappy about something. I don't want to pry—you can tell me to keep still if you like—but if there's anything we could help about—"

She looked at him without resentment, as far as he could see without any symptoms of anything seriously wrong. "Let's not talk about me," she said, "not now. There are things we all have to work out for ourselves, aren't there?"

∘ ∘ *8* ∘ ∘

What she had said to Arthur the other evening was true, Claudia thought, but it wasn't the whole truth. People had to work things out for themselves, and she among the rest, but she had worked out her problem as far as she alone was concerned. The difficulty now was to make Jim see that he didn't need to go on scrupulously treating her as just a friend.

She could laugh at the situation if it didn't strain her patience almost to the breaking point. Jim was taking her plea for time with dogged literalness. He was so fanatical about keeping to the plane of mere friendship that he almost fell below it. He took pains to encounter her two or three times a day in the museum, he helped her with unfamiliar work, he produced a quip or a turn of phrase, he was gone. On several evenings since the holidays he had taken her to dinner, followed by a movie or concert or a beer-and-talk session protected by the unwelcome safety of numbers. Each time he acted as though he were carrying out a carefully planned campaign. She could just see him jumping his hurdles and passing his fitness test.

228

She began to think she was contending with a real obstacle. Jim's resolutions were formidable; he'd made up his mind that he was on trial, and his mind was hard to unmake. He thought she lived in a little inviolable world of her own, a virginal Eden, and perhaps he'd been more right about that than she cared to admit. He'd stepped into that world and fouled it up, as he said, and so he'd taken it on himself to do penance, and God knows, now, when he'd stop or what would make him stop.

She couldn't blame him, in a way. She was surprised herself at how quickly her feelings had changed. As soon as she saw that she needed to grow, to understand herself and Jim and the world in general better than she had, she'd set to work on herself, and by the time she got home from Helena's on Christmas Eve she had just about come full circle. That was fairly prompt, wasn't it? She felt entitled to some self-congratulation. Of course it was her holiday visit to New York that she had to thank. Everything had played its part, the ride with Malcolm, the opportunity to meet Rosamund Temple, to watch her wonderful, fragile control, to feel her cool, tempered affection. She couldn't quite tell herself why Rosamund had been so important. Life could be lived in all sorts of ways. What happens matters less than what people are. Perhaps that was a way of putting it.

No doubt Helena had been the most directly persuasive force. She'd decided that she couldn't talk to Helena about Jim, and then she'd simply gone ahead and done it anyway. It started when she said that marriage seemed to agree with Helena, and Helena said that Claudia herself ought to have some plans of her own by now. Claudia said she wouldn't object to having plans, but they didn't always arrange themselves, did they? "Problems?" Helena asked. "Tell mother about them." The word 'mother' invited comment, and when they finished talking about when Helena's baby would arrive and what it would be named, Claudia found herself explaining about Jim. Not by name, of course, just the general posture of affairs. For a while afterward she was flabbergasted; she had no right to divulge Jim's confession, even anonymously, but she'd come out with it, and she felt better.

Helena took her misgivings lightly; in fact she pooh-poohed. It wasn't how you got into sex that mattered, Helena said; it was what you did with it as a mature person. Was Claudia sure the man in question had given up the older woman, actually made a final break? Then that settled the issue. Claudia tried to say she wasn't sure it settled the issue, but she knew she wasn't speaking with conviction. She just didn't want to give in too easily.

So she came home in an altered frame of mind, though now and then a qualm would return. If she and Jim were married, they would be completely intimate, physically intimate, and while that wasn't the whole of marriage, it was the foundation all the rest was built on. She'd got over worrying about Magda as a mental rival; would she have to worry about her as a physical rival? She'd have everything to learn, herself, from the start; when they got to that final point of intimacy, would she feel: This is how you used to do it with *her?* She decided that she'd just have to shut Magda completely out of her mind, be so wholly herself that Magda couldn't get in the way at all, on any plane. That would test her maturity, but she could meet the test. And she had to love Jim for what he was; she had to love real, fallible, good flesh and blood, not an ideal.

Now that she'd tried so hard to grow up to the challenge she faced, and succeeded, as she thought, it was ironic to be frustrated by Jim's obtuseness. He *was* a little obtuse. He could have risked, a dozen times, just saying: How about it? Am I back in grace? Do you feel any differently? He had the chances, but he didn't take them. She even tried to create them for him, by meeting his eyes and letting him read what must be written in hers, by standing close to him and allowing their shoulders to brush when he helped her check a reference or mount an exhibit. When her small ruses failed, she wondered whether he was cooling off, whether she had let him down so completely that he considered himself well out of a bad bargain. But no, she could see the tightening of his jaws, the whitening of the flesh around them sometimes when he controlled himself.

Well, she had laid down terms, or he thought she had. She could scarcely blame him if he accepted them, even with a conscientiousness that overshot the mark. She began to think the initiative must come from her. He was doing his part; how could he know that he was overdoing it unless she gave him an unmistakable clue? Next time he took her out she would say something. Jim, I haven't forgotten what you told me back in December. I know you were honest with me, and I know it took courage. I admit I was upset, but that's all over now. Magda is all over, isn't she? It's just something in your past, not something to be forgiven, but forgotten, so let's forget her, shall we?

Sitting in her upstairs room, clipping in a binder the pages of Jim's monograph that she had finally finished typing, Claudia felt an unbearable impatience. A gust of wind keened under the gable of the house, and she heard an eddy of snow whisk across the windowpane. Resentment rose in her against the long, tedious interval of the night ahead. How could she ever sleep? She wanted fiercely for the day to break. Tomorrow she would make an opportunity—tomorrow couldn't come too soon.

Down in the hall, cutting across her restlessness, the telephone rang. She heard Arthur's voice make polite responses, then call her name. She went to her door. "Yes, Uncle Arthur?"

"Jim Prescott wants to speak to you. Can you come down?"

"Thank you," she said. What could Jim want? Perhaps he had finished an evening's work and had a late movie in mind or the last hour of a talkfest in someone's apartment. If so, despite the weather—she imagined herself enclosed with him in his car, while the lines of flakes drove black into the headlights and piled up on sidewalks and lawns.

By the time she reached the telephone, Arthur had vanished into the living room. She picked up the receiver and said, "Jim?"

"I'm glad you're at home," Jim said. "Is the house full of guests or anything?"

"We're all by ourselves. Why?"

"Look, Claudia, I have some news. It's important—to me, anyway. I didn't want— This involves bringing up what I didn't mean to bring up again yet, but I've got to talk to you, if you'll let me come. I wouldn't ask except that time is on my neck, and I won't have a chance to explain tomorrow."

"You make it sound terribly urgent," Claudia said.

"It is, to me. Will it be all right if I come?"

"Of course, Jim. You aren't going to give me a hint?"

"I'd rather explain when I get there. Just as soon as I can hurdle the drifts in my jalopy."

She put down the telephone and stood thinking in a turmoil of alarm, hope, and uncertainty. What was his news? Bringing up what he hadn't intended—it must have something to do with Magda. Magda was sick, she'd been shut up in a mental hospital, Jim felt responsible, he was going to see her, going back to her. No, she was dead, she had committed suicide. Jim would think that made a difference.

Claudia tried to laugh down her melodramatic leap of imagination, but despite herself her body gave a shiver of presentiment. She would have him here with her, in the house; if he gave her a chance—but he'd sounded so urgent, so agitated, even.

She went into the living room, where Arthur and Rachel were sitting. "That was Jim Prescott," she said, and felt foolish. Of course it was; Arthur himself had told her so. "He says he has some very important news—he sounded urgent—and he wants to come over and tell me about it."

Arthur and Rachel were both looking at her intently. "He may have a time getting here," Arthur said. "The snow is piling up."

"Will it be all right, Uncle Arthur—oh, I'm sure he won't get stuck!—would you mind if I took him up to the study? That is, if he wants to talk to me alone."

"I was just going to bed," Rachel announced. "Arthur can have the study if he wants to read for a while."

"I do," Arthur said. "I'm not ready to turn in yet."

They both rose.

"Please, there's no earthly need for you to inconvenience yourselves," Claudia said. "I can just as well—"

"It won't inconvenience us in the least. You and Jim talk here," Arthur said.

She must be letting them see that she was disturbed, Claudia feared. The expression of anxiety came easily to Rachel's face, and it was there now as she went out with Arthur. When their steps had passed in opposite directions along the upstairs hall, Claudia went to her room to examine herself in the mirror and to pick up Jim's monograph. She would give it to him, and it would help break the first moments of tension.

The monograph served its purpose. Jim's eyes lit appreciatively. He said no opus of his had ever been dressed up in such an attractive and professional format. "I'll have to proofread it, though, and see how many times you've misspelled 'exogamy.'"

"Give me a dollar for every time," Claudia said, "and I still won't be able to buy a pack of cigarettes."

"Allow me," Jim said, holding out his own pack.

Was his hand a little unsteady? "Besides," Claudia said, "it isn't about exogamy. You don't use the word once."

Jim affected surprise. "You haven't just typed it, you've read it."

"That's one reason I was so slow getting it done. I think it's a fascinating piece of work, Jim. Of course I'm no judge, but it's so clear and interesting."

"Two qualities that won't recommend it to the professional journals," Jim said.

She motioned him to Arthur's chair and seated herself opposite in Rachel's. He was silent. His face fell into a brooding expression, its flat planes pale and introspective; he looked tired. Upstairs, only a few minutes ago, she had made a decision, chosen some words. Jim, I haven't forgotten what you told me— No, his urgency, his secrecy. She would have to wait until she had heard his news. When he remained silent, she asked, "Is there anything you'd like? A drink? Uncle Arthur wouldn't mind if I raided his liquor cabinet."

He looked at her, surprised, as if she'd confused a train of thought. "That wasn't on the agenda. I just meant—"

"Oh, Jim, you have a program again!"

233

"I'm sorry," he said. "I have, because I'm in a jam—a time jam. But I can pack all night, so if you want—"

"Pack?"

"I'll tell you about it. But if you'd like a drink, I'll keep you company."

"That makes me sound like a toper. I offered to keep you company."

"I'm in your hands," Jim said helplessly.

"You choose, Jim."

He'd uttered the word 'pack' and left it unexplained. He had a program, and it obsessed him so he could only shilly-shally about a little thing like a drink, while his whole face was tyrannically set on the news or decision or whatever it was he had come to tell her. He spoke abruptly. "Let's skip the drink, if you don't care. I've had a choice to make, a hard one. I try to stick to decisions once I've got there, but I don't always make them easily. Look, Claudia, I simply have to bring up something I know you don't want me to speak of yet, but it's—"

"How do you know, Jim?" she asked.

The interruption seemed only to throw him momentarily off the track. He looked puzzled, as though he hadn't properly heard her question. "Oh, I'm on pro," he said. "I realize that. I meant to stick to the rules, but something has come up—"

On pro! The ridiculous academic word! She felt an impulse to laugh hysterically. "Jim," she said, "if your news could wait long enough for me to explain—"

He made a prohibiting gesture. "You don't need to explain, Claudia. I'm not protesting, please understand that. I see I have pro coming to me all right. I've been trying to look at—well, at myself from your point of view, and I can see the landscape is messy. I think I can satisfy you about that, in time, but I can see other things too. I accomplished quite a lot all at once, didn't I? Muddied up my—let's say any favorable image you might have had of me, broke in on your world —your own life, the life you've had here with Arthur and Rachel, a good life, Claudia—broken in on all that with something you couldn't help seeing as pretty smirchy and questionable. I'm trying to do penance for what I put you through. I'm willing to serve out my pro, only—"

She drew a vigorous breath to speak, to try to begin setting him straight, but he wouldn't be interrupted.

"The only way I can work out my sentence, though, is by work. I've about run through what Rowley has to offer that I needed, and it's been valuable. So I've been shopping around —that's the advantage of the grant I'm living on. I can take the money wherever I want, if they'll take me in. I've scared up a chance to join one of the best departments in the country for the next term." He named it, and she knew enough to know he was right. "I'll be a research fellow, with some teaching on the side. As a professional opportunity, it's a beautiful piece of luck, and might lead to something permanent. So— that's why I felt I had to see you and say what I've said."

He looked at her hopefully, his face a plea for understanding. She said what on her side she obviously had to say. "It certainly is a wonderful opportunity, Jim. I'm glad for you. When—how soon—"

His eyes lit with gratitude that she found hatefully inappropriate. "I'll have to jump fast," he said. "Tonight I pack— clothes, notes, books. Tomorrow some last chores at the museum, then the noon plane. By sticking to an austerity program—that won't be hard for me—I'll be able to save some money and come East for a visit in June. Can I see you then, Claudia?"

"Why, Jim, of course you can!" She wanted desperately to go on, the more so now that he'd told her his news. Why should she hesitate? All this nonsense about doing penance— it was foolish and unnecessary, and she could just say so. And muddying up her image of him—perhaps he had, but that was temporary; she'd got over it quickly. Yet his penances and his pro and his sentence to serve—his own self-respect seemed to be bound up in them. It was all comically chivalrous and at the same time formidable. She'd have to think how to strike in so that the tremendous effort he'd made to behave as he thought she wanted wouldn't just look foolish. In her confusion, she played for time. "Tell me more about the job, Jim," she said, "what it will be like, what it might lead to."

"I'll keep the mails busy doing that when I get going on the spot," he said and suddenly got to his feet.

Was he really going to walk out without giving her a chance to speak? It was almost as though he didn't *want* to believe she might have changed. The moment of opportunity sailed by in hideous flight. Then, standing and facing her, he said, "Give me something to go on, Claudia."

She popped up, she didn't care with what unseemly haste. She must have jumped as if triggered, like a piece of bread from a toaster, done and ready on both sides. She was dizzy with reprieve. If he wouldn't let her do it in words, she had one final way to show him how mistaken he was, how foolishly, lovably in error. She could just let him crush her against his rib-cage, teach him by surrender what she couldn't by speech. Feeling her color mount, meeting the hunger of his look, she took a step forward. Then her eyes closed. The firm, long-fingered hands that should have dug into the small of her back and pulled her to him, length to length, rested lightly on her shoulders, and she felt his mouth on hers. He said hoarsely, "Thanks, Claudia. I can keep going on that." Then he was moving rapidly toward the hall, picking up his coat and scarf, pulling his hat-brim over his eyes, while she followed numbly, her legs like reeds of air, too dazed to seize control of a situation he had carried out according to program.

Even after the door closed behind him, she wanted to run out in pursuit, flounder down the snowy steps if she had to, so that she could catch his arm and pull him back and tell him what a blessed idiot he was. Actually she did swing open the panel and thrust out her head. Beyond the porch light swathes of flakes gyrated, hesitated, sank idly, gathered force again in a squall, and streamed slantwise across her view. He was a dim figure, blurred and bent against the wind, trudging toward his old car, climbing into it at a telescopic distance beyond the buried lawn. She shut the door and hurried to the living-room window, watching as the car began to buck through the un-plowed drifts, leaving its empty trail of tire tracks, vanishing soon through the lamplight at the corner. For a moment more she watched the black motes wavering and hurtling through the faint illumination of the globe on its solitary pike. Then she bent her head, resting her hair and her cheek against the glass, cold as a pane of ice between her and the night and the storm.

He was gone. She felt sick and empty and hurt, but she began to laugh convulsively in counterbalance to her disappointment. Could anyone imagine a more complete comedy of cross-purposes than the one they had just played out? But all wasn't over, all wasn't lost. In fact, she had the feeling that something had been gained. She felt Jim's lips on her mouth again. He would know that she was his; if he still tried to doubt, the doubt would break down. And June wasn't so far away. Only one academic term, and she'd survived a lot of them. She had a job, too; she could work, and he would write to her, and in a letter she might find a way to put the words he hadn't given her a chance to say directly.

To her surprise, she felt that now she could go up to bed and sleep. She went into the downstairs lavatory to see whether her face needed any repairs in case Uncle Arthur should speak to her as she passed the study door. He did, his voice apologetic. He had something she might like to see before he returned it to the library, a critical article about Malcolm Islay. Could it be the article Malcolm had talked about on the way to New York, she wondered, the article that really got under his skin? Arthur thought it well might be. Then, with obvious effort, he asked her, "What about Jim's dramatic news? Can it be told?"

She told him, and with a degree of composure she didn't expect to be capable of she added, "It's a wonderful professional opportunity. I'm glad for him." The act of saying the words gave them the force of truth. I *am* glad. I'm going to miss him like fury for a few months, but I *must* be glad, and I am.

Arthur was looking at her as though relieved that she had taken his question in good part. "He's coming back for a visit in June," Claudia said. She turned and went down the hall to her room. As she shut herself in, she heard Arthur getting up from his desk, going along the hall himself to Rachel's door, turning the knob, and entering. He would tell Rachel that it wasn't anything to worry about, that Jim had just gone off for the second term, that was all. Poor Arthur, poor Rachel! Other people had their troubles too.

∘ ∘ *9* ∘ ∘

Lamson Crocket, said the little green interoffice memo, had been called to Washington as a consultant on a board set up by the Undersecretary of Defense. He would be gone for at least a fortnight; would the Committee agree to suspend sessions until his return?

Agree? Arthur just escaped opening his mouth in audible gratitude as he wrote 'Heartily!' at the foot of the memo and routed it back to the Chairman. The next meeting, only two days off, wouldn't be held, and one for sure, two very likely, after that. His relief shamed him; and mightn't it be premature? At the next meeting his own proposals would have furnished the business. He should have insisted on holding it and pushing his case. That would have been the strong line; probably Lamson trusted him not to take the strong line.

He had an uneasy sense that he had allowed Lamson to reduce him to a state of paralysis. If he thought of Bi Sci 3, he thought of vested interest; if he thought of his intended book, he thought of popular preaching and wondered whether he wasn't indulging himself, after all, in a mere substitute for scientific work, a pretender's claim to creativity in a field he'd better leave to Malcolm Islay. Pritchard's words kept coming into his mind, but if Pritchard found reasons for going to Lapland they wouldn't make it appear that he was quitting under fire. Once Pritchard had said, with even greater bravado, 'The work I do, I'd do if I had a million dollars, and I'd do it if my family starved.' Well, Pritchard's family didn't pose the kind of issue Arthur faced; Pritchard didn't have Rachel to worry about.

Perhaps the wish was absurd, but he felt that if he could only get one other mind to see his predicament as he saw it himself it would cease to haunt him so obsessively. His brief attempt with Claudia had failed; he was grateful for her youthfully generous partisanship, but her understanding hadn't taken in what he was trying to convey. He could hardly expect better success with Rachel, but the impulse persisted in him to try. It was hard not to share with the wife of one's bosom a concern that occupied so much of one's mind, and it seemed as though he owed her some indication of what was going on in that aching area.

At home that evening, the atmosphere seemed propitious. Claudia had gone upstairs to write a letter; it was an open guess that she meant to answer one from Jim Prescott. Rachel's anxieties in that quarter seemed to be at least temporarily allayed, and, when she sat down with him in the living room, Arthur thought that he could at least lift the curtain on his internal scene and find out what effect a look behind it might bring.

"I had a great relief today," he said, "even if it's only temporary."

"I'm glad, Arthur. What was it?"

"I shouldn't feel as cheerful about it as I do, but one of our Committee members has been called to Washington, and we won't meet again till he comes back."

"I know you hate that Committee," Rachel said. "But I don't understand just what it is—you haven't hated other committees, even when you've said they were a bore."

"This one rubs me on a particularly tender point," Arthur said. "Let's not mention names, but one of the members— well, Lamson Crocket. I suppose we may as well mention names. At any rate, he's been accusing me—one of my courses—of being a vested interest. It's an awfully difficult charge to dispose of."

Rachel said fiercely, "But Arthur, that's outrageous! Vested interest! Why, anyone who knows you—" She came very close to duplicating Claudia's words.

"It's no good just denying an indictment like that," Arthur said. "It only plants the idea more firmly in people's minds. Don't you see? There isn't any effective answer."

"No, I don't see. All you have to do is tell him—tell him—"

"You know," Arthur said, "I thought you might be glad if I had to—if I gave up Bi Sci 3. That's what he's attacking, of course."

Rachel colored. "I may have said things—I'm sorry, Arthur, but if I have it's because—oh, you know why, and it doesn't matter how I—how I feel in comparison with your work. It *is* your work, and it's important, I know that. You can't give it up just because a wretched little man with an ax to grind— He's the one who wants to shoot us all off in rockets, isn't he?"

"Lamson is grinding an ax, or so I think," Arthur said, "but perhaps I'd be grinding an ax too, if I tried to hang on. That's an honor I'd prefer to leave to him."

"But that's absurd, Arthur. No one could seriously think, just because he makes an insulting accusation—"

"It's the difficulty of answering the accusation. Don't you see the position it puts me in?"

"I see that you have a distinguished position. You're one of the nationally known people at Rowley."

"I wasn't thinking of my position in general, but, as a matter of fact, what I do and how I stand at Rowley—well, Lamson is a very determined and very persistent—I was going to say antagonist."

"Surely the other people on the Committee, the people in the Department—they're your friends, they'll put a stop to it, or it will blow over."

"I don't want it just to blow over," Arthur said. "I don't want people just to vote Lamson down out of favor for me or dislike for him. I want to be vindicated by doing the right thing."

"What are you going to do, Arthur?"

She had asked the central question, and he wished he knew the answer. At least she was taking the conversation composedly. Her loyalty was aroused, but he couldn't see that her anxieties had been unduly touched. He would never have a better time to show her the full range of what he was thinking, if he could find the way. "Wouldn't you like to hear *The Magic Flute* in Salzburg sometime?" he asked.

She looked appropriately bewildered. "Of course, it would be wonderful, but I don't see what it has to do— Are you changing the subject, Arthur?"

"I thought we might go away for a year."

"A year? But would that really help? Wouldn't you find when we came back—"

"Where we came back to would depend."

He could see her begin to perceive the direction in which his mind was working. She looked at him gravely, her large eyes flushed with troubled light, her face appearing to narrow and stretch upward under the loose mass of her graying hair. "You don't mean—you don't think we may have to—to move away?"

"Not have to," Arthur said, "no. We might choose to."

"But that would be giving up! That would be letting— what's the wretched little man's name? I'm so angry at him I can't think of it."

"Lamson Crocket."

"That would be letting him have his way."

"In other words, the weak course," Arthur said. "I was wondering whether it wouldn't be the strong course."

"This house," Rachel said. "I'm so fond of it. We're so used to it. We've made our life here. It seems like deserting, forgetting—oh, everything we'd leave behind."

"Why cling to the painful that we couldn't help?"

"Oh, I don't know, Arthur. It's the way I feel. We'd be giving up so much. You would, too. You've made a position here that's brought you distinction everywhere."

"If that's true, I ought to be able to take my distinction with me."

"Of course I'd go with you, wherever you decided to go."

She whitened with such inner bleakness that Arthur quailed. "Let's not worry about it," he said. "I'm just turning over all possible contingencies, including very remote ones. I hesitated to bring the subject up, but if worst comes to worst—not that it will—you wouldn't want it to descend on you like a bolt from the blue. Let's forget the whole thing for a while. When Lamson gets back, the pattern may change."

Rachel's eyes watered suddenly. "So much trouble all at once," she said.

"You aren't thinking of Claudia?"

"I hope this Jim Prescott isn't just playing fast and loose with her. I hope she isn't making a mistake."

"He's taken what seems to be a fine professional opportunity," Arthur said, "and already, in hardly more than ten days, Claudia has had three letters from him."

"It isn't only Claudia. I was thinking of Abby and Kent. What *is* going to happen to us all?"

Arthur thought that he could afford to smile. "I think you can at least strike Kent off your list of worries. He's solidly entrenched in a big corporation, well toward the top. A change of presidents isn't going to hurt him. He may come out better for it."

"Abby is worried, I know she is."

"I suppose we all exaggerate our worries. I suppose I exaggerate mine," Arthur said.

Perhaps it had been a mistake to open his mind to her. He had feared all along arousing anxieties that might turn out to be needless. A way of alleviating her tension occurred to him. "Speaking of Kent and Abby," he said, "we haven't seen them since the holidays. Why don't we ask them to dinner? It would give Claudia something to do besides going to her job and waiting for letters from Jim Prescott."

Rachel welcomed the suggestion, and Arthur went to the telephone. "It's our turn to play host," Abby's voice insisted, and she asked whether Claudia wouldn't like to bring a friend. Who was that young man—Abby couldn't remember his name, but he was an anthropologist, wasn't he? Arthur explained why the young man wasn't available. If it didn't seem too much like naming guests for Abby's party, what about Malcolm Islay? Claudia would get on well with him as a partner. Abby's voice was cool, Arthur thought, but she agreed to consult Kent. She came back with the word that Kent would be delighted if Mr. Islay wanted to come. It seemed an accident had occurred while Kent was taking him on a tour of the plant, and while they could laugh about it afterward, someone might have been hurt. Kent could make amends for the narrow escape. Would Tuesday do, the first Tuesday in February? Rachel had no rehearsal on Tuesday; it would suit perfectly.

When Abby admitted them and led them to the study, Arthur was surprised by the lines of fatigue and strain that showed in Kent's face. He sat with his leg propped on its familiar cushion, his eyes looking dulled and shadowed, his clear skin drawn tight over the cleanly squared frame of his face. He livened almost at once as he got up to greet Claudia, and Arthur thought that in fact she appeared almost to her best advantage.

Kent supplied drinks, and they fitted themselves around the big inlaid table that crowded the study, momentarily expecting Islay's ring at the doorbell. He still hadn't come when Kent proposed a second drink. They all elected to wait except Kent, who said he could play host better if properly lubricated. Arthur recalled Rachel's dismay—could it have been as long ago as October?—when Malcolm had come early and she had to entertain him alone. Evidently he didn't mean to repeat the same error.

The door bell rang at last, and Abby said, "You can do the honors this time, Cappie." Kent got up, and they heard his voice in the hall urging, "Come in, come in, let me take your coat." Then he went on: "We've all parked our shooting irons at the door." He must be pointing to the mahogany gun-rack where he kept his shotguns, his rifle, his fishing rods for salmon and trout. "If you have a six-shooter on your hip, just add it to the rest of the armory. We'll promise not to put on any gunplay tonight."

Kent was grinning behind Malcolm's shoulder as they came into the study; he looked a little chagrined also. "We put Mr. Islay through a disgraceful risk to life and limb at the plant a while ago," he said, "absolutely disgraceful. The only excuse

I can make is that it was done by an advertising man. If he'd been an engineer, he'd have been fired on the spot." Kent wagged his head sadly. "He didn't know it was loaded!"

"You mean someone fired off a gun?" Claudia asked. "What on earth happened?"

Kent furnished Islay with a drink and told the story, adding further apologies.

"It all happened so fast I didn't know what was going on," Malcolm said.

"You remind me of the time we really had an accident. Chemical explosion. Some union brother who was paid expensive wages to watch a set of dials let his mind wander, and half a wall blew out, not to mention some high-priced equipment. We were lucky we didn't have to scrape up four or five corpses in slop pails. As it was, a couple of technicians were hospitalized for acid burns, and the company had to pay for some cosmetic surgery. About a week later an old mop-handler we had to clean sinks and floors in the lab caught me as he was lugging out a bucket of waste and fixed me at a forty-five-degree angle with his one good eye. 'Mr. Warner,' he says, 'about that accident. While it was goin on things happened so fast I didn't know what to make of it, but now I've had a chance to think, I've decided it mighta been serious.' "

Malcolm grinned, apparently unembarrassed by any analogy between himself and the mop-handler.

"I told that to Stocky," Kent said, "but he didn't think it was funny. Pounded the desk and tried to take it out on me. Accidents can't happen, company liability, bad for profits, who's responsible, you are, Warner!"

"I wanted to meet your Stocky," Malcolm said. "I've never met a captain of industry, and after your descriptions, I was hoping to see him at first hand."

Kent's face clouded. The lines of fatigue and strain returned. When he made no answer, Abby spoke for him. "I'm afraid it's too late for that now. Mr. Stockwell's days as a captain of industry are over."

"What happened?" Malcolm asked.

"Funny thing," Kent said. "Business is one crisis after another, but that afternoon, when they paged me and I turned you over to Shepherdson, I went to Stocky's office and found we had an outsized, gilt-edge, eighteen-carat crisis on our hands. Old Stocky was looking for a scapegoat. He tried out two or three candidates, including me, and then he got hold of the real culprit. I thought he was going to blow his circuits for good then and there, but by a miracle he got himself calmed down. I figured if he could survive that, he'd last another ten years. Instead, he goes home that night, where he can command all the comforts, and has a stroke, a major one. I guess the worst of it is it didn't finish him off. They say he'll make a partial recovery, but he'll be helpless for quite a while."

"I hope you aren't counting his daughter among his comforts," Abby said. "I wish you could have seen her when I called the other day. I took some flowers, but I had to force them into her hands. Even then she looked as though she wanted to throw them back in my face."

"She's a wild gal," Kent said. "She used to come to the office when she wanted money, wearing shorts and those open-front sandals, with blood-colored polish on her toenails. The talk at the plant is that she came home that night and announced she was moving in while she waited for her third divorce. I don't know whether that had anything to do with Stocky's crack-up or not."

"I shouldn't be in the least surprised," Abby said.

"Poor old Stocky. No more work for him," Kent said, speaking with what seemed to Arthur an odd mixture of envy and regret. "He raised this outfit from a piddling little company with a capital of a couple of million to one of the leaders in the field, and now he's out, just like that, a few years before they would have made him Chairman of the Board and he could have loafed out his time enjoying himself."

"It's just as well you can't retire and begin loafing," Abby said. "You'd go native."

"I'd go so fast you couldn't see me for dust, but I've got to stick with the worries and the uncertainties unless I blow a gasket myself or get run over by a taxi."

245

"You must have plenty of worries and problems, I know," Arthur said, "but surely you can't have any real uncertainty. I should think you'd welcome a new president, a new kind of management, from the way you've described life under the one you've had."

"Uncertainty," Kent said. "Insecurity. There are times when I envy you, Arthur. Academic life! A professor has tenure. Nothing to do but contemplate his navel and pass the results on to eager youth."

Arthur laughed. "Do you really believe academic life is as simple as that," he asked, "or as secure? It isn't."

Kent's face looked skeptical. To Arthur's astonishment, Rachel colored and straightened in her chair. She said, "Arthur's not just talking. There's a nasty little man on the faculty who's been making his life miserable." She turned to Malcolm. "I don't know whether you've met him—"

Arthur heard her with something approaching horror as well as surprise. "Please," he said. "Let's have no names. In fact, let's not go into the subject."

"Oh, Arthur, I don't care who knows what we think of him—what *I* think of him. His name is Lamson Crocket, and he's—"

"A scientist," Arthur said, "and competent enough in his field to be called to Washington to consult on space biology. Please, again—"

Once aroused, the partisanship of his womenfolk was hard to suppress. This time it was Claudia who spoke. "He's attacking Uncle Arthur's evolution and genetics course because—"

"I'd really be grateful if we could drop this whole business," Arthur pleaded.

"Tell us about it," Abby said. "It's all in the family. We'll include Mr. Islay in the family too."

"I'm just temporary here," Malcolm said. "I don't know anything about campus politics, but I must say I'm surprised, Arthur. That course—"

"It's a complicated story, and no doubt has two sides, at least," Arthur said. "I'd really prefer not to go into it at all, but suppose—" His mind searched desperately for a way to cut the talk short, or at worst to keep it safely general. "Suppose you were accused of maintaining a vested interest. How would you defend yourself?"

Kent grinned. "Step on it if it's the other guy's, make the most of it if it's your own. We have a case of the other guy's right now in our New Jersey plant. Tail trying to wag the dog. The local manager has been padding his staff, building an empire, till he thinks he can get anything he wants out of the main show. We'll have to cut the tail down to size and teach it to keep its place, which is small and situated at the rear end."

"I don't believe you spend your own time trying to build a personal empire," Arthur said. "You make the decisions you think are right for the interests of the firm."

"I don't think you need to defend yourself," Rachel said. "You only need to speak up and everyone who knows you—"

"I see Arthur's point, though," Malcolm said. "Some charges are hard, almost impossible, to meet. Deny them, and you only confirm your opponent. There's an idea there, if it hasn't already been done by Maupassant. You know that story of his, 'A Piece of String.' "

"Thanks, Malcolm." From an unexpected quarter, from the very man who maintained that human beings are fundamentally unable to communicate with one another, Arthur had received the understanding he sought. He must twit Malcolm about that sometime; it set a limit to the view that all men are islands. He wasn't sure, though, that the understanding would have the therapeutic effect he had obscurely anticipated. Perhaps it only confirmed the reality, the helplessness of his position. Arthur felt himself sinking into a private mood of depression. He hardly heard the talk going on around him until Abby rose and announced that if dinner were kept waiting any longer it wouldn't be fit to eat.

At the table he had the sense that he was the most silent member of the company and tried in vain to make himself more voluble. Fortunately the others all seemed able to keep their voices going cheerfully enough. He was glad, somewhat faintly and distantly glad, to see Malcolm drawing Rachel out. Malcolm made a favorable comment on the Civic Orchestra, and Rachel said she hoped she was helping with it a little, but she really preferred small chamber groups who got together just for the music and cared nothing about an audience. In fact the most congenial people to play with were those who simply came at an agreed hour to someone's house, hardly said more than hello, put their scores on their stands, played them, and went home. Malcolm laughed and said something about the New England temperament. Rachel began to defend it with a degree of warmth.

When they finished the brandy that Kent offered and went back to the study, Claudia asked him about the progress of his building program.

"Absolutely dead, my dear. The only thing we're putting up is a storage shed for maintenance. Four posts and a corrugated roof. A doghouse would be more of a challenge."

Kent smiled, but it was a down-in-the-mouth performance. Arthur felt the danger that the evening would bog down in personal frustrations and discouragements; it wasn't serving its purpose of diversion at all. He tried to think of a lead that would get them out of the trough, but while his mind was still searching, Abby made an effort of her own. "I'm glad to see you looking so well, Claudia dear," she said. "You're the only person here who doesn't seem to have a care in the world."

Claudia flushed, and her face immediately contradicted the assertion. "I'm glad you think so, Aunt Abby," she said.

Her effort to control herself was so obvious that Abby looked taken aback. She turned to Malcolm for a second effort. "Are you writing another book, Mr. Islay? Do you want to tell us about it, or will you keep us waiting till it comes out?"

"If I were writing," Malcolm said glumly, "I wouldn't be here, at Rowley, I mean. I'd be writing."

Abby was forced into silence, and Malcolm asked, "How about you, Arthur? How's your book coming along? Have you discovered God among the enzymes yet?"

"No," Arthur said, "and that isn't exactly my purpose. I

248

can't say I've got much of anywhere. Things haven't conspired to help, this term."

"What a waste of creative talents!" Abby said. "Cappie can't build his buildings, and you writers can't write your books. I think it's time you stopped crying in your beer and found something cheerful to talk about."

Arthur laughed. Abby spoke as hostess, and she spoke in character; in both capacities, she put them to the proper rebuke. At the same time, she touched off a susceptible trigger in his mind, and, without stopping to consider, he said, "Wasting our talents! Whether we are or not, it's a painful state to *feel* that way. Waste is the deadly foe of the creative, the sense that one is somehow being kept from using whatever talent he may have, yet, as a biologist sees it, waste is necessary to creation. As a biologist, I have to approve of waste."

"How can you say that?" Abby demanded.

The sharpness, the incredulity of her challenge brought Arthur up short. For more than one reason he didn't want to embark on a lecture popularizing his professional subject. He glanced at Rachel and said, "I assume that what we value about man is his creative talents—for tools, buildings, ideas, cultures, books, music, science—"

"I wonder sometimes," Abby said, "whether it's good to make just anything that can be made, regardless."

"In these days, it's entirely right to wonder," Arthur said, "but we don't want man to be *un*creative, do we? His talent for creation may get him into serious, even fatal trouble, but what would he be without it? Just on a practical level, it's going to be create or die, even more in the future than the past —create scientifically, technologically, socially, every other way. One of our creations may destroy us, but the kind of creativity that led to it is the only thing that can save us."

Abby was obviously unsatisfied, but she was reduced to the defensive. "Does everyone have to be creative?" she asked. "Isn't anything to be said for those of us who don't have the talent?"

"Of course there is," Arthur assured her.

He tried to think of a more adequate tribute, but Malcolm

spared him the necessity. "While you're talking about the creative, man the maker," he said, "don't forget man the unmaker. No one ever created anything yet that someone else wasn't waiting to belittle, destroy, steal, pervert, or undo. That's one way the creative gets wasted. But I'm still waiting to find out why waste is *necessary* to creation. You haven't told us that yet."

Arthur began to be seriously embarrassed by the theme he himself had tossed on the carpet. Malcolm wasn't going to let him escape. "Just remind yourself of what you know about the history of evolution," Arthur said, "from the molecular soup in which the first living forms originated to man as he is now. Remember the billions of years of slow variation and selection, remember the species that got left by the way because they couldn't adapt to environmental changes, remember the countless individuals in every species who had no chance of surviving until they could reproduce. Remember the impartiality of nature, if I may call it that—equally happy with predator and prey, parasite and host, the virus that to its victim is a disease, perhaps a crippling or a lethal one, but in itself is just another form of molecular organization and activity. Waste on a geologic scale, over a time span to which history is a tick on a watch. Without all this interaction and experimentation, wasteful as it is by any human measure, we wouldn't be here. The kind of consciousness that can entertain the idea of the creative would never have come into existence."

"But if all this waste and dog-eat-dog is biologically necessary," Malcolm said, "how are we going to get rid of wars and poverty and disease and the other inconveniences you're so noble about in your books?"

Arthur smiled. Here was his chance to give the conversation a turn toward the cheerful, as Abby had suggested. "You're going to push my inconsistencies to the wall, aren't you, Malcolm? If I am inconsistent! War, poverty, disease—of course, we're an animal species, like the others, and we have to live competitively in and on the environment where we find ourselves. But what about cultural waste? Is there a distinction? We have unavoidable biological waste, and we have avoidable cultural waste. Within the limits of cultural control, we have the resources to reduce poverty and disease, not to the vanishing point, certainly, but a point that would do us a lot more credit as a species than we can claim now. All-out war, on the world scale, with the possibilities that means now—if we don't reach some of these goals, we can't blame biological necessity. We can blame our failure to take advantage of our own evolution—anyone can who is left to blame anything."

"Jim Prescott would have liked to hear that, Uncle Arthur," Claudia said and colored a little.

"So we're headed for an earthly paradise. Is that the end of the road for creativity?" Malcolm asked. "That's the trouble with an Eden or a heaven. The devil has to get in to start the creative process going again."

"I didn't promise an earthly paradise," Arthur protested. "We'll always have plenty of waste to keep us inventive."

"But how? What kind?"

His reprieve had been short. Arthur felt himself being driven into the corner he dreaded. Genetic waste: the perpetual shuffling of the chance deck that keeps the human generations moving onward. You couldn't win on every deal; to get the good hands, you had to accept the bad. Arthur glanced at Rachel again. He decided to spare her even at the cost of hanging silent, but Abby came to his rescue. "I couldn't stand the thought of all the waste you talk about," she said, "if I didn't think there was a purpose in it somewhere, a Creator who meant something by his creation."

Malcolm shot her a sardonic look. "Teleology! The higher purpose in things," he said. "That's what you'd like to believe in, Arthur, only as a scientist you don't have the stomach to come out for it. That's your way to get God into the last chapter, though. I can see your book now, a bestseller, on the jacket a microscope overlaying a chaste Colonial steeple!"

Arthur was glad to laugh. "If I ever do write my book," he said, "some chapter will have to be the last, but I won't write it for the sake of putting God in—or, for that matter, keeping him out. You remember the man—a scientist, I think —who said atheism was a leap of faith too great for him to make? Of course I'd like to believe in a higher purpose—who wouldn't?—if I could understand it and it turned out to be one I could accept without loss of respect for myself and my fellow creatures. It isn't only as a scientist that I find such a purpose hard to define; it's as a human being, if you'll grant me that status. But isn't it odd that chemistry, enzymes and nucleic acids, can have some of the effects it does? What a piece of work is a man—a molecular system, but one capable of inner division and conflict, capable of ethical suffering, if I may put it that way. It used to be wonderful enough that he could remember the past and foresee the future, but now of course he builds machines that can virtually do that and plays checkers against them. One doesn't suppose the machine suffers personal anguish, though. That still seems to be a human prerogative. If molecules can produce that result, not enough has been said about molecules. I want to say some things about the higher faculties of molecules, some of the things I don't think have been articulated yet. It's probably a task where fools rush in, but how many precautions is it worth taking just for the sake of never being a fool?"

No one answered Arthur's question. Malcolm's face contorted like a particolored sponge being squeezed this way and that, but he remained silent. So did all the others in the room. Anxious as Arthur had become for a change of topic, the stillness made him uncomfortable. "I guess when I started," he said, "I hoped it would be a small consolation, when anyone is feeling frustrated, to remember that waste is the condition by which we come to have any creative talents at all."

Small consolation, in all truth. The theme went on reverberating in Arthur's mind while the silence prolonged itself, and the sum of human waste, dismal and oppressive, began to loom like an overhanging mountain. He was glad when Kent cleared his throat, grinned, and was reminded of a wheeze that might have something to do with the subject. It concerned an old gentleman whose capacity as a drinker was questioned. He surveyed his challenger contemptuously and said, "I spill more whisky before breakfast than you can hold in a day." And speaking of liquor, who would like a highball? Kent received orders, including requests for plain ice-water. When he came back from the pantry with a tray, Claudia asked him for one of his stories of engineering school.

"You must have heard them all before, my dear," Kent said, "but if you insist, what can I do?"

Arthur settled back in relief. He began to catch familiar phrases and to be amused by them. The story might be indexed: Education, Old-fashioned Attitude Toward. Faculty and students composed two unequal teams; an unending contest went on between them, a war in which all tactics were fair on the side of the students, and victory was the only measure of ethics. The faculty represented authority, whimsical and above law. Justice couldn't be expected of them. Faced with injustice, the student responded with diplomacy, conspiracy, chicanery, and sometimes came out on top. No one could guess from listening to Kent the pride he took in his technical education.

From engineering school, Kent worked easily back to high school in Amity. He wasn't in the habit of stinting his own glass when he dispensed hospitality, and the warmth of the whisky he poured himself began to be reflected in gesture and phrase. His eye lightened, his face cheered. He went from yarn to yarn, and a forgotten America grew about his listeners, the idyllic topography of a small town that melted into farm and river and pond and stands of pine and long-vanished chestnut, country where to man and boy, almost as in a state of nature, fish and game still offered themselves, where with a minimum of interference from the state the angler could take his string of trout or the hunter his fox or his partridge in season.

It was amusing to watch the faces in the room succumb to Kent's nostalgia. Arthur felt his own succumbing, despite his detachment from Amity. With Kent they hauled in a midnight catch of hornpout and went through the agony of skinning them. With him they contested desperate football games against the bigger mill town lower on the river, games in which no atrocity seemed to be barred, though the gladiators miraculously survived to play again. With him they celebrated the Fourth of July before explosives were forbidden, before safety rendered freedom dull. They accompanied the team of three boys and a horse who at four in the morning on the anniversary of independence hauled a cannon from corner to corner, murdering the sleep of patriots. At each strategic station, the first boy beat a stirring drum roll, the second rounded it off with a vigorous bugle call, while the third, at the delicately synchronized moment, touched a match to the charge in the cannon. Kent reckoned the broken windows in fabulous numbers.

Going farther afield, he recreated the November deer-hunting expeditions he was allowed to join at the august age of fifteen. He recalled the time when the wagon which hauled supplies to a deserted lumber camp lurched over a stump concealed in an early winter drift, tipping over the kerosene can and saturating a week's provision of potatoes and bread and bacon. He recalled the time when his old man, respected for his patience, forbearance, and godliness, came on their black and white hound, both its legs shot off, bleeding to death in the snow. That was one occasion when a legendary temper, kept under rigid control, burst its bounds. His old man, Kent said, seeing the dog with its red stumps of legs, looked for human tracks and, finding them, set off in pursuit, firing his rifle after them in the woods. It was lucky he didn't catch up with the culprit.

A vein of Tom Sawyer ran through Kent's yarns, a convention of mischief speciously deplored but actually expected of boys with any spirit. How beautiful the arc of a rising snowball, aimed at the back of a deacon of the First Congregational Church as he plodded unwittingly along the winter sidewalk! How majestic to watch as the trajectory of the missile, packed tight enough to keep its coherence in flight, but loose enough to spread and engulf its target on impact, brought the two moving bodies closer and closer to intersection! Then, from the shelter of a board fence, how marrow-tickling to observe the smack of the projectile on the deacon's neck, just above his coat-collar! How worthy of the talents of Malcolm Islay himself to describe the deacon digging the snow out of his neck, spluttering and threatening hellfire on the invisible miscreant behind the fence!

"It's a wonder your Grandmother Randall ever kept you from a life of crime," Abby said. "Think what she had to put up with, bringing up five sons of her own and then taking you on when your mother died."

"Five stalwart sons, that was the count," Kent said. "I can see how she brought them up. She was always in there pitching. Her arm never gave out and her control never failed. What I can't see is how she ever had them in the first place while maintaining an attitude of dignified disapproval of sex."

"People had a sense of duty in her generation," Abby said.

"I should think they could have achieved the same end just by pleasure," Kent said.

"I think it's time you elevated the conversation," Abby protested, but her plea was purely formal. Everyone's face, Arthur thought, reflected the common debt to Kent. Kent was a social being, naturally genial. He liked good spirits, he liked to promote them, and he had the gift. It might well be counted among the human gifts of superior value.

A movement of rising and saying good night began. Arthur waited for Rachel and Claudia and Malcolm to precede him into the hall. As they made slow work of it, exchanging words with Abby in the doorway, he turned back for a final acknowledgment to Kent and was startled to catch him looking abstractedly down at the photograph of Randy on the big center table. It was too easy to forget that no one was exempt from the deprivation of waste. Kent looked up, shamefaced, as Arthur's voice halted on a syllable. "Good party," Kent said. "Back to the grind tomorrow."

When Arthur reached the porch and the door closed behind him, Claudia said, "Malcolm wants to drive me home, and I didn't bring my key. If you and Rachel both brought yours, may I borrow one? We might stop for a cup of coffee somewhere."

Arthur looked at Rachel and saw that she was taken aback. "I'm afraid I didn't bring my key," she said. "I depended on Arthur."

"I'll leave the door on the latch," Arthur said. "I don't think we'll have any marauders, and you can lock it when you come home."

He must have shared with Rachel the impulse that held them motionless on the porch for an instant, watching while Claudia and Malcolm started down the steps toward the Mercedes.

∘ ∘ *10* ∘ ∘

"I should think some engineer could design an electric percolator that would work," Abby said plaintively.

"The engineer does his job. What he can't control is how the public will use it."

"All you have to do is plug the cord into the pot. I'm not mechanical, but I can do that much."

"There's a switch in the wall above the stove," Kent said. "Are you sure it says 'on,' not 'off'?"

"I never turn it off. I just unplug— All right, Cappie, I'll check."

Abby got up resignedly from the breakfast table and vanished into the kitchen. Kent looked out through the north window opposite his chair. Its large panes presented a uniformity of brownish fog that rose from rotting snow, from the colorless sop of turf patches around the rock outcroppings in the lawn. Heads of trees, gables of houses farther up the rising street showed muffled and indistinct through the blurred atmosphere. A persistent rain fell in vertical drops through the fog. If the weather held for another day, March would come in mildly, and if folklore ran true after that, a backlash of winter would follow and the world would have to live through a string of raw weeks worse than the forthright cold and snow of an unusually severe season. It would be longer than that, it would be months before the ice went out of the northern lakes and a man could troll for salmon.

From the kitchen Abby's voice said, "You win, Cappie. My face is red. Coffee in a few minutes now."

Perhaps this year, Kent thought, he and Abby could take his ten days' fishing vacation with Pete Blanchard and Mabel. Pete was a good man with fishing tackle, and the four of them played congenially competitive bridge of an evening. Besides, relations between Fullchem and Blanchard Tool and Die had gathered dust since Stocky had been forced to quit; it would do no harm to take them down from the shelf and polish them up a little.

This was one of the mornings when the *Times* failed to reach the doorstep; probably the plane that ferried the City Edition to Fullington had been grounded. Kent didn't want to begin thinking of the office before he had to; he was glad when Abby came back to keep him company while the coffee percolated.

"You won't forget to mail the check to the children today, will you?" she said. "They have to make the down payment on the house by the end of the week, and they'll want to bank the money."

"Thousands of smackers for do-good and uplift," Kent said.

"Now Cappie, it's for Ruth. You know they can't live decently without more space, and besides, you're unfair to Brainerd. He's making a name for himself with his articles, and he's doing better financially."

"Fifty dollars a month better."

"Money isn't everything. Recognition is something too."

Money and recognition. A man wanted both, Kent thought, feeling undefinably discouraged. Recognition came with money, though it might not be based on anything else; probably a man could attain recognition of a sort without any cash reward. The goals a man struggled for could turn elusive and raise doubts. Youthful anticipation never foresees the knocks and surprises. He himself had started out vaguely expecting recognition based on solid achievement and commensurably

257

rewarded with money. Compared with some of his engineer-ing-school contemporaries, he'd come near enough to the mark for envy on both counts; compared with others, he'd fallen a long way short of the target. A man could be haunted by the sense that he might have chosen other goals or found room for additional ones within his main choice.

Well, he didn't object to sending Ruth whatever she needed; he was glad he had it to send. He just couldn't help thinking of the retirement that closed in on him year by year, couldn't help thinking that in effect he financed Brainerd and his way of life as well as Ruth, not to mention the left-over product of Brainerd's first marriage. If he was forced into doing good despite himself, he hoped he'd get credit for it somewhere!

"I won't forget the check. I have a memo in my pocket," Kent said. He couldn't resist adding, "I'd bribe them with another thousand if they'd promise some family planning."

"That's more like it. That's my Cappie. You'd like a dozen grandchildren if you didn't have to see the girls till they were in sweaters and skirts and the boys till they could throw a football."

"That reminds me of a wheeze. You know the word the medical students use when they start doing obstetrics? They call it quarterbacking."

"I'm not that much of a football fan," Abby said. "I don't get it."

"You haven't watched a T-formation quarterback. He squats over the line, gets the ball from between the center's legs, and hands it to an accomplice."

"Really, Cappie, at the breakfast table! You're certainly getting a start on the day's work."

"All I need to be really ready is a cup of coffee."

Abby got up and went to the kitchen again. The coffee had finished percolating; she brought in two scalding-hot cups.

By the time he backed the car from the garage and began his drive to the plant, the rain had let up and the fog seemed to be shredding out. Hollows appeared in it here and there, like cavities in a soft cheese. Before the day was far advanced, the sun would burn it off entirely. He thought of fishing again, but it was far too soon to imagine spring, to imagine trailing a lure through the deep water off spruce-capped ledge, where it might tickle the nose of a waiting salmon. A lot of business would have to go over the dam before he could indulge to any purpose in reveries of that sort.

As he approached the plant, he felt himself drawn nearer mentally as well as physically to its problems. To all of them, Fred Abramson seemed the only key in sight, but Fred was a key who didn't as yet spring the lock. Fred's virtues had appeared reassuring when it first looked as though he would take over from Stocky. The sense of confidence in him, as far as Kent could make out, was general. He had good humor, steady judgment, thoroughness in weighing all the factors in a decision, including the personal equation. If he didn't exactly make status as a friend, if he didn't win a place as a regular member of a Sunday golf foursome, if no one had taken much from him or lost much to him at poker, he certainly didn't make enemies. The prevailing attitude held that Fred was a good guy; you could trust him, in or out of business. Yet in Kent's mind, misgivings were beginning to take root. Fred was marking time, going slowly until he was confirmed in office by the Directors; that was the obviously sensible course, but Fred was holding too much in abeyance, postponing decisions he might perfectly well have taken without so much caution and delay. Kent hoped the Directors would make their minds up before much longer; rumors of division within the board were beginning to seep round, though Fred, who was in the best position to know, kept a tight mouth about it.

The state of suspension would have been endurable in itself; what troubled Kent was that some elusive deterioration of morale, some subtle decline of efficiency, seemed to be going on in the plant. No specific failure had occurred that he could track to its root and hold someone accountable for. The shift in the feel of things was so nebulous that he could hardly be sure of its actuality, yet Shepherdson had noticed it, too, though he was no more able than Kent himself to make out a definite case. "What's going on around here, anyway?" was the most tangible question he could ask. Production schedules fell off in this or that department by percentages too inconsiderable to provide a basis for action. Equipment seemed to break down with just slightly greater frequency, and the maintenance force took longer to get it back in order than Kent and Shep thought it should, though the crew always came up with plausible defenses. The Grievance Committee ate up more hours of the week, and their grounds of complaint struck Kent as more than commonly frivolous. It was hard to believe that the loss of Stocky's unpredictable hand on the control knobs could account for a subtle slackening in the operation of the whole plant, but Kent began to wonder whether it mightn't be true. He and Shep and everyone else were sticking to their desks longer and keeping at the job harder, yet the results didn't seem to be the same as when Stocky, remote in his top-floor room in the old office building, stormed and fumed and hunted for scapegoats.

It occurred to Kent, as he parked his car and walked toward the main door, that perhaps he was sticking *too* close to his desk. Perhaps the way to find out what was going on around the plant was to nose into it a bit, show up at unexpected places at unexpected times, get a direct whiff of the morale. What did he want to do, turn himself into a Denis Prouty? That would be the end of the road for fair. It was odd about Denis. One thing Fred Abramson had accomplished that Kent wouldn't have believed possible was to detach Denis from even a nominal connection with engineering and give him a commission to improve the company house organ. Relieved of responsibility for any decision of the slightest importance, Denis flowered, in a small way and at exorbitant cost. He revealed unexpected talent as a gossip artist, collecting odd personal stories around the plant, running them as chit-chat stories, with photographs, in the *Fullchem Bulletin*. He even exploited his own dyspepsia by alluding to it humorously in print.

Well, if Denis had used his restless visits here and there as a way of avoiding his job, Kent could do some dropping in of his own for the real purpose of keeping a finger on the pulse.

He turned away from the main door that led to the elevators; he'd walk around to the back of the building, look in at the maintenance department on the ground floor, ask the chief in person what he'd done about the packing machine that had developed a vibration and interrupted the flow of facial cream. It would mean walking up three flights to his office, but if he could still use his football leg to play a salmon while standing in a boat, he could use it for climbing stairs.

As Kent circled the office building, he surveyed what he could see of the plant. The only sign of life visible at the moment came from a delivery truck backing toward the cafeteria. In the parking lot, cars by hundreds stood neatly aligned, vacant and immobile. A wedge of sunlight illumined for a moment, through the ragged fog, their beetle-shell tops, lacquered in red and blue, green and oyster white. No outward symptom of anything amiss, but for an instant the solid bricks of the older buildings, the new lab he had designed himself, its planes of glass intersected by colored verticals and horizontals in sheer lines, looked curiously insubstantial, as though the physical embodiment of Fullchem were a trick done with mirrors. Kent turned his eyes to the delivery truck again. A corrugated door in the wall of the cafeteria rolled up, the truck driver climbed out and let down the tailgate in alignment with the receiving platform. Two men in windbreakers appeared in the rectangle of the door and began handling the cartons of canned tomatoes, the crates of lettuce, the stacks of sandwich bread. Their small display of action, relaxed, habitual, reasonably efficient if hardly zealous, restored the sense of reality that for a moment Kent had almost lost.

Walking on, Kent turned the rear corner of the building into the dirt road along the fence by the railroad tracks. He found himself within a few steps of three figures lounging against the rail of a bulkhead that led down to the basement under the maintenance office. They were pulling on cigarettes and must have been kidding or conducting a bull session. It ceased abruptly as Kent bore down on them. One was Mike Hoague; a second Kent thought he had noticed working on minor maintenance jobs. The third was an unfamiliar gangling youth, a newcomer evidently, with a concave chest and a sepulchrally hanging jaw. They drew up straight, their faces taking on a wary and noncommittal look.

"Good morning, Mike," Kent said.

"Good morning, Mr. Warner." Mike's eye slid as he answered. He took a final drag at his half-consumed cigarette, dropped it in the mud, and ground it under his boot.

"How are Mrs. Hoague and your daughter? Are you keeping them in hand?"

Mike's face went glum. It said plainly that, as far as his womenfolk were concerned, he was currently in the doghouse. He finally confessed that the missis and daughter were the same as ever.

"Does Katy still like her job in accounting?" Kent asked.

Mike achieved a rueful grin. "She's that proud of herself for her pay envelope, you can't live in the house with her," he said.

Kent would have waited and given him a chance to introduce his mates, but Mike was in an uncommunicative mood. He spoke to his flankers over his shoulder, without looking at them. "Well, boys, let's go. The boss may have a job on the work sheet by now." He started down the steps of the bulkhead. The others ground out their cigarette butts and followed him, their shoulders descending in jerks.

Kent continued picking his way along the muddy road. Had Mike's eye looked a little bleared? Was he getting a trifle paunchy? Too bad if Mike had got tired of paying off his loan from the company fund and gone back to the money sharks in order to keep himself in beer and racing tips. Mike was too good a man to lose if a little pressure could keep him on the straight and narrow. If his women couldn't keep him under control—well, they probably pulled the reins too tight; that might be the root of the trouble.

Just as Kent was about to climb the steps to the rear entrance, his eye was caught by a glint of copper in the brown tangle of withered burrs and draggled vine stalks at the base of the fence along the railroad. Looking more closely, he made out a scattering of beer cans, old and new, half submerged in the weedy litter. They might have been tossed over the fence from the tracks, but the marshaling yards hardly seemed a convivial locality. If they had been thrown at an angle from the vicinity of the bulkhead, they would have every chance of escaping notice from the high first-floor windows of the office building.

Finishing his climb, Kent pushed through the rear door and made his way to the maintenance department. The chief looked up from his desk, surprised, as Kent entered. Denis Prouty came into Kent's mind again, and the thought of Denis didn't improve his temper. He asked what had been done about the packing machine. The chief shuffled papers on his desk uncertainly and said no order had come through about that.

"I thought Mr. Shepherdson phoned you yesterday afternoon," Kent said.

"He did call up, say something about it, but we had these other rush jobs, and we usually get a form—"

"Treat it as an emergency," Kent said. "You had an order from Mr. Shepherdson yesterday. You have an order from me now. You can get a piece of paper for your records any time."

The chief's eyes went blank, empty of everything except wounded astonishment. Kent regretted his sharpness. It didn't help morale to rile a usually dependable man; he was glad to see the chief recover. "I'll put a crew on it right away. I wrote myself a memo—don't know why I didn't see it first thing—" He got up from his desk and went to his secretary's door. "Get hold of Mike Hoague, will you, and tell him, whatever he's doing, drop it and come up here."

Kent welcomed an opportunity for a change of tone. "Speaking of Mike, sometime when you don't have him on a job, ask him whether he knows where those beer cans are coming from I noticed along the fence."

"Beer cans?" The chief looked bewildered. "Someone must be chucking them over from the tracks."

"I don't think it would do any harm to ask Mike," Kent said. "As a matter of fact, I saw Mike and two of his buddies doing nothing in a big way out there by the bulkhead as I came along just now. It mightn't be a bad idea to find out whether he's keeping up with his payments on the company loan he took out."

"Now that you speak of it, I have noticed lately—" The zest of righteousness lit the chief's eye. "Leave him to me, Mr. Warner. I'll ask him. I'll do some maintenance work on him. Trust me."

Kent was half an hour behind schedule when he sat down to the stack of mail, reports, and memos that Isabel had sorted and laid on his desk. He didn't count the time lost. His first personal inspection confirmed him in the feeling that he could well do more of it. He would request appointments, for one thing, with all production heads, diplomatically offering the help of the engineering department in any problems they might have. Everyone needed jacking up from time to time. If the lines of force weren't radiating with their former energy from Stocky's office, someone else would have to make them buzz from a different center. Fred Abramson wasn't making his hand felt yet. Reading one of Isabel's memos, Kent learned that Fred wanted to see him after he'd got through his mail. The message was very different from the kind of peremptory summons he would have received from Stocky. Well, there was always the chance Fred had heard the big news or reached a couple of decisions on his own that would start the wheels really purring again.

Stocky's office had undergone little physical change. The same immaculate and aggressive desk faced the door, the same conference table, surrounded by chairs upholstered in leather, flanked the desk to the right. Fred had introduced a larger and heavier chair at the desk to accommodate his bulk, but the chief visible difference in the room was the absence of Stocky's portrait from the paneling behind the executive seat. Its lower edge had left a faint, ineradicable line where it had hung for years in contact with the wood. Kent found it hard to keep from looking up and filling in the vacant area with its wonted occupant. When he did, the missing portrait sprang to life. For an instant, Stocky was there again in emphatic oil, the pale wedge of face, the turned-down mouth, the electric charge of the vividly blue eyes. Perhaps Fred's portrait would hang someday in the same spot. In the meanwhile, he had propped at the left side of the desk a photograph, framed in unassuming blue, in which he appeared as paterfamilias, with a comfortably blowsy Frau of a wife and with children that to Kent's eye looked unathletically fleshy but healthy as well-nourished cattle.

So little had changed outwardly that the total sense of change seemed disproportionate. Stocky's room had lost Stocky, that was the size of it; lost a source of energy, as if a powerful generator had been removed from its site, while its empty housing remained unaltered. In this empty housing, Fred appeared perfectly at ease. He didn't put on side, he didn't dramatize himself, he spoke in the same deliberate, unperturbed tones. He didn't even seem to lack force, though the current that ran out over the transmission lines was obviously depleted at the points of reception. From time to time, when he was summoned to the top-floor office and looked across the desk at Fred's large features, his nose only slightly prominent, his lips a little more than commonly full and moist, his eyes big and deep under heavy black brows, his expression even-tempered and cordial, Kent couldn't help wondering why he himself shouldn't be sitting in Stocky's chair in place of Fred. He would try to suppress the thought as soon as he felt it coming, but if he had been recognized at his full value— what was it that kept demonstrated ability from getting to the top? Was it the technical education without which you weren't qualified to do certain things at all, but which didn't necessarily open the doors to management in a broad sense? He could forget more than Fred would ever know about all phases of operation in the plant and still keep them running with superior efficiency. He could judge the practicability of a new product and set up the processes for turning it out at a lower cost and in a shorter time than almost any competitor in the business. He thought he had as much business and financial sense as Fred, and if he were sitting in the driver's seat he'd get the buggy rolling at highway speed and not wait for the road to come to him. Advertising, sales, promotion— that was the sphere where he was weak, and that was the way Fred had come up, and Stocky before him. Well, in a profit economy, in a private-enterprise system, that seemed to be the way things worked. It rankled him sometimes, but, if he believed in the system, who was he to complain?

Fred was dictating when Kent knocked on his door, but he told Kent to sit down, finished his letter with placid promptness, and dismissed his secretary. "How do things look, Cap?" he asked. "Caught any fish lately?"

"I admit my mind has been running that way," Kent said, "but the lid is still on the lake."

"Going to the usual place this spring?"

"I'd like to think of it when the ice breaks up."

"I'd like to take my family for the usual two weeks in Florida, but they'll have to do without me this year. I can't even think about it."

"Tough," Kent said, "but we need a hand on the controls."

"Yes," Fred said. "Well, there's one consolation. In Florida, nowadays, you never meet anyone but Jews."

He ought to be used to that kind of thing from Fred, Kent told himself, but he wasn't. The only way he knew to cope with it was to come back fast without thinking too hard. "I guess if you wanted to meet a Christian," he said, "you'd have to look in a museum."

Fred laughed and evidently decided that pleasantries had received their due. "Well, Cap, you keep an eye on our production reports," he said. "You must have noticed we're failing to meet schedules here and there. The gap isn't enough to worry about yet, but I don't like the trend. The worst of it is, sales are turning up after the final quarter of last year. It looks as though we'd make a record gross if we keep producing. Have you any ideas about what's going on?"

"That's the question Shep and I have been asking ourselves," Kent said, "and we haven't found anything we can pin down." He couldn't express his real suspicion, and besides, Fred was counteracting it, providing welcome evidence of alertness.

"We'll have to find out where the soft spots are. We can't let things go on in the same direction." Fred looked at Kent steadily through his black eyes, big as walnuts. "Sure, we're in a transition period. I know that. I may have to make some changes eventually. But meanwhile, I've got to work with what I have, and on this problem that's you, Cap. What do you propose to do?"

Kent felt a stir of zest. This was talk he understood, a graduated blend of trust and challenge. "The only way to look into things is on the spot," he said. "I'd about decided, if it's all right with you, I'd make appointments with production heads all around the board—get out of my hole and go see them where they live. You know, offer the services of the engineering department. If there's a problem, we'd be glad to help study it and iron it out."

"Good," Fred said. "Go right ahead on your own schedule. Take in the departments that are holding up as well as those that have fallen off. We're doing this for the future. No, wait. Maybe there's a better way to start. I don't want to send out a pep-sheet or a letter over my signature. That stuff just gets chucked into the waste basket. But how would it be if I called a meeting of all production heads here in my office? I could underline the facts, say I'd asked you to consult, give you some backing. I could mention sales and prospects for the year, too—hold the carrot in front of the donkey's nose. What do you think?"

"Fine, if you want to do it. A meeting would save me a lot of spadework trying to see that no one thought his toes were being stepped on."

"Then I'll set one up right away and send you a memo." Fred's heavy shoulders bent forward toward the desk; his large hand wrote words of reminder on a pad. "Bring Shep along if you think it would be helpful," he added, looking up. His eyes continued thoughtfully to meet Kent's. "I dare say you think I've been slow about a lot of things, Cap," he said. "You'd like to get to work on your building program, and you'd like to see Shep's position clarified, whether we let him take over New Jersey or whether we keep him here. Well, I don't like to keep anyone in suspense. I've had enough of it myself. But I've had to gauge the thinking of the Directors, and they haven't been too fast about showing their hand. As for the building program—" Fred paused, his full lips briefly smiling. "I have a notion the Directors may decide a lot of the plant is obsolescent, if not obsolete. If they do, there won't be any lack of construction going on."

Despite the fact that Fred hadn't committed himself to anything, had merely thrown out uncertain hints, Kent couldn't keep his mind from forming a vast, vague prospect: a lot of plant to rebuild, designs to work out, orders to place for steel, for concrete, for glass, for brick. Perhaps the wheels were really going to purr.

"As for Shep," Fred went on in his level, unexcited voice, "I think the Directors may have plans for New Jersey that will affect more futures than his. You can count on keeping him here until we all know where we stand."

Kent suffered a revulsion of feeling. For some reason, the words about New Jersey struck him as ominous. In Kent's view, the branch plant was tail of the dog, strictly subordinate, a profitable enterprise but a dispensable one. Did the Directors have expansion in mind? If so, for what product, to what end? Fred was holding back more than he was revealing.

"So keep your chin up, Cap," Fred was saying. "I think the whole position will clarify any time now." He spoke with a confidence that could only mean he was sure of his own part in the whole position. "As soon as a couple of pieces shake down in place, the future outlook—"

He was interrupted by a knock at the door. It opened, and the lank, sallow face of Denis Prouty appeared, his brass-colored lock of hair falling toward his left eye as he bent forward to look in. "I don't want to interrupt if there's anything hot on the fire," Denis said, "but if you have a minute—"

Fred Abramson looked at his watch. "Come in, Denis, if you can make it short. I have something coming up soon, but Cap and I were about done."

Kent got up as Denis advanced into the room holding in one hand what appeared to be a layout for the *Fullchem Bul-*

letin, but Denis said, "Morning, Cap. If you aren't in the middle of a scrimmage, you might like to look at this too. The more heads the better, right?"

"Okay, Denis, if I can help," Kent said.

Their eyes met, and Denis's cheerful self-satisfaction clouded over briefly. Kent was surprised at Denis's freedom from resentment. After all, he had displaced and unintentionally exposed the man. He could only figure that Denis was too happy with his layouts and his feature stories to bother with the grudge he might have nourished. Now and then Denis looked conscious that he *ought* to feel differently, but he was never much of a hand at living up to his obligations.

"I've got a spread here for a story about the lab," Denis said, laying the pasted columns and half-tones, mounted on their cardboard slab, under Fred's eye on the desk. "I think it's good, if I say so myself, but there's one thing I thought I ought to ask about before we go ahead and use it."

Kent looked over Denis's shoulder. Technicians in white, holding beakers, peering into microscopes, calibrating instruments, all grouped in front of equipment that would be standard in any lab. A portrait photograph of the Lab Director, with a thumbnail biography and a quote in italics underneath. The sort of spread every chemical company put in its quarterly report to shareholders to inspire confidence and awe. What was Denis worried about? He was probably looking for congratulations.

"Nice job, Denis," Fred Abramson said. "What's your problem?"

"Well, I got thinking. There's a lot of detail in those photographs," Denis said proudly. "That's one of the things I've been trying to do—raise the standard of illustration. This time I wondered whether we'd done it too well. Is there anything there the competition might get hold of? I thought I ought to get some opinions, though they don't seem worried at the lab."

Fred's face, as it seemed to Kent, gave an unusual twitch of impatience, but he said nothing. He simply looked toward Kent, waiting for him to speak.

"You're as safe as a church, Denis," Kent said. "The detail is good, but it won't give anything away."

"Then you think we can go ahead with it?" Denis asked, seeking Fred's ultimate confirmation. "I just wanted to make sure we wouldn't—"

Denis broke off at an interrupting sound. The door of the secretary's office, at the far end of the room beyond the conference table, opened suddenly, and Fred's new secretary, her face in a state of agitation, came forward a step or two. "They're here," she said, out of breath with nervousness. "Mr. Stockwell and his son. I couldn't make him wait. He said he knew his way around here and didn't need any help."

She looked apprehensively toward the door into the corridor. Fred got up from his chair with an abruptness that shouldered Denis aside. "They're early," he said, fumbling at his sleeve to expose his watch. "Ten minutes. Denis, you'd better—"

Before he could recommend a course to Denis, the knob turned on the corridor door. The door swung back, and Kent felt as though he were looking hypnotically through six pairs of eyes, instead of merely his own two, at the pair of figures in the entrance.

They stood there like a travesty of widely separated stages in the life of a single man. The same blue eyes peered out of each face, the faces made the same triangle of flat planes on either side of a sharp nose and mouth, the mouths turned down in the same pinched circumflex that forced the lower lip into a protruding arc. Young Herman was Old Stocky before the brunt of experience hit him; Old Stocky was a defaced survival of his own career. A seam, stiff as a crust of toasted bread, knotted his right cheek. His right arm appeared shrunken, and he had just flexibility enough in the fingers to manage a cane, while his elbow accepted additional support from Young Herman. For a long instant the pair stood frozen in a tableau; then they began moving painfully forward.

Kent was conscious of the secretary retreating to her office. His vision was momentarily blocked by Fred Abramson's big back and shoulders as Fred rounded his desk and advanced to greet his visitors. A faint irrelevant sound caught Kent's ear. Looking toward its source, he perceived Denis bracing himself against the desk, his arm vibrating like a plucked rubber band.

"Well, Stocky," Fred said, his voice booming out with unnecessary volume, "we didn't expect you quite so soon. Come in, make yourself at home." Fred held out his hand, and Stocky touched it with the two fingers that would not quite bend around the handle of his cane. "Fred," he succeeded in saying, with only slightly blurred articulation, his blue eyes lifting toward Fred's face with somewhat beclouded familiarity. Kent stepped forward to offer his own greeting. It seemed best not to go through the pretense of shaking hands. "Stocky," Kent said, "delighted to see you back at the old stand." He thought he could read in Stocky's expression a glint of approval and pleasure at the unexpected meeting. "Cap," Stocky said. "Haven't seen you too long. Still carrying the ball?" He would have answered, but Stocky's eyes concentrated as if by an effort at once intense and automatic. He moved forward toward the desk, still supported by Young Herman, until his dogged, singleminded purpose brought him abreast of Denis Prouty. Kent waited helplessly for what might follow. The possibilities of the encounter must have weighed on Fred and on Denis himself too, but as Stocky paused, turning his head and slowly coming to the point of recognition, he only surveyed the figure before him as though once, in another world, another time, Denis might have suggested to him an emotion he could no longer feel.

Denis appeared to swim in a solution of bewilderment and relief. "Stocky," he said, "glad to see you getting around this way. Glad to have you back. We've been missing you around the place."

"How's the wife, Denis?" Stocky asked. "She finish her—her—can't think what they call it."

"Analysis?" Denis offered eagerly. "I don't believe she ever will as long as I can keep on paying for it. She lives on it. She—"

Denis would have gone on about his domestic situation, but

Fred cut him short. "Stocky wanted to go through his personal files and see whether he can find something he might have left behind when he—took them home. The cabinet is just the way you left it, Stocky, so if you want to look—"

Reminded of his purpose, Stocky uttered the syllable "Key," fumbling at his coat pocket.

"Here it is, Dad," Young Herman said. "I took it for you. Remember?"

He extended a small key between thumb and finger, and with his help Stocky made his way to the cabinet behind the desk. With his left hand he succeeded in pulling open for himself one of the solid doors underneath the glass-fronted upper partitions, revealing a metal strong box on a shelf beyond. He was unequal to withdrawing the box, and still more to inserting the key in its lock. Herman carried the box to Fred's desk, placed it on the blotter, and turned the key. Kent felt a sense of indecent exposure as Stocky lifted the lid and began fumbling inside, but he couldn't turn his eyes away. With his left hand Stocky tried to select and remove a small bundle of papers and clippings bound in a rubber band. Herman tried to help, but Stocky brushed his hand away. "Do it myself," he said.

"He wants to be independent," Herman said with a mixture of apology and pride.

The words released Kent's captive vision. They seemed to release Fred and Denis as well. A common turning of heads brought a concentration of attention to bear on Young Herman. "He's getting better all the time," the boy went on. "The doctor says if he takes care of himself he'll get back most of what he's lost."

Kent looked at him with new interest. It struck him that the outlines of a man were beginning to take shape in Young Herman, perhaps not much of a man, but more than might have been expected. Kent glanced at Stocky, who had extracted his package from the strong box and was holding it down on the desk with the cane and claws of his right hand, more by weight than grip, while he tried with his other hand to slip off the elastic. Kent turned back to Herman. "I can see you're a big help," he said. "What are you doing yourself these days?"

"I've got a job," Herman said, "working on the paper. I'm going into journalism as a career."

"Fine," Kent said. "How do you like it? Have you got a by-line already?"

"I'm not a reporter yet," Herman said, looking a little downcast at the admission. "I mostly lug copy from the city desk to the press room, stuff like that. But I know the town better than most of the guys who've been on beats around here all their lives. I've given them some hot leads already, if they could spot a good story when they saw one."

The knowledge of Fullington that Herman had acquired, the exploits by which he got it, might have made a story in themselves, Kent thought; but if his acquaintance with the city gave him a foothold in journalism and helped him make a niche for himself, that was net human gain. "Are you studying days and working nights?" Kent asked.

"I'm through with the college stuff," Herman said. "I quit before they chucked me out. I'm going to stick to the newspaper game. If I need a degree later, I'll get it. I'll go to extension school if I have to." He paused, then added impulsively, "I'm getting married pretty soon," and immediately flushed.

"Congratulations," Kent said. "Who's the happy girl? Someone you met at Rowley?"

"I'm through with that stuff too. It's a girl, her father works for the paper, in the ad department."

Young Herman might have described his marital plans in greater detail, but he was interrupted by a sound of parting fiber and hoarsely drawn breath. Kent's head jerked toward the desk in time to see a litter of clippings, letters, and photographs cascading to the floor. "God damn 'lastic broke on me," Stocky said. He began to sway and crumple. His right leg was collapsing; his cane and half paralyzed hand made an inadequate supplement as he tried to maintain his balance by leaning on the desk.

Kent felt Fred Abramson's big figure bump him as they

sprang forward to help. Denis was trying to climb his back from the rear. A mob seemed to converge on Stocky all at once. It was Young Herman who moved in with efficient support, propping Stocky upright and holding him while he steadied himself. "Hang on, Dad, and I'll pick up for you," Herman said. He bent to retrieve the scattered mementos and assembled them in a coherent pile on Fred's blotter.

"Why don't you take the whole box along, Stocky?" Fred suggested. "That is, if it's not too much for Herman to handle. Can you manage it, Herman?"

"That's what I wanted to do in the first place," Herman said. "I was going to come down and get whatever he'd left, but he got it into his head he'd have to do it himself. He's stubborn sometimes."

He replaced the papers in the box, closed and locked the lid, and braced the considerable burden on his right hip, offering his left arm to Stocky. "Are you ready to go, Dad?" he asked.

Stocky appeared confused, as if he had unfinished business on his mind which he was trying to dredge up to the surface. He hesitated, but then the signal to action took effect. He accepted Herman's arm, and the two of them began a slow flanking movement around the desk and toward the corridor. Herman had to lean perceptibly toward his father, balancing the weight of the strong box. As they progressed laboriously toward the doorway, they almost composed a single broken figure, like two sides of a cracked arch.

They had taken only a few steps when Stocky paused and turned part way about. "Glad to see you boys again," he said. "Good team. Keep it up." His blue eyes came to rest on Denis, and it seemed to occur to him that Denis in his later phase had hardly qualified as a member of an effective team. "No hard feelings, Denis," he said. "All over now." His eyes continued their circuit until they reached Kent. "Counted a lot on you, Cap," Stocky said. "Never let us down."

"Thanks, Stocky," Kent said. He would have tried to say more, but for one thing it was hard to speak at all, and for another Stocky was turning toward Fred Abramson, looking as though he had brought his unfinished business to mind. "Sorry you didn't make it, Fred. Thought you would. Told them myself you were the man, but they called it the other way. Chairman of the Board came to see me last night, told me a lot of plans. Confidential. Hope they know what they're doing."

Kent felt the muscles of his neck rigidify as if with cramp. He was half aware that he was willing the paralysis on himself to keep from looking at Fred's face. The Chairman of the Board—of course, if he was in town, he'd call on Stocky, keep him posted about the company. He'd have no inkling that Stocky would come to claim his strong box and in doing it would spill the news to Fred. He'd expect to tell Fred privately. No doubt that was his mission. Kent had no time for the sickness of sympathy in his stomach. Stocky was speaking again. His lower lip pouted forward as he said, "Dynamic lea'ship, that's what they're looking for. That's what this company needs. That's what I tried to give it—dynamic lea'ship." His voice almost succeeded in bleating on the first syllable of the word he could not fully pronounce. His eyes lifted, searching the space above the desk where his portrait had hung. They dulled as he missed himself. He turned about, resuming his march with Young Herman toward the door. They were on the point of reaching it when a kind of yelp came from Denis Prouty. "I'll see you to the elevator, Stocky," Denis cried and flung himself after the retreating figures.

Kent wanted to follow, but his legs were sharing the calcification of his neck, and the abjectness of Denis's flight offended him. He forced himself to turn and face Fred Abramson. For an instant he had the blank sense that he had looked in the wrong place, or that Fred had somehow performed on himself a conjuror's vanishing trick. He looked where he thought he had left Fred standing, at the height where Fred's features ought to appear, and Fred was missing. Funny, he hadn't heard Fred move to the desk and sit down, but there he was, leaning heavily back in his chair, not moving a muscle, just staring at vacancy with an expression almost quizzical, as if in the extreme of defeat he found something incongruously comic.

Fred's eyes lifted and slowly came to a focus, acknowledging Kent's presence. His mouth formed a smile that was oddly apologetic. "One of our boys didn't make it," he said.

"I'm sorry. I was all ready for you to take over. We all were," Kent said. "We all had confidence."

"Well, that's that." Fred's eyes looked vacantly at the desk again. Then he thought to add, "Thanks, Cap. Coming from you, that means something." After a moment he began to speak again, a sharper note coming into his voice. "They took the outsider instead of promoting one of the team. They went outside for dynamic leadership." He snorted faintly. "Let me tell you, Cap. You've been a big support while I was—well, as Stocky said, you don't let the outfit down. You heard the other thing he said—'I hope they know what they're doing.' I hope so too, but from here on, Cap—I wouldn't want it repeated, but if I were you, I'd keep both eyes peeled. I can't say any more, but don't forget I told you."

Fred seemed to have discharged what it was in his mind to say. His look asked to be left alone with his blow, and Kent was willing enough to escape. When he reached his office, he couldn't shake the scene from his mind. 'One of our boys didn't make it.' What was the original? 'One of our boys did' —i. e., the Trinity. It was like Fred, in his black hour, to call on one of the Jewish jokes he liked to tell. If he meant to suggest that he'd been rejected because he was a Jew, Kent could hardly blame him for the thought, but he didn't believe it was true, or the whole truth. Dynamic leadership. The Directors might well have decided that Fred lacked precisely that quality; in their position, Kent might have agreed with them. On the other side, though, he ought to remember the warning Fred had thrown out; Fred meant well by that, whether it was based on anything solid or not. 'I hope they know what they're doing. If I were you, I'd keep both eyes peeled.' A common warning from Stocky and Fred could claim respect. Still, Stocky was out and had lost touch, and Fred had been let down hard, without a chance to prepare or put on the best face he could, and he was smarting from defeat. The Directors of a corporation like Fullchem must know their business. They had to judge men, they had to judge competition, they were all experienced themselves in management. Changes would come with new outside leadership, but that might be exactly what was needed.

∘ ∘ 11 ∘ ∘

If he knew how to ask favors of a deity, Arthur thought, he'd pray for an indefinite extension of Lamson Crocket's leave, which Lamson had already extended once. It was Malcolm's kidding that put such childish notions in his head, of course. Arthur found the kidding productive, but his spasmodic talks with Malcolm failed, like all half-serious fencing, to bring the difference between them clearly to the test. Arthur thought too late of apt replies or ways of putting the issue. Look, Malcolm, he wanted to say, this little contest between us isn't a matter of God in the last chapter, it isn't theological. You're tough-minded or ironical-minded enough to take the scheme of things as one big mare's nest of incongruities, and you're willing to let it go at that. You seem to lack the sense of wonder, or of empathy, the sense of the pathos of things that I'd expect of you as a literary temperament. I'm officially a scientist, but you force me to keep pointing out that there's another dimension to experience besides science.

Take me, Malcolm; consider me, as I sit here in my study, stealing a morning hour to think. I see colors and shapes, notably my books. I am aware of sounds. The day is so mild I have opened my window, even though it's only the last week in March; a flock of starlings are squawking and chattering outside, now and then producing long, surprisingly lyrical whistles. Color and sound—in one way science knows them very well. It can reduce them to wave-lengths and frequencies, can reproduce and transmit them to remote corners of the globe.

But in another way color and sound don't exist for science at all. Science can follow those still not at all well-known disturbances that travel along complicated nerve-paths from eye and ear to brain, but there it has to give up. These disturbances in themselves have no character whatever of color or sound or spatial configuration. They wouldn't *look* blue or red if you could see them, Malcolm; they wouldn't *sound* like starlings, they wouldn't appear like the extended surface of a desk, *my* desk, where I know I can lean and write. Yet when they reach the appropriate brain centers, what happens? Blue is suddenly present, not as a set of frequencies but as the color I perceive; and it's not just blue-here-now, it's the blue of a book-binding. I know what motions I have to make to pick up the book and open it. I'm spatially related. I know *what* book it is. No doubt we can build a machine to scan colors, distinguish between red and yellow, and behave accordingly. Can we make one to *see* blue as I see it? And of course it isn't only color and form and sound, the squawks and tremolos of the starlings, that science can only approach from the outside; it's our whole world of pleasure, concern, purpose—the pinch of destiny, as William James called it. No wonder a voice rises up now and then to ask, 'Isn't there a big discrepancy somewhere between the scientific view of things and what we know of reality by being directly related to it?' You think I lose caste as a scientist, Malcolm, by even bowing to the question. You're amused by the irony of *my* being the one to put it to you. Caste or outcast, I can't help it.

On the theological issue, we agree. The discrepancy can be as big as it likes and still not lead to the sort of God you accuse me of wanting to smuggle in. The world is process, and that means friction. What you call irony and laugh at, I call waste, and I view it with somewhat different emotions, though I hope I don't lack a sense of the ironic. Plato started the effort, didn't he, to explain how an imperfect world comes to be created by a perfect ultimate being? Take the other tack, try to work up from a world of waste to a benevolent and omnipotent God; either way the effort comes to grief on the same old snag; it winds up by making God responsible for evil, or by pretending evil is mere illusion, or that it's just the dark shadings of the picture put there by the artist to throw the light into relief. What actual sufferer in darkness ever willingly provided an aesthetic spectacle for those basking in the light? The only god who can emerge from cruelly wasteful process is a god who starts without even consciousness and evolves step by step with the animal species. A god like that is such an obvious self-projection that only a far-gone romantic egoist can take him seriously. So I suppose you're right, Malcolm, when you dismiss as unanswerable or even comic man's old question whether his faculties of seeing and knowing and wondering, his capacity for ethical strain and suffering, have any seat or station in the depth of things, beyond the throws of the dice that have given him his evolution among the animals and still give him his genetic start in life. What I can't share is your absence of *feeling* toward the question. I can never blame a man for asking it, even if it has no answer.

Arthur wished the starlings wouldn't make quite such a racket. He thought of closing the window; then he realized that the sound demanding his attention was the telephone ringing downstairs. Rachel had gone out shopping. He wished whoever was on the wire would get discouraged and hang up, but he rose and made reasonably conscientious haste down to the first floor. He reached the telephone table and spoke into the instrument.

"Arthur? You sound as though I'd interrupted something important."

"It will keep," Arthur said, recognizing the Chairman of Lamson's Committee.

"Well, too bad. The point is I've had a telegram from Lamson. He's leaving Washington and wants me to call a meeting next week at the usual hour."

Arthur must have grunted or groaned, for the Chairman went on, his voice warming with fellow feeling. "You aren't the only one who'd like to escape, Arthur, but don't forget your own proposals are coming up."

"So they are. All right, I'll jot it down and show up at the regular time," Arthur said.

The Chairman seemed to expect more of him, but when Arthur did not speak he said his good-by and rang off. The blessed interlude was over.

As he walked into the Committee room, Arthur mournfully noticed the ease with which the members appeared to slip back into their grooves of habit. Everyone seemed to pick up exactly where he had left off, even sitting in the same chair, assuming the same attitude. Arthur succumbed to the prevailing example, seating himself as usual at an angle across from Lamson toward the foot of the table. At the Chairman's left, the young secretary breathed on his glasses, wiped them, and aligned three freshly sharpened pencils by his scratch pad. Opposite the secretary, Pritchard nodded left and right as he came in late, sat heavily, and bent forward to pull toward him the mimeographed agenda containing Arthur's proposals.

Perhaps under the surface, Arthur told himself hopefully, a different temper would be working. Perhaps any success Lamson had achieved in Washington would diminish his bile, and they could get through the session amicably. He had everything to gain by succeeding with his own motions; he would try to argue them with all the persuasiveness he could, but also with sweetness and light. He looked across at Lamson, intending to utter a civil commonplace about his return. He waited until Lamson finished saying something in the ear of a henchman—well, of a junior colleague; then he caught Lamson's eye, and said, "Did you enjoy yourself in Washington?"

"I don't know about enjoyment. We had a job to do, and we did it. That's a satisfaction."

"So it is," Arthur said. "I'm glad if you got what you wanted."

"You haven't been letting the grass grow under your feet while I've been away."

"I don't know what you mean by that," Arthur said.

"If you don't, you're the only man around here who's preserved his innocence."

With astonishment that never ceased to be fresh, Arthur saw the little green thread of anger begin to tick in the hollow of Lamson's cheek. He looked at Lamson's colleague, who had turned away to speak to a neighbor and seemed to be somewhat ostentatiously not listening. "I haven't the slightest idea what you're getting at," Arthur said. "Will you put it in words I can understand?"

Before Lamson could answer, a settling of chairs and a cessation of neighborly talk around the table made a private reply impossible. The Chairman cleared his throat and announced that, since everyone seemed to be present, he would request order. "For a particular reason, which I'll try to explain in a moment," he went on, "I venture to suggest that we dispense with the reading of the minutes. I think, for the reason I referred to, we'll want to begin our discussion this afternoon—"

"Mr. Chairman, I'd like to point out that we have a docket," Lamson said. "It contains motions that strike at the heart of what this Committee was set up to accomplish. I think we ought to have the minutes, so we can refresh ourselves on the previous debate. I've been unavoidably absent, and meetings have been suspended—"

"We might at least let the Chairman tell us his reason," Pritchard said.

Arthur saw Lamson set himself to reply. His hope had been vain; another ordeal by acrimony was in store. Arthur felt almost ready to laugh. His inhibitions were giving way to a liberating anger, indifferent to consequences. "Wait a minute, Lamson," he said. "When I speak to my motions, I'll remind the Committee why I made them. If anyone's memory needs refreshing after that, I should think discussion would do it for him."

"Right," Pritchard said. "Meanwhile I suggest we let the Chairman conduct the meeting."

"I wait to be enlightened," Lamson said, leaning back glumly.

The Chairman flushed and glanced about the table with a look of resignation that showed his years. "The fact is, I received a communication just—ah, perhaps an hour before this meeting." He spread before him the two pages of a formally typed letter, flattening their creases with his palm. "Its contents are such that I was going to suggest postponing the docket and making this—ah, the first item of business. It's from the administration, from President Aiken, in fact."

Lamson leaned forward. His face, in its whittled hostility, looked as though it had thinned down until nothing was left but a pair of profiles welded together. "What's this? A letter from Aiken?"

"I believe I mentioned that," the Chairman told him stiffly.

"Is it relevant? What does Aiken know about the business of this Committee?"

"It's addressed to us, I take it," Pritchard said. "We might judge its relevance when we hear it."

"I don't like this," Lamson said. "Here we have a meeting to consider these motions on the docket—"

"I made the motions," Arthur said. "I think I have a right to yield, and I do yield, to the President's letter, whatever it contains, and I certainly don't know. I'm waiting to hear."

He received from Lamson a cynical glare. "I can understand your equanimity. Bi Sci 3 has always been a pet of the administration. It makes good alumni propaganda in the hands of a president whose innocence of science is virginal."

Arthur felt himself so nettled that his head seemed swathed in a fog. He fumbled for words to tell Lamson that, so far from aiding public relations, Bi Sci 3 often had to be defended against parents who charged it with instructing the young too well in godless and unwholesome truth about themselves, and that Aiken always defended it. Pritchard recalled him to the immediacy of the Committee table by saying, "Mr. Chairman, if we aren't going to be allowed to hear the letter, I for one am going to get up and go out. We've obviously got to put it first. That's only common sense as well as common courtesy."

Lamson sat back silent, and a gleam of weary relish came into the Chairman's eye. "Then if I hear no further objection," he said, and began to read the letter.

Arthur went to his office after the meeting broke up, but instead of immediately putting on his coat and hat to walk home, he sat down to think for a few minutes about the new turn of events. He had every reason for elation, and only a very small corner left for lingering discontent, or so it seemed to him at first. He'd kept his eyes averted from Lamson Crocket while the Chairman was reading; no doubt for that reason he remembered more sharply the expressions on other faces, the repressed twitch of mouth in response to an implication, the speculative pursing of eyes as the gist of the message became evident.

Arthur thought that Aiken had produced something of a masterpiece of administrative diplomacy. Without direct allusion or obvious irony, he showed that he'd been pretty well informed for some time about the acrimony of the Committee's proceedings. He was clearly trying to sponge up the bitterness by absorbing it into a larger context. He began by congratulating the Department on its initiative and courage in undertaking a voluntary self-scrutiny. Then he ventured a reminder: any major changes in program would naturally come up for review by the standing committee of the faculty on the curriculum as a whole, and, in particular, any substantial budgetary questions would have to be studied by the administration and the trustees. Then he announced his real news. He'd obtained a foundation grant to finance an *ad hoc* board of outside experts to study what Rowley was doing in *all* the sciences, and to make recommendations, in cooperation, of course, with the departments concerned. He was sure Biology would want to share in the enterprise and thought it wouldn't want to make a report that might look final before consulting with the *ad hoc* board, to which he would welcome nominations.

Aiken's letter might well have stopped there, but it went on. Candid self-criticism, Aiken said, was an intellectual virtue that universities ought to cultivate, but, in looking for shortcomings or possible improvements, we ought not to lose sight of what we were doing well. He thought the Department of Biology could take legitimate pride in its existing work. It was known well beyond Rowley for its high professional standards, and also for teaching that gave intelligent students who would never be scientists an insight into scientific methods and goals. The importance of this task in the modern world, Aiken said, was generally recognized.

What could he be referring to, when he said that, if not to Bi Sci 3? If Aiken had named Arthur and his course outright, he couldn't have made his point plainer. Vested interest! Aiken knew who was really trying to create a vested interest for himself, and he'd gone out of his way to pay Arthur a compliment and lend him a helping hand. The intervention was kindly meant; Arthur couldn't help responding to it, and yet he didn't relish the notion that he needed external aid. Who could have tipped Aiken off? Where did he get his information? No doubt it was part of the headquarters job to know what went on in the field, but could Pritchard or the Chairman or both have put Aiken up to making the gesture? Am I so vulnerable, Arthur asked himself, that I need a protective association to keep me from getting bruised?

Perhaps his elation had been premature, yet Aiken had got rid of the Committee more effectively than his own motions could have done. The discussion following the letter was brief and desultory. Pritchard's motion to report to the Department that any recommendations in advance of the *ad hoc* board would be wasted, and to ask for discharge or suspension, carried without dissent. Lamson kept unexpectedly quiet; perhaps he was mentally realigning his forces, making a calculus of future advantage. One foundation grant can lead to another; Lamson might smell money to windward. The relief of bidding the Committee good riddance was so great that Arthur was ready to wallow in it. In fact it would have been total if only—

Arthur heard a door shut and a lock snap in place down the corridor. Then he heard the familiar sharp click of heels uncushioned by rubber. The series of impacts receded, came to a halt, resumed, this time smartly approaching Arthur's door. Lamson Crocket. Arthur swung about in his chair and saw what he already knew, that he had left his door ajar. He thought of getting up and putting on his hat and coat, but if Lamson had anything to say to him he could say it as well walking as sitting or standing. In any case, he'd gain no credit with himself by shirking an encounter.

Lamson came in, pausing just long enough to look around the room and see that Arthur was present and alone. He circled the table, ran a fingernail along a row of books as he passed the shelves, and came to a stop near Arthur's chair. His face looked no more cordial than usual, but at least Arthur could see no sign of the green thread in his cheek. "Well," he said, "gloating over your triumph?"

"I don't know what triumph I have to gloat over," Arthur said. "I was thinking about Aiken's letter and what it would mean to the Department."

"I suppose you were pretty happy with Aiken's letter."

"If you mean it's a relief to me to get rid of these Committee sessions," Arthur said, "I admit as much. Beyond that I haven't the faintest idea what you're insinuating. My motions were on the docket. After we finally heard the letter, it wasn't necessary to argue them. So it hardly seems the triumph was mine."

"Quite a piece of administrative interference," Lamson said, "though it may work out all right. Do you suppose Aiken was responsible for it all by himself?"

Arthur had felt himself being baited without knowing where the attack was meant to strike. Now he began to see. "I think Aiken is fully capable of writing his own letters," he said. "Very literate ones, too."

"As to that, you're the judge," Lamson said. "I was thinking of the contents, also the timing. Hand-delivered just before we met."

"I don't know when he got news of this foundation grant. I should think he had good reason for letting us know promptly."

"You didn't miss his tidy little compliment to Bi Sci 3,

I hope," Lamson said. "It's all right to take a critical look at what the Department is doing as long as we don't disturb any sacred cows."

"Lamson, if you have an accusation to make, make it. Otherwise I'm going home." Released to this mild extent, Arthur's anger suddenly swelled in volume. "In particular, if you think I went to Aiken in any way, that I influenced, tried to influence, the letter he wrote—"

"Oh, I wouldn't think that, Arthur. I don't have to think. What happened is all over college. Everybody knows."

"Knows what? What do you mean? What's all over college?"

Lamson turned away, poking in turn with his fingernail, first left to right, then right to left, three books in the middle of a shelf. "Literature," he said finally, turning back to confront Arthur again. "Maybe you're right. Maybe I should pay more attention to it. A smart idea, to send your boy Islay as a secret agent to put the bee in Aiken's ear. Or it would have been smart if he hadn't done it where he could be overheard. Quite a pathetic tale he told. I've been persecuting you, it seems, and that shouldn't happen to a fellow author. Quite a tidbit for a presidential at-home on a Thursday aft—"

"Hold on. In fact, shut up, will you Lamson?" Arthur was stung to the point of dizziness. He tried to pull himself together, tried to think how anything of the sort Lamson described could possibly have occurred. When? what Thursday? who was there? he wanted to ask; he wanted to probe and verify and learn the worst. But no, he wouldn't submit to asking Lamson. If he asked anyone, it would have to be Malcolm. When could he ever have said anything to Malcolm— Then the dinner at Kent's and Abby's came back to his mind. Rachel and Claudia, that was it! The society for the protection of Arthur Comfort Scheuer at work!

Arthur's eyes cleared. He saw that Lamson had recoiled from him a step or two, was looking at him oddly, almost as if quelled or intimidated. Arthur got up from his chair and took a step toward his tormentor. "Listen, please, Lamson," he said. "If anything of the sort you say actually took place,

you can be sure I had nothing whatever to do with it. If someone—if a friend with well-meant intentions talked to Aiken—
well, I may wish he hadn't spoken, but I'm grateful for his
good will, and you're to understand that he did it strictly on
his own, not at any suggestion of mine. Is that plain?"

Arthur's breath was coming as though he had sprinted up
two flights of stairs. Lamson stood looking at him speechless;
he seemed to be trying to account to himself for the outburst.
"I don't want to talk any more about it," Arthur said, "in fact
I'd be obliged if you'd keep—" Keep your mouth shut for
good when you're around me, he was going to say. He
checked himself, walked carefully past Lamson to the corner
where his topcoat hung, and began writhing his arms into the
sleeves. Chagrin and the sense of exposure burned his flesh
like prickly heat. All over college. Persecution. Your boy
Islay. Fellow author. A reflex took hold of him and swung
him about toward Lamson, who was coming up behind him,
rounding the table toward the door, still not saying a word.
"You know, Lamson, there's something mystifying about you,
and I'll tell you what it is," Arthur said. "It's hard to figure out
why you treat people with the studied—the studied malevo-
lence you do, and the insufferable—the insufferable rudeness.
It's a puzzle what your motives can be. I should think you'd
find it wasteful. The time you put in on the art of insult, I
shouldn't think it would help you get your work done, or
even gain your ends in the long run."

Arthur finished in a thrill of exultation. For once he'd measured out the dose, and he thought he'd made it a good strong
plain one. Not only that, it had an intellectual character, it
was a lucid analysis and got to the root.

He was quite unprepared for its effect on Lamson, who did
not look repaid or outscored, but completely taken aback and
even, in a strange way, wounded. "Me?" Lamson said. "Ma-
levolence? Insult? Motives? You're losing your mind, old boy.
I don't have motives. I just have purposes. Motives are for literature. I don't have anything against anyone. I just try to get
what I want and what I believe in. I'll get the Project yet, if I
stay here. Aiken's letter doesn't shut the door, it opens it

wider. But I don't seem to be very well liked around here, do I? Well, I don't take things hard. I'm not personal about it. Sorry if you are, but that's your look-out."

Lamson belied himself by flushing suddenly. As he walked out into the corridor, he looked downright miffed. Was it possible he could really be unconscious of anything offensive in the way he treated people? Did he view himself in his own mind as a good fellow who simply drove hard at what he wanted to get? In human nature, Arthur reminded himself, anything is possible.

Pathetic tale. Everybody knows. All over college. The hideous phrases pursued Arthur during his walk home. Well, what would everybody know? That Malcolm had said such and such words, no doubt grotesquely distorted by now, in the course of a presidential at-home. Surely everybody wouldn't put the construction on the episode that Lamson had chosen to put? Surely *no*body would seriously believe that Arthur Scheuer had primed Malcolm Islay to intercede with Aiken and save him from persecution? The whole thing could be funny if it didn't actually make his joints ache. Unintentionally, Malcolm had subjected him to a severe humiliation.

Rounding the corner into his own street, Arthur saw the Mercedes at the curb outside the house. Malcolm must be calling to take Claudia out to dinner. He would have to steel himself to meet Malcolm. All right, as well now as ever, though he wouldn't bring up the subject of the Aikens' at-home until he felt better prepared.

As he came in, Rachel was standing with Malcolm in the hall, while Claudia was just coming down the stairs, buttoning her coat and pulling on her gloves. Arthur said his greetings and walked on past them to the cupboard under the stairs, conscious that he had avoided giving Malcolm a direct look. He hung up his coat and hat, and then he could hardly pursue a course of avoidance any longer. He went back to where they all stood in a group by the front door.

"How was the Committee meeting, Uncle Arthur?" Claudia asked.

288

He wished that for once her memory for his schedule could have been less retentive. "The Committee is dissolved," he said. "We've asked for our discharge without making any recommendations."

"But that's splendid, that's just what you want, isn't it?" Rachel asked.

"It didn't come about in the way I expected," Arthur said, "but I'm glad to be done with it."

"Did it go peacefully?" Claudia asked. "Did you put we-all-know-who in his place?"

He wasn't going to be spared; his best course was to answer as briefly and neutrally as possible. "We didn't begin very amicably, but after a letter from President Aiken was read, we were all sweetness and light."

"I thought your man Aiken would take a hand in the game," Malcolm said. "You can thank me for some spadework there." His face worked itself into an expression of self-congratulation that was almost smug.

Arthur gave him the direct look he had been withholding. "Did you know he was going to write us? Did you know what he was going to say? Did you know about the foundation grant he's got hold of—"

"I don't know anything about all that," Malcolm said. "I just thought he'd put an oar in on your side of the boat when he understood what was going on." His face changed, chopping this way and that, showing a puzzled awareness that something was wrong. He seemed to decide that a diversion was in order. "You know, I rather took to your man Aiken," he said. "He's a funny little sandy half-pint of a Scotchman, but surprisingly literate. For one thing, he had my books on his shelves, pretty nearly complete, and they showed wear, too. I promised to fill in a couple of items for him."

"But you discussed the Committee with him," Arthur said. "You went into personalities, it seems."

He felt Malcolm's eyes weighing him as though he were furnishing new and unexpected evidence against himself. "I wouldn't say we discussed personalities. I told him one of your —colleagues is what you say around here, isn't it? That he'd been giving you a rough time and I thought it was a damn shame. He said he valued you and your work highly. Anything wrong with that?"

Malcolm was on the verge of taking offense. Arthur perceived the fact clearly enough; less clearly he was aware of Rachel and Claudia standing rigid with embarrassment on either side. But hadn't they all contributed to his humiliation? Weren't they forcing the topic on him, against his will, at this very minute? It was talk that led to the whole mess; could they expect him to swallow it without talking back, at least to the point of letting them see the consequences? "I don't suppose you realized how many people might have overheard you," Arthur said.

Malcolm looked almost amused. "Arthur, my boy, don't tell me you've built such a shell around yourself it's a sin to mention your name in a friendly way where it might help out."

"It's not that, Malcolm. It's not that at all. I know you acted with the best of intentions, and I'm grateful for your good will, I assure you I am. You can take my name in vain anywhere, any time, call me any kind of damn fool you like, but there are some situations where it's better— What happened, if you want to know, is that a very different version of your well-meant words to Aiken has got around. It's all over college, I'm told. One that isn't flattering to either of us, certainly not to me." Should he tell them? No, he couldn't bring the words out, and to tell would only make a bad matter that much more public. Claudia, perhaps—but she too, all three of them, stood looking at him, speechless and frozen, flabbergasted by his outburst. "Oh, for God's sake, forget I opened my mouth, will you?" he said. "I'm sorry. It's just that I'd better be left to work this business out for myself as well as I can. I hope all—all of you—there's been enough talk, and I hope there won't be any more."

Arthur waited for one of them to move, to speak; a gesture or a word would relieve him of his exasperation, his contrition, his helplessness. Claudia recovered her powers of action first. She put a hand on his arm. "I'm sorry if anything I said or did—"

"Please forget the whole thing. I'm keeping you and Malcolm from your dinner. Why don't you go along and have a good time?"

"If you don't mind my carrying off your niece this way—" Malcolm bowed a little stiffly, including Rachel in his look.

"She tells us you're educating her at a great rate," Arthur said.

"She has a good instinct about writing. She keeps me on my toes," Malcolm said.

"I hope we'll see you again soon, Malcolm."

They went out, and Arthur was left standing in the hall with Rachel. Her face asked all manner of unhappy and bewildered questions, which he would have to answer as best he could, but at the moment he could only think that the demise of the Committee had done anything but put an end to his dissatisfactions.

o o *12* o o

Claudia was living two lives, or rather one was a life and the other a mere state of existence mechanically carried on between spurts of living. She lived in her letters to and from Jim Prescott. In them she felt her reality as a person with emotions and hopes and a purpose. Betweenwhiles, she went to the museum every day, did the chores her job demanded, came home, ate, slept, distracted herself as best she could. Perhaps she could call her evenings with Malcolm Islay a third life, or part-life, pitched somewhere between the other two, less routine than merely going from home to job and coming from job to home, but still only a distraction as compared with the letters she and Jim wrote each other.

Even her real life, of course, could hardly be called real. Letters—a substitute, if there ever was one! Not only that, but Jim's letters put her in a quandary. She was sure that when he began writing he would be bound to use some word, let fall some expression, which she could seize on to let him know how she felt. But he wrote as he had behaved around the museum before he left, still sticking to the fitness test he was so determined to carry out to the bitter end. He'd got hold of that stick and he wouldn't let go if his knuckles turned white with the effort of hanging on. He was amusing, newsy, and horridly, stupidly silent on the main issue. He never said, 'I love you, Claudia. Are my chances looking up?' He never said any of the thousand and one things he could have said to give her the opportunity she waited for.

She thought often enough of taking matters into her own hands. 'You've made all the amends you need to make, Jim. There aren't, haven't been, any to make, for that matter. I was upset, I'll admit, at first—" She had any number of easy ways to tell him, but she became confused and hesitant when she set out to do it. She didn't quite feel able to estimate just how all the effort he put into doing penance, redeeming himself in her eyes—as if he had to!—how important that effort was to him, in just what way. If she'd made such an effort herself, about *anything*, she thought she'd feel pretty deflated and even angry if she was told it was unnecessary, in fact foolish. He was coming back in June, and, no matter how time limped along, June wasn't so far off. He must have worked it out in his mind that June would be the critical point, the moment when he could ask if he'd jumped enough hurdles. Perhaps, till then, it would be better to play the game his way? That is, unless he gave her an opportunity. If he did that, she'd cut his schedule short for him! She certainly wouldn't stop watching.

So she wrote him such trivia as the museum provided, wrote about Arthur and Rachel, wrote even about the weather. Spring was making up for winter. The forsythia had come out full, lighting even the dusk with left-over sunglow, and the lilac buds were fattening by the hour. She wrote a good deal about her evenings with Malcolm. Wasn't it a comic chain of coincidence, she asked Jim, that she should find herself sitting in his room, listening to him talk about his work and his problems, actually asking her opinions and advice? She had to admit that as time went on she grew more and more overpowered by his egotism. He was quite frank and ingratiating about it, in a way. He said one evening, "I have a monumental ego, but practically no vanity." She thought it was true up to a point; at least he didn't expect to be flattered and buttered. What he seemed to crave was harder to give, just an absolute, total, whole-souled absorption in himself and his work while he was talking about them.

Now and then Claudia wondered whether she was making too much of Malcolm as a topic of correspondence, but what else did she have to write about that was half so interesting? For the first time within her conscious memory, she felt dissatisfied with the whole pattern of her life. Fullington was a small puddle; Arthur and Rachel were sweet and wonderful people, but she couldn't stay with them forever. The japonica put on its coral bloom; nesting-lyrics drifted ingenuously down from the maples along the streets. They made her chafe and ache with restlessness. Oh, why didn't Jim break down and say, 'I love you, Claudia. Can't you take me back?'

Through a particularly enervating afternoon of late sunlight she drove Arthur home from his office, put her car away, and followed him into the hall. Rachel came from the living room to greet them, but when Claudia saw the familiar typing on the envelope awaiting her by the telephone she pounced on it, waved it at them, and bore it off upstairs to read without losing a minute. One of her problems would be to break the news to them if the time ever came. They might as well have some advance warning, if they hadn't already. Poor Arthur, poor Rachel!

She had learned to absorb at a glance what Jim was talking about page by page, whether chit-chat about his new campus or comment on her chit-chat to him. Her eye was always looking for the sentence or paragraph that would set things off on a different course; it would leap out if it was there. This time the familiar hope seemed about to be followed by the familiar disappointment; then, in a postscript, the note of difference rang out.

Jim's old portable had run true to form:

> This I slay. (There goes Jumping Je sus again, but it produced a go od one that time, didn't it?) He must be a fasc inating character. You've given him five and a half

p ages in three letters. I hope there's a limit to his fascinat ion.
What's the secret of his charm?

Jim was jealous of Malcolm. Jim was suspicious of her, he
didn't trust her, he was still so blind— For an instant she was
outraged. Her entire innocence rose up to defend her; but in
almost the same breath she saw that here was her opportunity.
She squeezed the letter against her breast and, in the privacy
of her room, laughed aloud. Then she laid the letter on her
desk, got out a sheet of stationery, and hunted through her
purse for her fountain pen. Before she could so much as write
his name, Rachel's voice called her down to dinner.

By the time she had struggled through conversation at the
table and returned to her room, she had sobered and was
ready to go at her task less impulsively. The mildness of the
afternoon had continued. She opened her window and stood
for a moment inhaling the soundless aroma of dusk, drugged
with the languor of growth and bloom. Then she sat down at
her desk, unscrewed the cap of her fountain pen, and wrote:
"Dear Jim."

This was a letter she would do by hand. Her trained typing
would make it look too professional and impersonal. In every
way she wanted it to come from herself.

She considered how to begin, and felt temporarily at a loss.
He trusted her so little he could seriously think, could he, that
she was carrying on with another man, or, even worse, pretending to in order to keep him on tenterhooks? If he were
only within reach, she would punch him in the ribs for that,
make him howl in mock anguish, make him see how unfair
his suspicions really were. But he wasn't within punching distance. She could only reach him through words, and she
wouldn't waste her opportunity trying to make him feel con-
trite. She would just try to disabuse him of his misunderstand-
ing, to make her own position so plain that he would take the
next step; she would think of nothing else.

She brought her attention back to the sheet on her blotter,
but, though her purpose felt clear and settled in her mind,
words did not immediately follow. She found herself studying
her hand, the hand that had just written "Dear Jim." It was a

competent-looking hand, she thought, the fingers neither long nor stubby; the palm, when she turned it over and stretched it out, appeared rather broad and firm without being mannish. The hand merged into a wrist and forearm, rounded out in curves both familiar and new: *her* hand, *her* forearm. She took note of the barely perceptible down on the turn of the flesh. She became suddenly conscious of herself as an entire vital organism, felt her legs doubled beneath her and crossed at the ankle, her left toe braced against the floor as she leaned toward the desk, felt the pressure of the chair cushion supporting her weight, felt a thrust of consciousness rise all through her, into her breasts and shoulders and the pulse in her temples, until her existence as a self, a person, seemed to come all together and hang at a point neither quite inside her nor quite out. Her very self hovered around her so that she could feel its uniqueness in a new way. It seemed warm and rich; it seemed to radiate from the blood that quickened its beat beneath her skin. But this sense of richness in being what she was needed something to complete and fulfill it. Sometime it would have to be *given;* otherwise it couldn't be kept. Glancing at her closed door, confirming her privacy, she spoke aloud the name of the something, *his* name: "Oh, Jim!"

Then she buckled down to work. Her fingers took up her pen and began to write. "I could hardly believe it, Jim, but when I read your last I almost thought—" How would she put it? She couldn't say 'your nose was out of joint,' or 'you'd got the idea Malcolm is a rival.' She didn't want to use the word 'jealous' outright. He'd drawn inferences, he'd deceived— misled, that was the word. "—you'd misled yourself completely about Malcolm. The reason I've written so much about him is just that he's the most interesting thing I have to write about these days, and I thought he'd interest you. It's as simple as that. What can I say to prove you were wrong if you thought anything else?

"It was fun going out with Malcolm as long as he took me to dinner and then a concert or movie or something. You wouldn't want me to go to a nunnery while you're away." Jim deserved that; and besides, wasn't it practically an outright avowal? "Lately he's been taking me up to his apartment so he can talk, talk, talk about his problems. That's what we do; we discuss him and the 'missing element' in his work. It's flattering up to a point; he wants *me* to solve his problems, he keeps asking *my* advice. But I've begun to feel as though I had a large and formidable albatross tied around my neck.

"I know perfectly well Malcolm isn't interested in me as me. He's using me as a stand-in for Rosamund Temple. He'd do the same with any reasonably literate woman who'd listen to him. I judge he doesn't consider his wife reasonably literate. He talks about her in the most scandalously uninhibited way, how she insisted on marrying him, he doesn't know why, and how he feels like a stranger with her and their two boys. What it comes down to, Jim, is that it gets exhausting at times, but I can't refuse Malcolm's invitations when he's a friend of Uncle Arthur's and is as nice to me as he knows how to be. So now I've tried to explain, and if I mention Malcolm again, you'll know it's because I don't want to write nothing but chit-chat."

There, that should do it! Claudia addressed and sealed her letter and carried it out to the corner box to catch the last collection. She thought of the three or four days that would pass before she could expect an answer.

She climbed the porch at the end of an afternoon of raw weather. The lilacs had come out on the old bush by the steps, and she brushed her nose against a cluster that hung heavily down, weighted with spangled wetness. Jim's envelope was lying on the hall table. This time the heart of the message was right at the foot of the first page. Her eyes took in what preceded by a synthetic squint—Jim all contrition, oh, very apologetic. Then, in the best style of Jumping Jesus:

> But I hope you can unde rstand, Claudia, why I let myself get worked up. You se e, it means so much to me. I didn't want my pro bation closed by default. I want my chance to be reins tated and finish the curricu lum.

That idiotic word 'probation' again! All the same, she wanted to whoop as she read it. Here was her opportunity, complete and wide open, and in just the form she'd told herself it would someday occur. In the midst of dinner, another phrase came back to her: finish the curriculum. She could see it, in the inspired typography of Jumping Jesus, as clearly as if it were printed on her place mat. *I'm* the curriculum, she thought. Her face grew warm, and she began to laugh uncontrollably, while Arthur and Rachel looked at her as though she'd lost her wits. The worst of it was that she couldn't explain. She could only say something Jim had put in a letter had amused her; it was just his way of phrasing it that set her off.

In her room again, she began writing immediately. "Dear Jim: I wish you'd stop using that ridiculous word probation! I never want to hear it again. Can't we just forget it for good and all? Just before we dismiss it, I'll say this. If anyone has been on pro, it's been me as much as you. I told you I needed time, and you said you'd give me time. You gave it generously, Jim! You might have found out how I was using it if you'd asked me, but you never gave me a chance to speak. You might have found out that night in January when you stomped off in the thick of the snowstorm. It's a fine quality to be able to make decisions and stick to them, but decisions don't have to be all one-sided, do they? So now let's never use that *word* again, *please!*"

Coming back from the post box after mailing her letter, Claudia sniffed the lilac heads that turned the drizzle itself fragrant, and wondered how she'd survive until Jim answered.

"I got an idea for a story today," Malcolm said. "I wondered what you'd think of it."

They had come back to his apartment, a reasonably pleasant suite in the house of a faculty widow, after ladies' night dinner at the downtown club where Malcolm had a visiting membership. He was slouching in a big upholstered chair covered in a shade of blue that accentuated the mottling of his face.

"Tell me the idea," Claudia said, "and I'll see whether I have any thoughts."

"This is something that actually happened, something I saw myself. I've always wanted to use it, but it's a problem how it can be treated."

"I doubt whether I could help with that," Claudia said.

"Well, this is what happened, just as I saw it. I was coming back by train from San Francisco, years ago, and I went into the diner early for breakfast. Just as I sat down, the train rolled into a Godforsaken Midwestern town and stopped. I looked out the window and couldn't see a thing in motion, not even a dog or a pigeon scratching for garbage, until I caught sight of an old man coming along a street toward the tracks. The street ran at an angle to the train—the angle of vision is important. It was a grubby, empty street. On the near side it bordered an open square by the station. On the far side it was framed by a row of nondescript buildings. I noticed one in particular because it was especially dreary and had a false front that tried to make it look five flights instead of three. Beside the building was a cobblestone alley, and on the false front I could make out some letters in what looked like faded whitewash. Everything was in tones of gray. The weather was gray, the street and the square looked gray, even the brick buildings wore a gray patina. Everything was absolutely static except the old man coming along the street before anyone else was up. It was all like a stage set from the *Street Scene* period. You could have framed it in a proscenium, and every detail, every angle would have been just right. I *was* seeing it through a proscenium—the dining-car window."

"You certainly give me the picture," Claudia said. "Is it only a picture?"

"That's the question. The old man kept coming along the street, slowly, not tottering, but setting one foot after the other carefully, walking on eggs. He looked decently dressed, but he didn't have an overcoat or gloves, and the weather looked raw. He had an old derby on his head, and a white mustache that drooped at the ends. I thought he had a sort of pathetic dignity, and at the same time the absent-mindedness of age, there but not wholly there, you know. He toddled along, coming closer and closer, until he reached the building with the false front. The door was right at the near corner of it, next the alley. He stopped when he got to the door and turned very slowly to face it, pivoted, you might say. His hand went out, and I could see him give a tug at a bell handle. No answer. He tried the doorknob. Obviously the building was locked. So, very slowly again—you've got to visualize the tempo—he braced his left hand against the door post and leaned out until he could see around the corner and into the alley. Nothing there, nothing but the usual iron fire-escape, totally empty, climbing up zigzag to the top floor. He pushed himself upright again and turned his back to the building. He seemed to look vacantly around for a minute, and then he caught sight of a piece of paper or trash on the sidewalk. He stooped over, slowly and carefully, as if he might be rheumatic, and picked it up. Then he made the one motion in the whole scene that was quick, almost violent. He flung whatever it was away from him toward the gutter. Flung is the word. I can still see it, that gesture of senile resentment and repudiation against a universe where doors don't open and things are untidy or out of place. He went back and leaned against the building, not collapsing, but huddling into it, his chin coming down on his chest until his face was hidden by the rim of his bowler. The train began to move. The picture began to slide away. It was then I looked up and read the washed-out letters on the tin false front."

"What did they say?" Claudia asked.

"That legend on the false front, that's one reason I've never been able to use the whole thing. The irony is so obvious it's hard to see what to do with it. I suppose it must have been a Salvation Army joint, something of the sort. What it said was: JESUS, THE HOPE OF THE WORLD."

Claudia could not repress a gasp and a slight shudder. The misery of the scene caught hold of her.

"Well, what do you think?" Malcolm asked.

"I think it's a very vivid incident, and a rather painful one."

"Painful? Nothing's painful that's well written. But of course it *is* just an incident, just a vignette. The technical problem is how to get a story out of it."

"I suppose the story is in the old man," Claudia said. "I suppose you'd have to imagine a life for him, how he came to stand outside the door, whether it ever opened—"

"I don't see it that way," Malcolm said. "The problem is to preserve the picture, the vignette, and at the same time make it something more. A lot of biography of the old man, or any *direct* sympathy for him, would swamp the picture."

"How are you going to treat it, then?"

"It only occurred to me today that what impressed me about the whole thing, made it stick in my memory all these years, was just the staginess of it, the theatrical quality. No designer could have created a more perfect set, no director could have controlled the timing with such perfect rightness, no character actor could have improved by a hair on the pantomime, every motion and gesture just completely so. That's the quality I've got to get in. Maybe I can do it by the language, by writing it so that it all comes out as an extended stage metaphor, from beginning to end. Maybe I'll have to put in a perceiver who can bring it out, say a producer or a dramatic critic who can sort of egg the old man on or review the show while he watches."

"Then the poor old man will be nothing but a puppet worked on strings in front of a train window?" Claudia asked. "You see, I can't forget him."

"There we are again," Malcolm said. " 'The missing element.' Islay doesn't understand a simple human emotion. I thought—you heard me give him credit for pathetic dignity. Everything about him was so shabby-decent. And then that fierce fling he gave when he threw away whatever it was littering the street. I thought for once you'd grant I was on the track of some human understanding."

"I do. I'm sure, when you come to write the story—you don't really mean all you say, do you, Malcolm, about the impossibility of understanding? Men and women aren't such—such absolutely isolated islands as you make them out?" Claudia became aware that her voice was rising and growing warmer. She was trying to talk to Malcolm, but she was thinking of Jim. It struck her how little Malcolm knew about her, how little he troubled himself to learn. He had no idea that Jim was a part of her life. He never asked, nor, so far as she could tell, speculated or showed curiosity about any independent concerns of hers. "We *have* to understand each other, don't we?" she said. "Even if there's a limit to it, we have to try, and the trying makes it possible to live together—get on together in the same world."

She must have sounded terribly earnest. Malcolm was looking at her queerly, his face working sidewise and up and down, deciding what expression to put on. "Well," he said finally, "I'm asking you to help me try. I need something to get over this block I'm in. What is it?"

She was becoming more and more impatient as the weight of his demand on her grew more oppressive. She took refuge in what seemed a justifiable evasion. "What does Rosamund Temple tell you?" she asked.

He surprised her by looking a little let down at the question. For a moment she thought he wasn't going to answer at all. His face chopped mournfully back and forth; then he said, "You might be surprised if you knew, or again you might not. She tells me I might begin by trying to get closer to Beth and the boys." He tried to smile at the irony of that, but produced what was more nearly an unhappy smirk. Claudia was startled by the look that followed. It seemed for once utterly transparent, utterly defenseless and appealing. She felt as though she had noticed a stranger on the street and suddenly perceived that he was *hungry*. "You know, Rosamund keeps a stable of writers going," he said. "I may be a bit of a prize boy, but I'm only one." And that, his silence added, isn't enough, not nearly enough; I want impossibly more.

Claudia was appalled by his revelation of the depth of his need and his dependence; but what could she do? Her mind was crying inwardly: Oh, Jim, come back and take me away from all this! It's more than I can deal with, more than I should be called on to deal with! "I'd help in any way I could, Malcolm," she assured him, "but I wonder what I could possibly say that Rosamund mustn't have said many times already?"

He accepted the words as though they disappointed but hardly surprised him. She was sorry, but the amount of regret she had to spare was limited. She wanted overwhelmingly to escape. To her horror, she began involuntarily to manufacture the means of escape. She felt a yawn invade her deep down and start to work its way up. It was forcing itself on her relentlessly. It reached the base of her neck, it seized on her jaws, and she clamped them shut by a ferocious exertion of will. She covered her lips with the back of her hand. The spasm passed on, up and out by some avenue in the top of her head. "Lord, is it getting late?" she said. "It's been a fascinating evening, Malcolm. I hope you'll let me see your story when you write it, but I'll always remember it just as you told it."

He made polite small talk as he drove her home. She had a premonition that their têtes-à-têtes would become less frequent, and felt a mild compunction. Jesus, the hope of the world. The old man, his face hidden by his bowler, leaning against the shabby building, beside the locked door. Suddenly a transposition occurred: it was Malcolm himself, an old derby absurdly tilted over his forehead, who slumped against the grimy wall under the false front. Well, tomorrow she would find Jim's letter waiting for her on the hall table. She'd counted the days and knew it would be there. Jumping Jesus! She could hardly wait.

The letter lay in the usual place, but it wasn't from Jim. Her disappointment was so extreme it tempted her to unreasoning anger, but she fought against it, telling herself a thousand trivial accidents could account for delay in the mail. She'd simply have to wait, somehow, another night, another eight hours on her job, another dinner, breakfast, and lunch. With faint curiosity she picked up the letter she *had* received and carried it to her room.

It was addressed in precise, delicately thin strokes, in an unfamiliar hand, obviously a woman's. Claudia turned first to the signature: Rosamund Temple. Now why on earth should Rosamund be writing to her? "Claudia, dear," the letter began and it explained itself quickly enough:

You'll wonder why I'm writing you, but I remember so well the day Malcolm brought you to lunch, and he has referred to you so often since, I simply can't resist. As an incurable writer, he is also a prolific correspondent, as you can imagine. I just wanted to say I'm so glad Malcolm found you and your Aunt and Uncle during his year at Rowley. It would have been an uncomfortable year for him, perhaps a failure, if he hadn't. You're aware that he's in a crisis about his work. I don't know whether you realize how much it has meant to him to talk with you during these recent weeks. Malcolm is self-centered, but he's a dear soul all the same. If he accepts more than he gives, he rewards us all with his books. I think you deserve a vote of thanks for the way you have listened to him. Trying to satisfy psychic needs can be a burden, and one that isn't always repaid with gratitude, but I know Malcolm is grateful in his way, and I am too, for his sake.

It was such a pleasure to see you I hope it will be repeated. Perhaps Malcolm will drive you down for a week-end during the spring. On account of limited strength, I am much alone, and new voices in the house are a delight to me. My husband (who, incidentally, understands Malcolm much better than Malcolm understands him) would enjoy a week-end visit also.

Affectionately,

Rosamund Temple

What a lovely, what a flattering letter, Claudia thought; but the feeling that came with the words was tepid. If only Rosamund had written *after* she'd heard from Jim she could properly appreciate and answer her much too generous tribute and her invitation. Of course she'd have to say that Malcolm wouldn't be bringing her for a visit, because she was afraid she'd let him down just last evening and destroyed any usefulness she might have had as a listener. Could she suggest that possibly, in June, she might call for an hour with a different escort? That is, if Jim actually wrote and things were settled; oh, why hadn't he written?

When, next afternoon, the letter actually lay waiting for her by the telephone, Claudia governed her motions very deliberately. She went to the table as though she had all the leisure in the world, picked the envelope up unhurriedly, and held it at her side, her palm itching with the contact, while she exchanged the commonplaces of the day with Arthur and Rachel. Then she climbed the stairs at a controlled pace and went into her room. She put the letter on the desk, set her handbag neatly on the bureau, straightened a picture that hung unevenly, smoothed the pillow on her bed. The impulse on which she had been waiting to act took over at last. She made a leap across the room to her desk chair, slit open the letter, and spread it out. She saw the first words: "Darling Claudia," and they were enough. She knew that everything after that would be what she wanted, and so she could begin noticing at once that Jumping Jesus had really outdone himself:

Lord, what fo ols these mortals be, and I be the b egodammede st big one of the lot. If I didn't understand you this time, I gues s I'm doomed to be a fool for goo d. Anyway, when I read your last, I thoug ht the circumstances called for cel e bration . The opportunities here are limited, but I did what I could. I gue ss I really tied one on. All yesterday my tong ue was packed in a mud p oultice and my head was stuck in a revoling door studded with spi kes. That's why this is late getting of f. I don't do this kind of thing regularly, but you 'll never know what you r letter meant. It was a bright torch and a casement ope at n ight, it launched a thousand shi ps, it outcomp ared any summer's day that ever burned too ho t. My mind is a disc playing all the world's clichés, and the best and tru est is "I love you." We'll make up for lost time, wh at? When I come east, I'll have plans, but this time I'll give you a chance to ratif y them. More, and more ra tionally, tomorrow.

Jim

The second time Arthur summoned her to dinner, Claudia managed to respond. She was afraid her face looked imbecilic, and while the substance on her plate was undoubtedly food, eating seemed an act utterly foreign to her experience. How she had ever performed it she couldn't imagine. She was aware that Arthur and Rachel studied her furtively. At last she couldn't stand it any longer. Poor Arthur, poor Rachel! A great feeling of tenderness for them came over her. She took advantage of a pause in the talk to look at them and say,

"There's something I want to ask you both. Will you mind very much if I—if Jim and I are married one of these days? Will you be able to get along without me?"

∘ ∘ *13* ∘ ∘

Arthur thought mournfully of the sniff of disapproval he would receive if Lamson Crocket came into his study and saw him looking over his lecture notes. Year by year, as the end of the course approached, Arthur tried to set his subject in something of a philosophical perspective. Is it really possible, he would ask, to believe in the process of evolution without believing in some guiding hand, some agency of meaning or purpose, that has led it along its humanly incredible path? By now, he would remind the students, you know that for science any such assumption isn't merely unnecessary, it's an impediment. It tempts us to take refuge in metaphysics before we have to, dampens our sense of what we can achieve by experimenting and verifying up to the limit of human powers. But science isn't the whole of life. Even where its discoveries are most certain, its explanations most satisfactory, it doesn't touch bottom, it doesn't exhaust mystery. Perhaps a scientist ought to leave it to non-scientists to say these things, but it was important, Arthur felt, for a *scientist* to say them now and then, not always leave them to the layman.

What about that evolutionary chicken that half-developed wings and half-flew? In other words, at what point in the development of an organ by minute successive changes does it acquire selective value, what *keeps* it developing from the first slight difference up to the stage where it has the obvious selective value, say, of binocular vision? A layman's puzzle; any student in the course could answer it for himself by now. But as a matter of fact, the human eye made even the great Charles Darwin gulp a little in his chapter on "Organs of Extreme Perfection and Complication." Had Darwin's difficulty ever been

305

completely put to rest? Illustrate, said Arthur's notes, not from Darwin but from Sherrington. Remind class he's writing on embryology here, but point is suggestive for evolution too.

Arthur reached for his copy of *Man on His Nature* and looked over the passage to which his notes referred. Sherrington not only described, he evoked vividly. A cluster of dividing cells, enclosed within the uterus; from it a human individual will take shape. In the cluster, certain skin cells, carrying out their marvelous inherited blueprint, begin forming themselves at the locus of what will become a forehead into the wonderfully refined camera structure of what will become eyes. Nerve processes, originating at different points, worm toward each other, like approaching ends of tunnels, to connect the developing eyes with the developing brain. Work of extraordinary coordination and complexity, this, harnessing eye and brain to each other; and, as Sherrington put it, all this work goes on in darkness as a preparation for light.

Take over from Sherrington, Arthur's notes told him. We can inspect all this work from beginning to end; we can see it in the long stretch of evolution or in the nine-months' growth of the embryo. While the work goes on in darkness, we know that light is on the way. Our knowledge is really hindsight, the result of study; but it can feel like foresight. Often we feel almost irresistibly that this foresight of ours must be paralleled by some supreme foresight in the universe that has known all along and still knows, has intended and still intends, the miraculous outcome that science attributes to the chances of mutation and selection.

Descriptively, on all current evidence, the account biology gives of evolution compels acceptance; no mind that really understands it can reject it. Don't forget to say that firmly, Arthur reminded himself. But the account science in general gives of the world in general isn't the whole account of reality. What happens when the eye finally gets ready to receive light? A nervous excitation travels from the retina back into the brain. This excitation isn't in itself light, or space, or form; yet when it reaches the appropriate brain centers, a rose is seen to be in bloom, or a Picasso is perceived for what it is. Science has no access to this phenomenon, can't deal with it, still less account for it. Reality includes not only what science can experiment with, but a whole other world, which no philosopher these days seems able to bring into unity with the world of science: our human world of perception and feeling, of looking before and after and trying to make choices that may diminish evil and increase good. What sort of underpinnings, physical or metaphysical, can this world claim in the vast scheme of things? On that point Arthur would close by saying that, after all, it isn't merely scientists who are agnostic; many men in many walks are glad to acknowledge their humility, to say 'We don't know.'

Arthur put his notes in his brief case, looked at his watch, and found he still had upwards of half an hour before he needed to leave the house. He heard Rachel's distant practicing come to a halt, heard her going to the front door. Voices became audible, the second one Abby's. The two of them came upstairs and went into the bedroom. The door closed; he went to it and knocked.

"Arthur?" Rachel asked. "We didn't want to interrupt you, so we shut ourselves in. It's so much sunnier up here than in the living room."

"May I join you for a few minutes?"

"Of course," Rachel said.

Arthur went in. The room was in fact so bright that Rachel had pulled an upholstered chair for Abby to the middle of the rug, away from the window, and seated herself at the foot of her bed. "What were you gossiping about?" Arthur asked.

"Abby has been telling me what Kent is going through with the new management," Rachel said.

The mention of the topic brought nervous tension into her voice. Arthur looked inquiringly at Abby, but she seemed reluctant to go on for the moment. She was silent; at last she said, "I hear we're going to have a wedding in the family. I hope Claudia is gloriously happy."

"It seems to me I've detected symptoms of euphoria," Arthur said.

"Have they made any definite plans yet?"

"Not that I know of," Arthur said. "I suppose that will wait till Jim comes East in June, won't it?"

Rachel answered his question obliquely at best. "There'll be so much to do. You'll have to help me, Abby."

The nervousness of her tone sharpened; it wouldn't be easy for her to lose Claudia.

"Cappie and I would love to help all we can. Claudia is a lovely child, and Cappie has had a crush on her ever since she was in pigtails." Abby paused and seemed almost to be gathering her courage to continue. "I'm afraid what we can do will depend on where we are when the time comes."

"Where you are?" Rachel asked.

Again Abby delayed her reply so long that Arthur said, "Things are really troublesome at the plant?"

"Fresh, dynamic leadership," Abby said. "That's the priceless quality the new President was supposed to bring, Mr. Bracket, Cyrus Bracket. So far dynamic leadership seems to mean making heads roll. Denis Prouty—has Cappie ever mentioned him to you?"

"Yes, I think so," Arthur said.

"Of course no one was surprised when Denis was let go, but the way it was done, after all his years with the company, just being told on a Friday that he needn't report on Monday. Not even a hod-carrier would be treated that way in these day of unions. Then Fred Abramson—"

"Wasn't he the man Kent expected to be made president?"

"Yes. There was no reason in Fred's case except fear of a rival or pure spite. Cappie can't see any other motives."

"I suppose such things are administrative decisions," Arthur said. He felt that he was speaking lamely. "I suppose a new President coming in—"

"The cruelty of it is that Denis and Fred were getting toward their last years, looking forward to retirement with pension and benefits. Now they've lost all that, or a lot that they expected. And they aren't the only ones who've felt the ax. It's the senior men who are being lopped off, men who thought they'd earned some comfort and security by a lifetime of work."

The bitterness with which Abby spoke was having its effect on Rachel. Her nervous alarm was mounting. "Surely Kent doesn't feel his standing is in any doubt," Arthur said.

"Cappie doesn't believe Mr. Bracket would dare to meddle with the engineering department. Cappie says he doesn't know an engineer from a pig's eye. Besides, he has confidence in his record, and he's entitled to. But the atmosphere he has to work in—we used to think it was bad enough at times when Stocky was in charge, but we didn't know how well off we were. If Cappie weren't getting old enough to look ahead toward retirement himself—he's given so many years to the company he can't afford to lose his own pension and benefits. Did Cappie tell you what Mr. Bracket said when he made a tour of the office with the new Vice President he put in Fred's place?"

"What did he say?"

"He said—I'm quoting Cappie literally—'As I walk around here, I notice on the doors a lot of brass plates with names of executives on them. I want a man to take them down and write the names with a piece of chalk instead. He'd better carry a sponge so that he can wipe them off, too.'"

"I don't see how such a man got to be President," Rachel said.

"Cappie has wondered himself. He got some light the other day by asking Fred Abramson to lunch. Fred was willing to talk, though Cappie said he'd never seen a man lose his grip so fast. Fred looked ten years older and three times as Jewish —that was how Cappie put it. Anyway, Fred told him all he knew about what went on in the Board of Directors. They had a long battle over whether to promote someone from the ranks or bring in a completely new man from outside. Fred thought up to the last minute that he'd won out himself, but he hadn't. He'd seen something of Mr. Bracket before they chose him, and said he acted very differently while he was trying to get power from the way he acts now that he has it. He can turn on a smooth tongue, apparently, when he wants to, and he sold a majority of the Directors on a big plan for expansion. It will involve a stock issue, and Cappie thinks there's an element of risk, but he says no company can make progress without taking risks."

"But even if things are temporarily uncomfortable, Kent thinks it will all work out?" Arthur asked.

"Cappie has lost his assistant," Abby said. "Shepherdson. I

don't know whether Cappie has mentioned him to you, but he picked Shep out and trained him, advanced him as fast as he could, and relied on him completely. Shep was devoted to Cappie, but the other day he came in and said he'd had an exceptional offer and he'd lost confidence in the way Fullchem was being run from the top. He was getting out when he could. Cappie asked Mr. Bracket to authorize an immediate replacement, and what do you think he was told? 'This company is under reorganization, and I'll see about replacements in my own time.' Just like that! So Cappie pointed out if there was any thought of going ahead with the building program, he simply couldn't do the work without a reliable assistant in his office. Mr. Bracket smiled and said the company might undertake even more extensive building, and Cappie would find out what his part was when the time came."

"Design and construction," Arthur said. "That's just the work Kent takes most pride in." He tried to strike an optimistic note for Rachel's sake; actually, he was feeling himself the effect of Abby's bitterness and seriousness.

"Of course Cappie wanted to find out what Mr. Bracket was hinting at," Abby said, "and he got some light from Fred Abramson about that too." Abby paused. She seemed about to impart the news she had really come to tell, and it promised to be unwelcome. "Mr. Bracket hasn't yet breathed all he has in mind to anyone. You know we have a branch plant in New Jersey. What he wants to do is move everything, all the manufacturing and research operations, down there, and set up the main business offices in New York."

Rachel's repressed apprehensions came out in a gasp of dismay. "But Abby, that would mean—you wouldn't be here, you and Kent. You'd have to give up your house—"

"It hasn't happened yet. Fred may be wrong, or the Directors may modify the plans. Of course," Abby said, looking at Rachel with sober reminder, "New Jersey would have compensations for us. We'd be closer to the children. And it isn't as though we'd vanish out of each other's lives."

"When do you think," Rachel asked, her face flushing darkly, her mouth held firm by an effort, "when do you think it might happen?"

"We don't know when or whether," Abby said. She rose and stooped to kiss Rachel's face. "I just thought you both ought to know how the land lies. Do tell Claudia how happy I am for her."

Arthur followed them down the stairs to the door. Rachel kept her composure until Abby said her good-bys, climbed into her car, and drove off. Then, confronting Arthur in the hall, she gave way to her incertitudes, her eyes growing moist, her lips trembling. Arthur provided what reassurance he could by drawing her physically against him, but while she accepted his touch, she didn't really yield to it. "What's going to become of us?" she asked.

"What a question!" Arthur said. "I know it would be a major loss to you if Kent and Abby had to move away, but Kent will naturally have to go where it's financially and professionally best, and as Abby said, they won't be vanishing from our lives."

"But if all those other men, men who've been with the company as long as Kent, and some longer—"

"His head might roll too? I can't believe it."

"Just when Claudia has told us—"

Arthur spoke as gently as he could. "Haven't we always known she'd marry someday? You wouldn't want her not to."

"I'm being absurd." Rachel gave her hair a shake and straightened away from him. "I don't know why I'm so nervous today. I've had a presentiment. It's not just the thought of losing Abby and Claudia both. You're so discontented yourself, Arthur."

"I'll admit I've had a trying year," Arthur said. "But I'm making an effort to control my dissatisfactions, and I've got them fairly well in hand. I'll be here to count on for what I'm worth."

"You don't still want to resign, do you?"

Arthur allowed himself a sigh and a smile. "In an absolutely free world, I might want to," he said. "But it isn't a free world. I have ties and commitments, and I value them. I've put any serious thought of resigning out of my mind, so please don't worry about that."

She seemed to take comfort a little. She said that if she really meant to play in the concert that evening, she'd have to go on practicing. "But I don't see how I can, Arthur. I feel so—just so unstrung. I'd make a wrong entrance or something and disgrace myself."

"Don't you think the very best thing you could do would be to play as usual?"

She agreed reluctantly to try. Looking at his watch, Arthur saw that he would have to leave at once and quicken his pace to reach his lecture on schedule.

What Rachel had said about discontent brought his mind back to his own problem, finical as it might seem in comparison with the very practical trials that Kent was facing. Ties and commitments; he shouldn't be chafing at ties, Arthur told himself. He should be feeling like a liberated man. He was spared the ordeal of the defunct Committee. Lamson Crocket was keeping out of his way. If he were ever going to make progress with his book, he ought to be getting ahead with it now, but he was still allowing himself to be frustrated by interior obstacles. Malcolm's well-meant officiousness with Aiken would come sharply back to him and singe him with shame from time to time, and he still couldn't tell himself that he'd done anything to allay the rankling charge of vested interest.

After cooling off somewhat about Malcolm and getting back on an easy footing with him, Arthur had made up his mind to seek a direct talk with Aiken. He thought he could say a few things that would help to square his position, at least with himself. But before he could make an appointment, Aiken went off on an annual tour, speaking to alumni clubs. Well, time enough when he came back.

He came home at the end of the day wondering in what state he would find Rachel, but she was wearing a concert costume and he could detect scarcely more than the customary nervousness that beset her before the conductor's downbeat absorbed her safely in the trained momentum of performance. As usual on concert evenings, dinner was served by their thrice-a-week helper, who had a taste for festivity and arrayed the table to the best effect she could achieve with the resources of the household. Instead of place mats and paper napkins, they sat down to linen. Candles gleamed on the blue and gold glaze of china from Rachel's Rumford forebears, on silver from generations of bourgeois Scheuers, on the crystal of goblets needlessly elegant for the mere purpose of containing water. They were using objects of value that ought to be handed on intact to Claudia, yet a departure from the stainless steel and throw-away tissues of a do-it-yourself world could be salutary now and then.

Claudia gave off a bouquet appropriate to the setting. Her tongue chattered effortlessly, but she seemed to be talking and thinking on parallel tracks. Now and then she would pause, and heightened color would come into her face as she dwelt on a private image. Emerging, she would shake her cropped hair lightly and put on a businesslike expression. In another family, Arthur thought, if she had brothers, or the cousins who might have been older brothers to her in effect, she wouldn't have got through this period in her life without some twitting, but if she had missed this part of her birthright, she didn't seem to have suffered from it.

They had nearly finished dessert when the telephone rang. "I'll go," Claudia said and got quickly up from her chair. She went out into the hall, and they heard her make the responses necessary to completing a long distance connection. Then she said, "Jim!" In the silence after the name, Arthur was conscious of Rachel involuntarily straightening and straining to listen. "No," Claudia said, "only the three of us. We've just finished dinner. Why?" A longer silence, then the sharp sound of Claudia's breath as she gave a disheartened gasp. "Wait a minute, Jim, please. Can you hold on for just a minute?" They heard her footsteps, and she appeared in the door. Her face had undergone a transformation. It was white and puzzled. "I'm awfully sorry," she said. "Would you mind if I closed the door? Jim has something important—I want to be sure I hear everything—" She produced a smile of dazed apology. They watched the blank panels of wood swing to behind her, sentencing them to indefinite confinement with the dregs of their coffee.

"Arthur!"

"Steady," Arthur said. "We don't know whether anything's really the matter, whether it isn't just some minor hitch."

"I wish we knew more about him," Rachel said. "I hope she isn't rushing into something—"

"I don't see that she's been rushing. She's known him for a whole year now, a college year."

"But something went on, oh, back in December. She was so unhappy."

"Young people's troubles don't bring the world to an end," Arthur said helplessly. He tried to think of a diversion, but they were both too intent on the progress of the telephone call. They could hear Claudia's voice rising and falling, now uttering a sentence, now a monosyllable. "They're running up a bill that would start them off with a month's rent," Arthur said and received a look of wounded reproach for his levity.

At length Claudia stopped speaking. Silence continued for so long it could only mean the call had come to an end. She must be standing alone by the telephone table, digesting whatever Jim had told her. Then they heard her footsteps coming evenly along the hall. The door opened, and she stood looking at them as if through a scrim that made them appear distant and unreal. "I'm awfully sorry," she said. "I shouldn't have shut you in that way. I—Jim—we had something—something we had to talk about." She paused and then appealed to them. "Would you mind if I didn't come to the concert with you tonight? I've got to think, and I seem to have developed a headache." Claudia turned, and her steps receded through the hall. They heard her climbing the stairs.

Arthur shut the bedroom door as quietly as he could, looked at his watch, and was surprised to discover the evening so little advanced. Only a few minutes past nine; certainly not too late to invade Claudia's privacy. He looked at her door. It was closed, but a thin band of light showed along the sill. He crossed the hall and tapped, asking, "May I come in?" She said, "Yes." He turned the knob and entered.

She was sitting in her small upholstered chair, in an attitude of rumpled dejection very different from her usual regard for appearances. She looked at him vacantly and distantly, accepting his presence in the room with indifferent tolerance as he pulled out her desk chair and established himself opposite her.

"I don't want to intrude," Arthur said, "but for Rachel's sake even more than my own, I'm constrained to ask what's the matter, Claudia? Can I be told? Can I help?"

She had been absently meeting his eyes, but now her vision moved to a different focus, or none at all. "It isn't that I want to hold anything back. It isn't that I have anything to hold back," she said. "I just can't talk yet, that's all. I have to meet my problems in my own way. You said that once yourself, Uncle Arthur. You agreed."

"I'd be glad to still, but sometimes, when others are affected—you know Rachel hasn't been able to keep her concert date."

The words penetrated the subjectivity in which she was wrapped. She looked penitent and seemed to become directly conscious of him for the first time. "No," she said. She sat upright, then she rose, smoothed down her skirt, and reseated herself. "What time is it? I thought— Oh, I guess I didn't think. I assumed you'd both gone."

"I persuaded her to go to bed and take a pill," Arthur said, "on the promise that I'd try to talk with you. I'm sorry, but you know you mean so much to Rachel that she can't bear to think you're disturbed or unhappy."

"Poor Rachel," Claudia said faintly.

"A number of things have conspired to—shall we say arouse her anxieties lately. I'm afraid I've been one of them myself. I've tried to reassure her on that score, but she's also worried about Abby and Kent—excessively so, perhaps, but not without some cause."

"I know."

Arthur waited, and presently Claudia seemed to reconcile

herself to laying bare her situation. "Oh, well," she said. Then she paused before she could begin again. "I suppose I've been acting like a child, thinking only of myself, but really, Uncle Arthur— About Jim and me. It's perfectly simple. It's just that our plans have changed. Jim has had a wonderful professional opportunity—he's always having wonderful professional opportunities—no, that's unfair. Anyway, he's been invited to join a big expedition, a really major anthropological do, with archaeology and sociology thrown in—all the ologies you ever heard of. He only got the chance because another man had to drop out on account of illness. They offered Jim his place, and he says it would affect his whole future—*our* whole future—to turn it down. He'll be leaving in a week or two for I don't know how long—a year, he thinks."

Arthur plied her with the obvious questions. Where was the expedition going? New Guinea, she said miserably, as if it were Tierra del Fuego or Ultima Thule. She would have married him and gone with him, but the expedition wouldn't tolerate an unqualified supernumerary female. Jim made that clear, though he tried to be apologetic about it. Would Jim have to leave before she could see him again? No, by all sorts of finagling he'd arranged to come East for three days next week. The graduate student who'd taken his apartment was leaving early to go abroad, so Jim would occupy his old digs for those three days, which were all they'd have of each other before he vanished.

Arthur said he understood her disappointment and felt for her, but after all, a valuable professional opportunity was worth sacrificing for, and long as a year might seem, it wasn't forever.

"I know, but it makes me feel everything is up in the air," Claudia said.

"If this is the right marriage for you, and you're both serious about it," Arthur said, "it won't stay up in the air."

"Oh, it is, if it ever happens." After a moment she added, with a bitterness Arthur could hardly blame her for, "Jim will have his work. He's already head over ears in it."

"You wouldn't really want him to be otherwise, would you?"

316

"Oh, no, of course not. I'd just like to share it with him."

Arthur's relief at the reassurance he thought he could give Rachel occupied so much of his mind that he was unprepared when Claudia said, "Remember when we all ate dinner at Uncle Kent's, and you talked about waste?"

"I remember talking too much."

"I don't want to be wasted."

Arthur felt for her at last the full twinge of sympathy he should have felt earlier. "Remember you aren't wasted on us," he said, "on Rachel and me, as long as we have you."

She smiled faintly and said, "I'll try not to let myself go again."

∘ ∘ *14* ∘ ∘

"You were sweet to Rachel this morning, Jim," Claudia said.

"Rachel is easy to be sweet to. I had no idea your aunt and uncle had been through all you've told me about. They're remarkable people, both. If I could help a little by just being decent, I'm glad."

"It was an inspiration to ask her to play. She'll trust you a lot more now. She didn't at first."

"So?" Jim said. He looked surprised, and then suspicious of her meaning. "What did she *dis*trust me about?"

"Oh, that was my fault, not yours. I'm afraid I showed I was upset at times—you can guess when they were. Rachel worries easily, and she thought—well, she held you responsible."

"I see. I can't blame her, but I'm glad if her confidence has risen. It can hardly be my talents as an accompanist, though."

"I especially appreciate your being sweet to her," Claudia said, "because I could see you were impatient all the time."

Jim flushed. "Honest, now, weren't you?" he said.

She studied him as he sat on the edge of the bed in the same apartment where, a spring and half a winter ago, he had invited her to his ill-fated steak dinner. Everything unchanged,

317

the same tiny, decently ugly living room, the same box of a bathroom, the same utility furniture, the yellow oak desk, the chalk-white straight chair, the decrepit easy chair in which she herself was sitting again. She studied the planes of his face, wide at the forehead, narrowing down to his small humorous mouth; she measured with her eyes the breadth of his shoulders, the efficient compactness of his hips. Oh, Jim, darling, if everything was only different! If it only hadn't worked out this way! The power of her resentment at the way things had worked out possessed her like an inhabiting demon. She was afraid it would lead her to lash out, to make him angry; yet it wasn't Jim, surely, she wanted to anger or punish. It was the situation she found herself in. She couldn't punish that; Jim was the only thing she could attack. He was simply in the line of fire. Perhaps she *needed* his anger to break down her own resistance, needed to attack in order to be forced into retreat and surrender.

The trouble was that she had no sooner met him at the airport that morning and driven him home to cook him a breakfast than she knew what he not only wanted—she could hardly be surprised at that—but what he counted on, what he had deliberately planned for. They had hardly crossed the sill when he held out both arms to her, and this time he didn't merely kiss her abstemiously at arms' length; oh, no, not at all, and for that matter she hadn't been abstemious herself, not in the least. So she knew well enough what he expected, though she didn't find the phrase for it until later, while he was playing accompaniments for Rachel: he expected to begin the curriculum. She was confronted with Helena's choice without Helena's time to make it. Time, she thought; Jim was impatient with time. He wanted to squeeze it dry on the instant. She needed, apparently, to use it more slowly, to consider and decide what she was really prepared to do. But didn't she want what Jim wanted? Hadn't she covertly known all along how it would be? Oh, if things were only different, if they hadn't worked out as they had! If Jim didn't veer from one extreme to another because he made up his own mind how she must feel without letting her work things out at her own pace!

He'd left a question hanging in the air: hadn't she been impatient too, while he labored through obbligatos with Rachel? She didn't feel capable of saying yes or no to that; she said, "Wasn't it lucky your friend just happened to be giving up his apartment?"

Did he read the storm warnings in her voice? Apparently not. He grinned with self-satisfaction and said, "Call it luck. It was, but I don't trust luck implicitly. I gave it a nudge in the right direction."

"What do you mean?"

"Well, I knew he planned to go abroad, I knew he was working on his thesis and had no finals, so I called him up and used a little persuasion to make him vacate early."

"Did you tell him why you wanted him to get out?"

Jim flushed again. "You wouldn't think I'd implicate you?" he said. "For God's sake, no. I can be discreet. I put it on grounds I had to see some things here before the expedition gets under way, and it would help like hell to have a room near the college."

"I see."

"I thought—well, all we have is three days, Claudia, less than that now by some hours. I thought a place where we could get away by ourselves—"

He looked at her inquiringly. She supposed he should get credit for the manoeuver he had made, but the complicity in which they had both been engaged, Jim by conscious purpose and she by an acquiescence she hadn't let herself face, all at once struck her as cynical and transparent. She had insisted on taking a week of accumulated vacation time; the museum had been irked and inconvenienced. Eyes would be watching. She felt batteries of eyes smirking in on the two of them through the dusty afternoon windowpane. She felt as public as if they had set up a bed in the middle of a basketball court. What if gossip got back to Arthur and Rachel?

But the coin had another side. Here was the man she loved and expected to marry. If she didn't want what he wanted, in defiance of convention or suspicion or even the risk of hurting others, what was wrong with her? The answer seemed obvious, but somehow she had never envisioned her life as taking the course to which it had brought her, and she felt unprepared. She must be one of those people who just naturally like standards or ceremony, something like that, something open and recognized, about the major steps in life. The pressure of haste, the mockery of circumstance, made what she apparently had to do seem not a consummation but a defeat. "You've worked out what you want very cleverly," she said, "haven't you, Jim?"

"I thought it would be what we both want."

"You always know what I feel without asking me."

"This time it's different," Jim said. "You've told me you love me. I have it in writing."

"Oh, Jim, you have everything! You have your work—just to hear you describe it to Rachel this morning, the maps, the tents, the trucks, the movie cameras, the tape-recorders, the God knows what, down to the last tin of dried prunes! That's what you're really in love with!"

She expected him to be incensed at that, but his answer was merely plaintive. "Honey, we've been all over this before," he said. "This is an opportunity on which we build our whole future, hard now, but it means everything in the long run. You wouldn't want me to give it up? That's maybe the one thing you could ask that I wouldn't do. I didn't mean to gloat when I talked about it, as if it didn't cost me anything to put things off for a year, but yes, I'm keen on my job. The day I'm not, you can begin to worry about me."

"So I'm just sex. I'm just a passing convenience on your way to what you really want to do."

"Did you want me to skip off without so much as a good-by?" Jim said. "Did you expect me just to give you a fraternal peck on the cheek, as I was fool enough to do once before? You told me I was a fool."

She had angered him at last. One brief show of it was enough. The punitive impulse had exhausted itself, and she felt her eyes run. "I'm sorry, Jim," she said. "I'm appalled at myself. It's just that—just that I love you so much, and I didn't want things to go this way."

"No more did I." Jim got up from the bed and bent over her

chair. She lifted her face to be kissed and wished that she could respond with more than passivity. He went back to his place, and she felt his eyes gravely studying her. "What is it, Claudia? If I'm not good at understanding how you feel, tell me. Are you afraid? Is that it?"

Afraid of what? Pregnancy—he might think she was worried about that, but he would be provided, and if there was a chance, a very off chance, even so— Afraid to go through with it; timid—that was what he meant. She smiled at him. "No, honestly, it isn't that." She paused, feeling helpless. "I'll stop being a fool. We're letting our three days go by."

He looked at her, unsatisfied. "I don't want to do anything you don't want to do," he said slowly. "Would it help—I don't know the laws in this state. There might be a five-day rule, but we might be able to get a waiver. We could get the standard tests—I thought you'd want a wedding, a real celebration, when we can."

She was grateful, despite an added twinge of distaste. "I do," she said. "Let's have a wedding when we're married, not a splurge, but—it would look like a shotgun affair if we just went to a JP, and I'd—I'd hate that."

Again he said slowly, "I don't want to do anything you don't want to do."

She saw by the extreme bleakness of his face that he meant what he said, or believed he did. "Now you're being noble, Jim. I don't want you to be noble, or I don't want to be the cause why you have to be. I just want—I only want to love you." Her breath began to come quickly, her voice to waver. "So let's make use of our time." He still sat looking at her gravely. "Did you hear, Jim?"

"I don't know whether that's what you really want," he said.

She was so deeply entrenched in the all but springless easy chair that she had to struggle to extricate herself, but she succeeded and sat down on the bed beside him. She put her arm across his neck and shoulder and lowered her head to his chest and leaned her weight against him, and at first she felt as rigid as if she were swathed in a cast. She tried to command her body to turn pliant, and after a moment the message reached its goal. She went limp so suddenly that she threw him off balance; he had to thrust out an arm and a bracing hand to keep from collapsing. Then both his arms were holding her, and his chin was grating on the top of her head as his voice spoke out across her free ear. "Are you sure, Claudia? Are you sure?" She couldn't answer that, even to herself, but she burrowed against him with her breast, and that sufficed. He went into his box of a bathroom, and she got up and looked down at the bed, trying to imagine what sort of appearance she would make lying in it with nothing on.

So they began the curriculum, but the school reputed easy turned out to contain unexpected possibilities of failure. By the time they had showered and dressed in turn in Jim's tiny bathroom, she was already reflecting on the results of the first test. She shouldn't be surprised, she told herself; she was inexperienced, and she hadn't started in the right frame of mind. Jim confessed apologetically that he'd been banked up too long and had allowed himself to hurry things too much. He was chagrined. He drove her home to dinner and protected her against the sense of transparency she felt by talking about his expedition and asking Arthur intelligent biological questions. After dinner he offered his services again as an accompanist, and Rachel responded with an alacrity that obviously moved Arthur in Jim's favor.

Finally Jim went to pieces completely over Beethoven. He laughed and said he'd better stick to Handel until he could revive his lost technique. Rachel smiled at him with tolerant reproach, and Claudia said she and Jim had thought of going out for the evening. She had to swallow hard as she said it. She spoke for Jim's sake, not for her own. A dread had begun to define itself in her: what were they going to *do* for the rest of their time? Short as it was, they couldn't spend it *all* on one single thing, could they? To go to a movie would be idiocy. To look up some of the set they used to talk the night hours away with—she thought she might like that best, but Jim, as she foresaw, had his own ideas. He hadn't secured his little apartment for their exclusive use without meaning to use it.

She thought sadly that they'd gone at one step from being friends who weren't yet lovers to being lovers who had no time to be friends.

Fear of failure was not a good preparation for the second test, nor was trying too hard more successful than inexperienced passivity. Jim drove her decorously home in her car at midnight, and she fell into an exhausted sleep, grateful and alone in her own bed. In the morning she examined her face for signs of haggardness or traces of guilt, mildly surprised to find none. She made Jim a late breakfast when he called at ten o'clock. They drove out into the country and might have learned to be friends again if she had not heard the clang of time at her back. After lunch Jim played another sonata or two with Rachel, and then they were climbing up to his apartment again; it was afternoon of the second day.

So a pattern almost established itself; but briefness and urgency seemed insurmountable obstacles to its fruition. It wasn't until the last and most hopeless moment that by some stroke of luck or abandonment she suddenly discovered in full what she would be missing while Jim was away. A great quantity of tears, not separate drops, but an entire cascade, ran out of her eyes all at once and wet the pillow, wet Jim's face and his bare shoulder and all down his chest, until they were swimming in it and his cheek was glued to hers by a sticky fluid. It was all right, she told herself; they would be lovers, they would know how to satisfy each other completely, if only Jim came back to claim her for good. It seemed as though the thought had no more than formed than he was fishing with his bare arm on the ghastly little white table by the bed, looking at his watch, and speaking of the plane he had to catch. She felt as though it were literally beyond the limits of the possible that she should be able to dress and drive him to the airport and drive herself home; after she had done it, she had to go up to her room and cry bitterly again, but she remembered her last redemptive moment and began to build on it as on a cornerstone of confidence and promise for the future that surely would come.

The football leg seemed determined to give increasing trouble these days. It produced sensations Kent had never felt from it before. It tickled or grew numb, as if it weren't getting enough juice. It wanted to go to sleep all the time. The shoe down at the end of it bound the ball of his foot; the pinch after a time became a steady throbbing.

Kent got up, went to the bedroom, and by rummaging in the cupboard behind Abby's clothes managed to open the locker in which he kept his camping equipment. He pulled out the pair of old felt slippers he found comfortable for lounging in at the bridge or poker table after a day's fishing, took off his shoes, and eased his feet gratefully into the slippers instead. Then he shuffled back across the hall to the upstairs desk room where he had been sitting, the only free room in the house since the children had driven up yesterday at a summons from Abby.

He let himself down again into the armchair across from the towering cabinet desk, a relic handed down from Grandmother Randall, a cumbersome mass of drawers with brass locks and keys, of pigeonholes in tiers, all surmounted by a superstructure of shelves behind casement doors. The spectacle of the desk faintly suggested the activity of writing; in one of those pigeonholes a stack of his personal stationery was neatly wedged. But he wasn't ready yet. A man could be driven only so hard and so far; his will needed time for recovery, didn't it, before it could be goaded to exert itself again?

A sound reached his ear with just enough strength so that his mind sluggishly identified it: the vibrating globe bowled out by a clapper meeting a bell-rim in a steeple. Sunday morning services. He felt the inadequately cushioned oak pew of the First Congregational Church in Amity grinding his youthful hunkers again, while Grandmother Randall sat beside him with stiffly erected backbone and face resolutely fixed toward the pulpit. The First Congregational Church gave way to more congenial arenas. He was fishing for trout in the pools of the brook that wound down through the wooded ridges and eventually fed into the river; he was jumping up and down on top of the sand banks above the bright, lazy bend of the channel to make the startled cliff swallows come pelting out of their holes like bats. But no, he wasn't in any such cheerful state; he was walking out to the pitcher's mound in the last of the ninth inning, knowing that he was through, absolutely done in and finished, knowing that he had to pitch and lose the game because he had no stuff left to serve up. His arm was a toothache; it felt like the crucifixion.

The recollection was inadequate. The state he was in now admitted of no localized image. His whole body, and his soul too, if he had such a thing, had turned into a raw tooth. He was a total ache, as if he had been stretched by ropes and winches until his tendons had pretty nearly parted from his joints. He realized that he was clenching his jaws; that was part of the ache. He forced them to relax. Then the numbness of his leg seemed to mount and spread through him in a kind of soporific haze. He stretched the leg and wriggled his toes inside the gray felt slipper, and a sense of life came back.

He heard the study door open downstairs, heard footsteps come out into the hall. Talk was going on inside the room, and his mind made a halfhearted effort to distinguish words. Then Ruth's voice called out clearly, "What are you doing out there, Randy?" The boy made no answer. Kent thought he heard him lift the cover of the cushioned bench under the window, looking for birthday and Christmas toys kept for visits under less constrained circumstances. "Come back, please, Randy," Ruth said, but she was too late. Randy had found the extravagantly loud policeman's rattle and was whirling its wooden tongue and ratchet in a barrage of sound that grated like a file-blade driven into a man's skull.

The noise wavered and turned spasmodic as Ruth came running from the study. A chase ensued. Randy took to the stairs, Ruth baying on his trail. "Randy, come back, you mustn't disturb Grandpa!" The boy outscrambled her to the second floor and dodged from room to room, probably under beds and around furniture. He appeared in the doorway and stopped suddenly, meeting Kent's eye. His own eyes enlarged and grew solemn; the policeman's rattle dangled motionless from his wrist. Ruth caught him by the shoulders and took it from him. "I'm sorry, Daddy," she said.

"It's all right. Let him have his fun." Kent heard the words, but he had no sense of speaking them. They seemed to float from his mouth like bubbles.

"Now, downstairs," Ruth said, "and I think you and your brother had better play outdoors for a while."

He could hear bustling in the lower hall. Ruth rounded up young Kent to take charge of Randy in the yard, issuing off-bounds instructions; then the front door closed behind them. The study door must have been left open for a moment, because he heard Abby with startling distinctness, almost as if she were at his elbow. She must be speaking to Brainerd; her voice was distressingly unsteady. "It's the blow to his pride, it's the injustice—I wish you could help persuade him—" The door closed, and he could hear only the faintest shapes of sound to tell him that they were all still talking to one another.

So they had names for it! He felt a sense of surprise and illumination. Pride. Injustice. He might have thought of the words for himself. Did they define the total ache that was worse than any joint spiked by exhaustion? A man felt galled by what he considered unfair treatment, no doubt of that; but he couldn't expect complete justice at every bend in the road, so he learned to discount injustice in advance. Pride —he supposed that came nearer to the mark. After all the years he had put into the company, the money he had saved the outfit by efficiency, the record for building and production he'd established—funny, he hadn't really thought the blow would fall, but if it did, he hadn't expected that Dynamic Leadership would deliver it in person. He didn't think Dynamic Leadership was man enough. He thought he'd get a dictated note, like the others who'd been thrown out. He was really surprised when he was told face to face. In the new table of organization we're drawing up, looking toward the transfer of operations to New Jersey, we don't seem to have a place for you, Mr. Warner. But the new building program, the expansion of plant that will be needed? Oh, as to that—the smirk that went with the words was the hardest thing for pride to take. As to that, a nationally known firm of architects, one of the leading industrial construction companies— You see how it is, Mr. Warner. Severance pay in recognition—annuity up to the value of current accumulation, or lump sum payment, whichever— Could it have happened just the day before yesterday? Yes. Write it down as pride's Black Friday.

He could still feel in his head the buzz of Randy's police rattle, like a wood-rasp scraping between his ears. The picture he made in the doorway after his pursuit by Ruth defined itself again to Kent's view: the round, solemn, enlarging eyes just staring in arrested awe. No wonder he'd been startled, coming that way on his grandfather, who was himself just sitting and staring, alone in a room he seldom used. The other Randy, the real Randy, had got into his share of scrapes, none too serious, none that left behind any nasty pieces to pick up. He'd smashed the car one time—every kid had to do that. He'd gone beyond his capacity two or three times while he was learning to drink. No girl trouble, none at any rate to cause more than ordinary concern, though Kent could remember driving Randy and his date home from a fifteen-year-old dance when the whole back seat got in such a tangle you couldn't tell what arm or leg went with what sex or individual. He'd spoken to Randy about that, and Randy had accepted his cautions reasonably. Then the pure accidents, of course: the time Randy dived into a pothole, only to discover that the water was deceptively shallow, so that he had to spend three days in the hospital recovering from a concussion. The recurrent dream Kent thought he had left behind came back to him, suddenly vivid, the sense of frantic effort against insidious obstacles, of legs that lifted like pig-iron as they tried to flounder up a mountain like a breaking wave, through snow that offered no more grip than a bottomless fog. He

327

shifted in his chair, as though he were rolling over in bed to forestall the end of the dream.

Another series of footsteps was climbing the stairs. He hadn't noticed them until they nearly reached the top. Slow, even, and heavy, they carried Brainerd across the hall and into beetling visibility in the doorway. His big face peered apprehensively over a tray bearing what had every appearance of being a highball. Kent returned his look with faint surprise.

"We thought you might like a drink before lunch," Brainerd said. "As a matter of fact, since it's a—a family Sunday, we're all having one downstairs. We hoped you'd join us."

Kent reached toward the glass, or his arm reached for him, without any accompanying sense of volition. He tried a swallow and found it welcome. "Thanks," he said.

"Is it mixed right?"

"The chief ingredient is there. I don't know about lunch, but I'll come down and sit for a while."

His leg was numb enough so that he had to brace himself for an instant against the arm of his chair when he got up. After a step or two it began to prickle and function as he followed Brainerd into the hall. He slid one hand along the banister as they went down, gingerly carrying his highball in the other, but he hardly needed support. In the study, the whisky began to have a salutary effect. It enabled him to sit through lunch, even to eat a few bites and to share in the talk, though he seemed to speak by a set of automatic circuits rigged up somewhere outside the ordinary control centers.

After lunch he excused himself on the plea that he had things to do at his desk. As he headed out through the hall, Ruth's baby woke from her midday nap and began a thin, imperious wail upstairs. At the same moment the doorbell rang. Kent turned by reflex to answer it. He was conscious of Ruth hurrying behind him toward the stairs, pausing long enough at the foot to see who might be ringing the bell.

The face Kent confronted when he opened the door was familiar enough, but something seemed to have gone wrong with it. All would have been normal if it had looked thirty-five years older. Then the belated recognition caught up with him. Of course, it wasn't Old Stocky, it was Young Herman. "Well, Herman," Kent said, "what can I do for you?"

The boy extracted a reporter's notebook from the side pocket of his crumpled wash jacket; a pencil was strapped to it by a rubber band. "I don't want to interrupt your Sunday or anything," he said, "but I wondered whether I could ask you a couple of questions, Mr. Warner?" He put one foot, then both feet, on the sill, and stood in the frame of the door. Short of offering bodily opposition or bumping the door shut in his face, Kent could hardly dislodge him. He gave back a step and said, "If it doesn't take too long. We're having a little family reunion, or I'd ask you into the study."

"Oh, it won't take long," Herman said, slipping the pencil from the rubber band.

"Are you a reporter now?" Kent asked.

"They won't give me a chance yet, but I'll tell you what I'm doing, Mr. Warner. I'm trying to get the facts on Fullchem. After all, it was Dad's firm. I guess you were one of his righthand men."

"How is your old man?" Kent asked.

"He's quite a lot better. He's more independent all the time. The doctor says if he takes care of himself he can last for years."

"I'm glad to hear it."

"About the company," Herman said. "What I think is, here's one of the biggest stories this town ever broke, but the paper won't touch it. They just take the handouts from this new guy, this Cyrus Bracket who's stepped into Dad's place, mostly about himself and what a tycoon he thinks he is. Now I'm trying to get all the dope, everything—what it will mean to the town when this guy Bracket pulls out to New Jersey, the people who've been thrown out in the cold, the human interest—you know about the suicides?"

Kent stared at the pale wedge of face looking up at him. Denis Prouty—he'd heard about Denis; the surprise was minimal in his case, but had others done the same thing?

"Mr. Prouty was the first," Herman said with sepulchral relish. "Then Mr. Abramson—"

"Fred Abramson?" Kent said. The shock came as sharply

as his general numbness permitted. "You know that for a fact? When did it happen?"

"The obit will be in the morning edition. Body found in his car with the windows shut and the motor running. 'It is believed he became despondent as a result of financial reverses since his retirement'—that's what the obit says. Retirement, crap! This Bracket axed him as soon as he thought he could get away with it. This story has everything! The unemployment it's going to mean in this town! There's a lot of people, they've worked for Fullchem all their lives, they've still got mortgages on their houses. They can't afford to pull up stakes and move to Manhattan or wherever, even if they get the chance. When you figure the New York, New Jersey angle, it's practically national. I tell the paper if they wrote it up they might get a Pulitzer Prize, but they're afraid of losing some advertising lines. I thought if I got all the facts and put 'em together in a feature story, they might have to print it. If they don't, I'll stay here till I get some experience and then I'll get a job on some paper that really wants to print the news."

"I hope you'll get a Pulitzer Prize yourself someday, Herman," Kent said.

"Well, who knows?" Herman grinned a little sheepishly. "Anyway, Mr. Warner, I'm trying to get all the cases and details, and I thought—I got the idea you might be willing to talk, make a statement about how you see it."

Kent inspected the down-turned mouth, the blue eyes that looked at him inquiringly. A stir of anger began in him, but it did not gather head. The features he saw were those of Old Stocky; for a moment the two so closely similar faces pulsated back and forth, replacing each other in uneasy superimposition. Then he became aware that someone was approaching from the direction of the study. Abby drew up at his elbow. She smiled at Herman, but Kent could see two white spots of tension on either side of her chin.

"Isn't it nice to have you pay us an unexpected call?" she said. "I'm glad to hear Mr. Stockwell is improving so. I hope he'll soon be able to join us for a rubber of bridge."

"He might, at that," Herman said. "He'd like it."

"You're married now, Herman. How does it feel to be the head of a household?"

"It's still a bit new, but it's okay."

"You must bring your wife to call on us one of these days," Abby said. "We'd ask you to join us all now, except that Cappie is exhausted by all the extra work he's been doing, and he's loafing with his family today before going on a fishing trip. Perhaps it would be better if you talked with him after he gets back."

"Why don't you do that, Herman?" Kent said. "There isn't a thing I'm in a position to say now."

Young Herman looked crestfallen, suspicious, but hardly surprised. For a moment he stubbornly held his place, then he reconciled himself to the inevitable. He snapped the rubber band over his pencil and notebook and put them back in his pocket. The motion brought his eyes downward briefly, and Kent had the feeling that his old lounging slippers were being observed and filed away in a reportorial memory as possible data for a feature story. "Well, thanks," Herman said. "I'll be around again. How long will you be gone?"

"Two weeks, at least," Abby said quickly.

Kent turned to her when the door closed. "What's this about a fishing trip?" he asked.

"We don't have to settle it now," Abby said. "But we've been talking about it. We think it's what you ought to do."

So they had all been talking about him behind his back, deciding for him what action he ought to take. Ruth, coming down the stairs with the baby's chin resting on her shoulder, added her voice to the conspiracy. "You simply must, Daddy. We all think you must. You'd come back healthy and brown and full of energy for whatever you make up your mind to do next."

"The ice wouldn't be out of the lake yet," Kent said.

"What, in the middle of May?" The baby uttered a healthy ourp, and Ruth added the encouragement of a thump on the small of her back.

"It depends on what kind of season they've had."

"Well, you wouldn't have to start right away, but please, Daddy, promise."

"I'll think about it," Kent said.

He found himself contemplating the exposed leg of his granddaughter as it dangled down Ruth's front; the other leg was doubled into the hollow of her arm and shoulder. The knee joint revealed itself only as a double crease of fat; the tiny calf hung slack and mottled, like an uncooked sausage, not yet a usable limb, except for thrashing and kicking when she got in a fury. A human cub took a long time to shape up and get started. Ruth turned and carried her off toward the study.

If Abby would share a fishing trip with him, if they could coordinate schedules with Pete Blanchard and his wife—for a moment Kent considered the possibility as though it could be taken seriously; but no, it wouldn't do. Their plot was having an effect on him, though, even if not the one intended. Together with the main item of news Herman had divulged, it had set a change of current running in him. "Did you hear what Herman said about Fred Abramson?" Kent asked.

"Isn't it awful?" Abby said. "I wonder what I should do? I've hardly met his wife more than once or twice, but I feel as though I ought to call."

"Maybe we'd better let the dust settle."

"I don't know anything about Jewish funerals. Do people send flowers?"

"Let's wait and see whether there's any indication in the paper."

"You ought to write a note, at least, Cappie."

"Later," Kent said. "I've got other things to do first."

Later he would write to Fred's widow; later he would feel the force of Fred's tragedy. Right now he was postponing too long what he had to do for himself and those who depended on him. He climbed the stairs again and stood for a moment in the doorway, looking at Grandmother Randall's monstrosity of drawers and pigeonholes and cabinets. Then he sat down in the ladder-backed chair that faced its available writing surface.

Pete Blanchard was one of the first people to whom he'd have to bare the facts. He wished now that he'd accepted Pete's proposal of a partnership when Blanchard Tool & Die, years ago, was just a gleam in Pete's imagination. He hadn't thought then that Pete could raise the capital to make a go of it, and he would have been right if Pete hadn't profited by a couple of early breaks. Now Pete had his own flourishing organization, though a small one; he wouldn't have room for an out-of-work engineer whose middle age wouldn't last many years longer.

Of course, if there was anything in the notion of setting up shop as an independent consultant, as he'd always wanted to do—Fullington would make a poor headquarters for such a risky enterprise, too small, too off-center, but he could try. He had some solid accomplishments and some reputation to give him a start. He'd need an office, a secretary, a letterhead. Kent Warner, Consulting Engineer. Pete might use him now and then, perhaps give him an initial push ahead. No, you couldn't count on friendship that way. Kent saw himself breaking the news, the initial incredulity in Pete's eye, the quick spasm of sympathy, then the protective hardening of expression that would mean: Jesus, man, you're in a fix, and I'm sorry, but I can't take over your troubles. Or Pete might say: Sure, Cap, we've got a little job right now we could use some help on. The job would turn out to be some piddling problem Pete's outfit could just as well solve for itself. Add it all up, it might come to a couple of hundred bucks at *per diem* rates. The main hope with Pete was that he had contacts. Let me call up so-and-so, Cap; I've heard about a change there. Well, he'd have to get in touch with Pete tomorrow. Pete might be free for lunch. Meanwhile, he could start writing letters.

Even before beginning, he foresaw the standard answer. Would like to take advantage of your availability, but with our existing organization we cannot make an offer consistent with your experience and qualifications. However, we are placing your letter on file . . . Experience. Qualifications. Call it age, call it years. Getting on toward retirement. Everyone wants youth nowadays.

Still, he had to begin somewhere. He got up, his leg numb again, lifted his seldom-used typewriter to the desk, opened its case, and slid a sheet of stationery into the roller. It took him a long time even to type the date with his hunt-and-peck system. Don't sound overeager. Reorganization at Fullchem makes it advisable to consider other opportunities. That was the line to follow. No suggestion of appealing under pressure; the note to strike was the note of confidence. A wheeze at the end would help establish that. He got up and went to his clothes cupboard in the bedroom, fished through the pockets of his business suits until he found his little black book of jotted reminders. He carried it back and put it beside his typewriter for reference.

Hunt and peck, hunt and peck. While he was looking for the *i* to follow the *n* of opportunities, Abby came to the doorway and surveyed him. The percussion of the keys must have carried downstairs and aroused curiosity. "What are you doing, Cappie?"

"Getting to work on my correspondence."

Abby came and leaned over his shoulder, seeing what he meant by his correspondence. "You won't go fishing?"

"Every day I'm a day older."

"That's nonsense. You're in the prime of life, and everything is going to work out all right, but you owe yourself a rest so that you can come back stronger."

"Tomorrow I get in touch with Pete Blanchard," Kent said. "Then I begin pounding the pavement, knocking on doors—"

Abby put her arms on his shoulders and her face against his. He felt the incontinence of her eyes. "You're a fighter, aren't you, Cappie? I hope you aren't asking more courage of yourself than a man has to give."

Pride. Injustice. Courage. Abby seemed to have words for the whole situation. Fighter—that was the one he liked best.

○ ○ *16* ○ ○

As Arthur emerged from the Administration Building after his appointment with Aiken, the rectangle of turf that formed

334

the Rowley campus presented one of its hourly scenes of activity. The bell had just stopped ringing in the chapel belfry. Lines of figures intersected one another on the blacktop walks, most of them on their way to lunch at dining halls or fraternities or Faculty Club. The weather was getting into its Commencement stride, hot and bright, though a few puddles were left from the rain that according to the adage began before seven and cleared before eleven.

Arthur heard a clicking of uncushioned heels and saw Lamson Crocket, his head screwed slightly to one side, rounding the corner of the building just as Arthur himself started down the steps. They met at the foot. Lamson hesitated. For an instant Arthur thought he was going to go on with no more than the briefest nod and a flicker of his eye; for an instant Arthur was on the verge of doing so himself. Then Lamson stopped and looked significantly up at the windows of the President's office on the third floor. "A little log-rolling with the administration?" he asked.

"I've been seeing the President," Arthur admitted. "We talked about a number of things, but mainly I had a piece of news to tell him."

"Local news?"

"I guess the answer to that is yes and no."

"You looked pleased," Lamson said.

"I am," Arthur confessed. "I won't deny it."

"Must be something big, to judge by your face. Have you had an accolade?"

Arthur laughed. "Something like that, modestly proportioned to my case."

"You aren't saying what?"

"Not till it's official."

Lamson looked downward. With his left toe he tapped in order five of the bricks that bordered the walk at the foot of the steps. He tapped them again in reverse and said, "I may as well add to your pleasure by some news of mine. I won't be here next year."

"Any pleasure I might take in that I'll have to take from a distance," Arthur said. "I don't expect to be here myself."

The words slipped from his mouth before he could check or consider them. He hadn't intended to be sharp, but, now that he'd spoken, he couldn't help being amused at himself. Lamson flushed, and the injured expression that Arthur had seen on his face once before took shape again. "Where are you going, Lamson?" Arthur asked hastily.

"Government," Lamson said. "They seem to value me in Washington."

"A year's leave?"

"It might be for good."

"I hope you find it rewarding," Arthur said. "Whatever you think, I've always recognized the importance of your work."

"I suppose you're going to philosophize or be literary somewhere," Lamson said. "I hope you find that rewarding. Well, so long, Arthur."

He turned and bustled off. Arthur felt uneasily that in his own way Lamson had offered a personal olive branch and had considered himself rebuffed. Arthur almost set out to overtake the retreating figure as it clicked off in the direction of the Faculty Club. He could have walked along with Lamson, lunched with him even, to show that he could dismiss bygones as bygones, but he was too full of his own mood to try to patch over relations that weren't of his own making. He went on toward his office and midway across the patch of green campus met Pritchard, heading from another angle toward the club.

"Hello, Arthur. Not going to lunch?" Pritchard asked.

"I'll join the one-o'clock shift," Arthur said. "I have some things I want to do first."

Pritchard looked at him inquiringly. "You look as though you'd just swallowed the canary," he said. He began to smile, as if by contagion from Arthur's own face.

"I've had some good news," Arthur said.

"I'm glad to hear it. Is it under wraps, or public property?"

Arthur's impulse was to say that he couldn't divulge his news yet, but here was a man who had shown him a friendly disposition and taken a crisp part in battles he hadn't fought any too effectively for himself. Reserve and caution ought to acknowledge some limit. "As a matter of fact, I've been invited to give a series of lectures abroad, and the invitation comes at a time when, I must confess, it couldn't be more welcome. I've cleared everything with Aiken. I haven't anything to worry about except possible private obstacles."

"You'll take a Sabbatical?"

"The whole year—work up and write the lectures in the first half, give them in the second, travel if there's any time left."

"Whereabouts? Oxford, Edinburgh, Strasbourg?"

"Nothing so exalted," Arthur said. "Provincial British. A foundation open to both public and university. What makes it desirable to me is that it's practically a mandate to write the book I want to write anyway, and I'll have time and opportunity to do it."

"What about Bi Sci 3?"

"Aiken is willing to bring in a visiting lecturer, if we can find one at this late date. Otherwise my chief assistant can do it for a year."

"You'll keep on giving the course when you come back?"

"I'm trying not to look that far ahead, but I'd expect to, unless the Department or the outside board of review decides that Bi Sci 3 is a dispensable luxury."

"Improbable," Pritchard said, smiling.

"As a matter of fact I told Aiken some of the charges more or less tacitly or openly aired in our defunct Committee. I told him I'd welcome any fresh assessment by any board or group. He said—I don't think I'm violating a confidence, because I believe he intends to write the Chairman. He said he thought he could give an assurance that any extra cost of Bi Sci 3—my assistants and secretary and so on—wouldn't stand in the way of any new projects or changes the Department might want to propose. He made it clear he wasn't just handing us a simple increase in budget. He just said that fresh undertakings would be considered on their merits. I don't mean I think this ought to be a factor in any review of the course, but it did make me think I wouldn't be, *hadn't* been, an obstacle to any new proposal of any value."

337

"You never needed to feel you were an obstacle," Pritchard said. "Well, Arthur, I'll envy you next year, and I'm delighted for your sake."

Somewhat to Arthur's surprise, Pritchard thrust out his hand. Arthur accepted it gratefully, and then they parted, Arthur going on to his office and Pritchard to the Faculty Club.

Janice had gone out for the noon hour. Arthur unlocked his office door and sat down at his desk. Things he wanted to do before lunching, he'd told Pritchard, but the only thing he really wanted to do was gloat over his luck and ask himself whether he faced any serious hindrances to its fulfillment. Rachel was his only genuine concern. He was afraid the prospect of upheaval in itself would arouse her anxieties. To make matters worse, she was badly disturbed at the moment about Abby and Kent, as she had a right to be. He'd simply have to argue that they couldn't possibly help by staying home, nor would Abby and Kent want them to. Rachel would think at once of Claudia, too, but that problem should prove easy. Claudia would come along; in fact, she would be almost indispensable. She could tide Rachel over any feeling of disruption, help her get settled and secure, perhaps travel with her on the Continent now and then while he applied himself to his lectures. Surely Claudia was at a juncture in her life—Jim away, a year of waiting before marriage—when she would leap at the chance. It was part of his luck to be able to offer it to her.

Thinking of Claudia, he wondered, as he had a number of times already, about floating impressions left in his mind since the three days of Jim's visit. He couldn't put his finger on anything; he didn't know, he couldn't ask, it was none of his business. He couldn't tell whether Rachel shared any suspicion with him; he certainly wouldn't drop a hint, he would leave it to her to speak first if she chose to. So far she hadn't; partly, he thought, because Jim had won her over. For that matter, Arthur had been considerably won himself. Jim had brought Claudia home at a sufficiently seemly hour on each of the two nights he had been in town, and he *could* have ousted a friend and reclaimed his bachelor quarters without ulterior purpose. Well, it wasn't for an aging if not aged biologist to be surprised at any conjunction of the human sexes, except that when a man stood *in loco parentis*, when for all his scientific pretensions he had perhaps never shaken off, at the deepest level, the moral bias of an earlier place and age— Times change, and we with them, Arthur thought. Mores had undergone a mighty revolution since he and Rachel first discovered each other in an Amity kitchen and made such diffident progress thereafter. If he looked into himself honestly, would he detect a little envy of Claudia and Jim? But there, of course, he was supposing what he didn't really know.

At the end of the day, as he neared the house on his walk homeward, Arthur remembered that at his own urging Rachel had invited three friends to make up a quartet and spend the evening reading scores. She had withdrawn temporarily from the Civic Orchestra, and that might well be for the best, but she certainly mustn't withdraw from all her music. The quartet, as it happened, worked to his advantage. As soon as it got actively absorbed, he was able to signal Claudia and take her up to his study for consultation. He gave her the letter inviting him to serve as the next incumbent of the Sir James Allison-Titchfield Lectureship in Natural Science. "I want you to see something that reached me this morning, right out of the blue," Arthur said. "It's lucky I went to my office and discovered it before keeping an appointment with President Aiken. You'll see it calls for planning."

Claudia took the letter from him passively; as she read, her face grew alert with interest. "Why, Uncle Arthur, this is a tremendous honor. Doesn't it sound British, though? And they've come all the way over here and singled you out—"

"Now, now," Arthur said. "I'm really not showing it to you for flattery. William James really broke a trail when he was the first American asked to deliver the Gifford Lectures, but since then the two-way, or multi-way, traffic has become commonplace."

"It *is* an honor," Claudia insisted. "Don't pretend it isn't. Of course you'll accept. You must."

"I'm only worried about uprooting Rachel. I can't think of leaving her behind with Abby and Kent in their current state of uncertainty, but I'm afraid she'll be upset at the mere thought of going."

"I can see that," Claudia said, "but I think I can help persuade her."

"You could help most of all if you wanted to come along," Arthur said. "You could get Rachel settled, then you could do some traveling on your own, or perhaps take her for a swing or two on the Continent while I keep my nose to the grindstone in a provincial university town, with a run up to Cambridge or London now and then for books. How would you feel about that?"

For a moment Claudia looked almost in the bloom again. "Why, it would be a Godsend, Uncle Arthur! I'd simply love to, and I could help, I know I could. I almost feel as though I could live through—" Her underlying ordeal of patience broke through and showed in her face.

"That will be the greatest possible reassurance to Rachel," Arthur said. "I hope it won't be asking too much of you, but I'll have to work hard and steadily and put work first. You two can go gallivanting as much as you like."

"We'll tell her just as soon as the quartet breaks up," Claudia said.

"I'm afraid we're in for a wait. They've just got started." Arthur listened while the distant polyphony issued faintly from the living room, thinking that, to anyone who doesn't happen to be caught up at the moment in the charm of the music, the repeats and *da capos* of a classical minuet can take on a character of the relentless. He was about to speak when the quartet suffered the rivalry of a non-musical sound. The doorbell rang. Arthur welcomed the physical diversion of going to answer it.

"Malcolm! Come in."

Malcolm's eyes turned toward the source of the *allegro* that vigorously launched its opening notes from the living room. "You're having a musical soirée. I'd better drop by another time."

"I've been talking with Claudia in the study," Arthur said, "about some plans we have to make. Come join us for a while."

Malcolm looked uncertain. "I don't want to interrupt."

"I think we've settled the main issue," Arthur said.

"Well, then." Malcolm allowed Arthur to take his hat and put it on the cupboard shelf. In his hand he held a folder obviously containing a typescript. "I brought this along. I talked about the idea with Claudia, and I thought she might like to see the result."

They climbed up to the study, and Malcolm proffered the folder. "You may want to see how I worked the problem out. It's the 'Jesus, Hope of the World' story. I haven't given the old man a biography, the way you wanted me to, but maybe I've given him some life. You can see what you think."

"I'd love to read it," Claudia said.

"I've sent the ribbon copy to Rosamund, but this is the first carbon. You won't have any trouble with it."

"How is Rosamund?"

"She keeps her sense for copy," Malcolm said, "in the midst of her luxurious fetters."

Arthur thought that Claudia's nose wrinkled slightly with distaste at the words. He thought Malcolm looked as though he had come with a hope of detaching her and bearing her away for a renewal of their private sessions. "Arthur tells me you were making plans," Malcolm said. "I don't want to interfere."

"Show him your letter, Uncle Arthur," Claudia said. "Uncle Arthur has received a tremendous honor."

Arthur tried to make light of his honor, but Claudia refused to be put off. "If Arthur won't show you himself, I will," she declared and handed the letter to Malcolm.

Arthur winced. Malcolm had got him into trouble once before; no knowing what might happen again. "I haven't accepted yet," he said, "so it will have to be considered confidential."

"What are you afraid of, Arthur, old boy?" Malcolm asked.

"I'm superstitious. I have a strong sense of *absit omen*," Arthur said. "I knock on wood when a piece of luck threatens."

341

Malcolm laughed, and his eyes went back to the letter. Then the mottling of his face clouded, and he said enviously, "I can see what this means to you, Arthur. It means you get your book written. You'll be a writer who's writing, not wasting the one talent that it's death to hide." Before Arthur could speak, his loose flesh shuttled into a new expression, gleefully sardonic. "Listen to this," he said. "I quote: 'According to the will of the donor, Sir James Allison-Titchfield, first consideration is to be given to an authority who can relate the findings of natural science to the religious, philosophical, or ethical interests of mankind.' Arthur, you're under a mandate to put God in the last chapter!"

"Notice the saving 'or,' " Arthur said. "I have my choice of words. I can be as agnostic as I like."

Malcolm rose abruptly and put the letter down on Arthur's desk. "Well, I'll leave you to your planning," he said.

Arthur had the uncomfortable sense that Malcolm's figure had lost height. He seemed crestfallen, even disheartened, but he thrust out his hand, and for the second time during the day Arthur extended his own for an unexpected clasp. "Congratulations, old boy," Malcolm said. "Go ahead and do your book and rock everyone with it."

Arthur offered a drink and hoped he would stay till the quartet finished so that Rachel wouldn't miss him, but he insisted on taking his leave. Arthur and Claudia followed him down to the front door. In the hall he said, "There was one other thing I dropped in for. I'd like to give a little farewell dinner at the club downtown, you and Rachel and Claudia and the Warners. Just a little return on the hospitality you've offered me. How about it?"

"Speaking for ourselves, we'd be delighted, I'm sure," Arthur said. "About the Warners, they'd love to be asked, but Kent has been under—well, more than common business pressure. I hope they can come, but I wouldn't be certain. You'll understand if they can't."

Malcolm looked as though he were going to ask questions, but he thought better of it and said, "I'll try to get them, anyway."

After he had gone out, Claudia said, "I hope Uncle Kent can come. It would do him good. We'll start him telling yarns, and everyone will have a time."

"If there are any Malcolm hasn't heard by now," Arthur said.

"Remember the one about the first 'man-dance' when he was courting Aunt Abby at college, and it had just got over being called a female seminary? How he was looking for the building reserved for men and blundered into a dormitory where the girls were all dressing and met a real old dragon of a dean of women?"

"That's right," Arthur said. "We haven't heard that yarn for a long time."

"Shall we listen to the end of the concert and then tell Rachel?"

"Yes," Arthur said, "let's do exactly that."

When the performers at last folded their scores, when Rachel ushered them to the door and came back to shut her violin case and put it carefully on the piano, Claudia spoke first. "We have some wonderful news, Aunt Rachel."

"Wonderful?" As usual, when she was taken by surprise, her first response was one of alarm.

"Uncle Arthur has received a terrific honor."

She was relieved by that. Then she listened to the unfolding tale with bewilderment, misgiving, doubtful excitement. She brought up the expected apprehensions; Arthur and Claudia joined forces to beat them down. In the end Rachel decided that she really might survive listening to *The Magic Flute* in Salzburg if Claudia would keep her company.

The main issue settled, Arthur remembered Malcolm's proposal of a farewell dinner. Perhaps it would actually come off, and, if it did, it would represent something of a culmination, even a terminus. They would sit together at the club table, the Scheuers, the Warners, Malcolm Islay himself, a mixture of elements, an unstable compound the ingredients of which had for a time entered into solution and affected one another. Could any parting of the ways in human life escape a strain of melancholy? No telling where another year would find Kent and Abby; as for Malcolm, he seemed certainly the most volatile particle in the mixture. It was unlikely that he would play a part at Rowley again. Still, separations turned out often enough less final than they threatened to be, even in an uncertain world. Lines unexpectedly re-formed and crossed in different patterns; reunions occurred in defiance of probability. As for himself, Arthur felt that his mind had already performed whatever act of farewell might be in order. For a year he was liberated, free to enslave himself to a task he welcomed. He was itching to get at his work. He hadn't always been fortunate in the course of his life; no one was always fortunate; but for the moment he could count himself a fortunate man.

PART THREE

○ ○

The Whole Creation

The homing plane, smaller and more sensitive to turbulence than the transatlantic jet from which they had disembarked in New York, shuddered slightly and then dropped through a hollow in its atmospheric support, smacking on bottom as it found a floor of buoyancy again. Green lights belatedly instructed the passengers to fasten their seat belts. The plane was descending on a patch of cloud as it nosed down toward Fullington. The portholes turned gray as it settled into the flying vapor, the air roughened, the cabin bounced and fluttered. Arthur turned to Rachel, who sat beside him next the window. She was composedly adjusting her belt and smiled at him, undisturbed. People are subject to different forms of queasiness, Arthur reflected; Rachel's weren't physical. For that matter, she had considerably enlarged her range of independence and confidence in the course of a year abroad. With Claudia's help, she had learned to travel freely and enjoy it. That was not the least of the satisfactions he was bringing home with him.

The overcast thinned suddenly; the vapor shredded out, vanishing altogether as the plane emerged below cloud level. Arthur leaned against Rachel's shoulder to look out. The wing banked, and straight beneath it he saw, as if selected and focused by a skillful lens, the athletic fields of Rowley thrusting into the river in a green bell-shaped peninsula. A baseball game was going on. Arthur had time to perceive minute figures put themselves in motion, as if activated by cams; they scooted, absurdly slow, along the formal paths of the diamond, while others watched from the stiff small diagram of the bleachers. Then the wing lifted and leveled, and he could see, farther westward, the Rowley campus, the chapel belfry rising from gabled slate, the yellow stone forms of lab and lecture hall and library shouldering each other about the cramped central space of turf. Here was his locus of activity from now on; he was a homecomer. Home looked very unreal and parochial, viewed on this aerial scale which made it appear a comically tiny table toy. He felt unrelated to it, but by next fall he would slip back into harness as if no interruption had occurred. He would need harness, and Rachel would need all the musical connections she could revive. Claudia would be married. A new phase of life would set in.

The plane was following the river southward after coming in on a wide swing over the city in order to land upwind at the airport. Cars in double files moved in opposite directions along the river drive, as if carried on belts that alternately stopped and started. Claudia leaned forward from her seat behind Rachel. "Can you believe we're actually home again?" she said. "It doesn't look much like Vienna or Paris or even Bristol, does it?" Under the tip of the wing, the railroad bridge, the traffic bridge, the hospital took shape and sailed away to the rear, vanishing from the outspread map. The smoke and grit of the industrial district spiraled up. The plane banked and made a half-turn; it growled and strained as its landing gear was forced into position; then the wheels touched with a brief lurch of friction.

As Arthur signaled a cab and indicated the baggage he had piled on the curb, he felt familiarity invest him with its comfortable but numbing influence. Already the images of Europe in his mind were beginning to recede and grow faint. The cab driver was stowing the luggage in the trunk of his car. With his melting-pot face and heavily pelted arms, he stood no higher nor lower on any scale of value than countless millions of human beings on the continents or islands of the habitable globe; but he certainly gave a sharp reminder that they had touched down again on local American soil.

The driver stopped behind a trailer truck at an intersection,

348

and Arthur, looking out through the window, found his eye caught by an immense and lofty sign strung on a cross-hatching of steel across an impressive span of sky: FULLINGTON CHEMICAL AND PHARMACEUTICAL CORPORATION. He thought how seldom occasion had taken him through this part of town before. So far as he could remember, he had never visited the scene of Kent's former activity. A few of the buildings looked as though they might still be in use, but one, in the style of an old brick armory, wore an aspect of dejected emptiness; a number of its lower windows were broken, the jagged holes leering witlessly at the street. Might it be the antiquated central office that Kent was to have replaced? Never mind; Kent was far better off now than before, despite Abby's complaints that they had no home, no headquarters, living in a hotel in Detroit for a week, an apartment in New York for a month, camping wherever Kent's field missions took him. Kent had been forced to lower his sights financially, and that galled him more, Arthur thought, than it should. He was being paid for the exercise of his best talents, and being paid on the scale of a top professor at one of the stronger universities. He ought not to count that a disaster. The only alarming note about him in Abby's letters concerned his football leg; Arthur suspected the symptoms were more ominous than Abby would confess outright to Rachel.

The cab lurched ahead and for several traffic lights gained uninterrupted ground. When they surmounted the bridge over the river, they could see on the other side a vast lava bed of devastation. Bulldozers, bucket shovels, cranes, and trucks were making puny efforts to reduce the chaos to order. "What's this?" Arthur asked. "Is the city building a new link to the river drive?" The cabby swiveled his neck briefly and launched on a profane indictment of the whole project, especially the graft that was changing hands between contractors and politicians.

"I hope the tenants have left the house in some sort of decent condition," Rachel said, cutting short his invective. "I suppose we can't expect too much when we had to turn them out early. It's lucky they could find another place to go."

349

"I'm afraid I've inconvenienced everyone," Claudia said. "If it weren't for me, you and Uncle Arthur could spend the whole summer abroad."

"We'll go back next summer," Arthur said. "I'd like to see some of the places you visited together while I was sticking to my last. Right now we have a more important event in prospect."

"I don't see how we're going to do all we have to do," Rachel said. "There's the house to put in order, and everything for the wedding, from invitations to flowers. If only Abby could be here to help!"

"I can do a lot of things myself," Claudia said. "I'll shop like mad when I drive down to New York to meet Jim."

"Are you sure you ought to do that?" Rachel asked. "I don't like your driving all that distance by yourself, alone in the car."

"I'll be perfectly all right," Claudia said. "I want to see Jim again the minute he lands. It's just lucky that Helena can put me up and Jim has a place to stay while he takes care of some loose ends of work."

"But driving down all alone—"

"I'm a good driver, Aunt Rachel, and we'll want to be free to do things, take a spin out into the country or look up friends of ours in Connecticut and Long Island."

"It would be different if I could count on Abby."

"I'll only be gone a few days. We can manage everything before and after," Claudia said. Then she added, "I hope they can come to the wedding at least. I want Uncle Kent to drink a lot of champagne and tell all his stories and be the life of the party, and I want Jim to begin really knowing him."

The little altercation between them over Claudia's insistence on meeting Jim in New York had become familiar. Rachel might well view the management of a wedding with some trepidation, Arthur thought, but it was unlike her to oppose Claudia so persistently. He wondered whether her concern didn't have other roots as well. If she was worried about propriety, Claudia had secured her position by arranging to stay with Helena. Whatever misgivings Rachel might feel, she always wound up in defeat. Claudia was determined.

The cab swung westward, away from the river, and skirted the edge of campus. The familiar chimneys and gables, now that Arthur peered up at them from close range, looked at least more solid and imposing than they had as matchbox models on a flat distance under the wing of the plane. "This is the street," Arthur said, and the cab squealed around the corner into the last blocks before the house.

By the time Arthur paid and tipped the driver and carried the bags into the hall, Rachel and Claudia had vanished. He heard Claudia moving about upstairs in her room and discovered Rachel unlocking the piano and examining its surface for scars. It seemed unblemished, and she directed a critical look on the room in general. "The whole place will have to be cleaned," she said, running her finger over the drop-leaf table, "and they've moved the furniture all around." She began pushing at a displaced chair and saying that the old slip-covers she had left for the tenants would have to be taken off first thing in the morning and the good ones restored.

"Wouldn't it be a good idea to unpack?" Arthur asked.

"I have to see what sort of condition the house is in," she protested and went out through the hall into the pantry. He could hear cabinet doors being pulled back and drawers opened and shut. Arthur thought he might as well carry the bags upstairs and start on his own unpacking. He had almost finished sorting out laundry and hanging clothes in his cupboard when the telephone rang, a surprising sound when they had scarcely taken possession of the house again. He heard Rachel going to answer, and then her delighted cry of recognition: "Abby!"

He listened from the head of the stairs till the long and exclamatory conversation came to an end. Rachel called up to him. "They're right here in Fullington, Kent and Abby both. They're going to open and clean the house—their tenants have gone too—and then Kent is going on a fishing trip, his first vacation in two years. Abby will be here for several weeks, at least."

"We couldn't be greeted with better news," Arthur said.

"Abby got the letter I sent to Saint Louis, even though it had to be forwarded. She's gone shopping for us and wants to bring over some eggs and milk for breakfast. And they want us to go there for supper."

"I'm glad we'll see them so soon," Arthur said.

In due time Abby appeared with supplies to stock the ice-box for the morning, and they drove back with her. She apologized for the state of her premises. Rugs were at the cleaners and floors bare, windows uncurtained or hung with makeshift. Moreover, she and Kent had suffered worse luck from tenants than Arthur and Rachel. They had found a broken dining-room chair lying with uncollected trash in the cellar, their liquor cabinet was full of stale bottles, and cigarette butts had burned holes in table covers and bedspreads. Kent seemed to be bearing these depredations philosophically. His house might be reduced to a camp, and his stay brief, but he had provided the generally acknowledged means of hospitality. He was sitting in the study, his foot braced on his stool, a high-ball in hand, a well-equipped bar table at his side. He rose, despite all protests, as they came in. "Rachel, have you been playing before the crowned heads of Europe?"

"Not quite," Rachel said, laughing. "I hardly touched my violin, except toward the end, when Arthur was giving his lectures and I found a little college group that let me play with them."

"Claudia, my dear, you're more beautiful than ever. I hear you're about to take the most important step in life."

"Jim and I want you to be there, you and Aunt Abby. We'll promise lots of champagne if you'll promise to come."

"Cross my heart and hope to die," Kent said. "I'll come if I have to crawl on hands and knees."

"Rachel kept writing what a success your lectures were, Arthur," Abby said. "I should think you'd be feeling very proud and happy."

"A lecture is a lecture anywhere. I was certainly treated cordially."

"They were a brilliant success, and you know it, Uncle Arthur. The letter you got from the foundation afterwards was proof."

"I won't deny I was pleased," Arthur said.

"It's a horrible confession, but I'd never heard Arthur lecture," Rachel said. "I don't know how well I understood, but I couldn't help being impressed."

"I'm glad I can impress my own family, at least." Arthur was glad when attention scattered away from him to busy itself with inquiries about transatlantic flight, cities and sights, hotels and *pensions*, menus and prices. When had they left London? Did they really feel that they had come down to earth yet? Was it a horrible anticlimax to be back in Fullington again? Abby went out to the kitchen to inspect the progress of supper; Rachel and Claudia pursued her with offers of help. Left alone with Kent, Arthur tried to fuse the impressions he had been gathering sidelong during the talk. Kent had aged a little, he decided; the fine light hair at his temples had begun to gray at the roots, he had thickened at what he called the midsection, and barely perceptible lines marked the clear skin at either corner of his mouth. The football leg was not merely propped up; it wore a wool sock despite the mild late-May weather, and the foot was encased in a gray felt slipper.

"How's the leg, Kent?" Arthur asked.

"Miserable," Kent said genially, but his eyes darkened and turned away momentarily. "No immediate distress to amount to anything. It's the prognosis that's a damned uncomfortable thing to have hanging over you."

"What is it? What's the diagnosis, to begin with?"

"I don't know what Abby put in her letters."

"Nothing very definite, to tell the truth, but enough to indicate you were having trouble."

"It's the artery," Kent said. "It's going to pot, deteriorating. No elasticity. It won't carry the pumping load, so the subsidiary lines have to take over, and they can't do an adequate job. Low circulation. That's what they tell me."

"What about prognosis and treatment?"

"I may be able to struggle along the way I am, keeping the temperature even, doing exercises every day, having a check-up every now and then. I could go under the knife, but I don't like the look in the surgeon's eye. He's trigger-happy, if you ask me."

"What sort of operation would you be in for?"

"Transplant," Kent said. "From all I've heard of the results, I don't want to play ball, but the big club they hold over my head is an amputation. I guess they don't want to risk a clot breaking loose and traveling around my system. That would ring down the curtain at one tick if it got to the right place."

Kent spoke with detached evenness, as if he were making an engineering appraisal of his own organism, not without amusement at the unfavorable findings. He raised his highball to his lips. Was it the whisky that enabled him to speak as coolly as he had? No; Cap Warner might have his limitations, but a need for false courage had no place among them.

Arthur found his mind taking flight in a defensive fantasy under Kent's disturbingly level glance. He hadn't come down to earth yet; he was in a plane cabin, bouncing through the overcast, banking over the Rowley playing fields; rather, he was back in the lecture room of a provincial British university, feeling dwarfed by the barrel-vaulted roof, its carved supporting beams filigreed faintly in the shadows overhead with gilt and color, while he tried to draw the audience within the range of his voice. He forced himself back to the study where he sat with Kent across a quadrant of the big center table. No man would want to lose one of the members of the body he was born with; for Kent the deprivation would be more severe than for others.

Abby came back from the kitchen to announce that supper was ready. Kent gave a look of mock despair and asked whether she couldn't keep it on ice while they all had one more drink. He was denied the privilege; he could bring his glass to the table, but the meal wouldn't wait. It proved to be heartier than Arthur could cope with. Rachel and Claudia seemed to labor under the same difficulty, but Kent helped himself freely; his appetite hadn't suffered, nor had his readiness to talk.

By a tacit impulse, they continued to sit at table over liqueurs instead of going back to the study. Arthur asked what had happened to Fullchem as a result of all its changes, and Kent said he didn't know at first hand, but he understood the honeymoon period for the new President was over. Production hitches developed in the transfer to New Jersey; sales fell off, and the Directors were definitely uneasy. Kent was glad he had been heaved out in time; his luck had broken right, though the outfit he was with now certainly differed from the company Old Stocky had built up. Did they know that Old Stocky had cashed in his chips? He'd suffered another stroke, and this time it was fatal.

What about Kent's new outfit, Arthur asked; Micklejohn Industrial Research, wasn't that its name? M. I. R. certainly made a contrast with Fullchem, Kent said. For one thing it had no fixer. One of the bright young lights in the lab, who was working on an improved method for distilling sea-water, got an idea in the middle of traffic a week or so after Kent joined the firm. He drove through a red light, barely avoided a multi-car collision, and had to go to court, settle his ticket, and pay his fine like any ordinary citizen. M. I. R. took a different attitude toward profits, too. It was a profit-making concern, but old Micklejohn, who founded it, willed the controlling stock to his alma mater, so that it was really institutionally owned. Salaries reflected its academic ownership, but nobody seemed to care. The incentive lay in the job, whether the job called for a fringe discovery in physics or an elaborate mathematical and statistical method of selecting names from a mailing list for the most profitable distribution of a thousand-page catalogue. As an example of the Micklejohn temper of mind, Kent told of a client of the firm who got involved in a breach-of-patent suit. Some work M. I. R. had done bore on the alleged infringement. The case was highly technical; neither judge nor jury understood the expert testimony on each side. By shading the evidence a little bit, not lying but tipping the emphasis this way or that or just not saying too much, Micklejohn could have got a better verdict for its client, but everyone from the company who was put on the stand testified as if he was a professor lecturing to a class and trying to drive the subject into their heads from alpha to omega. Result: the client had to accept an expensive compromise.

"Aren't you glad you're with people who don't cheat, Cappie? You've been made an honest man after all these years."

"Honesty is the best policy when it's the most profitable," Kent said, grinning.

"You don't believe that," Abby persisted. "You know you didn't like some of the things you were asked to do at Full-chem."

"We didn't cheat. We just outsmarted the other guy."

"You're a lot happier now when the job is all that matters."

"I'd be still happier if it paid more," Kent said.

"How did you come to join Micklejohn?" Arthur asked. "I thought, when we left last year, you were going to set up as a consultant."

"I saw right away I couldn't make a go of that," Kent said. "I scared up a few *per diem* jobs, not enough to meet the overhead on a room and a girl with a typewriter. It would have taken five years and a peck of capital just to get started, and by then I'd be decrepit."

"Micklejohn approached Cappie. It wasn't the other way around," Abby said. "They'd been asked by the government to help design that big new medical research center under the A. E. C. You must know about it, Arthur. It's for all the applications of atomic energy and radiation in medicine. They'd noticed the write-ups in the engineering magazines of buildings Cappie has put up, and they got in touch with him. They had hard work inducing him to meet their salary scale, though."

"Not as hard as I wish they'd had," Kent said. "Something looked better than nothing right then."

"It seems to me you're building yourself a national monument," Arthur said. "That will be one of the great research centers anywhere."

"An anonymous monument," Kent said. "It won't have my name on it the way your book will have yours." Despite his deprecatory grin, he was obviously pleased.

Arthur asked what else he was doing for his new company. He was being used a good deal, Kent said, to scout up jobs and bring in business. He'd spent a month in Seattle looking into the possibilities of opening a West Coast branch. He'd written reports for the fertilizer industry and the brewing industry, and he brought home all sorts of problems he couldn't solve himself for the longhairs with their test tubes and slide rules to work out. He was beginning to know American business from one shore of the continent to the other.

"Will you have to keep hopping from place to place forever?" Rachel asked in some dismay.

"We hope we've come to the end of that, don't we, Cappie? We're thinking of keeping the house open as headquarters from now on," Abby said. "Cappie is going to insist on not more than two or three months' travel a year, and he's going to try commuting to the office three or four days a week. The rest of the time he can prop his leg up and work at home."

"Oh, I hope you can do that!" Rachel said.

"When are you going to start on your fishing trip, Uncle Kent?" Claudia asked.

"Day after tomorrow," Kent said.

"I hope you have a wonderful time."

"I'm no good for stream fishing any more," Kent said, "but I can sit in Pete Blanchard's boat and troll for salmon."

"And you'll be back in time for the wedding?"

"Promise," Kent said. "I'll kiss the book if you want." He proposed that they all go back to the study and give the coming event a preliminary consecration by drinking a couple of toasts, but Rachel demurred. She was tired; they'd been on the wing for the better part of two days, and had ever so many things to do in the morning. She and Claudia would stay just long enough to help clear the table and wash the dishes. Abby wouldn't hear of assistance, but she did agree to let them walk the few blocks home. She followed them out to the porch, and as Arthur turned for a final good night he saw that Kent had followed also as far as the doorway. He stood in the lighted frame, his white shirt rolling out a little with unfamiliar paunchiness over his belt, his left foot encased in its wool sock and gray slipper. He raised his hand in salute, and Arthur waved back. Then Kent's eyes seemed to look out over and beyond them, occupied with some private vision. Arthur hoped it might be his fishing trip, but he feared it might equally well be the leg and its discouraging prognosis.

357

∘ ∘ 𝟤 ∘ ∘

She would have met Jim anywhere, Claudia told herself; she was driven not only by the urgency of a year apart, but by a special urgency, the product of that year, about which she wouldn't even be able to speak until she and Jim had learned what it was to be together again. Perhaps then it wouldn't be necessary to speak, or perhaps the words would come easily.

For whatever reason—could it be a sense of guilt or subterfuge toward Arthur and Rachel, even toward herself?—she expected the worst of the apartment a senior member of Jim's expedition had lent him in New York. A grubby cell somewhere; cockroaches crawling out from under the sink. Instead, Jim ushered her into space and comfort she could hardly take in at first. Room after room, immaculate, beautifully appointed, the rugs, the curtains, the dining-room and bedroom furniture, the Mexican paintings, fabrics, and artifacts obviously chosen by someone who knew and loved them. When Jim, smugly playing the impresario, pulled the traverse cord of the big living room windowpane, she almost pitched forward with dizziness, finding herself looking far down on the flat panorama of the East River scalloped into tiny stitches of whitecaps by the hot afternoon wind. A fleet of barges made stiff headway upstream, the tugboats that propelled them trailing black horse-tails of smoke. Gulls made sidelong sallies on the wind or beat with measured labor against it, their smooth heads and hooked bills turning this way and that, their eyes impersonally peering downward.

Jim led her on a tour of exploration, holding her against him so that she tripped and stumbled, explaining that the owner of the apartment had been an important figure in the expedition, very friendly and helpful from the beginning. He'd gone out West to summer with his family and seemed really pleased to offer the premises so that Jim could finish ticketing artifacts and indexing files. Would he have been so generous, Claudia wondered, if he had known she was included in Jim's plans? Wouldn't the walls have eyes to watch them and tongues to report on what they did? But she might as well forget a compunction too frail to influence her actions. She had got Jim back; everything had to yield to that.

After their inspection, they sat on the couch in the living room to undertake the serious business of rediscovering each other. "Oh, Jim," she said, "you're really real. You actually exist."

"From now on I'm going to be frighteningly real."

"Sometimes I've been afraid you were only a dream I had long ago."

"I'm not the stuff dreams are made of. Feel that squeeze?"

"Ouch, you're twisting me apart."

"I'm just making sure *you* exist. That's the main thing."

"The main thing is, you've come back. Are you going to stay?"

"For keeps. The main thing is, we're here together."

They had so much news to exchange that the enterprise seemed hopeless. Had the expedition lived up to his hopes? Begin at the beginning and go right through; tell everything. Well, that would be quite an order! On the whole, he was more than satisfied. He'd worked closely with professionally important figures, many of whom he wouldn't otherwise have met. He'd come back with solid work to his credit, and he'd be starting his career—*their* career—a notch or two higher than he could have expected. He was already in demand at a number of desirable campuses. But chiefly he'd come to know and in a number of ways to love the region and people they'd been studying. If the government ever wanted to do anything for that part of the world, they'd have a systematic body of materials on archaeology, folklore, religion, language, mores, economy; you might compare it to the work that had been done on Japan as a guide to the occupation. But *she* must have a lot to tell, with all her gadding around Europe! What about that? Were Arthur's lectures a success? Did she and Rachel hear a lot of music?

359

Oh, there were lots of things she would remember bit by bit—it was funny how far away they all seemed now! And it hadn't been entirely gadding. She spent a lot of time with Arthur and Rachel in England, especially at first, helping Rachel to settle down and make herself somewhat at home in a new environment where she didn't know a soul, typing Arthur's lectures, checking references for him—not technical ones, of course, but all sorts of books he wanted to quote from. She and Rachel had made two musical pilgrimages, notably to Vienna. What she'd been doing didn't seem in the least important beside his expedition, except for the little help she'd given Arthur. His lectures were a tremendous success, and his book would be out in the fall.

They kept the exchange going until it began to be perfunctory. With two worlds and a whole year to talk about, talk became increasingly forced and needless. After a silence that could have only one issue, he disentangled himself from her and got to his feet, retaining her hand. He didn't need to tug on it; she rose with him almost simultaneously, and he said, "Is it time, Claudia?" She said, "Oh, yes, Jim," and followed him into the room she knew already he had chosen for their encounter.

If she had felt any lurking fear that it mightn't go well, she could have spared herself the apprehension. She found herself appeased not only of the urgency of a year of separation but of that special urgency she had worried about. In a corner of her mind a ghost was exorcised; or if he didn't entirely disappear, he shrank into a wry, frail little ghost, so unimportant that she could think about him, even talk about him if it ever seemed necessary. She satisfied herself that she hadn't been wrong; she was Jim's, utterly, his from the first.

They went out to a late dinner at a restaurant of Jim's choosing, and when they came back to the apartment they found their tongues loosened so that they could rattle away at each other exchanging news. Jim groused mildly when he was called on to take her back to the more modest but still comfortably attractive apartment where Helena and her husband lived. She could make an excuse and spend the night with him, Jim urged. No, she'd practiced enough subterfuge, Claudia insisted. She'd said she was going to stay with Helena; stay she would, and they'd have to get there at a decent hour, besides. Helena's second baby was due within a month or so. Helena would need her sleep, and her husband deserved some consideration too. Hadn't Helena given her a key? Yes, but she wasn't going to risk waking them up by trying to creep in at dawn.

Jim proved sweetly reasonable. He understood and assented, Claudia could see, with the part of him that respected work and responsibility. Helena's husband let them in, and, when Helena herself appeared, he politely offered a nightcap. Claudia declined, and they chatted briefly. When Jim began to describe some of his New Guinea adventures and interest threatened to grow too intense, Claudia intervened and brought about a general good night.

So she lay alone in the bed Helena had provided for her use, and a great luxury of bodily lassitude surrounded and suffused her, a lethargy of flesh in the midst of which her mind floated at a distance, content, detached, yet fully aware. Her first thought was that the quality of time had changed. Time no longer hustled and compelled her into actions that she had no real opportunity to assess or choose by the sanction of her own full assent, as in those desperate three days with Jim before he set off on his expedition. Time was no longer a dreary load, as during her year abroad, to be carried down endless milestones of days toward a future she couldn't make real. Of course, Claudia told herself, that was putting it very melodramatically; many a day abroad she'd been interested, usefully occupied, next door to happy. She mustn't forget that. But other days, other hours—

She could remember thinking more than once that perhaps those three days before Jim's departure had been a mistake; perhaps she would have done better to refuse him, after all. But wouldn't he have gone off so disappointed, so outraged, in fact, that he would have found someone else? Didn't she have some obligation to the fact that she loved him and had told him so? Perhaps, if it hadn't gone so well just that once,

361

that last time when she'd given up expecting anything at all, she would have escaped those occasions when she wanted Jim so much it seemed the gates of hell were trying to burst open inside her, with all the devils pushing at them. At such times she could at one minute have plucked Jim out of the air and made him materialize right in front of her, and at the next he would seem so unreal, so impossibly far away, she could have despaired and thrown herself into the nearest friendly arms that offered. It wasn't as though friendly arms didn't offer! For that matter Jim must have had opportunities too, and he might have, must have— Well, she didn't want to think about whether he might or must. That was his business. But somehow she wanted him to know that it hadn't been easy for her. If he understood that, she thought she could permanently and completely exorcise that already reduced little ghost that had been troubling her.

It was natural enough that she and Rachel should encounter a music student in Vienna who spotted them as fellow countrymen and made himself known after a concert. He was really a very polite, gentlemanly, attractive music student, who somewhat shocked and considerably entertained Rachel by his irreverences toward Viennese teachers, conductors, real and alleged virtuosos, toward the frequent complacency and mediocrity of Viennese musical taste. Claudia thought he compared very favorably with the young European students and listeners with whom they rubbed elbows. He took to squiring them about, and even turned up rooms for them in a private house he was sure they would find more congenial and much cheaper than their pre-engaged hotel quarters.

Claudia retained a vivid impression of the tiny sitting room, a bourgeois family cell bulging with lumpish furniture and crowded with knickknacks, that separated her bedroom from Rachel's. On the night when the music student turned into a ghost to exorcise, Rachel had announced that she was tired after the opera. If they'd excuse her, she thought she'd go to bed, but it wouldn't disturb her in the least if the two of them wanted to sit up and go on talking. The music student for a while continued to demolish the sacred cows of Viennese music; then he began to grow more personal, and Claudia could see excitement and expectation building up in him. The change of manner made him look suddenly younger and rather appealing; at the same time she perceived the lines of not yet fully developed virility under the smooth good looks she had first suspected of being just a trifle effeminate. She thought fatally of Jim and had to bite her lip to repress the wish that ensued on the thought.

She would have handled the situation better, she told herself afterward, if she could have kept Jim out of her mind. She told the music student that she and her aunt would be leaving Vienna in the morning; she thanked him for helping to make their stay so enjoyable. But she was feeling rather tired herself, and if he'd forgive her— She got up, and he rose too, looking even more hangdog and expectant. She thought she was making it clear that she was dismissing him, but she gave him a smile that tried to say: If I'm not accessible, never mind; some nice girl will be sometime. When he advanced on her, she turned her cheek and passively allowed him to kiss it. What happened then? He must have gone out; she was sure he had, although she retained no mental image of seeing him go. She crossed the tiny parlor to her bedroom, closed the door behind her, took off her necklace and laid it on the bureau, and reached behind her neck to unfasten the top button of her dress. Then the door opened. She thought Rachel must have waked and come to ask her something, but when she turned about, there he was, quietly shutting the door, shutting them both in. "I thought we said good night," she told him, and he said, "Yes, but you didn't mean—" He added as if by sophisticated inspiration, "There are better ways—" and couldn't finish the sentence.

Claudia found it hard to remember the complete sequence of what she did and didn't do. She remembered taking steps to get around him and open the door. She remembered being seized and awkwardly grappled with. At that point the scene went totally dark in her mind, not with the darkness of extinguished light, but with a black emanation that welled out of herself and blotted everything external from view. She was in a lightless cave, except that the cave contained a gap or inset in another perspective, as in a surrealistic painting, and through it, at an infinite distance, the face of Jim appeared, remote, inaccessible, unreal. She hated it with a burning anger and desired it with an impossible desire. She said to it desperately and silently: Oh, Jim, what's the use? I need you, need someone. I can't hold out.

Or did her mind form any such words or any such thought? She couldn't really remember. She must have stood still and let her intruder go on making his inexpert efforts to arouse her while, already aroused, she tried to call Jim from half a globe away to her aid. She could remember swaying and shifting on her feet; she could remember pressures and constrictions that had nothing to do with the way she was feeling, that were as impersonal as if she were being cramped in the frame of a machine. She said something eventually, she couldn't recall what, except that instead of threatening or forbidding or crying out, she *appealed* to him. Please don't go on, I don't want you to, I hope you won't—something of the sort. Perhaps an instinct guided her, because he stopped and stood off, looking puzzled and chagrined. "What's the matter?" She remembered his asking that, and she remembered saying, "There's a man I'm going to marry. Does that explain?" He was inexperienced enough, or decent or diffident enough, to accept her appeal. He was sorry, he hadn't known, he'd thought she meant— He went away, definitely this time, accepting defeat, pouting and looking a little spoiled and pitiable, now that she could survey the whole thing in retrospect. But what if he had been more experienced, what if he had detected the state she was in and known how to play on it?

Stretched safely in her bed in Helena's apartment, feeling the approach of sleep in every gently sagging fiber of her flesh, Claudia indulged a small luxurious tremor of gratitude for her escape. The ghost needed only one more fillip to be dismissed forever, and best of all, it seemed, time had become neither a tyrannical force, in a hurry to get things done, nor a long, dreary deferment of waste. Time had turned kindly.

It had grown into a season that allowed things to ripen toward their fulfillment at their own pace, in their own way.

Claudia pursued her forenoon shopping while Jim made progress with his labeling, classifying, packing, and filing. They used up two afternoons driving out on visits in Claudia's car, and she made him pay a suitably formal tea-and-cocktails call on Helena and her husband. She bought Helena a house present, a vase of clear crystal, and Jim whistled at the cost. What was the use of her having a modest income of her own, she demanded, if she never bought or did anything nice with it? Then he wanted to add flowers himself to go with the vase, and the joint gift was gratifyingly received. Helena praised the engagement ring he had bought, and Claudia felt that he was regarded by her hosts with genuine approval. She added that to her list of satisfactions.

A handful of afternoons, followed by dinners together, followed by evenings in the apartment overlooking the river; it was surprising how they could pass so quickly without any sense of struggling to hold the door against inrushing time. The eve of their return to Fullington arrived almost like any other day, not as the last stand against doom. They sat in the living room of the apartment, and Jim looked about a little ruefully. "This is a standard of living we won't become accustomed to all at once," he said.

"Hasn't it been fun?" Claudia asked. "It makes me feel guilty, though."

"Guilty?" he said. "How?"

"I guess I feel that if we're living in sin, we ought to be living in squalor."

Jim laughed, but then his eyes began to study her attentively. He was really trying to learn his lesson, trying to find out how she felt, without just making up his mind unaided. "You aren't really suffering from a sense of guilt, are you?"

"Have I acted as though I were?"

"If you have, you've kept it pretty well secret. I hope it hasn't been gnawing away inside. What is there to feel guilty about?"

"It was mean to go off and desert Rachel with all there is to do," Claudia said defensively, "and sometimes I suspect they wonder, or I wonder whether they suspect— Sometimes *I* wonder, Jim."

"About what?"

"Well, the way we've been behaving, there won't be anything new after we're married, will there?"

Jim considered the question. "I can think of one or two things," he said. "I've never been a bridegroom, and you've never been a bride. That will be new, won't it?"

"You'll still feel that I'm a bride?"

"At least till you're a grandmother," Jim said. He considered again. "There's another novelty we've got to learn, too."

"What's that?"

"We've got to learn to sleep together."

She looked at him, puzzled, ready to be indignant. Could he possibly mean, especially after these last few days— Then she saw that his mouth was holding back a joke. "I'll grant we've occupied the same bed, but I can't recall we've ever slept in it. Want to try?" he asked.

She could think of no better answer than to give him a solid punch in the ribs. He doubled up in mock agony, protesting that, with his corrupted constitution, she might have killed him.

"Seriously, Jim, you realize we're driving back home to Fullington tomorrow."

"And that's going to be awkward, isn't it? This is the time I ought to have a family to go to, so that I could vanish and reappear at the last minute. But anything else aside, I can't afford to fly out to California for three weeks and listen to my brother talk advertising, even if he needed me as an audience. I could stay here alone, I suppose, and maybe you could sneak down again—"

"I won't desert Rachel another time, and there's too much to do," Claudia said. "I don't want to leave you alone, and I don't want to be left. I want to show you off, Jim, and I want you to get to know Uncle Arthur and Uncle Kent."

"Well, if you can put up with an encumbrance around the house—"

"You know we don't feel that way. What I actually had in mind was something else."

"What would that be?"

"We'll have to be good."

"Good for what?"

"Just good."

"I don't know the word," Jim said, grinning. "We'll be discreet. I'll settle for that. Times and places—"

"There might be times and places, but I'm not going to let you have any expectations. We'll be in the house with Arthur and Rachel, and it won't be long now. Besides, we have a life to build together, Jim, and it can't all be one thing, important as that is."

"All right," Jim said. "I understand. I'm on your side, really, in principle. I've taken the course once, and I can take it again, for good cause. You make the rules. I'll keep them."

"Don't put it that way, Jim," she pleaded. "I don't like to make rules, and it isn't as though *I* didn't want— Oh, Jim, was it hard for you when we were away from each other?"

"If you imagine otherwise, you're a hundred and eighty degrees off truth and heading in the opposite direction. It was work that kept me reasonably sane. I'm a natural worker, or I have been. My only worry about marrying you is that I'll be tempted to turn lazy and sit around looking at you all day."

"I'm not going to be an obstacle to your work. I'm going to help. But was it really hard, Jim, more than you could bear sometimes?"

"Are you asking for confessions?"

"No," Claudia said, "no. You'd tell me anything that was really important to us, and I don't care about anything else. I guess perhaps I'm *making* a confession. I just wanted—"

"What do you want, honey?"

"I wanted you to know how hard it was for me." She found herself leaning against him, practically forcing him to put his arms around her and support her, while an unexpected trickle ran from her eyes. "So hard—you were so far away— I almost once or twice might have—"

The heat of his cheeks burned through her hair. "Don't say

it, honey. It's all right, it doesn't matter, it's all over now. I'll try and make it up to you any way you like. I love you, honey."

She straightened up and found a handkerchief to wipe the sniffles from her nose. Then she could laugh and apologize and say she guessed she just had a little ghost to exorcise. Why, it was actually getting on toward midnight! It was high time he took her back to Helena's apartment.

She studied his hands, crossed over each other on top of the wheel in the way he liked to drive; studied his profile, alert to the road without any strain, responsive when she commented on a scene they passed or remembered a travel anecdote she hadn't told him. They were on their way home; they were going back to Fullington, and the day of the wedding was drawing steadily nearer. They were settling back into the relation of companionability that for her had been violently foreshortened and almost destroyed. They could call each other's attention to things by the road and share the delight of noticing them, simple things, a run-out hayfield blazing with weed-flowers, the abjectness of an old barn with a broken rooftree, the absurdity of a file of ducks waddling toward a farmyard pool. It was wonderful how the fact of so many different existences could be enhanced by mutual perception.

"You're going to be awfully bored by all the preparations for the wedding," Claudia said.

"I'll be bored if you're so obsessed you can't even look at me."

"There's a lot to do. I can't be with you all the time."

"I can get started on a monograph if there's a desk I can hole up at."

"You'll find a desk in your room, and you can use my typewriter while I'm dress-fitting and things like that."

"Anyhow, I'm a student of tribal customs and ceremonies," Jim said. "No matter how outlandish they seem, they have a rationale to the discerning eye."

"If you think it's a tribal ceremony you're going through—"

"Isn't it? But I don't object. I've watched a lot of initiation rites and things like that. Why shouldn't I be a protagonist for once?"

He was twitting her. She gave him a good thump on the shoulder, and he howled with pretended injury, saying that white Protestant America was the only culture where a woman was allowed to beat her man. In all sensible and advanced cultures, a man was encouraged to beat his woman. Claudia told him that, in this respect and a number of others, she intended to stick by her own culture.

They could enjoy silences as well as talk. Claudia's mind began to occupy itself with a question which took something like a mile to form. "Jim," she said, "how much does it really help improve our own culture to know all about how other societies behave? I mean, I've read a little about initiation and puberty rites and sex and marriage customs and population control and all those things, and the implication always seems to be that the more we know about other cultures, the better we can make our own. But because they all do things differently, should we imitate them, and which ones should we imitate? We can't be like them all."

Jim smiled. "You're raising the question of relativism," he said, "and it's pretty hard to answer. But when you see the variety of cultures, when you see none is completely successful and maybe none is completely *un*successful, you're at least shaken out of the complacency of any one parochial system, aren't you?"

"Yes, but where do we stop being shaken?"

Jim drove on for some time without speaking. Then he said, "Claudia, I hope you aren't really feeling guilty. I hope you aren't holding it against me that we— Right from the start I wanted to marry you, meaning by that everything a marriage is supposed to mean in our culture. You know that. I didn't want—"

"I'm not feeling guilty, Jim, not for anything I've done with you, and I don't hold anything against you. Whatever I've done I did because I loved you and—" Claudia paused.

"No regrets, then?" Jim said.

"No regrets. At least not the kind you're thinking of. I feel

369

lucky, maybe. I'm glad things worked out. They might not have, you know. And I feel—"

"Yes? What do you feel?"

"I feel like a fool when I try to say what I mean."

"Say it, Claudia."

"Well, you with your anthropology and your relativism—the cultures you study, Jim, they all had rules, *some* rules. It's one thing to give up a bad set of rules for a better one, and another to give it up for none at all."

"Catch as catch can and anything goes," Jim said. "Sometimes it seems as though that's the only rule left, doesn't it? Well, I don't hold that anything goes. When it comes to rules, though, who's wise enough to draw them up? In this age of the oncoming female pill—"

"The oncoming *male* pill," Claudia said. "Pretty soon I'll be able to slip one in your coffee and you won't even know."

"As long as you slip an aphrodisiac in with it."

"I haven't noticed you need anything of that sort."

"You win. With you around—"

"Seriously, Jim—"

"Seriously, I was going to say everyone has to get launched on a career of sex at some time in his life, and it won't be and never has been always by a formal introduction with the blessing of the elders. Oh, sure, adolescents tumble into some pretty ghastly scrapes—any high school or college is full of them—and it isn't a good start for a ten-year-old girl to get raped by the gardener. Some rules with real social force would keep some people from getting hurt. But there are risks and horrors and perversions in everything the human animal can do. The point is, just sleeping together doesn't matter as people used to think it did."

Claudia couldn't argue when she so nearly agreed, but she felt obscurely unsatisfied. "What does matter, Jim? Sleeping together matters to me, more than I thought it was going to. I didn't know—"

"You had natural gifts that just needed a little cultivation."

"All right, then, don't be serious if you don't want to."

"I'll be serious. Go on, Claudia."

"You make it sound so *negative*. I wasn't thinking about not getting hurt. Maybe I've lived a protected life, but I wasn't *asking* for protection. I'm not afraid of taking risks when they have to be taken. I was trying to get at something *positive*. Rules is the wrong word. I don't mean rules you obey just because they've been laid down and there they are and you don't have the courage to break them. I mean ways of acting that people can agree on and expect of themselves and each other, so they can do what it's right for them to do openly and not be hypocritical about it."

Jim fell briefly silent again. Then he said, "You know, Claudia, if you went in for religion, you'd be an Episcopalian or a Catholic. You don't like the untidy or the irresponsible or the hypocritical, but it's more than that. You like form. You'd like the sacraments and the collects and the prayers for special occasions."

"You're making fun of me."

"I'm not. Ceremonies, observances, rites. As an anthropologist, I understand."

"How can you live up to anything if there's no agreement anywhere about anything to live up to?"

"You're one of the few people who could be trusted with Shakespeare's dubious maxim, Claudia. 'To thine own self be true.' Just go on being yourself, honey, and you won't have to worry about images to live up to." Jim's hand strayed from the wheel and reached toward her lap. She took it and explored its fingers and palm until, at the next curve, it had to go into service again.

They passed through a village where a brick Colonial house with a delicately wrought fan window above the door caught Claudia's eye. It started an association working in the back of her mind that eluded her like a well-known but momentarily forgotten name. A mile or two onward the link snapped into place. "Jim," she said, "I think it's just a little beyond here there's a turn—it's out of our way, but not far, and we don't have to get back by any particular time. I've just had a thought."

"What is it?"

She reminded him of Malcolm Islay and Rosamund Temple, of Rosamund's wonderful house, her isolation, and her cordiality. She had an impulse, Claudia said, to see whether Rosamund was at home. She wanted Jim to see the place, wanted them to meet each other.

Jim was a little nonplused. Did she really want to go out of their way to introduce him, a perfect stranger, to this woman who was apparently a big thing in Islay's life? Why?

"It's part of the tribal ceremony, Jim. I want her to see you," Claudia said. "Besides, you'll understand when we get there."

Jim pulled over to the shoulder of the road, studied a map, and memorized route numbers. It was a shock, a really nasty turn, when they discovered at the end of their detour that the house stood vacant, its windows boarded up, its lawns and gardens unkempt. A sign with a realtor's name leaned dejectedly beside the driveway: "Estate for Sale," it said. Claudia thought at first that the difference between summer and winter, the lapse of a year and more, had led her to choose the wrong road from the village or fail to recognize the place when she saw it, but she was finally convinced. She shivered, and said, "I feel as though a rabbit had run over my grave."

"If they're the sort of people you make out," Jim said, "They've decided to retire and live in Bermuda or on the Riviera."

"I suppose so." With Jim in the car beside her, driving her home to Fullington and marriage, the impression of the deserted house did not last. It slipped rapidly back with the stretches of concrete and macadam that flowed under the wheels.

○ ○ *3* ○ ○

Kent stood up to relieve the knots in his legs and back, feeling the cork grip of his salmon rod and the deep drag of line and lure pleasantly evoking a mild resistance in his hand and arm. Behind him Pete Blanchard kept the outboard motor turning over at its minimum rate. The way the northwest wind was pushing them down the lake, they hardly needed engine power at all for trolling, just enough to keep them off-shore, winding at a sinuous parallel to the shingle and the spruce-crowned ledges that defined the flat wilderness to the east of them.

Kent twisted toward the open lake and looked back over his shoulder. Quartered off there, north of the lower hills behind which the sun would go down, bulged the small mountain that served as a local weather gauge. Its bulk showed black except for its bare granite top, which looked almost like a snow cap. Above and behind it, a darkening density of sky, not yet shaping into outright cloud forms, gave a threat of increasing wind. Turning forward again, Kent resumed his seat on the thwart. The bow of the boat was heading into the narrows, a passage between the eastern shore and a longish island tufted with a pelt of stunted spruce. In the lee of the island, the water was calmer, scalloped into a flowing blue chop that broke only mildly into whitecaps. Beyond the island, in the exposed stretch that continued all the way to the bony finger-point behind which the camp buildings and cottages nestled along their crescent of beach, the wind was really at work, trying to pick up fifteen miles of open water and throw it at the opposing shoreline. The sun was bright, but it had a brassy tinge, as if it didn't mean well. The surface of the lake, out there in the stretch ahead of them, seemed broken into shifting quarter-moons of white, all writhing one way, like an enormous school of fish hurtling in an endless column against a weir.

"Pete," Kent said, "they aren't treating us right."

"You're damn toot'n," Pete agreed amiably. "Let's see, how many days of this weather, and we've hardly had a strike?"

"I don't know whether the water's too cold, or the fish are getting educated, or we aren't using the right tactics. Maybe the fish are smart and we're dumb."

"The water's cold, that's for one thing," Pete said. "Even

camp admits the ice hasn't been out more than a week or so."

"If we aren't making out with the salmon, at least we've hooked a couple of indoor suckers. We certainly creamed that gang of fourflushers last night."

"The best poker player in the bunch was that dame whose husband chickened out and went to bed."

"A few better deals," Kent agreed, "and she might have come out with a pile."

"Have you seen her down in the corner of the dock, out of the wind, pretending to take a sunbath?"

"I don't happen to have noticed," Kent said.

"Her goggles cover more than anything else she has on."

"Maybe she thinks she's invisible with those things over her eyes, like an ostrich with its head in the sand."

"I always thought the ostrich put its head in the sand to show its tail. Anyway, there's plenty of ostrich showing if you stop to look. I felt like hanging around to see whether she really wants to double-time her husband."

Pete was doing a little fourflushing of his own, Kent thought. A wheeze or a good yarn, even on the raw side, was one thing; it was a little different to pull the stops out about a particular woman, even if she asked for it. "If you want to get back and sit in on the game tonight," Kent said, "we'd better get started. I think we're in for some weather. You know how fast it can come up with the wind in this quarter."

"It's blowing a bit, but it's clear over where the sun is."

"Take a look behind you, at the mountain," Kent said. He turned to verify himself what he expected Pete to see. The diffused atmospheric density had spread and deepened over the summit, over the entire ledge-capped profile. It now made a vague overhanging pyramid, black at its widening base, thinning out to a light, ragged pallor at the tip.

"I see what you mean," Pete said, "but it won't get here for a while. Tell you what, with all the money we've shelled out, we ought to get some return on it. I'd like to see one of us tie onto a good one. Why don't you keep trolling at least through the narrows? Remember the twelve-pounder you hooked off the big split rock, four, five years ago? If we don't have any luck by the time we've run the island, we'll quit."

Kent had his doubts. Even if Pete gave the engine full throttle and they chugged right on, they'd have to make a quartering run across the open, beyond the island, in order to clear the point. They'd be taking spray if not water, with the wind at present strength, and if it got worse and rain came with the squalls—well, that wasn't exactly what the doctor prescribed for his leg. Still, he was game. He'd like to see a fish himself.

In the lee of the island, the wind kept mostly overhead. It wasn't lathering the surface. Opposite the big split rock, where a fissure opened into the woods and a spit of sand had formed, a doe was standing in the shallows. She swung a dripping muzzle up as the boat drew abreast, then whirled and rocked off into the spruces, the white down of her flag showing briefly. They could hear her belling snort of alarm as she disappeared. If it was autumn, with two or three inches of trailing-snow on the ground, they could be out with rifles looking for the buck who would be keeping her company. No, Kent told himself, he wouldn't be good for that kind of thing any more.

"Not a strike?" Pete asked.

"Not a tickle," Kent said.

"This is just about the place. Actually, we've passed it a bit, but it's usually good all along here if it is anywhere." Pete was silent a moment, then he said, "There's something I've been wanting to tell you, Cap. It's just that I'm damned glad you got on your feet again after that raw deal at Fullchem. It took guts to rally the way you did."

"I didn't do anything but what I had to do, and by the grace of God, it paid off," Kent said, "though the grace of God doesn't pay very high."

"I wish I could have helped more," Pete said, "but as it is, you've made a permanent contribution with what you did designing that A. E. C. research center."

"You did everything you could."

"If I'd been in a position—" Pete said, and it was in that instant that Kent felt the strike.

"You wanted a fish," Kent said, getting to his feet, the arched tip of his rod oscillating with tension, "you've got him! Yes, sir, that bastard is hooked."

"Look at that line run out," Pete said. "He's going to take it clear across the lake."

Somehow the most magnificent sight of the trophy was the most distant one. Far out toward the island, when Kent snubbed the line, thinking his victim had run far enough to be ready for a change, a solid silver eyebrow of life and vigor broke from the surface and hung, briefly splendid, against the dark rocks of the shore. Whatever he might go to on the scales, and it would be plenty, this one was game and sly. He took a long time to play before Kent could tease him, exhausted, alongside the boat and Pete could dip him out and dump him in the bottom.

They could admire and display their catch when they got to camp. Right now it was time to cut and run. "I guess we're going to get the weather," Pete said. Kent qualified the statement. "I guess we've got it already." The black area that had been building up behind the mountain was flying almost overhead now, and it was flounced along its advancing front with sickly pale ruffles of cloud. The sun was a livid circle in soft focus off the fringe of the broadening squall. The water in the open stretch beyond the island had turned from white to black, except for the foam caps that whipped from the pitch and toss of the waves.

Pete gunned the motor, and Kent estimated the amount of lee they could still expect from the island. "There's quite a sea running out there," he said. "We ought to be in the Queen Mary."

"I guess this buggy will take it," Pete said.

The line of demarcation between the shelter of the island and the full drive of the wind beyond was oddly distinct. They moved toward it, then, with a shuddering chop and a sudden increase of pressure on their faces and noise in their ears, they were taking the full brunt. The boat rode ahead by a sort of vertical loop-stitch, with an added sidewise moment of force, lurching in two planes as it quartered over the steep fresh-water roll toward the tip of the point. Spray whipped across Kent's knees and mist flew like frosted breath around his head. Every now and then a slop of solid water came aboard; it slid back and forth in the bottom of the boat, cold as melting snow. Kent turned his back to the wind and sat crosswise, propping his left leg against the leeward gunwale. The squall, not content with half-measures, began to deliver black rain that drove across the churned-up lake surface in slanting rods.

Pete howled to make himself heard above the wind. "All this is just to make that Scotch and soda taste better when we make camp."

"I'm not waiting for soda," Kent howled back. "I'll take a shot of bourbon right out of the bottle."

"You always were an impatient cuss, Cap."

"Pete, if you want that Scotch and soda, better head up farther off the point. The wind is slewing us inshore all the time, and we're getting pretty close to the ledges."

Kent had been worrying for some distance about the low reef inside the tip of the point. He watched the bow swing out to give greater clearance, but the change of course brought the boat full broadside to the wind. It began to roll more violently and to gulp solid water by the bucketful.

"This isn't so good," Pete shouted. "I'd better run down past the ledges and then see whether we can beat up inside them, straighter into the wind."

"All right if we don't pile into them." Kent was thinking that they might have to beach the boat and walk back to camp, cutting through the spruce woods, crossing the base of the point, and picking up the wood road that wives who didn't care to fish all day used for picnics and nature walks.

The bow swung toward shore till it brought the wind almost dead astern. They were outrunning the waves now; neatly divided, the rolling backs and crests, though moving in the same direction as the boat, slid backward along the gunwales and fell away behind them. Every now and then a white lip poured thinly over and added its deposit to the slop in the bottom. Then a curious reversal occurred. For a moment they kept even pace with the waves; at the next moment the waves began to outrun the boat, rolling up from the stern and sliding ahead to subside beyond the bow. At the same time the boat began to yaw and swing broadside to the weather again.

"Goddamn it," Pete yelled, "wouldn't you know the motor would conk out in the middle of this?"

In his concern for the reef, Kent hadn't heard the engine choke and give up. Now he became aware of the missing throb, and it was like missing a beat of his own heart. "Get out the oars," he called back to Pete. "See whether you can steady her a bit. I'm going to keep an eye out for the ledges."

Bracing his hands on the gunwales, holding his left foot doubled up to keep it out of the water, he hobbled one-legged up to the bow seat. He heard the motor turn over as Pete fussed with it in the stern. Once, twice, three times it compressed without result. "No spark," Pete called.

Kent thought the wind was yawing them dangerously close to the reef, though it was hard to tell, in the pother that was going on, how near they might be. "Get out the oars," he shouted again. "We may need them to dodge the rocks. I don't want to swim for it in this water."

He braced his left knee on the bow seat and tried to take a survey of their prospects. The black rain, the lathered lake, the premature dusk, the broadside heaving of the boat didn't make for visibility. He heard Pete stumble and curse; after an interval he felt the oars take hold and steady somewhat the medley of motions they were undergoing. Then he caught sight of the ledges, like so many molars of granite on which white water broke with a thicker turbulence than the surrounding upheaval. They might clear; half a dozen yanks of an oar would certainly get them around what Kent could see. The danger would come from submerged outriders on the fringe. He took in a breath to make Pete hear. "Pull like hell on your right oar!"

Before the message could take effect, the boat rose on a wave mass, lurched forward, and sat down hard. Kent's left kneecap, supporting half his weight on the bow seat, took a sharp blow. Wood splintered and wrenched underneath him. Water squirted over the calf of his right leg where it kept its stance on the bottom. His braced arms gave way at the elbows, and he barely kept himself from being pitched out as the forward motion of the boat came to an abrupt halt and the stern began to swing sidewise into the wind. The sense of torsion as the hull twisted and strained was like the whole force of inertia applied at a single point. The bow, impaled on its hidden spike of rock, wrenched and splintered still more; the boat canted over until it took half the lake aboard across its submerged gunwale. Then the bow lifted as a wave passed under; it tore loose, and the whole craft wallowed free. It would have swamped under them on the spot except that it grated on rock again and came to a tilted rest, wedged in a tight crevice.

Kent writhed around on his front perch. Water was lapping now at the seat of his pants. He hardly knew whether Pete would still be in the boat. With some surprise, he observed him sitting at the oars, twisting backward to survey the disaster with comic chagrin. "Cap, we're in a fix," Pete said.

Kent knew that for him the fix was critical. He recognized a moment for decision. "I guess we swim for it after all," he said.

"Hold on, Cap. With that leg of yours—"

"That's why. Leg won't take it, sitting out here in this temperature. Doctor's orders." Kent unzipped his windbreaker and began pulling it off.

"It's a quarter of a mile to the point," Pete said.

"Nothing like it. A couple of hundred yards. You stick it out if you want, Pete. You'll be safe as in a church if you can stand the exposure. I'll walk into camp and they can send out the launch." Kent shook off his boots. He had long johns on beneath his heavy wool pants; they might give him some protection, if any protection was possible against the shock of the water.

"We could work our way over to the high point on the ledge," Pete said.

"I can't hang around till they miss us and start looking. It may be hours."

"Jesus, Cap, think twice." As Pete spoke, his teeth began to chatter.

The cold was what Kent feared; the cold, and the fact that swimming wasn't his sport. He could swim, all right, but he'd never been taught the way the kids were nowadays, the way Randy was taught, for example. Nothing but his old frog-stroke to keep him going. If the challenge had been football or baseball, and he was twenty years younger— "What about it, Pete? Coming, or shall I send out the rescue squad?"

"If you can make it, I can," Pete said.

Kent eased his legs over the side of the boat, and the cold caught him instantly. It almost numbed sensation, except for a total agony that seemed to begin at the marrow and work out as much as to pierce in from the ice-packs that encompassed his flesh. He felt ledge with his feet, worked toward deeper water, and lunged forward.

Sitting in the swamped and wedged boat, Pete Blanchard underwent a moment of indecision. He watched Cap make his start, hauling himself away from the rocks with his anti-quated breast stroke in almost vertical convulsions of effort, his head and shoulders rising half upright as he flailed with his arms and lifted on a wave, then slid out of view in the trough. Pete could even hear, two or three times, the sough of breath that Cap sucked in and expelled. He looked ahead at the spruce-capped point, dark beyond the dark rain, looked at the stretch of water in between, and didn't like what he saw. He guessed the percentages lay with taking to the lake, though. He was beginning to flap with cold himself; the water couldn't be much worse. And Cap might need help; either one of them might, once they were both in the lake, though he was a better swimmer than Cap and ought to be able to overtake him in twenty yards. He ought, that is, if he'd kept in any sort of condition.

While he was stripping off his poncho and boots, he noticed the salmon they had caught sliding out from under the seat and bobbing toward the gunwale on the low side. It picked up speed as a wave sloshed through, teetered briefly on the just submerged wood, then slid off into the roll of the waves. "Go ahead, you bastard, you swim for it, too," Pete said. He let himself into the water, felt no footing, and struck out.

The cold was a shock beyond expectation or belief, worse

than a man could imagine. It almost paralyzed effort at a single blow. His condition was worse than he could believe of himself, too. He couldn't establish a breathing rhythm. A wave rose right in his face before he'd gone half a dozen strokes, and he took aboard enough ice water to sink him at the start. After that his lungs agonized for air on a beat of their own, out of phase with the forward reach of his arms and the up and down paddling of his feet. He couldn't use his crawl stroke, that was obvious. He rolled on his side, his back to the weather, and began using a side stroke, a slower mode of progress, but at least he could breathe, and even this way he ought to be able to overtake Cap before long.

He felt himself lifted on a higher wave mass, and from the summit he tried to catch a glimpse of Cap. Nothing in his line of view but whitecaps and slanting rain and the still impossibly distant file of spruces on the shore. He tried again from another crest, twisting his neck to take in a wider span. Cap was there, ahead and to the right, still thrashing along in those half-vertical frog-lurches that lifted his shoulders and scalp an instant before they sank out of sight in the trough. Cap was taking the shortest line to the point. With his own side stroke and his back to the wind, Pete saw, he was drifting downweather, angling away from Cap's course. He tried to head more upwind to bring their paths together, but a new sort of cold began to take possession of him, a cold at the center of the will, a kind of indifference and withdrawal of any sense of reality or purpose in what he was doing. He was just a set of flippers that had even ceased to ache, and by some initiative of their own went flogging mechanically on through a fluid glacier.

The frantic automaton he had become seemed to have worn out hours, generations, life sentences of senseless, agonizing exertion in the water. He could feel the propulsion that made the idiotic thing work giving out; for an instant a real despair took hold of him. Then once more a stockier wave lifted him. From its crest he snatched a lungful of air and craned his neck up and sidewise. Even farther to windward, but almost opposite to him now, he made out Cap Warner hauling himself along in the same almost perpendicular spasms, wastefully rising, wastefully sinking, but washing with each roll and each stroke a little nearer to shore. And incredibly, shore was not far away. The spruces had risen up until their tops were almost overhead. Cap must be pretty nearly there, almost touching bottom. Pete put his face down and plowed on until he felt another lift of extra power beneath him. He looked again from the highest point of buoyancy. Cap's face, in profile, and his lunging and climbing shoulders, rode into view just beyond the spot where a big hemlock had toppled from the bank and stretched into the water. Cap looked as though he could put his feet down where he was and walk up the narrow strip of shingle. Cap had come through; Cap had made it.

Pete pulled in a breath, rolled on his belly, and whipped himself into a furious crawl. Just as his lungs were ready to explode, the fingers of his forward-reaching hand touched stone. He lifted his head and breathed. He let his legs come down in the wash of the waves, and his feet grated on the pebbled bottom. Now that he had reached shore, it seemed almost impossible to haul himself up on it. He bent over and worked himself out of the water on all fours. With safety came his real moment of collapse. He was suddenly lying flat, his whole length shaking from weakness as much as cold, his legs unable to straighten and support him. He couldn't tell how many efforts he made before he managed to stand upright, or how long the struggle had taken. He looked along the narrow strip of beach for a sight of Cap Warner, but Cap was nowhere visible. Had he cut immediately into the spruces, to cross the point and reach the wood road back to camp? It wasn't like Cap to leave the scene before making sure what had happened to the other guy, but probably he'd waited till he saw Pete scramble out of the water and then taken off for shelter.

Pete hesitated. His teeth were rattling and his thighs were jiggling, but the big fallen hemlock was only a couple of dozen strides up the beach. It might be well to make a quick check. He set off at a staggering trot, and when he reached the tree, he had to get down on his belly and wriggle under the butt. He didn't have the strength to climb over or fight his way up the bank and around the tangle of upheaved roots. It wasn't until he got to his feet again on the other side that he saw Cap Warner, face down on the slanting shingle, his chin and chest and one outstretched hand lifelessly grasping shore, his feet still gently heaving in the wash of the lake.

∘ ∘ 4 ∘ ∘

"This is just the way Cappie would have wanted it," Abby said.

Rachel, seated next to her on the sofa, put her hand on Abby's arm. "It's wonderful so many of his friends could come," she said, "and a lot of them from so far away. But you mustn't let it tire you out utterly. Don't you think you could excuse yourself and rest for a while?"

"I want to be here while his friends are," Abby said.

"But you've already been through the service. You mustn't overtax yourself."

"Ruth and Brainerd are taking care of me, and I'll have plenty of time to be alone."

Standing next them beside the arm of the sofa, Arthur agreed inwardly that Abby was right. Kent would have approved of the gathering that occupied most of the first floor of the house, flowing in and out of the living room, crowding the dining room and the hall. Arthur had seldom seen the living room in use; as a family group, they had always sat in the small study, cramped around the center table. The image of Kent, relaxed in his usual chair, his leg propped on its leather hassock, came into his mind and gave him a wrench. The image seemed more at home in the study; but no, it was fully as natural to think of Kent circulating among his guests, and he would certainly want them to be convivial. The sight of highballs rising to ready lips would give him nothing but pleasure. He would find nothing inappropriate in the talk of business deals, taxes, golf, bridge, talk that now and then reverted to the occasion long enough to remember how Cap Warner told a story or to comment that, for all his fighting spirit, he hadn't left an enemy behind him in the world.

Arthur noticed the Congregational minister who had conducted the service talking with Brainerd Hitchens. He had to keep reminding himself of the name of Kent's son-in-law, whom he had hardly encountered since Ruth's marriage. Hitchens and the minister made two abstemious figures in a company which presented the external appearances of a cocktail party and might have been mistaken for one, except that the participants had the air now and then of keeping somewhat on guard. If Kent could have considered anything superfluous or uncongenial, it would hardly have been the party, but the service preceding it. Arthur doubted whether he would have found a redeeming feature in that, not the evangelical hymns played on an organ slightly out of tune, not the miscellany from Scripture, not the eulogy nor the prayers, most of them fortunately traditional. He would have been gratified only from family loyalty by the solo that Rachel played on her violin, her customary taste hampered by an obbligato limited to the more saccharine organ stops. If there was a sacrament appropriate to Kent's passage, he would have found it himself in this breaking of bread and imbibing of spirits by friends who could not long conceal their ordinary interests in living. The very appearance of cheerfulness in it would have delighted him.

Arthur felt himself a misfit in this company largely made up of Kent's business associates, golfing partners, classmates from engineering school. He could identify no more than a handful. Two or three executives from Micklejohn Industrial Research had come up, spoken to Abby, and been introduced, and the man called Pete Blanchard, who had shared Kent's fishing trip. The rest, husbands with or without wives, wives with or without husbands, formed an anonymous mass with whom Arthur had no links. Now and then a fragment of the mass would detach itself and advance to make a profession of sympathy or an inquiry about future plans. After listening to a litany of such attentions, Arthur decided that Claudia had found words as fitting as any for what words can be expected to do. She had simply burst out, without the slightest affectation, "Oh, Aunt Abby, I wanted him to come to the wedding," wiping her eyes as she spoke. "You'll come, won't you, if only to the church? We'd love to have you come to the reception too, even if you only looked in for a minute." Jim had been commendably straightforward also. "I think I only met your husband once, Mrs. Warner, but I remember him from then, and Claudia has been telling me so much about him I feel as though I'd lost a big slice of my future."

Standing by the end of the sofa, Arthur was beginning to grow conscious of his isolation when he felt Abby's touch on his arm. "Don't you want to sit down, Arthur?" she asked.

He suffered a twinge of chagrin. He'd almost forgotten where he was. "Perhaps I will," he said. He crossed in front of the sofa to seat himself next Rachel, but remained standing when he noticed Ruth approaching her mother with a plate and napkin.

"I've brought you this, Mother," Ruth said. "You ought to nibble something to keep your strength up. You didn't eat any lunch, you know."

"That was thoughtful of you, dear," Abby said. "I suppose if I must, I must." She accepted the plate, with its buttered rye bread and ham and mustard, but she was obviously not tempted. "How are the children?" she asked. "They're behaving wonderfully, keeping so quiet and taking care of themselves. This is a hard day for them."

"I've tried to make them understand as well as I can," Ruth said. "Do eat something, Mother. Would a drink help?"

"Something to wash it down with. A glass of water, perhaps."

"With a little whisky in it?"

"Just a little."

"Let me get it for you," Arthur said. Without waiting to be formally commissioned, he made his way through the living room and hall to the dining room, where the bar tray had been wheeled into position beside the door. It was being liberally patronized; Arthur could hardly edge into the room, and once inside he circled the walls to try a less crowded approach. In the space beyond the bar, he found Claudia and Jim talking with Blanchard.

"Mr. Blanchard was telling us how it happened," Claudia said.

Blanchard diverted his eye from Claudia long enough to nod. "I was so sure he'd made it you couldn't have told me anything else," he said. "I remember thinking, the last glimpse I had of him, 'Cap has made it.' I think that's what gave me the spurt I needed to reach shore myself. Oh, I suppose I would have got there somehow, but knowing Cap had come through was a big help." Blanchard swallowed generously from his glass. "Because he did, you know. The thought I keep coming back to is, Cap won his last fight. He got to shore, there's no doubt of that, and just as he made it the clot or whatever it was hit him, and his ticker quit, just like that. The local doctor up there at camp put down heart failure as the cause of death. It wasn't drowning. All those years Cap put in with guns and rods and football since he was knee high, it would have been —well, ignominious, if he'd gone under in an ordinary drowning accident. Cap was a fighter, and he won his last big one."

"I'm sure you're right," Arthur said. "I'd like to hear more, but I'm getting a glass for Abby. She's trying to eat a little and wants a small drink to go with it."

Blanchard moved aside and gave Arthur access to the bar. As he edged his way out with the glass, he heard Blanchard describing the salmon that would have been Cap's biggest trophy ever if he'd only been able to bring it home.

The Blanchards of this world—doubtless useful and decent enough citizens, Arthur thought, twisting his way through the hall; but as spokesmen for Kent's life they turned in a woefully inadequate verdict. A fighter who made friends, not enemies—good, as far as it went. But Kent was a builder; go further still, and grant him his share of the creative. He liked to design, to make, and didn't like to undo. So he had mind and imagination, and the professional pride that set them productively to work. Allow for some prejudices and attitudes, early implants reinforced by his associations; call them as deplorable as you liked. Kent could always transcend them in practice; and there was that other quality about him, so easy to feel, so hard to define adequately. Most personal bonds of any warmth, Arthur thought, spring up between those who share a way of life. They are products of similar tastes, joint efforts, or a common occupation. Seldom do the lines cross and the elements mix; but Kent, as he might have said of himself, was a mixer. That was why his talents as a raconteur pointed to something beyond themselves. Kent didn't yarn to hold the stage; he yarned because he wanted to create a kind of hearth on which a moment of life could burn more genially. That was why all sorts and kinds came within the radiation of his charm; that was the fire that had gone out, the hearth that wouldn't be lighted again.

Arthur thought of the pleasure Claudia had taken in Kent as a story-teller. He had been forced to let her know what he himself had barely heard almost as soon as she and Jim stepped through the door on their return from New York. Claudia took the news hard. When she got a chance, she asked him privately whether they should postpone the wedding. No, Arthur said; he didn't think it would be feasible, even if desirable, and he didn't think Aunt Abby would want them to. Upstairs, in her mail, Claudia had found an envelope in Kent's hand containing what she thought an excessively generous check as a wedding gift. Arthur heard her cry out. She brought the letter down, in a state of distress no doubt partly due to the fact that she was inexperienced in the ways of death. Couldn't she return the check? Wouldn't Aunt Abby need it? Arthur felt a little rueful at discouraging her impulse, but he really thought a call of thanks would be more welcome, and he was sure that, for all the self-deprecation about money that Kent was given to, he had left his family more than decently well provided for.

Claudia was among those outside Kent's business and professional circle who responded to his personal qualities. It occurred to Arthur that Malcolm Islay was another. The thought of Malcolm wasn't entirely welcome at the moment, yet Arthur recognized that it was appropriate. If Malcolm had happened to be in Fullington, at Rowley, he would have made one, Arthur felt sure, among the company who gathered to break bread and to be convivial in Cap Warner's memory.

∘ ∘ *5* ∘ ∘

"Professor Scheuer?" said the voice on the wire. "President Aiken's assistant speaking. I'm making some of the usual arrangements for Commencement, and the President wanted me to ask you—he knows you're just recently back from Europe and officially off duty, but he wonders whether you'd be willing to act as faculty sponsor for one of our honorary degrees —you know, steer him through the protocol, and so on."

"I hadn't planned to come to Commencement this year," Arthur said, "but if the President wants—" The prospective honorary would be some biologist, no doubt; a respectable choice, Arthur hoped. A wild notion struck him: Lamson Crocket. Arthur had picked up enough gossip since his return to know that Lamson's name had begun to radiate from Washington, not conspicuously, but in a way suggesting some degree of bureaucratic power. Lamson had given press conferences, in which a subdued trace of his acidity made itself felt. Perhaps the trait made him attractive to story-hungry reporters. He had apparently launched one or two calculated leaks or trial balloons, no doubt at the behest of the policy-makers. Rowley might well want to ingratiate itself with a former faculty member now close to the sources of government money, but would Aiken ask Arthur to sponsor him at Commencement? "You can tell me who it is?" Arthur asked.

"Confidentially, of course. It's Malcolm Islay, the writer. The President thought it would be highly appropriate, if you're willing—"

"I see," Arthur said. He was both relieved and taken aback; his immediate impulse was to beg off, but he could give no

388

good reason. "Very well. Since the President wants, I'll be glad to do what's expected."

Arthur turned away from the telephone, remembering the small literary magazine he had picked up in a British bookstore on the eve of homecoming. The name *Malcolm Islay* appeared prominently on the cover in green ink, but last-minute packing had limited Arthur to a hasty skimming of Malcolm's contribution. Malcolm had made a quite unexpected use of his view that a writer is a selfish egotist, taking all human experience as his meat but living on it as a parasite lives on its host. In his hurried sampling, Arthur might have missed a sentence or two that gave him a sense of betrayal and raw exposure; but he'd blundered on them and been outraged. Then he shrugged off his resentment; no harm done, and Malcolm had to exploit his talents as he could. None the less Arthur was left with a disinclination toward trying to sustain what had promised to be a friendship. Now, thanks to Aiken, he was going to see Malcolm in Fullington again.

Arthur went up to his study, found the magazine where he had shoved it beneath an unsorted pile of books and papers, and sat down for a closer look. The beginning of Malcolm's fable—it was a fable rather than a story—went as he remembered. New twist to a very old idea: In a sort of prenatal limbo, a swarm of lives were waiting to be shipped to earth. The undistinguished mass were simply rattled together in a bin, where the common chances of life stuck to them like confetti, determining their humdrum fates. A select number were specially dealt with by two very important personages. The Secretary for the Talents endowed them with superior gifts, but, before they could embark on their voyage of incarnation, the Secretary for the Ironies attached to each gift the cross most subtly designed to mock it. As Arthur glanced through the chillingly ingenious catalogue of endowments and crosses, one struck him more forcibly than it had on his first hasty reading. Here, said the Secretary for the Talents, is an imagination who will delight his contemporaries through the written word. We have the prescription for him, said the Secretary for the Ironies; we shall make his imagination dependent for support on a woman, and he shall find her and crave to possess her utterly and exclusively, but she shall belong to another man and shall be as cool, as inaccessible in her kindness as the air that all breathe and none can arrogate to himself alone.

Hadn't Malcolm betrayed his own case? Wasn't he alluding to the woman—what was her name? Claudia knew. If so, Arthur had the less reason, he supposed, for resenting his own inclusion in the gallery. Could he possibly be wrong in thinking that Malcolm had worked him in? No, the words were right on the same page, plain and visible, however Malcolm had come by his knowledge: Here, said the Secretary for the Talents, is an intellect who shall be wise in the secrets of life and shall increase men's understanding of their origins and heredity. Then, said the Secretary for the Ironies, he shall be mocked in his children; they shall be such as men conceal and make no mention of.

Arthur's first sense of outrage flared again. It subsided, and he read on, not recalling how Malcolm had ended his fable. The Secretary for the Talents grew weary of his work, threatening to go on strike if every gift at his disposal continued to be crippled or mocked. Whereat the Secretary for the Ironies reminded him that they were both mere agents of an Ulterior Power, and neither was at liberty to resign his commission.

It occurred to Arthur that he hadn't asked when Malcolm would arrive or where he would stay. He made a return call to Aiken's assistant and learned that this time Malcolm wasn't coming to Rowley alone. Mrs. Islay and their two boys would be with him.

"After the way he's talked about her," Claudia said, "I'm dying to see them together."

Certainly it would hardly do not to invite the Islays to the house. Arthur made another phone call. Malcolm's time had been pretty well charted, but the chart left room for tea or a highball on the afternoon before commencement.

Malcolm looked odd unwinding his legs not from the Mercedes but from an unfashionably tall station wagon, its wooden ribs and panels rubbed largely bare of varnish. He looked even less familiar stalking up the walk behind a rather short, rather pretty woman, pretty in a blond way that struck Arthur as a bit washed-out, the two of them flanked by a pair of surprisingly compact and round-headed small boys, who gave off an impression of curbed animal vigor. Malcolm identified Beth as his wife and Bruce and Wallace as the two boys before he fully took on his own appearance again. Introductions completed, his face began to work in its accustomed way, settling into an expression of pleased reunion. "Arthur, old boy, I don't know why you aren't still in Europe when you had the chance to get there," he said, "but I'm glad you're here."

Arthur shepherded them all out through the living room to the screened porch overlooking the yard, and the question what kind of woman Beth Islay might be began promptly to answer itself. She made a quick survey and disposed the boys on a wooden bench which they might succeed in tipping over but could hardly injure by squirming or kicking. When Arthur wheeled the tea tray into position, she kept them active passing cups and plates of nut bread, and saw to it that they didn't wipe cake frosting on their clean shirts. Meanwhile she talked pleasant but rapid civilities, which seemed to have the effect of reducing Malcolm to speechlessness. She almost appeared to think that unknown hazards might be lurking for Malcolm in ambush. Presently she dismissed the boys to the yard, where they began a game of pursuit around the inviting features of knolls, tree trunks, and outcroppings of ledge.

Arthur couldn't help studying her with interest. She had a firm jaw under rather soft cheeks, but something about the lines of decision that framed her mouth gave the impression of being acquired as much as natural. The character of her face was concentrated in her remarkably fine eyes, of a shade neither quite gray nor blue, and capable of a look that at first sight seemed very direct and clear, but on a second glance became opaque, as if revealing no more than it chose to. It was a look everyone received who spoke to her. Rachel received it when she asked how long Beth and Malcolm meant to stay.

"I'm afraid we'll have to start back the minute we're free,"

Beth said. "I'm so glad Arthur is going to take charge of Malcolm. He isn't at ease with formal ceremonies, and it will help ever so much to have Arthur tell him where to stand and what to do." When no one spoke, she went on. "Malcolm is working very hard, and he doesn't want to be interrupted longer than he has to. Also it's hard to keep the boys out of mischief. I want them to see Malcolm get his honorary degree, but naturally enough they don't make a trip easier. They're already straining at the leash like puppies."

Arthur turned toward Malcolm. "Are you working at home?" he asked.

"He's hired a room where he shuts himself in by the day," Beth said, "so that none of us will interrupt. I'm afraid he's really working too hard. We're all going to take a family vacation together when he's finished."

Malcolm looked rather like a man obediently prepared to swallow an unwelcome dose, Arthur thought. He wanted to ask what it was Malcolm was working on, but he found himself being put through an inquisition about his lectures and about all the places the Scheuers had seen abroad. Arthur began to feel as withdrawn from the talk as Malcolm seemed to be. He became very conscious of Claudia and Jim, sitting in adjacent chairs, largely silent spectators. Their relation almost screamed for recognition, but who was to make the announcement and explain why they hadn't sent the Islays an invitation? None of them supposed the Islays could come—of course if they'd had any idea—and people think an invitation means a present—

At last Beth's vocal energy spent itself long enough for Malcolm to put in a word. He asked after Kent. He'd at least like to call up the Warners before he left. Arthur was compelled to explain; he was grateful for the simplicity and genuineness of Malcolm's response. Malcolm was sorry; he had hoped to see Kent again. Kent belonged to a very different sphere, but Malcolm remembered him. He stood out, he had a quality it would be hard to replace.

In the pause that followed, Claudia found an opportunity to speak. "I've been wanting to ask about Rosamund Temple," she said. "You haven't mentioned her, Malcolm. When Jim and I were driving back from New York recently, we went by—"

"It's very tragic about Mrs. Temple," Beth said. "I'm afraid her health has given way completely. It's affected Malcolm so that he doesn't like to speak of it at all."

"Oh, I'm sorry," Claudia said, her color mounting vividly.

Arthur heard a smothered sound from his left, where Malcolm was sitting. He was appalled when a quick glance revealed Malcolm's face. He perceived suddenly that the surface Beth had spread over the scene and carefully maintained had been a disciplined work, not a mere gush of triviality. He didn't know what would happen; Malcolm might go to pieces on the spot if someone didn't leap forward with another commonplace.

It was Malcolm's boys who were inspired to provide the needed diversion. An outraged cry came from the branches of a maple tree in the yard. "Leggo, leggo, goddamn bast—leggo!" Through the porch screening a novel spectacle presented itself. A double figure dangled grotesquely from a stout limb at about a man's height above the ground. The upper figure clung desperately to the limb; the lower swung from the thighs of the upper, dragging shorts and underwear down until a rounded white division of young male buttocks began to show. Suddenly the upper figure lost or released its grip, and the united pair descended as one to the turf. They seemed to bounce, and, in the act of rising, separated. Two hands made a frantic grab, pulling up the displaced shorts, and at once four fists began to lacerate the air, now and then making contact with a feature that blundered into the way.

Before Arthur could sort out his confused perceptions, Beth Islay was on her feet, opening the screen door and marching down the steps, remarkably unflustered. "Boys!" she said, hardly raising her voice. "Bruce, Wallace!" The scuffle stopped at once. "What have you done to each other this time?" Beth asked, bending over to inspect them for contusions or bloodletting.

Jim got up with the rest of them, but he had a hard time to

keep from doubling over. "That's a real little pair of Scottish chiefs you have," he said to Malcolm. "It's lucky they didn't have their claymores with them, or they might have lopped off a couple of ears."

Malcolm was uncertainly following Beth part way across the porch. "Beth knows how to handle them," he said. "She's used to it. They fight all the time."

Jim was still laughing. "They're real brothers. They'll fight like wildcats while they're growing up and then stick to each other like two valves of a clam."

Malcolm turned abruptly and, as if fearing he couldn't get the words out fast enough, said, "I want to talk to you, Arthur. We may not have another chance. Is there somewhere we could go?"

"Of course. We'll go up to the study," Arthur said, "if everyone will excuse us for a while."

Malcolm set off into the house before Beth could climb the steps, and Arthur followed him through living room and hall and upstairs to the study. While they were in progress, Malcolm's long legs carried him impatiently, but when they sat down, Arthur at his desk, Malcolm in the easy chair, Malcolm seemed unable to begin the conversation he had asked for. "Well, you gave your lectures, Arthur, old boy," he said at last. "You wrote your book."

"Yes," Arthur said.

"I used to kid you about getting God into the last chapter."

"I never took the kidding at face value," Arthur said, "but it was useful to me as an indirect stimulus. I was grateful for it, whether I said so or not."

"You didn't do it, then?"

"Come, now, Malcolm. You didn't really expect I would?"

"It doesn't matter," Malcolm said. "Men don't have to travel by the same road to get to the same place."

Arthur looked at him, mystified. Malcolm's facial play, the loose, expressive flesh that made a continual study in suspense, went dead, hanging slack and haggard; the bones looked through. "I tell you what, Arthur, there are some things— things that make art look cheap. You can't *do* anything with them! I'm supposed to be an ironist, and I don't know why I shouldn't be when you think of the things— Hell, what's Christendom founded on? The Son of God crucified—that's an irony to start with. But at least it's been written about— four gospels, not to mention a lot of pious trash and a lot of blasphemy. Some things, though—I don't know why I should expect you to listen to me. It's just that I haven't anyone else to talk with. I can't talk with Beth about—about this. I've got to get it off my chest to someone."

Arthur summoned his endurance and forced himself to say, "Go on, Malcolm. Talk to me."

"I don't blame Claudia, please understand that. I mean for asking me about—" Malcolm's voice refused to produce the name that struggled in his throat.

"Rosamund Temple?" Arthur supplied.

Malcolm gave him a brief look of gratitude. "Claudia had no idea, naturally, but when she asked that way, just when I was least expecting— You didn't know her, Arthur. I—I depended on her. I always knew it, but I didn't know how much. I'm learning about myself, too late, the way most learning comes. Anyway, she had the best critical mind I ever met, I mean the sort of critical mind that can help a writer, not just crab him after he's in print. But that's not the half. I—she—I can't describe her. Ask Claudia. Sometimes when I wonder what music means to people like Rachel, I think of her voice. Now and then I think it's the only voice I ever heard, really heard. I wish to Christ I could stop hearing it now!"

Malcolm could speak only in spurts. Finding the silence insupportable, Arthur prodded as gently as he knew how. "Beth says her health has failed?"

"She has—you'd know the name of it, Arthur. I've heard, but I can't remember—don't want to. They call it a degenerative disease. You retrogress, you go backward through all the stages till you're a child again, or worse. Till you're a vegetable. On the way you lose control of your functions— Oh, God, a woman like that! The worst of it is, it can go on for years. The only hope would be if her heart quit, but with all the care she's getting . . ."

Arthur wondered what he could say or do to break the silence again for any purpose beyond merely sparing his own distress, but now that Malcolm had struggled through his revelation he seemed to begin manufacturing his own relief by an outpouring of uninhibited speech. "You know, Arthur, there's one story I wish I'd been born to write. Once you've heard it, you don't see why anything else needs to be written. Well, perhaps that isn't quite true, but anyway, it's an old folktale. I don't know where it comes from, all over the Orient probably. It's about the young Shah of Persia, or wherever you want to put him, who asks his savants and soothsayers to compile an encyclopedia of human wisdom so that he can study it and learn to rule well. They go off and come back in five years with enough scrolls to fill the Alexandrian library, and by then the young King is head-over-ears in budgets and policy-making and appeals from the district court. He sends them back to make a digest, and in a couple of years they show up again with half the amount of vellum, but the King has a war on his hands and he tells them to bring him the most concise epitome they can put together. Well, the cycle goes on till the King is old and tired and almost at the end of his days, when the savants appear in court with a single small sheet, and they say, 'Sire, we have reduced all wisdom about the life of men to one sentence,' and the King takes it and reads it. You know what it says? You've heard the story? It says, 'They are born, they suffer, and they die.' "

"It's a moving story, Malcolm, but you concede yourself it isn't quite all that deserves to be written."

"I'll tell you what, Arthur. They've made the point, the critics have, that I've never put a human emotion in my books. Maybe they've been right. Maybe I've never had the gall or the courage or the humility. Maybe I've been dodging, protecting myself, afraid to go all out. Well, I'm showing them now. Oh, I'm doing a book—I've known what human suffering is. I could tell them about it. I *am* telling them. That's what I'm working at, what Beth is keeping me at, though she hasn't any idea what the result will be like. She may not understand much about writing, but she believes in me, Arthur, God help her, and in her own way she's going to bring me out on top yet."

"I'm sure of it," Arthur said. He took thought for a moment, then ventured, "I hope this new book won't be—well, merely a pendant to the folktale you told me. There are other things men do from time to time, aren't there? They laugh, they marry, they create?"

Malcolm's face regained in full its flexible powers of suspense. It shuffled this way and that, settling into a familiar look of enigmatic inquiry. "What would you say if I did what you didn't?"

"What I didn't—?" Arthur had to think back to the beginning of the conversation. "You don't mean—"

"Why not? Beth has always been one of the faithful. I'm just joining her, that's all. We're regular communicants at Saint Michael's Episcopal."

Arthur couldn't keep from asking, "Is this a matter of belief?"

"Lock, stock, and barrel. The whole works. Immaculate conception, virgin birth, harrowing of Hell, the resurrection and the life, the Trinity—"

"*Credo quia impossibile.*"

"How do I know what's possible and what's impossible in this universe? How do you? I've come to the stage where I have to believe something, and there's no halfway house between your scientific universe, without point or plan or purpose, and a church with a creed. I dare say all creeds are equally wide of the mark in detail or taken literally, but there's got to be a purpose in it all. I've read your stuff and other stuff in your line, and I'll grant evolution is true if you'll grant it's incredible. Darwin himself pretty nearly admitted that. You know where he says—you know better than I do—says that to believe the human eye got here by blind evolution requires a man to let his imagination be overcome by his reason. Well, I have too much imagination. I'll string along with what Byron said about the Creed and the Trinity. He was half joking, saying it's easy to scoff when you're healthy, but a few attacks of the gout turn any man into a believer. In my case it was just—well, let's say it was need. I needed something to survive on, but it comes to the same thing. Anyway, Byron winds up:

> I devoutly wished the Three were Four
> On purpose to believe so much the more.

Are you shocked at me, old man?"

Arthur considered and said carefully, "I hope you understand it isn't science, in itself or taken alone, that prevents me from making an affirmation of belief like yours. There are things I wouldn't want to hold God responsible for, things in my own life, things everyone encounters. I'd be a seriously embittered man if I thought that a conscious, guiding purpose in the universe brought about—whatever catastrophes you want to mention. I'm less embittered to think otherwise. Of course, at the heart of things, there's mystery. Even a scientist can recognize that."

"You've got the stick by the wrong end," Malcolm said impatiently. "You try to turn the reason why we have to have God into an indictment of Him. If there weren't any suffering or wrong, we could do without Him. It's because there is we can't. There's got to be a purpose and a possibility of redemption. 'I believe in the life to come.' What's a redemption but a reversal? Reversal is the soul of the plot."

"I'm sorry, Malcolm," Arthur said. "I don't in the least object to your being a believer. I'm glad, if you can get there with a clear mental conscience. But don't expect the same of me."

"I haven't lost my mind because I've found something to believe in," Malcolm said. "When is your book coming out? You'll send me a copy?"

Arthur's eyes turned involuntarily to the batch of galleys waiting on his desk to be corrected. Malcolm saw the direction of his look, rose abruptly, and picked up the galleys. "Is this it?"

"The final batch. I proofread the earlier ones in England."

"Good, I want to see what's in the last chapter." Malcolm sat down, shuffled the long sheets rapidly. "Here it is," he said. "I see you begin with a recapitulation. The line where strictly biological evolution puts on a different face, begins to look like cultural evolution, with cultural responsibility for it. What we do with the race from here on is up to us, or we can affect it, at least. Ideas we've batted around before, right?"

"Right," Arthur admitted.

"This looks new," Malcolm said, and began to read aloud.

Arthur underwent the novel and somewhat startling experience of hearing himself intoned in Malcolm's hoarse, expressive voice. While Malcolm read, Arthur's mind blocked the words as they would appear in type, and at the same time he felt himself delivering them in person from his British rostrum and wondering what it would be like to see himself at work on the platform and hear his own voice uttering the words instead of Malcolm's. He half winced and half approved as Malcolm began:

"I sometimes think that underneath our anthropomorphic desire to find a single, inclusive, conscious purpose in the world—"

"Don't declaim me so, Malcolm, please," Arthur begged.

"You would call it anthropomorphic," Malcolm said. "Let's see, where were we?

". . . purpose in the world, lies a simpler and even more fundamental craving. How deep do we go? How profound is our station in nature? Is it central in any way, or are we the flimsiest chance froth on the periphery, no more than a frail scum on the random splash of things—

"You aren't afraid to swing a metaphor, are you, Arthur? It's all right. Let's go on and see what's next.

". . . or have we, with our faiths, terrors, and hopes, our sensual and ethical anxieties, a seat of greater dignity and moment?

"That's the right question, Arthur, old boy. 'How deep do we go?' I wish I could hope you'd give the right answer.

"Many of you will say that only religious conviction can reply to such a query, and its reply will be unequivocal. But as a scientist, and as a man who by temperament finds himself compelled to stop short of any such conviction, I should like to suggest, if not a reply, at least an appropriate reflection."

Malcolm looked up, disappointed. "So you aren't going to answer. You're going to dodge. Better make your appropriate reflection a good one," he said, and went on:

"If all evolution began in that primeval molecular soup we have spoken of, then we go at least as deep as chemistry goes. Our ultimate seat in things, as forms of life, is in the habit molecules have of banding together briefly to outwit entropy, the endless raveling out of things into progressive disorganization. It is in their habit of associating in systems of the most elaborate organization, systems that can reproduce and perpetuate themselves, can walk about the world and look at it with pleasure and purpose, can even suffer ethical anguish. How much deeper-seated do we want or need to be?"

Malcolm raised his eyes again. "Is that the gist of it? Is that where you come out?" he asked.

"Read one more paragraph," Arthur said, or perhaps it's two."

"Here goes.

"As astronomy opens the universe more and more expansively to view, it brings within calculation extremely large numbers of suns like our own, brings the virtual certainty of many other planets with temperatures and environments favorable to life. Though we are as yet incommunicado on our small, local earth, it is unlikely that we are alone. We may be not only deep-seated, but widespread. We do not know, of course, whether life elsewhere has any of the ethical or creative traits we think characterize us at our best, but we cannot exclude the possibility. If molecules can suffer ethical anguish in one corner of the universe, I see no antecedent reason why they may not in another.

"Chemistry, it seems, has a tendency, given the right conditions, to organize itself as life. But of course, wherever we caught it in the act of doing so, we might expect to find waste and destructiveness in the process. Whatever novel region we may some day look into or look out from, we shall be sure to learn there again, in the words of Saint Paul, that the whole creation groaneth and travaileth together. We can ask to be grounded in the depth of things; we can hardly ask to escape waste and mischance, and I do not think any profound moral literature has ever encouraged us to make such a request.

"Is that where I stop?" Malcolm asked.

"I think that will do as a stopping point," Arthur said.

Malcolm lowered the folded galleys to his knees and sat silent. Then he said, "Stet?"

"Stet," Arthur said. He added, "As being the best I can do."

"In my credo, there's a little wicket gate with redemption on the other side. You'll send me the book when it comes out?"

"Nothing would please me more, if you'd really like it."

"Of course I would. I ought to apologize to you for putting you through all this, Arthur," Malcolm said, getting up and replacing the galleys on the desk, "but you've done me an act of charity, given a cup of water. I wish I'd ever done as much. Perhaps I'll at least learn to write about it."

∘ ∘ 6 ∘ ∘

Everyone said the bride was beautiful. For once, Arthur thought, the expected commonplace was hard to deny. He had got through his part in church, duly bestowing his niece on Jim Prescott, who had audibly and firmly uttered the prescribed promises. He had got through most of the reception, which was dragging to an end. Claudia had thrown the bridal bouquet from the stairs. Now she was in her room, with Rachel and Abby, changing into her traveling clothes. Most of the guests had already gone. A few diehards, determined to squeeze ceremony to the last drop, sat with bridesmaids and ushers in the living room or stood in knots on the front porch, waiting for the departure of bride and groom.

Arthur judged that the interval of waiting would continue for a few minutes yet. After the press of the receiving line, the effort of moving about and trying to make himself agreeable, trying to see that no one was overlooked who called for recognition or attention, he felt that he could use a snatch of solitude. He went out through the hall to the screened porch at the back of the house. In the marquee that had been set up on the most nearly level stretch of lawn, the caterer's corps, their faces cynically busybody and anxious to finish duty, were carrying off stacks of soiled plates, trays of champagne glasses and coffee cups. The champagne had served its purpose, Arthur thought, despite the fact that Kent wasn't on hand to drink his share. Rachel had taken a glass or two more than she ordinarily would, with the result that, after the receiving line broke up, Jim persuaded her to play her violin, and she rendered a Brahms rhapsody with an abandon that Arthur didn't suspect she commanded, while Jim and Claudia danced.

Arthur was afraid that Rachel was trying to keep her courage up, letting herself go a little desperately in view of the years ahead without Claudia. He was depressed by the prospect himself more than he cared to admit. Of course it was the worse for Rachel because she might not even be able to count on Abby for long; Abby might well decide to live with or near her children. Well, he and Rachel would live differently in the future; they would revisit Europe, they would enlarge their range of activity. Rachel would always have her music, and it wasn't as though Claudia would vanish from their lives.

Leaning against the porch rail, half conscious of the efficiency with which the caterers were striking camp, Arthur felt himself slipping into a fit of melancholy and abstraction. He supposed it was natural enough to have a sense of a watershed passed, of life turning into memory. It seemed as though a lot had happened in the few weeks just gone by, Kent's death, Malcolm's visit, Claudia's marriage. The events resonated in his mind, all in their way contributing an undertone of finality, of losses not to be restored. He faced about toward the screen door into the house, wondering whether he should go in. As he did so a gust of summer wind arose and shook the scalloped flaps of the marquee, stretched its peaked fabric on its guy ropes, and made the supporting poles lightly sway. He heard a door slam in the house, then another. Looking up at the sky, he decided that the weather was going to change, though the sun was still bright. A second gust followed the first, and a scurry of paper napkins blew across the grass. He would have problems to think about, challenges to meet, in the days and months ahead.

He must have let himself sink into abstraction for longer than he had realized, for suddenly the screen door opened and he saw Claudia looking out. "We couldn't find you, Uncle Arthur," she said. "We looked everywhere, and here you are on the porch all by yourself. Aren't you going to say good-by to me?"

"I must have lost all track—I didn't imagine—" Arthur said. "I thought I'd been here only a minute." He started to advance toward the door, but she closed it behind her and came toward him across the porch.

"You're all right?" she asked.

"Of course."

She seemed to study him earnestly, even tenderly. "Will you get along, you and Rachel, without me to take care of you?"

Arthur laughed. "It hasn't been long since we were taking care of you." She looked a little disappointed, he thought, and he added, "We'll do our best. We'll manage."

"You must, for my sake," she said. "It seems silly to say thank you, Uncle Arthur, but that's the way I feel—for the wedding, for everything you and Rachel have done for me always."

"You know what you've meant to us," Arthur said.

"You don't too much mind my going off and leaving you?"

"Never think that," Arthur said. "It's your life we want you to lead, not ours. As long as you're making the right marriage—and I'm sure you are. I've taken to Jim very much."

"Oh, it's going to be a good life with Jim," Claudia said. "You needn't worry about that." She met Arthur's look with her own, holding him with its youthful directness and candor. "We aren't a pair of innocents, Jim and I. We know each other, and we're starting out with our eyes open."

She continued to fix him with the same forthright look that seemed partly to challenge him and partly to await his judgment, if he had any to offer. Could his almost irresistible impression be right? Could she be making an acknowledgement, inviting him to condemn if he chose to? "I'm sure it will be a good life," Arthur said hastily. It was no time for *absit omens* or faintness of heart, certainly no time for judgment. "You and Jim will make it so."

She looked happy at that, perhaps just a trifle relieved, and suddenly Arthur was overtaken by a fit of envy, bitter and deep. To be starting out again in Jim's shoes, starting out with a different set of chances—Arthur's own life hung before him briefly, a maimed, half-wasted thing. He and Malcolm and Kent, in their efforts to share the creator's laurels, had never included one important form of creativity. Perhaps it couldn't be called that; the names for it were plainer and more physiological, but it did result in new, unique existences. Everyone talked about the population problem nowadays, and nothing was more important; yet the race had to be recruited, and those old lines— Two or three words escaped Arthur's throat. He tried to stuff them back.

"What did you say, Uncle Arthur?"

"Nothing. Just my bad habit. I was quoting something, that's all."

"But what was it? Tell me."

Arthur summoned his courage. "You really want me to say?

> "From fairest creatures we desire increase,
>   That thereby beauty's rose might never die."

She looked at him, completely taken aback. He supposed he'd been scrupulous not to tell her that he, like other people, considered her beautiful. He supposed it might not have occurred to her that he had his share of ordinary sensual imagination. "Why, Uncle Arthur!" she said, and she laughed. Then her color mounted, her eyes moistened, and she laughed again, her voice ringing out wholeheartedly this time above a banging gust of wind. "You're an old dear," she said. He felt himself taken into her arms, felt himself kissed, felt her youth pressed against him for an instant.

Her laugh must have been sufficiently unrestrained to call attention to their presence, for, as she drew away, the screen door opened, and Jim appeared. "So here you are!" he said. "We've had a posse looking for you both."

"I was just saying good-by to Uncle Arthur," Claudia said. "A private good-by."

"Well, if he's ready to give us a final blessing, I think we're expected to make an exit, showered with rice and old shoes."

They might have been showered with more rose leaves and confetti, if not rice and old shoes, Arthur thought, had Kent been present to do his part. He followed Jim and Claudia out through the hall, across the porch, where Claudia stopped to cling briefly to Rachel among a small cluster of remaining guests, followed them all the way down the walk to the curb. He helped stow baggage in Claudia's car, watched while Jim felt through his pockets and discovered the keys entrusted to him, watched while the car began its passage down the curving street toward the corner where it would vanish.

It's your life we want you to lead, not ours. Arthur remembered his words; they were true, but he had spoken in a double sense. Underneath he had meant almost the reverse: let the life you are going to lead be mine. His impulse to envy had been natural and harmless, but he couldn't live on it. To the car and its occupants, now quite beyond view, he said again, with single purpose: it's your life we want you to lead, not ours. Then he turned back toward the house, toward his own future, encountering the last guests as they scattered down the walk, noticing that Rachel had vanished from the porch and gone in alone. Where he was needed, Arthur told himself, he could try to serve; for that matter, he could still try to create, if he had it in him. The double thought pressed in his mind as he climbed the steps, opened the door, and called out Rachel's name.

HOUSTON
PUBLIC
LIBRARY